W9-CHY-628

ANGELS
ALL
OVER
TOWN

LUANNE RICE

ANGELS
ALL
OVER
TOWN

New York ATHENEUM *1985*

Library of Congress Cataloging-in-Publication Data

Rice, Luanne.
   Angels all over town.

   I. Title.
PS3568.I289A8 1985   813'.54   85–47612
ISBN 0–689–11616–0

FOR THOMAS FARRELL

ANGELS
ALL
OVER
TOWN

THE problem was not that I believed in ghosts. I did not believe in ghosts, but I was visited by one. I could not deny it. When I least expected to, I would see my father, solid of body, curly of hair, in true corporeal splendor, even though he had died months earlier. Once I saw him across the floor at the Rose Room in the Algonquin Hotel. I spotted him from behind. He was dining with two other men, and his greying golden-brown hair looked as springy as ever. I made no attempt to speak to him. I sat in my seat, not eating my chef's salad, watching his familiar movements: the way he drank his martini, smoked his cigarette, gestured expansively. I guessed that he was trying to sell some land to his table companions. I had no doubt that he would pick up the tab.

The next time I saw him was at the apartment I shared with my sisters in Newport. It was a small, dingy, second-floor walkup, made cool by a breeze off the harbor. One close August morning Lily and Margaret had left for the boatyard where they worked, and I had just finished another cup of coffee. I grabbed an old *Redbook* and headed for the bathroom. There I found my father, seated on the toilet, reading the New York *Daily News*.

"Oh, I'm sorry," I said, backing out and slamming the door behind me.

"Hang on a sec, I'm almost through," he called. My heart was racing, but from embarrassment, not shock. I did not ask myself how my father, a man who had died wearing two colostomy bags, could be taking a normal shit. Nor did I wonder why he was reading the *Daily News*, a tabloid he had considered vulgar in life, and which, besides, was not readily available in Newport. I just sat at the kitchen table and waited.

Presently he flushed the toilet and opened the door. He wore a white dress shirt with the sleeves rolled up and a pair of faded madras shorts. Now that detail shocked me: he had pale, bony, freckled legs covered with curly reddish hair, and I had *never* seen him wear shorts.

"Sweetheart," he said, opening his arms to embrace me.

I raced toward him and gave him a huge hug. "Dad, are you real?" I asked, feeling queer for asking: he felt solid and sweaty.

"Yes, sweetheart, I am. Unfortunately, I can't stay long." He checked his watch, a cheap Bulova, the one he had worn ever since I could remember.

"Tell me everything. What has it been like?"

We sat opposite each other at the kitchen table. Lily's plastic birth-control Pilpac was open beside the pepper shaker, and I tried to surreptitiously glide it under a napkin. My father waved his hand.

"Don't bother doing that," he said. "I've seen it already. That's the sheer hell of it. I can see everything, the good along with the bad, and I can't tell you a damn thing about what to do."

Instantly my mind was flooded with images of things, the good along with the bad, that I had done since he had died. Alastair "Boom-Boom" Brady's face kept swimming to the forefront, and I kept blinking my eyes to push it away.

"That puke you're thinking of now, for instance. What is he, Australian?"

"Yes, he's a sailor. He's the bowman on a famous racer."

"I don't give a goddamn if he won the America's Cup, for godsakes. He's no good. You're a fine actress, even if it is for a soap opera. If you aren't going to have respect for yourself . . ." He patted his breast pocket and removed a pack of L&Ms. He glanced around, and I handed him a matchbox from the Candy Store. Examining the logo, one gilded mermaid with two graceful tails, he lit his cigarette and handed the matchbox back to me. "And you should stay away from that place. The Candy Store. A bunch of guys with their hands in the cookie jar."

I fought to keep my mind blank. "Mom's good," I said.

"I know. I like the way she finished the living room. Tell her the beam's sagging, though. She'd better get a brace. In fact, have her call Creighton Albemarle—he owes me money. He'll do a good job."

"What do you mean, the beam's sagging? Is there any danger?" Just before my father died, he and my mother began renovating our summer cottage on Long Island Sound, converting the old screen porch into part of the living room, replacing the screens with huge Thermopane windows, removing the wall that had separated the porch from the living room, leaving one beam to bear the weight of the house. My mother lived alone there, year round now, painting watercolors. My father's words frightened me; I thought I had noticed a slight bow myself.

"Nothing immediate, my angel. But have her take care of it before winter. I don't like the thought of snow on the roof."

"Dad, can I tell her I've seen you?"

He grinned then, a wide, easy grin that lifted his hazel eyes and made creases in his pale cheeks. He had a lean face and a long, straight nose. The Cavan nose. I had it myself. When I was young I once looked in a mirror and called my nose long. "Aristocratic," my father had corrected, only partly pretending to be angry.

"Telling people could be a problem, couldn't it?" he said now. "They'll wonder why I don't stay."

"Why don't you stay?" I asked.

His face went sad. My father's expression could run through emotions the way a flutist plays scales. "I just can't, Una," he said.

"But you'll come back?"

"If I can."

I stared at him, thinking that he needed another haircut. The day before he died, I had given him a bad haircut. He was lying in his hospital bed, weak and shrunken from cancer, and his thick, curly hair made his head itch. "They won't get me a barber," he had said. So I had picked up a pair of scissors, the crooked kind used by nurses to cut bandages, and chopped off all his hair. The remaining tufts sticking out on his skull, combined with his wide, darting eyes, had made him look like an owl.

"Whooo!" he said to me now. Then he rose, hugged me hard, and left through the front door.

I RAN down Brewer Street to The Yard. Lily was making fast a long white ketch to a floating dock. Boom-Boom stood at the bow, a line in his heavy hands. He called my name, making it sound like "Ina" in his Australian accent, but I ignored him. "You have got to come with me," I said to Lily. "Where's Margo?"

She looked at me as if I were crazy. "I'm in the middle of something here."

"You've got to come now."

Lily gauged the situation. She knew I didn't often make demands unless they were urgent. Throwing the remaining untied line to Boom-Boom, she walked along the dock with me. We found Margaret driving the Travelift, a huge apparatus used for moving huge boats. "Margo!" Lily called. "Come on down."

Lily was our middle sister, two years younger than I, but she had seniority over Margaret at the boatyard as well as in our family. Margaret hurried across the hot asphalt parking lot, and we went into a ramshackle shed at the far end of The Yard.

"Una has big business," Lily explained.

"You won't believe this," I said. I remember twisting my hands, trying to find a clear way to tell them what had happened. I settled on directness. "I saw Dad."

"When?" Lily asked, her voice giving nothing away.

"Today—ten minutes ago. He looks great. He misses us all." I looked into both my sisters' faces. Lily's eyebrows were arched, her mouth thin and set. Margo ducked her head, patting the pockets of her khaki shorts for cigarettes. They both had wild yellow hair, unlike mine, which was reddish. The sun shined through the open windows behind them, lighting their heads like halos. I tried to breathe more steadily. "He was in the bathroom, reading the paper. I didn't buy the *Daily News*, and I know you two didn't, so how else would it be there? It's right on the floor, soaking wet because he dropped it on the bathmat." I gave Margo a dirty look because she was notorious for forgetting to hang up her wet bath things.

"Dad hates scandal sheets," Margo said.

"He used to, but apparently he likes them now."

"What did he say?" Lily asked.

"Okay. He said—" I laughed. "Typical. Guess what he said about Boom-Boom?"

" 'Stay away from that no-good punk,' " Lily said.

" 'Puke.' He said 'no-good puke.' "

"That *is* typical," Margo agreed.

"He also said that the Candy Store is bad, and also that Mom should get the beam fixed."

"No kidding. The house is ready to collapse," Lily said.

"What else?" Margo asked.

"That's about it. We just sat and talked."

I noticed, of course, the looks my sisters exchanged. I couldn't blame them for not truly believing me, no matter how badly I wanted them to; I hadn't told them about the time at the Algonquin for that precise reason. But this time seemed more compelling. Our father had appeared to me in their apartment.

"Listen," Lily said. "We'd better get back to work. You can finish telling us about it later."

I walked back up Brewer Street's small hill, disappointed that they hadn't felt more inclined to keep open minds. My day stretched emptily ahead, until five that evening, when they would come home. All three of us were on leaves of sorts. They from Brown University, where they were both graduate students in the Art History Department, and I from my role as Delilah Grant on "Beyond the Bridge," a soap opera which filmed five days a week, with occasional weeks off during which we were supposed to make public appearances at shopping malls and guest spots on game shows. But my character had disappeared for the summer. In September she would reappear, fleeing to Lake Huron, to an isolated cabin where she could forget a painful episode with her long-term lover, and where a psychopathic fur trapper would eventually corner her.

It had seemed like a perfect time to reunite with Lily and Margo. Our father had died in January; except for the two weeks surrounding his death when we had converged on our mother's house in Connecticut, we hadn't lived together for eight years. Presence is everything.

I used to say texture is everything while Lily and Margo would say color is everything. We would have fantastic debates. Driving past the marsh at Black Hall I would say the texture of the cattails and grasses, spiky and tubular, was the most beautiful. Margo and Lily would argue for the color: the shades of blue, green, and gold. (Although they preferred wilder colors with evocative names: apricot, persimmon, tea rose, vermilion, emerald, azure.) We invented names for our preferences. The color school was Karsky (named for a boy Margo had known in high school) and the texture school was Schlumberger (pronounced shlum-bear-zhay, an extremely textural name).

Then we invented Vuarnet. Once when I went to Providence to visit them, we walked down Angell Street to the Rhode Island School of Design. The students there dressed like anarchists in black leather, skinny cotton shifts over black tights, white oxford-cloth shirts worn as dresses with studded leather belts, tight pedal pushers worn over plastic thongs. They had razor haircuts. They wanted to keep their skin pure white, so they wore sunscreen and walked on the shady side of the street. Margo and Lily told me the sunglasses they favored were Vuarnets and Raybans, so we started calling that cool, new look "Vuarnet."

I remembered that day perfectly. They took me to the graduate student show at the RISD Museum. There were mammoth geometric paintings that resembled daggers on one wall; narrow, meticulously drawn architectural-type renderings which, when carefully regarded, showed men in lewd positions with each other; a video segment in which a TV screen was set into a dog house and, when the viewer pressed the button, an image of feet pacing a room would appear on the screen and a whiny voice berating its father for neglect and mistreatment would blare out. One student had hired a crane to hoist a brand-new white Lincoln Continental into an interior courtyard, and that was his project. There were ceramic vases, enameled jewelry, furniture including a teak bed suspended from the ceiling in the midst of matching dining room table and chairs. Its title: Dining with the Invalid.

One student was walking through the show with his parents. Margo whispered to Lily and me that the father reminded her of a coal miner from West Virginia: he was brown and wizened, as if he spent much time underground, and he wore a thin, short-sleeved, green nylon shirt with a pack of Camels showing through the pocket. His posture was stooped. He walked around the gallery scowling while his wife, a proud fat woman, walked ahead with her son. "How do you like it, Willard?" she asked the man, and he said, "Too many doodads."

That cracked Margo up. She wanted to think of a school we could call "Doodad." We tried to connect it with Dada, but nothing sprang to mind. It seemed to overlap Vuarnet too much. On the way to their apartment, I stepped on a wad of gum. By the time I noticed it, it had stones, hair, and grass pressed into it. "My RISD thesis," I said. "Very Doodad."

"Vuarnet," Lily and Margo said at once.

Crossing the Brown Green, students recognized me from "Beyond the Bridge." "Hey, Delilah," some of them called. Some of them just stared, but many asked whether I was planning to marry Beck Vandeweghe, my starcrossed lover and editor of the Mooreland *Tribune*. One girl asked for my autograph and said she had planned her entire spring semester around the show. I was used to such attention. I signed the autograph, secretly pleased that my sisters should see me adulated, but one thought nagged at my mind. As Delilah, I had another family: my father, Paul Grant, and his scheming new wife Selena, my sisters Nicola, Stephanie, and Bianca, my half-brother Scott, and my illegitimate baby Jennifer. But walking across the green that day, listening to people ask me about the Grants, I thought of my own father who had died two months earlier, and whose ghost I had seen the week before at the Algonquin. I was walking between my two real sisters, but that meant nothing to my fans.

AT five-thirty, Lily and Margo came quietly into the apartment. They looked tired from working on the docks all day for the wages they stretched to cover their summer expenses. The sun, an orange ball over Newport Harbor, blazed through our west-facing windows. I was lying on the couch, with a smooth cotton sheet between me and the upholstery. Itchy wool upholstery.

"Hi," I said.

Both sisters sat beside me on the floor. "Do you know you sleepwalk?" Lily asked.

"I wasn't sleepwalking. Go into the bathroom—the paper's on the floor."

Margo walked out of the room, returning in an instant with a rumpled *Daily News*. "You sleepwalked up to Bellevue Avenue, bought the paper, came home and read it on the toilet, then sleepwalked down to The Yard."

"Unie, Unie, Unahhh," Lily said, throwing her keychain at my legs. "You couldn't have seen Dad. Dad got cremated, and now his ashes are in the ocean. You weren't swimming, were you?"

"Please don't joke about it. He knew about Boom-Boom. He also knew about your birth-control pills, and I'm pretty sure he knows about the Wild One."

Lily looked terrified for a second, but then she relaxed. The Wild One was a French sailor, extremely handsome in a dark, mysterious, sex-crazed way. He had black curls and hooded eyes. He was noted in Newport for his reticence and distance. Currently he was seeing Lily exclusively, and that did not go unremarked on the docks. Margo and I, and even Lily to some degree, regarded the situation with mild disgust. That a man known for his aloofness to women could be so compelling to Lily.

"Why do you think he knows about the Wild One?" Lily asked. She gave slight emphasis to the word "knows," as though she wanted to convey true skepticism, but she was nervous. I could tell.

"Because he seems to know everything. It's horrifying, if you think about it. He actually read my mind at one point."

"What were you thinking?" Margo asked.

"About Boom-Boom."

"God, to think that Dad could read our minds," Margo said, shuddering. "After he died, I secretly hoped he would come back for visits. It seems lousy that he won't know what we do for the rest of our lives. I mean, when Lily and I get master's degrees, and when Una moves from the soaps to the movies. When we get married. In a way, I'd like to think that he could know about all that."

"I'd like to think it too," Lily said. "But it's crazy. It cannot happen."

"If that's all there was to it, that would be fine," I said, and suddenly my voice sounded as if it was blowing through a tunnel. "But he can read our minds. We'll have to live practically like nuns."

"Nuns can't do anything, so they think the dirtiest thoughts," Lily said.

"Una, are you dis or something?" Margo asked, peering at me.

"Dis" was a word we had created years earlier to mean disgruntled, dismayed, disenchanted, distressed, disgusted, disheartened, disengaged, distant.

"I think so," I said. Prickles were racing around my lips and nose.

"Do you think we should call Mom?" I heard Margo ask Lily.

"No, we'll keep her right here," Lily said.

I heard that, and then I went to sleep for two days.

M Y father made real estate deals. Books on success tell you that real estate is one of the fast tracks to fortune, but in my father's case it was mainly an excuse to wear good suits and have lunch at places like the Algonquin. He was tall and handsome and had an easy charm that flattered everyone and made them feel grateful for his attention. His name was James Francis Xavier Cavan, and no one ever called him anything except "James." His mother had made that clear from the day he was born into a family of seven girls. "Jim and Jimmy and Jamey—pansy names," she had reportedly said to anyone who asked about the baby's nickname. One of his sisters had called him "Radio Ears," but never in front of their mother.

My father's protruding ears were the only blight on his beauty. He was not beautiful in the smooth television sense; he had freckles and scars and a slightly crooked profile. But everything merged well, and photographs prove that he was an extremely handsome man. My mother was beautiful, the all-American college girl. She painted watercolors and wrote poems. She was my father's shy, quiet counterpart. How often had my sisters and I heard the story of how they met? It was summer, the year he returned from serving in the Eighth Air Force in England during World War II. It was raining. My father was earning some fast money as an ice-cream man. My mother, wearing her shiny red raincoat, bought a Creamsicle. My father watched her stride away (the words they always used when telling the story: "I stood there and watched Grace stride away") and then he drove his ice-cream truck right after her and offered her a ride home. Only instead of going home they drove along the Connecticut shoreline until they ran out of gas.

Unfortunately my father drank. He said he didn't know why, but on certain nights he would fail to come home. He suffered from black moods, fits my sisters and I called "Black Ass." When I was old enough my mother would take me out to look for him, and we would find him at bars like The Blue Danube or The Wonder Bar, buying rounds for everyone, charming the waitresses, telling stories. One time my mother stayed in the car, keeping it running, while I went inside to get my father. He was sitting at the bar, telling a story to a rapt audience of the bartender and two patrons. I stood in a dark shadow behind a coatrack and listened.

"He's sitting on a fortune in real estate," my father was saying, "and there's nothing anyone can do. He's a hell of a guy, a real gent, but he doesn't have a clue about what I could make happen. I mean, it's waterfront property, honest to god waterfront. You can see clear to Orient Point. New London's a halfway point for—what? Boston and New York? Providence and New Haven? Hartford and Riverhead, for godsakes. On a train line with ferries and a major airport nearby. But will the guy sell? No way." My father chuckled and slugged from his martini. He whirled his finger in the air, a signal for the bartender to pour another round. "He wants to sit on the goddamn place, just because he was born there. I can see his point. He's a sentimental guy, a real family man. He wants to keep the place for his kids. But I'm telling you, so help me god, you put a hotel there, or a big marina, or even a *heliport*, and the sky's the limit. That bastard could buy twenty waterfront parcels and give them to his kids and all their goddamn friends."

I hated to interrupt. His friends were drooping slightly, but they were all nodding in sympathy and admiration: here was a guy who could throw the word "heliport" around in general conversation.

"Dad," I said. "You have to leave."

"What the—" he said, spinning around on his stool. He smiled when he saw me. His eyes grew bright for an instant, and he looked proud. "Fellas, will you look who's here? Wasn't I just telling you about this one?"

Both friends glanced up from their drinks, and the bartender nodded.

"This is my daughter Una. Just graduated from high school and next year is going to drama school in New York. What an actress! Ever seen the play *Wonderful Town?*"

No one replied.

"I mean it—you, Fred? You ever seen *Wonderful Town?*"

"I sure have," Fred said. "It's a really good show."

"Bullshit—pardon me, Una angel. But you haven't seen a good show until you've seen Una in *Wonderful Town*. She brought down the house. Wasn't I just telling you fellas how she brought down the house?"

"And now she's off to the big city," the bartender said. "Where are you going to study, hon?"

"At Juilliard," I said. I remember barely pronouncing the *ll*'s. "Dad, we have to go."

"Where are you taking your old father?" he asked, still smiling.

"Home. You have a conference call."

"Oh, a *conference* call," Fred said, nodding and making an exaggerated frown. "Big-shot papa you got there."

"We'd better go before they hang up," I said.

When we were outside my father sped up, leaving me behind. "What the hell, coming in and embarrassing me like that. You damn kid. You get your own ride home." He tried to open the door to his car, but it was locked. He didn't notice my mother's car idling in the space beside him.

"That car," I said, pointing at my mother's. "You can't drive —you'll kill yourself."

"Damn smartaleck. Embarrassing me like that."

"This place is a sleazehole," I said just before opening the front door to let him in.

He wheeled to face me. "What are you talking about? You were inside."

"It's a dump."

"Right, a dump with paneling like that. You don't know anything about real estate, Una. Your father goes first class or he doesn't go at all."

"Oh, I know *that*," I said. Then I climbed into his car and drove it out of the parking lot behind him and my mother, leaving the sign with the words "The Blue Danube" and the bubbling champagne glass flashing in blue neon behind us.

At home my mother no doubt threw him into bed, said a few words over him as if he were a cauldron and she could actually affect its contents, and settled down with a cup of milky tea at her easel. I would find my sisters. For years it seemed that they had no idea at all of what was happening. In those days we would sit on our beds in the room we shared and play Hubbabub or Antique Store (games we had invented) or talk about places like Los Angeles, South Africa, New Orleans: places that seemed too bizarre to be real.

Years later, when they understood the truth about our father's late nights and could see how sad it made me to drag him out of places like The Blue Danube, they became violently protective of my well-being. They became my emotional Mafia.

"Look what that creep's doing to you," Lily would say, angrily gritting her perfect teeth when I would walk into the house sobbing behind my wobbly father and silent mother. "Why do you let him get you? He's got a real bad case of Black Ass—you should just let Mom go alone. Let them pick up his lousy Cow tomorrow." He drove a Volvo station wagon, and to us it had the noble, graceless lines of a cow.

"I can't," I would sob. "They need me."

"This is what he needs," Margo would say, tipping an imaginary bottle upside down and glugging.

"Yes, that is all he needs," Lily would say. Then she would walk into his bedroom and stand at the foot of his bed, glaring at him while he smiled and waved and said things like "Hey, sweetheart, what's doing?"

One Christmas Eve day, during an ice storm, my mother, Lily, Margo, and I went shopping for nuts, cranberries, stollen, figs, turkey, and white onions. On our way home from the market I noticed Margo nudge Lily. Both heads snapped to see something out the window. They glanced at me but were silent. "What?" I mouthed silently, but they only shook their heads. Our mother was concentrating on not sliding off the road. Glare ice made the asphalt gleam like a black river. At home we unloaded the car. My mother and I started making figgy pudding.

"Where are the girls?" Mother asked.

"I'll look." I ran upstairs but they were not in our room. Then I checked the living room and TV room and finally all the rooms in the house. *That look.* Suddenly their secret glance made sense. It had something to do with Andrew Wilson or Aldo Fabbiano or some other current loved one. I returned to the kitchen.

"They're doing homework," I told my mother.

"On Christmas Eve? They have the entire vacation."

"They're also wrapping presents."

We stirred the pudding and added a small dose of rum. Presently, because I had been listening for it, I heard the front door close quietly. I heard my sisters go upstairs.

Forty minutes later, when it was past six and becoming increasingly clear that it was going to be a night out for our father, the front door opened.

"Goddamn pukes slit my tires," his voice croaked.

"James, what happened?" my mother asked, hurrying into the front hall. She stood there, regarding her rumpled husband with a thin-lipped stare.

"Goddamn pukes slit my tires. Four sixty-dollar Michelins *kaput*."

"Where did this happen?"

"Down at Frank's. Down the corner." He meant Frank's Tavern, a mile from our house. He rarely drank so close to home, but he apparently figured that he would make it the first of several Christmas Eve social calls: Ebenezer Scrooge spreading cheer to one and all. He rubbed his hip, and I noticed that his Chesterfield coat was torn.

"What happened to your hip?" I asked.

"Slipped on the goddamn ice. Fell flat on a stick."

"And you tore that *coat*?" my mother asked. "Did you break anything?"

"I don't know," my father said, patting his pockets for cigarettes. He walked into the living room and sat heavily down on a green horsehair chair. "Walked the whole way home in a damn ice storm." For the first time since coming in, he met my mother's and my eyes. "Did you know that? Ice is coming down, but it'll turn to snow. Santa needs a nice snowfall for midnight, sweethearts. We'll hear the angels singing tonight."

Upstairs I found Lily and Margo. "Can you believe it? Someone slit his tires."

"Meet Vigil," Lily said.

"Meet Ante," Margo said, giggling.

"You two slit his forty-dollar Michelins?"

"You bet we did," Vigil said, slipping her strong arm around my shoulders. "Couldn't have our little search party going out on Christmas Eve."

"*Sixty*-dollar Michelins," Ante said.

"You're both going to get coal in your stockings," I said.

But the next morning, sober and happy, our father wakened us at sunrise with mugs of hot chocolate in our beds.

"Hohoho," he said, bearing a tray. "What happened to the old days when my girls couldn't sleep past three A.M. before they had to check for Santa?"

My sisters and I snuggled under our separate quilts and sipped our steaming-hot chocolate. I felt it burn a blister on the roof of my mouth. Our father sat on my desk. "Come on, come on. Drink that stuff and get hopping. Your mother's downstairs waiting for you."

Ice covered the inside of our windows, making feathery patterns through which the pink light of dawn shined. We all yawned. Downstairs bacon crackled and the odor of woodsmoke drifted up. Our father walked to one window and made circles in the ice with a nickel. I looked across the room at Lily and Margo, snug in their beds. They shrugged, and Lily did what all three of us wanted to do: blew apologetic kisses to our father, behind his back.

ON THE second day, after my long sleep in Newport, Lily and Margo stood over me. I opened my eyes and asked for juice.

"Jesus, if you didn't wake up tonight, I was going to call the ambulance," Lily said.

"We were starting to think you were in a coma," Margo said. "You kept waking up but not *saying* anything."

"I think I'm fine."

"Something is wrong. Very wrong," Lily pronounced. "Say 'I dreamed I saw Dad.' "

"I did see him."

She shook her head. "Then something is wrong. Do you want us to find you some therapy?"

I thought about it, then shook my head.

"We have some cold borscht for dinner," Lily said. "We're having it with sour cream floating on top."

"The Wild One's coming for dinner," Margo said.

I closed my eyes. "Lily, you've got to get rid of him. Are you in love?"

"I might be."

"He's using you. You have—"

"Dad's poisoned your brain. And not two days ago, either. All your life. Sex is bad, bad, rotten. You're going to turn into a Holy Roller if you don't straighten out."

"Straighten out!" I laughed at the irony.

"It isn't funny, Una," Margo said sadly. "We love you, but this isn't like you."

I stared at my sisters, at their soft, monochromatic yellow hair. Their hair had been pure blond since birth, as if they shared a secret Scandinavian heritage that had nothing to do with the rest of us Irish Cavans. But Lily's face was soft and voluptuous, like a Raphael madonna, while Margo's was sharp, like a bird's.

"Do you want borscht in bed?" Lily asked.

I shook my head.

"Toast, then. I'll fix toast with honey."

Margo sat next to me on the bed. "Want to glance through the new *Vogue*?" she asked. The magazine was open on the covers. I wondered whether one of the girls had been reading it at my bedside while I slept. I liked that idea. Only sleeping for two days straight seemed too close to death.

"The last time I was in a coma was on the show," I said.

"I remember. Beck was cheating on you with that cub reporter, and she hit you with a bookend. Are you going to marry that loser?"

"Well, I hope not. I'm sort of hoping they fire the actor who plays him—he has a miserable personal life and keeps flubbing his lines. It's constant improvisation when I have a scene with him. But he is a nice guy."

"That must be fun, though. You're always saying you love improvisation."

"I do, but not that kind." I wanted to fall asleep again, and I fought to keep my eyes open.

"When do you start filming again?"

"In the fall. Right around my birthday."

"Late September, good. Lily and I will cure you before you turn twenty-nine."

"Of what?" I asked, but then we heard Lily's voice in the kitchen. Occasionally it was answered by a primal grunt.

"Who's she talking to?" I asked, and we listened.

"The Wild One," Margo and I said at once.

In Newport there were many racing yachts, most with all-male crews, ready to leave New England as soon as the first autumn breezes started to blow. That signaled the great exodus to the south, the start of the Southern Ocean Racing Circuit, known to sailors and followers of sailors as the SORC. Yachtsmen were fond of nicknames. For each other: Boom-Boom, the Wild One, Spearchucker, Big Bird. For boats: *Yankee Girl* was called "Girl," *China Doll* was called "Dollface," *Different Drummer* was called "Ringo," *Tempest* was called "Tempo." The diminutives were a shrewd method of telling SORC insiders from pretenders. People who know a little about yachting know the terms *mast*, *deck*, *crewman*. But an insidious trick of reversal made, to a true racer, the mast a "stick," the deck the "floor," a crewman a "boat nigger." It struck me as puerile and racist, but one had to abandon judgment to last in Newport.

The Wild One opened my bedroom door and leaned against the doorjamb. His messy black hair fell into his dark eyes; he stretched one long, muscular arm up the wall. He nodded at me. I nodded back. That was the extent of our communication. Lily and Margo, art history scholars, spoke fluent French, and Margo carried on a lengthy conversation with him. His answers were brief.

"What did he say?" I asked when the discussion was over. The Wild One remained in position, burning me with his eyes.

"He hopes you become well soon. I told him you have a virus."

"Maybe we should tell him it's catching," I said, turning my head to the wall.

"No, he's really concerned. He says he hopes you become happier."

I looked back at him. He wore a white sweatshirt with the sleeves cut off and a pair of navy shorts. Sun-lightened hairs glinted on his golden skin, and there were shadows in the valleys of his muscles. His taut mouth lifted in a semismile. I felt like my father; I thought I could read his mind. "I bet I know what he thinks can make me happy."

Margo slapped the bedcovers. "Una, you sound like a Vibbert." The Vibberts were unmarried sisters who referred to themselves as "maiden ladies" and lived next door to my mother, complaining nightly of sleeplessness caused by noise on the beach, any noise, all of which they attributed to sexual frolicking.

"I'm serious," she went on. "You'd better watch it. Mom says both of them liked men until they were thirty or so and then went frigid. And you're twenty-eight."

"I'm not frigid. I just don't like the Wild One looking at me that way when he's supposed to be Lily's boyfriend. Besides I completely *hate* the word 'frigid.' It was created by men to make women feel guilty just because they're not in the mood one night."

"That's not what I meant. I meant hating sex."

"I don't hate sex." It seemed extraordinary that we were having this discussion with the Wild One standing in the doorway, a paragon of seduction, not understanding a word.

"No, but you're feeling guilty. Isn't that what this is all about? You imagining Dad reading your mind, watching you and Boom-Boom in bed? And what about John?"

I tried not to think about John Luddington. He was part of the reason I had decided to go to Newport. He was the curator of Achilles House, a small museum on East Eighty-third Street devoted to ancient art. It had once been the private residence of an obscure robber baron. For one year I had thought I loved John. I had spent nearly every night at his brownstone in Brooklyn Heights while my own apartment in Chelsea gathered dust and attracted burglars. During my time with John, it was burgled twice.

John, tall and pristine, wore a gold stickpin to keep his collar together beneath his narrow pale-silk ties. He kept his hands still, just so, on top of his desk, as if he were posing for a sculptor. His black suits never lost their creases or picked up hairs. He took me to every four-star restaurant in the city, then every three-star one. He drew the line there; except for mad forays into Chinatown or Little Italy, excursions which he called "slumming," he had no desire to try the two- and one-star establishments. The exception to this rule was any place that was very in with the art crowd, like Café Brillat and the Silver Star Diner. Often I would be unaware of a restaurant's rating until we were in the cab, heading across the Brooklyn Bridge, when he would say, "If only they gave *five* stars, they'd move that place into the stratosphere," or, "What a charade! *Three* stars? That place was no more than *fair*."

But in spite of his outward refinement, John had loved me messily. He would bring me croissants in bed and let me eat them amid his pressed white sheets (his cleaning woman, finding nothing to clean in the Luddington apartment, would press his sheets and then stack them in the cedar chest, tied with yellow grosgrain ribbons). On our weekend trips to the country, he would tromp through mud in order to show me the largest-known patch of lady-slippers in New England. He would follow me into the dustiest stacks of my favorite library. He would hold me tight, without apparent fear that my makeup would smear on his shirt, whenever I told him I was afraid my father would die of cancer. He adored hugging me.

His widowed mother was rich and lived year round on Monhegan Island in Maine. John would often charter a plane and we would land at Brunswick, drive to Port Clyde, and ferry to the island for a visit. It was there, on a new spring weekend in April, that I discovered the strange sexual stirrings that went on in the Luddington household and sent me running, alone, to the ferry across Muscongus Bay to the first Bonanza Bus headed for New York and sanity.

"John Luddington was a very sick man," I said to Margo.

"In what way?"

"Well, he was . . . troubled. He was driven by success and a need to please. Those two goals are not always compatible."

"Quit talking like a principal. Tell me, Una."

Had the time come to tell? I lay on my back, feeling a hot breeze blow through the open window, and stared at the watermarked ceiling. My youngest sister sat beside me, tweaking my big toe, urging me to talk. The Wild One leaned against the door and stared at both of us.

What I knew of the truth sounded nearly innocent. But my conclusions, my suspicions, and the sum of it all made for a sordid tale. "John and his mother had a weird flirtation going," I said.

"How weird?"

"Well, pretty weird. John's a night owl, and on Monhegan I would go to bed even earlier than I usually do. Probably from hiking all over and swimming in freezing water. I used to wake up and wonder where John was and find him sitting on his mother's bed, having a chat."

"You went swimming in April in *Maine?* You must have been crazy."

"Well . . ."

"So, they were having a chat."

"It never bothered me at first. I thought it was nice—a man who cares about his mother. You know how they say a man who loves his mother will love his wife?"

Margo nodded.

"She had a very frilly bedroom, with scented things all over the place and lots of pink, even though her clothes were quite tailored. It seemed incongruous, seeing her sitting up against about fifty pillows, wearing a pink negligee, with John cuddled around her feet as if he were a little boy."

"This is sounding strange, Una. What else?"

I felt grateful to her for getting my drift, though I shouldn't have been surprised. All three of us had strong powers of intuition when it came to each other.

"She started pushing him on another man."

"You're kidding."

"I'm not. Things were getting serious for John and me. Jemmie could see that; I mean every time John went up there, he took me." The memory of it made me start to cry. At the first sign of tears, the Wild One left the room. "In April we went up, and I had the strangest feeling he was going to propose to me. We had discussed marriage a million times, but he was conventional. He'd go to Tiffany's and pick out a ring by him-

on "Beyond the Bridge" every day between two and three. Because he would pass up big parties because I hated them. Because he had comforted me before and after my father had died. And because, for one year, from one spring till the next, he had given me all the love I had thought I wanted.

W H E N I first felt better after what Lily and Margaret had come to call "The Awakening," I took a book to read on one of the docks. The day was clear and fine, a brilliant day with a stiff offshore breeze. Beneath my long white pants and billowy shirt, I was covered with sunscreen. I wore sunglasses and a wide brimmed straw hat, tied on with a blue silk scarf. Perhaps I looked like a reclusive movie star, but my purpose was more urgent: cancer runs in the Cavan family, especially in the fair among us, the ones who freckle easily. And I have red hair.

"Delilah, can I have your autograph?" asked one girl in a group of high school girls clustered around The Yard's entrance. They moved nervously while I signed the covers of their paperback books with someone's eyeliner: no one had paper or pen. Why did that act have the strange effect of lifting my spirits so high? Because it told me I was loved. It didn't matter that the man I had loved was perverse, that I had twice seen my father's ghost, that I believed the Cavan women had the power of witches. Nice high school girls liked me, and that counted.

"Una!" I turned to see Boom-Boom hurrying toward me from the *Manaloa*. Instantly I resolved to call him "Alastair." I would never call another man, even a sailor, by an idiotic nickname. I would learn the Wild One's first name and call him by it.

"Hi there," he said, grabbing me in a hard, close hug. His body was stout and muscular, and he anchored it to me. Grains of salt clung to his short, curly brown hair. He smiled a three-cornered smile, like Elvis. "Your sisters keep telling me you're off limits. You feeling any better?"

"Yes. Much better. Thank you for the daisies."

We kissed, and I touched his hair. It felt warm, and his scalp felt hot. We were sheltered from the wind behind a tool-shed, and the sun beat relentlessly down from a cloudless August sky.

"I've missed you," he whispered, his mouth on my ear.

We walked toward the *Manaloa*. I felt brave, as if I had fallen off a horse and was daring myself to get back on. A sense of adventure: desire tempered by terror.

The *Manaloa* was an eighty-foot racing sloop, owned by a rich Floridian and crewed by twenty-five men. It always won most of the SORC trophies. Boom-Boom—no, Alastair—and I stepped down the gangway into the main salon, a fabulous room with teak walls, an enormous leather settee, a gimbaled teak table at which a party of twenty could eat without spilling a drop while ten-foot seas battered the hull, and a door that led to a well-stocked wine cellar. Alastair went through it and emerged with a bottle of Cristal Louis Roederer champagne.

"We've got to celebrate your return to the living," he said. I loved the way Australians talked, the way they made "celebrate" sound like "celebright."

We walked into the crew's quarters where Alastair, as one of the senior men, had his own compartment. He undressed me tenderly, as if my absence had made me more fragile. Unhooking my bra's front closure, he spent ample time nibbling my nipples, circling them with his pink tongue, cupping my round breasts with calloused brown hands, murmuring "beautiful, beautiful." We climbed into his bunk with the champagne and two champagne glasses shallow as fingerbowls. They reminded me of the sign at the old Blue Danube.

Alastair opened the bottle the way I knew he would: with one mighty twist that sent the cork ricocheting off the teak walls and bubbly cascading over our naked bodies.

"Can't waste a drop!" he said, bending to slurp champagne out of my navel. Then he poured two glasses and we toasted to health.

I needed that champagne. It blazed on my tongue like fireworks fizzling on the surface of a bay. It went straight to my head and transported me. If Alastair had set sail and pointed east, I couldn't have felt further from Newport.

"You need a tan," Alastair said, tracing my pale shoulder with one big finger. He smelled faintly like the medicated powder he used to combat the dampness on board.

"I hate the sun."

"You can't hate the sun, Una."

"But I do." The banality of our conversation soothed me somehow. It was nothing like what had gone on between me and John. What went on between me and Alastair was pure sex, and the conversation was filler.

"You're sure you're feeling better?" he asked.

"Oh, yes. Much better."

"Well, you're going to feel much, *much* better," he said, a devilish grin on his handsome, tan face. When he grinned, the tiny white creases around his blue eyes closed up. I liked that. It meant he spent most of his time in the sun with a big grin on his face.

We kissed, and Alastair turned serious. Every time we made love, it was as though he was going for the Anaïs Nin award. With his eyes on my face the entire time, he stroked my body, hardly smiling even when I squirmed and giggled when he got to my belly. He went down on me, eating me until I came once, pausing, then making me come again even after I protested, telling him no, it's *your turn*, then finally fucking me. Still, he kept his eyes on my face as he moved slowly. What was he watching for? Signs of passion? I felt it, so he saw them. When he was finished, he kissed me and fell asleep. I knew he'd be awake in ten minutes. For ten minutes I lay there, eyes on the teak ceiling, wondering what, in the largest sense, comes next?

That was Newport: fucking handsome sailors. Everybody did it. Climbing off *Manaloa* we met Ian, another crew member, with a woman I recognized from the Candy Store. We smiled as we passed. On the dock I couldn't help glancing around, nervously expecting to see James Cavan standing by the power station, blocking my passage. But he'd had it wrong. It wasn't sailors with their hands caught in the cookie jar— it was his daughters.

THAT night Margo had to work at The Yard office, so Lily, my protector, took me out to dinner at Christie's.

"I still can't believe what that rat did to you."

"John?"

"Yes, John. If I ever meet the guy, I'll break every bone in his body."

"The worst part of it is, I thought he'd be a pretty good contact for you and Margo in the museum world."

"That's bad, but it's not the worst part. We'll get jobs."

Our waiter brought oysters on the half shell. We stared at them for a few seconds. All of us loved raw oysters and clams, but it took a minute to get used to the idea of something slick and raw sliding down the throat.

"Dear little oyster from the bottom of the sea," Lily said, holding it between two fingers. She always had to say that before eating oysters, the way other people say grace or "bottoms up" or "skoal."

"I don't know what the word is at Brown," I said, "but jobs are fairly tight for art history types."

"I think Margo will wind up staying in Providence, to tell you the truth. She has a good thing with Professor Allen, and she'll probably teach and become more of a Rodin expert."

"Do you still want to move to New York?"

"I have one more semester to go."

"I know, but after that. You can share my place."

"Listen, Buster, when you were with that asshole, you told me I could *have* your place. I'd like to kill him."

"Don't bother." The subject of John was making me nervous. "Do you still want to be a conservator?"

"Yes. Don't get excited, but I have an inside track to the Tate Gallery."

"Don't go to London—you have to come to New York. Who's the inside track?" I asked.

"Guy I met at a party. I know—I know how that sounds. But he's really nice. He's on the Tate's board. He says the department at Brown is regarded very highly at the Tate."

"Forgive me for asking," I said. She knew what I wanted to ask.

"Did I sleep with him? Yes. But so what?"

"And is he married with four children and a country house in Hampstead?" My sister Lily was at that instant staring at me with vivid anger in her green eyes. She was brilliant, even without her degrees, but she was naive. "How does the Wild One figure into this, by the way?"

"Why should he figure into it at all?"

"I thought you said you're in love with him."

"His family lives in Marseilles, and Marseilles is only a plane ride away from London. But who knows what will happen? I'm not about to tie him down," she said with unconvincing detachment. More than either Margo or me, Lily teased herself with dreams of marriage.

Tie him down, Lily? I wanted to say to her. You could be his sails. "What's his real name?" I asked instead.

"Bruno." She giggled.

"No wonder he'd rather be called 'the Wild One.' Do you call him that even in bed?"

"No. In bed I call him 'Wild.' "

At that moment we were interrupted by Sherry Adamson, Queen of the Sailor Fuckers. She collected sailors the way other women collect stamps or commemorative plates. She was short, tan, with long blond hair and huge breasts. She most often wore halters or bikini tops over tight shorts, but that night she wore a backless sundress. For some reason she amused Lily, and Lily tolerated her. Sherry loathed me. Before my arrival in Newport, Alastair had been at the head of her list of new acquisitions. When Lily had introduced us, telling her that I was Delilah on "Beyond the Bridge," Sherry had said snidely, "Oh, I watch 'All My Children.' "

"Hey, Lil," she said. Her eyes flicked at me. "Hi, Una. I thought you'd be back in the city taping by now."

"Not for a couple more weeks." Sherry's loathing for me was blurred by a desire to break into television. She acted with a group that did farce at a bar on Long Wharf. She loved jargon like "taping," and she cultivated any person who might turn into a connection.

"What's up, Sherry?" Lily asked.

"Party on *Vamp* tonight."

"What's *Vamp?* She's not at The Yard, is she?"

"No, she's a Swan 48 over at Treadway. Owned by Bill Grumbacher—doesn't that ring a bell?"

Lily shook her head.

Sherry exhaled impatiently and sat down at our table without invitation. "Grumbacher *Precision?* They build *instruments?*"

"Like trombones?" I asked.

"No, high-tech. This guy was a pioneer in Silicon Valley. Big buckaroos at the Treadway tonight, girls."

I felt like one of a trio of whores planning to scout the automobile dealers' convention at the Hyatt.

"I don't think so, Sherry. I'm meeting Bruno later," Lily said.

I smiled, noting the "Bruno."

"Your loss, but I must admit that *I* wouldn't let the Wild One out of my sight either. Mind if I order a drink?"

The waiter brought rum-and-tonics for all three of us. Then he brought our dinners. "Sorry," Lily mouthed to me while Sherry used her pointy fingernails to eat scallops off my plate and shreds of swordfish off Lily's. The sun had set behind Jamestown, and a fake Dixieland band had started to play "Won't You Come Home, Bill Bailey?" on one of the wharves. Wind sang in the halyards of boats on mooring and lining the docks. I ate my lemony scallops and listened to my sister-protector tell Sherry about the Emmy "Beyond the Bridge" had won for best daytime drama the year I had joined the cast. But, nevertheless, I felt jealous that Lily had allowed Sherry to stay with us at all.

AFTER Labor Day the crowds left Newport. Children returned to school, tourists went back to work, and the sailors headed south. Every day docks at The Yard were lined with women and girls, some crying, all waving goodbye to the boats.

"Why don't they just go along?" I asked Alastair one afternoon. We were sitting on the bow of *Manaloa*, half in and half out of the next boat's shadow, watching two woman hold onto each other and sob as *Twister* heeled out of the harbor.

"What, the girls?" he asked.

"Yes, those women. Why don't they just sign on and crew their way through the SORC? Then they wouldn't have to go through these painful separations."

Alastair fixed his eyes on my face and laughed. He wanted to see whether I was serious. In retrospect I realized that I was picking a fight, but at that moment I felt innocent, even blithe. "Girls in the SORC?" he asked.

"Those two are not girls, Alastair. They are at least twenty-five."

He looked at the two women, still waving at a fast-retreating white blur. "Una, a lady doesn't like attention called to her age. I call 'em girls to give 'em a lift. I call my aunts 'girls.' "

"Don't do that anymore. Would you like me to call you a boy?"

"Sometimes, sure. That's okay."

He wasn't reacting the way I'd hoped he would. I switched tacks. "Well, what's wrong with women in the SORC?"

He laughed again, this time nervously. "Una, I know you're a women's libber, and that's fine with me. But you don't know racing. A girl—a woman—can't live the way she's meant to. Most of the boats don't have the right—facilities. Know what I mean?"

"You mean bathrooms, don't you?"

"Well, sure. I mean, say you're sailing an upwind leg, and you're heelin' as far as you can go, and you have to—relieve yourself. What's a lady going to do? She can't hang over the side the way a guy can. And no one would ever want her to. And there's no way the skipper's going to let her go below to use the head." He shrugged his wide shoulders. "I mean, pissin's not all. It's not the most important thing. Sure there are some lady racers, but none you'd want to share your bunk with. You need muscles to sail, Una. It's not like flapping around in a dinghy, you know."

"I know that," I said solemnly. It was clear that Alastair

considered his use of "lady" instead of "girl" a concession to
my feminist sensibilities. As I have said, I had previously
found comfort in Alastair's and my banal conversation, but
at that moment I felt that he was being used. By me. The way
my father had accused me of being used by Alastair, the way
I had accused Lily of being used by Bruno. It was a sad revelation. I sat in the shade and Alastair sat twelve inches away
in the sun. Our hands touched. I felt fond of him, and even at
that moment of disturbing insight, a growing desire. But I
found myself sneaking glances around The Yard, just in case
my father had come back. I felt dirtier as a user than I ever
had felt during any moment of forbidden sex. The thing I
despised most was manipulation.

I was deep in dire thought when the two women who had
been crying spotted Alastair.

"When do *you* go south?" one of them asked.

Alastair smiled. "Not till next week. Our stick needs work."

"Your stick?" the taller, darker woman asked.

"Our mast. It's that really big one over there." He pointed
at the massive silver mast, horizontal on The Yard's black-
top, glinting in the sun. He winked at me. Alastair's favorite
gags were Monty Python silly walks and double entendres. I
shrank farther into the shadow, but the tall woman saw me.

"Oh, good god. Aren't you Delilah Grant?"

"Yes."

"I *love* your program." She stepped closer to the *Manaloa*
and grasped the lifelines. "I haven't seen you for a couple of
weeks. Have you run off for good?"

"No, only for the summer. I'll be back."

"Will you marry Beck Vandeweghe?"

"I'm not sure." I leaned against a sail bag and smiled.
Alastair puffed with pride, tucked his chin down to his chest,
and grinned at me. In my billowing white garb and dark
shades, I felt very glamorous, the way I almost never felt in
New York. Classmates of mine from Juilliard and actors I
knew from dance class were performing for pittances Off-Off-
Broadway, burning with the sense that they were creating
real art. The day I left Juilliard to accept the part of Delilah

I knew how lucky I was, but even then I had the slightly slimy feeling of selling out.

"Well, we don't want to intrude," the tall woman said, still holding *Manaloa*'s lifeline. "Give my regards to that hunk of a father you have!"

For a second my heart stopped, but then I realized that she was talking about Paul Grant, my soap father, not James Cavan. The women walked off the pier toward Thames Street, glancing as they went at me and the headland jutting into Newport Harbor which blocked their view of *Twister*, now doubtless taking a right turn into the Atlantic Ocean.

O N E week later I stood in the spot where the women had stood waving to *Twister* while Alastair made final preparations to get under way. His fellow crew mates ran back and forth across the white fiberglass deck stowing provisions; checking sparkling stainless-steel winches, halyards, blocks, and cleats; waving goodbye to the gathering throng of women. I felt as if we should all be standing in cupolas or white gingerbread-decked widows' walks atop the houses along Spring Street, waving farewell to our men with lace-trimmed hankies.

"Sorry, baby, the season's over," Alastair said to me, leaning across *Manaloa*'s lifelines to give me a final embrace. I hugged his solid body, feeling the muscles on his back, furrowed as a ribcage. His lips tasted of salt and zinc oxide. "Write me a letter in Lauderdale?"

"Of course. You have my address in New York?"

"You bet."

"Hey, Boom-Boom, kiss her goodbye and get crackin'," Kanga, the skipper, commanded. He smiled sadly at me beneath his damp brown moustache. He had seen these tender farewells before. He knew about women's aching hearts.

The men of *Manaloa* hoisted her sails which filled instantly, cracking like gunfire, and she shot away from the dock. Alastair stood on the bow, hidden from my view by the jib. My sisters waited for me at the end of the dock. They wore

identical khaki shorts and navy shirts: The Yard's uniform.
Lily filled hers more fully than Margo.

" 'It hurts too much to say au revoir, So let's just say hors
d'oeuvre,' " Margo said to me.

"It is sad," I said, surprising myself. How tender I felt!
How deserted! Robbed by the sea of love, alone and lonely.
But perhaps my feeling had more to do with the fact of being
left than with the man who was leaving.

"Wild leaves tomorrow," Lily said. "I'm thinking of bag-
ging this place and heading for Fort Lauderdale."

"You can't. You have to be in Providence in two weeks," I
said.

"Just for one more semester. Maybe I'll go to Florida in
time to miss the snow."

"You love the snow," Margo said.

"I love Wild more. I am serious about this."

"How serious can you be?" I asked. "You have one semester
of graduate school left. What about the Tate Gallery? What
about New York?"

"I know, I know." Lily's eyes were scanning Dock 2 for
signs of the Wild One. The boat he sailed on, *Dauntless*,
looked deserted.

"Lily, he's a sailor. Sailors don't get married, or if they do,
they don't stay at home," Margo said.

"Just like Dad," Lily said, smirking. We all laughed. Our
father and his vagabond ways were always good for a chuckle.
"Speaking of which," Lily said, looking at me, "any more
sightings?"

"No. Not since that time in the apartment." I spoke
steadily, without wavering. I ran through the facts in my
mind. Dad's ghost had dropped in for a visit. He had also
been to the Algonquin. It might be possible for me to see him
at any time. But at the same moment a feeling of craziness
clouded my brain. I knew how it sounded. It made no sense.
Before I had seen him I had not believed in ghosts, reincarna-
tion, or heaven. Perhaps I still didn't. Perhaps he had been
no more than a foggy dream after a bad year of death, John
Luddington, and loveless, guilty fucks. I envied Lily for her

raw love of Bruno, but I also wanted to warn her: men die or defect, but they leave you one way or the other.

T H E following weeks passed in a late-summer haze. Early mornings were chillier, but the sea retained heat and kept the air warm. Restless air currents carried autumn down from Canada, and by our last week in Newport, the trees along Ocean Drive had started to turn.

"Let's take a sea cruise!" Margo announced one morning when my anxiety about returning to New York had reached fever pitch and Lily's empty longing to see Bruno had plunged her to her nadir. We piled into the front seat of our father's old Volvo wagon and, with Lily driving, me wedged beside the gearbox, and Margo smoking a cigarette out the open window, we drove away, six breasts abreast, toward Ocean Drive.

The drive winds for approximately six miles along Newport's southern coast, beginning at Hammersmith Farm, where Jacqueline Bouvier spent her girlhood summers, and ending at Bellevue Avenue, where the robber barons' glittering palaces erected during the last century still remain, each "cottage" now either a museum or a packet of twenty or so condos. In between stretched wonderful Ocean Drive. It bordered the wildest stretch of Atlantic south of Maine. One could see: crashing surf, craggy rocks, dories, calm bays, swans, pheasants, hedgehogs, bowers of wild roses and orange day lilies, owls hunting over fields of dry grass, marshes, fishermen catching striped bass, ships coming home from Liverpool-Genoa-Tangiers, flocks of gulls chasing schools of blues, trawlers with their nets out, couples kissing on the rocks, scrubby pines, stone ruins, sheep, Canada geese. The houses were huge, but wonderful, unlike the gross castles on Bellevue Avenue. One looked like a retreat in Normandy, another like a haunted house with sixteen chimneys. One was a saltwater farm, and every Christmas the owners would hand out eggs, milk, and lamb to the poor of Newport.

Lily, Margo, and I drove along it whenever we had free

time. That day we shared a six-pack of beer. We had the car radio turned up. It felt like all the times we had driven together in years past when we had lived in the same house, when our parents had been distracted by their own troubles and left us to our own devices. I didn't know that day that Lily had already started receding from me, and that it would be our last drive in the front seat of that Volvo—the last drive together in any car for a long, long time.

I remember that we didn't talk much that day. We all watched the scenes pass and thought privately. Occasionally Margo would change the radio station. We were preparing to part. It had been our first August together in—how long? I tried to figure it out. Five years? Six? We were grownups. We paid rent for our own apartments, even though Lily and Margo shared theirs. Our father, our patriarch, was dead. We fell in and out of love with men, and we shared advice on birth control. Margo and I favored diaphragms (the safest method) while Lily used the Pill (more convenient, less likely to interrupt the spontaneity). Looking back at that entire summer in Newport, it seemed that all three of us had regressed. Each of us had chucked the real world and woven a cocoon around ourselves in Newport, the raciest port in New England. We found security in promiscuity, in the transience of sailors, in the Here Today, Gone Tomorrow school of love. If you knew what to expect, you could not be hurt. You could go happily to sleep at night in the arms of a man you knew would be gone by September. There was no mystery about it. You said goodbye on schedule, at a predetermined place. You didn't have to say "so long" because of revelation about one man's sexuality; you didn't have to conjure up a vision of your father's ghost in order to say a civilized farewell, to replace the one you had said to his comatose body. You only had to lower your expectations.

But it could not last. We had been raised by parents whose Catholic beliefs had not stopped until our father was ravaged by cancer, and parents with Catholic beliefs raise daughters with Catholic consciences. So what if we Believed Not? The guilt was there. You didn't fuck without love for long before guilt snuck up on you. It hulked overhead, waiting until you were at your weakest, and then it sent hallucinations that looked like your father to yell at you, shame you, tell you to pull yourself together. Cruising blithely along Ocean Drive, the September wind blowing warm whiffs of salt air, pine, and Margo's cigarette smoke through the car, we didn't speak, but we were all thinking the same thing. Our thought was a fourth person, sitting in the back seat. Una, Lily, and Margaret Cavan were past twenty-four. Time was moving on, pressing on, passing by. We had to get it together, pick up the pieces, fish or cut bait. *It was time to get married.*

Dance class. Fourth floor of a converted factory building on Tenth Avenue in New York. Enormous black windows along two walls holding sepia-toned reflections of thirteen stretching bodies. Liver-colored linoleum floor. Garish fluorescent light illuminating the cavernous room. I look around, and I see: our instructor, a woman last seen on stage dancing the role of the Sylph; four women who have taken time off from avant-garde companies like the Lulie McLeod Ballet, Nancy Kramer Dancefest, and STRUT! to have babies; eight men and women, actors and actresses (three of whom I knew at Juilliard) who act, direct, or act and direct for experimental, dirt-poor theater companies; me. Una Rose Cavan. Soap Opera Actress Extraordinaire. I am the only person in the room who wears new, expensive, matching leotard and leg warmers. My leg warmers have gold threads in them. The neckline of my leotard plunges so that the beads of sweat between my full, pale breasts gleam in the harsh light.

The camera is not kind. If I gain a pound in life, it looks like two on television. I must move with extreme grace, with perfect posture, as if I had a bowl of raspberries balanced on the crown of my head. Right on the crown. I must not spill one piece of fruit. I envision the bowl: it is blue-and-white Canton china, made in a dynasty so long ago that the bones of its maker have turned to dust and sunk to the center of the earth. If you try to dig to China, that is what you will find.

Dance class helps me make the grace, the posture, the thinness possible. Plus it fills the hours between six and eight when I should be sitting at a cozy candlelit table, gazing into the eyes of a loved one.

One of the people I knew at Juilliard is still my friend:

Susan Russell. The other people I knew there have not exactly renounced me. Their replies to my inquiries about
health, career, family, etc., however, could be described as
"curt." Susan has spent much of the last year and a half out
of work, but next spring she will have the lead role in a wonderful new play at the Charles Place Theater. She will play
the sister of a woman accused of witchcraft in Salem.

Susan Russell: tall; skinny (always thinks she's fat); gently
frizzy brown hair; hazel eyes whose myopia she corrects by
wearing untinted contacts; loves the idea of living on Nova
Scotia; loves her husband, her parents, Princess Diana, and
me. Beside my sisters, Susan Russell is my best friend in the
old-schoolgirl sense of best friends. We tell each other everything, and we are envious when the other does better in the
profession or has lunch with another woman. Susan dances
beside me. She is five inches taller, she wears a black leotard
with balls of grey fuzz all over it, and I can hear her breathe
out but not in.

Who would *you* say is doing better? *S*, who struggles daily,
who waits and hopes for a great part or even a terrible part,
who once every twelve months or so gets a part, only to have
the play close after a short run, but not until she's gotten good
notices and given her husband a chance to tell her she's the
best? Or *U*, who was grabbed out of drama school by the producer of one of TV's hottest soap operas just because she had
the right pale, red-haired, vulnerable Irish looks, who must
speak essentially the same melodramatic lines on each episode,
who makes a veritable fortune for her troubles, who is recognized at least twice every waking hour on the streets, and who
goes home alone? *Think carefully before you answer.*

S U S A N and I showered side by side in the smelly locker
room. I stared with unbridled envy at her long, thin ribcage.
"Don't look at me that way," she said, turning her back to me.
"I'm fat."

"You are not fat. Quit saying you are. Do you still throw
up?"

"Not often. Don't talk about it."

"Okay. How is your part coming?"

"Really great." She squeezed water out of her hair, which started to fluff the second she stepped out of the shower. We dried ourselves on the threadbare pink towels supplied by the dance studio. "My character isn't sure herself whether her sister is a witch. But she has to find out—not that it will make her feel different or change their relationship in the long run."

"Witches," I said.

"I know. Louis and I are going to Salem in October, just to walk around and get the feeling. I remember going there on a school vacation with my family. I wrote reports about it for the next three years."

"Places like that are haunted."

"I know. Just thinking about what they did to the women. Atrocities. Places like that make me feel as though the things could happen again, or that they're still happening. As if there's a secret society in Salem, meeting every sabbath to talk over the witch list—who's bad, who's evil."

"I could never go to Germany," I said.

"I know. Germany would be the same. Betrayals and torture."

"Just like Monhegan. Only there, Jemmie Luddington was the witch *and* the tribunal."

Susan looked at me, deciding whether to speak, then did. "I saw John, by the way. Louis and I took my mother to Achilles House last weekend."

"I don't want to know, but you'd better tell me." I slipped on my jeans and started buttoning my yellow cotton shirt. I moved slowly, with great deliberation, but hearing John's name took my breath away. I felt as if I might never get it back.

"He's the same. Dark suit, Gucci loafers, perfect manicure. He's moving into Manhattan."

I snorted. "What a joke. He was always talking about 'land values,' and the quality you could get in Brooklyn Heights for half the price." I thought then about my father and his real estate deals, of how the men in my life always seemed to be unduly concerned with the price of property. "Where in Manhattan?"

"TriBeCa."

"God, *TriBeCa.* He's about ten years behind the times. What an asshole! He doesn't even have any imagination about it. I've heard about these *row* houses in *Harlem* with unbelievable original detail that you can buy for a *song*—why doesn't he buy one of those? Then he could be in the *vanguard.*"

"Una, he was *really* embarrassed to see us. He asked all about you."

"What did you tell him? That I have Hodgkin's disease, I hope."

"No, I told him that you are perfectly wonderful. Doing A-OK. Aren't you?"

"No." I tied my shoelaces. I felt like total shit. Three minutes of conversation about John Luddington could reduce me to a shivering, furious, vengeful wraith. I wanted to spread black batwings and fly to Brooklyn Heights before he had a chance to hide in TriBeCa. I wanted to clutch his pate in my teeth, fly him far, far out over the Atlantic, and drop him into the murky deep.

"He's alone, by the way."

"What do you mean, 'he's alone'?"

"I mean, he's not seeing anyone else. He made that very clear. He repeated it three times."

"Of course he's not seeing anyone. That's the whole point—Jemmie wanted me to think that within three weeks he'd be cruising the bars on West Street, but I knew what was happening. She's ruining him for *anyone.* She couldn't bear to see him with me or anyone else."

"Well, anyway, he's the same," Susan said quickly. "What do you think of Lady Di's new hairstyle?"

"I like it." The mention of Lady Di melted my black heart a little. I still remembered how young, how innocent she had been when she married Charles. She had reminded me of Lily and Margaret.

"How's the show?" she asked me.

I shrugged. Usually it helped to talk to Susan, but I envied her new part in *Hester's Sister.* I had visions of her taking it

to Broadway where she would become an overnight sensation
and wind up playing parts like Lady Macbeth, Mary Tyrone,
Hedda Gabler, Amanda Wingfield, Joan of Arc, even Lady
Di when the time came. "The show is fine."

She watched me shrewdly. She had soft features that
molded to any character she tried to play. "You're in a rut.
But this should help—Louis and I are having a party—a
small party," she amended, glimpsing my expression, "on
Saturday night. You are coming."

"I am?"

"You are."

It was settled.

I SAT in my dressing room at Soundstage 3 and prepared to
go before the cameras. My face was made up with snowy
powder covering my cheeks and violet crescents beneath my
eyes. Delilah was on the lam. I wore a snorkel coat, one of
those bottle-green nylon jackets with orange lining and a ratty
fur-trimmed hood that unpopular boys wore in high school,
the sort of boys who belonged to audiovisual club or played
sousaphone in the band. Today a blizzard would trap Delilah
in a cabin deep in the Michigan woods, and she would be
"rescued" by a fur trapper with murder in his heart.

"Paler, hon," our director, Art Panella, was saying to the
makeup woman, Abby Schwartz. "She's been freezing in the
elements for eighteen hours, for heaven's sakes," he said.
"She's lost all her color."

"Art, wouldn't my face be red, not white?" I asked, thinking of the way my nose had flamed the last time I went skiing.

"Una, try to think of the effect: you're going to be surrounded by the whitest snow we can make, and night's coming on. We're gonna turn on the blue lights."

"Whatever you think." I stared into my blue eyes and
didn't cough when a puff of white powder went down my
throat. Art left the room. On the set he called directions to
Leonard, our lighting man. "I want a bluish cast on the snow,"
he was saying. "Think winter in the north woods." The studio
lights were already heating up. A trickle of sweat ran behind

my ear. I sat straighter in my padded seat, stared into my own eyes, and spun back eight years.

I was a senior at Juilliard. I was playing Gina in Ibsen's *The Wild Duck*. My parents, Lily, and Margo had come from Connecticut to see me perform. My auburn hair was swept up into a French twist, and I wore an old-fashioned long dress of pale green silk. It pinched at my waist and flared slightly, and when I walked it swished against my legs. I remember standing in the wings, having the bold, naive thought "I was born for this." Overhead lights blazed, and although the audience was invisible in the dark, I could sense their expectancy. My cue came, and I flew onstage.

After the performance people came backstage to kiss the actors and tell us how fine we were. My father gave me a slightly wilted bouquet of long-stemmed red roses that he had held on his lap throughout the performance. My mother gave me a leatherbound edition of *The Wild Duck*. Lily and Margo begged me to tell them everything I knew about the actor who had played Gregers. Into this Cavan family scene enter Chance Schutz, six feet two inches of Prussian will and demeanor. He wore a suit so dark and tailored, so obviously full of silk threads that, although I had never seen a custom-made suit or been to London, I immediately thought "Savile Row." His silver hair was impeccable, his grey eyes gleamed out of dark sockets like a wolf's, and his ageless face was that of a man thirty or sixty. He stood in our midst and stared at me. Later Margo told me: "He drank you with his eyes." He took my hand in a painfully firm handshake.

"I want you for Delilah," he said.

"What?" I asked.

"I produce 'Beyond the Bridge,' and I will create a character for you. Very vulnerable, just right for you. Come, let's talk."

My father chuckled and stepped forward. His suit, although not custom-made, was of the finest wool and fit his lean body perfectly. His curly light-brown hair was merely bordered with silver, and he figured that that gave him the edge. He shook Chance Schutz's hand.

"Sorry, but not tonight. Una's got her family in town."

My head filled with blood and I thought I would explode or pass out from embarrassment. It was so typical of my father to take charge of his daughters, even when one was standing at the crossroads of her career.

Chance engaged my eyes and said, "I shall call you." He handed me his business card and walked away.

My father, fuming, pulled out his cigarettes. "That bastard, what does he think he's up to?"

"Excuse me, sir, but you can't smoke in the theater," said one of the stagehands.

My father herded all of us into a taxi and directed the driver to Le Perigord. Lily, Margo, and I sat on the pink banquette while my parents faced us in chairs. My father could not forget Chance Schutz. "When I think of that guy, what a lot of gall—telling Una he'd call her. That puke. You know what's on his mind, don't you?"

"James, he wants to offer her a part," my mother said, looking past me as she spoke. My mother, during those years, had a difficult time focusing on anyone.

"A part, yes, but on a *soap* opera! What a lot of cheap trash. Una's a trained stage actress. She could be another Katharine Cornell. You stay away from that troublemaker, Una."

"Television is a perfectly viable medium," I said loftily, the way I said almost everything that year.

"Sure, television's okay. Television's *fine*. But not a soap opera. I'd be ashamed to tell people my daughter was on a soap opera. That would really make me sick." My father sipped his seltzer water. He almost never drank when the family was together.

"Una would be *great* in soap operas," Lily said.

"Don't let me hear you say that," my father warned sternly.

Because it was a celebration my father ordered for everyone: rack of lamb, baby green beans, and Pommard. I can remember every bite I took. Lily and Margo kept finishing their water because they liked the looks of the young waiter who came to refill their glasses.

Later I drove with them in a cab back to the Westbury. In

the lobby my father and I said goodbye. He hugged me, and I smelled his characteristic odor of wool, sweat, and stale cigarettes. "Sweetheart, you know I only want you to be happy," he said. "You know that, don't you?"

"Sure I do."

"That's why it's important that you don't talk to that jerk. You don't really want to be on soap operas, do you?"

"Not really."

"I mean, you didn't go to the finest drama school in the nation in order to spend the rest of your life crying over this or that. You're the best damn actress I've ever seen."

"Thank you, Dad," I said, and I meant it.

He kissed me and gave me money for a cab. When I arrived at my apartment on West Seventy-fourth Street I didn't wait for Chance Schutz to call me. I found his card and called him.

"Ah, hello, Miss Cavan. Family obligations all squared away?" he said the instant he heard me speak.

His quick recognition shocked and flattered me. "How did you know it was me?"

"You have a distinctive, may I say, lilt to your voice. Very pretty. A very pretty voice."

"Thank you."

"You are calling about my offer, are you not?"

"Yes."

"Wonderful. I am prepared to offer you a part on 'Beyond the Bridge.' A part that will lead to a starring role."

I held the smooth black receiver and listened to this man promise to change my life. He was going to make me a star. Adrenaline stung my veins. "A starring role?" I repeated dully.

Chance Schutz laughed. "You think about it. It's a bit much to consider all at once. You come by my office and I will give you more details. You come by tomorrow, how's that?"

I had dance, singing, and playwriting classes the next day, but I told him of course I'd be there. He took me to lunch at the Russian Tea Room. I ate blini with Malassol caviar and listened to his ideas. He had seen me act in previous Juilliard productions and had snuck into several rehearsals. For the part of Delilah Grant, he wanted a new actress, one who had my "chiseled features" and a gentle way about her. Delilah was to be a victim; she would be misunderstood by her stepmother and sisters, taken advantage of by the men in her life, and frequently placed in mortal danger. But as her character expanded she would find reservoirs of inner strength. She would turn the tables, and in five years Chance Schutz saw Delilah becoming one of the show's two main characters.

He didn't need to tell me that Rachel Moore, Kurtz Drago, Corey Levinson, and Cecile Van Vliet had stepped from "Beyond the Bridge" into major stage and screen roles. Yes, it was a soap opera, but its scope was greater than that of most soaps. It demanded more of the actors; its plot lines were not as contrived as other soap plot lines. "Truthfully, 'Beyond' has the most artistic integrity of any soap opera today," Chance told me that afternoon. "We strive for something one usually finds in film or even theater. We are not pap."

I sat beside him on the cozy rose-red banquette and popped fish eggs against the roof of my mouth with my tongue. Chance's perfect hand rested on the tablecloth beside mine. His nails were clipped straight across; he wore a weighty gold crest ring on his pinky finger. Occasionally he would turn to smile at me, and I would see a softness in his wolf eyes. I found myself leaning forward, to see whether he wore a wedding band on his left hand. He didn't, but I knew that meant nothing. Many Juilliard professors were married and didn't wear rings. With dessert we had Russian tea in a glass, and I found myself in the middle of an elaborate fantasy. Chance Schutz would take me to his apartment in his limousine and invite me upstairs to continue discussing his offer. We would lounge on a glove-soft leather sofa. I envisioned yards of heavy brocade draperies at the floor-to-ceiling windows, soft lamplight, classical music on the stereo. Chance would say, "If you want the part, there is only one thing that you must do . . ."

Instead he handed me cab fare and told me to think things over. Then he hurried off to meet his wife, who taught a pottery class at the New School, leaving me to pocket the money and take a subway home. Riding through the tunnel beneath Seventh Avenue, I tried not to think about my fantasy. Only a daughter of James Cavan would expect sex demands from every man she met. I felt ashamed of myself. Chance Schutz cared about artistic matters, not sleeping with actresses. He had described in loving detail the sort of pots his wife created: huge, cockeyed things that looked like umbrella stands and spittoons. I began a new fantasy in which "Beyond's" cast members were like a family with Chance Schutz and his wife as the loving, benevolent parents. Before I reached my stop at Seventy-second and Broadway, I had already made my decision: I would take a screen test for "Beyond the Bridge" as soon as Chance Schutz could arrange it.

We set it up for the following Tuesday. I walked from my apartment to the studio on West Fifty-sixth Street, growing more nervous with each passing block. I was to read a scene with Stuart MacDuff, the actor who played Paul Grant, Delilah's soap opera father. Paul Grant was a former bank president as well as the mayor of Mooreland. Delilah, his middle and favorite daughter, had run away from home five years earlier. During her absence she had been a victim of the white slave trade in Singapore, rescued by a ship's captain who had turned out to be the first transsexual Rhodesian, and finally returned to Mooreland. The scene I read for my screen test was the first meeting between Paul and Delilah Grant in five years.

DELILAH (*anguished*). Dad, don't you know me?
PAUL (*hesitating*). Not . . . Delilah?
DELILAH Yes, I've come . . . home!
PAUL (*embracing her*). Oh, Delilah, Delilah. You don't know how much your mother and I missed. . . . And now your mother is dead. I have remarried. (*Slaps his head, looks deeply into her eyes.*) But all that can wait. You *are* going to stay?
DELILAH (*shy, eyes downcast*). If you'll have me. If you'll forgive me.

PAUL Darling, forgive you? These years have been hell
for us, not knowing. Tell me everything.

DELILAH Oh, Dad, they've been hell for *me*. I didn't
really mean to run away, you know. I just had to
think, to be alone for a few days. (*Becomes agitated.*)
That man, that man—I'll never forget . . .

PAUL (*embracing her again, this time roughly*). Don't
talk, don't think. We've all the time in the world for
that.

Art Panella, the director, told me I had played the scene
with more reserve than he would like. But basically he
thought I was fine. Chance, dressed in khaki pants, a peach
silk shirt, and a golden chamois leather jacket, leaned against
one of the huge cameras. "I beg to differ, Arthur," he said.
"She is perfect. Quiet, shy. Perfect. And she comes to us via
Juilliard. She will be a feather in our cap."

I beamed proudly. Stuart MacDuff stood beside me until
Chance handed me the contracts. Then he kissed my cheek
and walked away. My starting salary seemed immense.
Chance promised there would be better scripts as soon as they
could lure a certain writer away from a competing show. I
thought of hiring a lawyer, of showing the contracts to my
father, but excitement prevented me. I signed on the spot. I
would start two weeks later, leaving me just enough time to
withdraw from Juilliard and inform my family.

T H A T was seven years ago. Now I sat before my dressing-
room mirror, made up for the wilds of Lake Huron, and prepared to film my scene with the fur trapper. As far as Delilah
was concerned, I perceived no vast difference between a psy-
chotic fur trapper and a white slaver; my character's character had not changed as much as I had hoped it would.
Chance had hired several new scriptwriters who were period-
ically replaced by other new scriptwriters. The truth, which
I hadn't wanted to face in my wide-eyed days, when I had
hoped to revolutionize daytime drama, was that soap operas

had to be formulaic. The audience liked them that way. Tears, love, and angst. "Make them laugh, make them cry, and make them wait," one of our longest-lasting writers professed.

Art was having some trouble getting the lighting exactly the way he wanted it. One of the stagehands told me there would be a fifteen-minute delay. I did what I always did during delays: I called Lily and Margo in Providence.

Margo answered. As soon as she heard my voice she called for Lily to pick up the extension.

"Baby, baby, baby, have I got news for you!" Lily said.

"She's in love," Margo said drolly.

"Oh, you miss Bruno?" I asked.

"No, he's gone forever. I've faced that. This is someone new—a *New Yorker*."

"Really? Tell all."

"He's a man of medicine," Margo said. "Our Lily's going to marry a doctor."

"No one said anything about *marrying*," Lily said.

"But you're seeing quite a bit of him," Margo said.

"Tell me! I only have a few minutes," I said. I could hear Art making happy, satisfied grunts in the studio, and I knew he'd call for me soon.

"Okay. He's forty. He's a heart surgeon at New York Hospital, and he's giving a seminar here in Providence."

"A heart surgeon," Margo said gravely.

"Also, he loves art, especially Cinquecento! I met him in Professor Bachman's office—they're close friends."

"What's his name?"

"Henk Voorhees. He's Dutch."

"You should hear him," Margo said. "He's always scoffing at everything. He looks at our white paper towels and says 'Eh, you should get a color.' "

"He's forty?" I asked.

"Yes, but a very young forty," Lily said.

"Married?"

"No, divorced."

"His ex-wife lives in The Hague," Margo said.

"Well, it sounds interesting. When did you meet him?"

"Just last Thursday. He's in Rhode Island for another week, and then it's back to New York."

"Do you think you'll visit him sometime? I'd love to meet him."

"Definitely."

"She took him to Newport, and they had brunch at the Candy Store," Margo said. We all laughed, thinking of the secrets about Lily known by the Candy Store waiters, of the things Henk could have learned if he'd known whom to ask.

"So, our Lily's living dangerously," I said just before Art rang the bell in my dressing room, indicating that I was wanted in the studio. We said goodbye, and I hung up smiling. Perhaps Lily wouldn't go to London after all. My secret wish was that all three of us could live in the same city, if not under the same roof.

SATURDAY night I went to Susan and Louis's party in their loft apartment snuggled beneath the Brooklyn Bridge. They shared one floor of an old warehouse with two other couples. All except two were actors, and they were painters. The loft, divided into three separate living areas with a communal kitchen and bathrooms, had windows on only one narrow wall, so most of it was very dark. Susan and Louis combatted this by painting their rooms white, but one of the other couples said that the cavelike aspect had drawn them to the loft in the first place, and had painted their walls black. The noise of rushing bridge traffic was constantly overhead, rattling the old building's foundations. But the rent was cheap, and that was why Susan and Louis stayed there.

I wore snug black jeans, battered black boots, and a big blue corduroy shirt. I put more kohl around my eyes than I usually do, and I wore huge, dangling silver earrings. Whenever I go to parties at Susan's I feel super-aware of my clothes. I make at least three times as much money as anyone else there, so I don't like to look affluent; also, it is the most artistic crowd I know, and their clothing is as much a means of self-expression as paper, canvas, or the stage. That night I stood in the stairwell, listening to Talking Heads music blare from inside, patting my hips and wondering whether I looked too casual, not funky enough, or too contrived.

Louis Pease, Susan's husband, opened the door. He hugged me tight, and I kissed his lips through his soft brown beard. Louis, a composer of avant-garde string music as well as an actor, looks more like a husky cowboy. He wears jeans that flare, flannel shirts, and string ties. He could stand to lose some weight.

"Hey, Una," he said. "You've arrived."

I looked into the room behind him and saw masses of dancers. "Oh, Susan said this was a small party."

"You've seen our big ones—it's relative."

It was true; I had never been to their place with fewer than seventy-five other people, many of whom Susan and Louis didn't even know. Word got around about their parties; to people who loved parties, theirs had the right chemistry or something. Susan, Louis, and the loftmates left bowls of fresh popcorn, pretzels, cherries in season, M&M's, Fritos with hot dip, and chicken wings around the room. You brought your own liquor. You couldn't even get a gingerale from the hosts.

I recognized several Juilliard classmates right away. Susan, lithe in a turquoise turtleneck over black tights which made her legs look as if they went on forever, ducked between dancing guests to greet me. She stood with her back to Louis and squirmed with the music against his body.

"Glad you're here," she said, leaning just far enough away from Louis to kiss me.

"Una is saying you lured her here on false pretenses," Louis said.

"This started out to be a very tiny party—dinner for thirteen people. I was going to make paella. But then I started figuring—hors d'oeuvres, the shellfish, *saffron*, which costs a veritable fortune per pinch, wine, dessert . . . I would have spent as much and worked six times as hard as I did for this party."

"It's okay," I said. I knew that in an hour I would be having a good time, but entering a room filled with people terrified me. Sometimes I wondered whether that fact lay behind my choice to act before cameras instead of a live audience; the reactions of crowds were immediate and brutal. Standing within one, you could see what everyone thought of you by the expressions on their faces. I always acted confident as hell, as if *I* knew I was wonderful and therefore couldn't give a shit for what anyone thought of me, but secretly I constantly scanned faces for clues: did they think I was too flashy, too conceited, too reserved, too quiet, too eager? I honestly didn't know. So I acted as if I didn't care. Only Susan knew.

After showing me their stash of Scotch, since I hadn't been forewarned and therefore couldn't be expected to have brought my own, Susan and Louis left me to my own devices. Intimate orange light shined from small table lamps. I stood against the old refrigerator, its metal skin yellow and its edges round, and watched the dancers.

"Hi, Una," a husky female voice said. It belonged to Jane Valera, a woman I hadn't seen since Juilliard. "How is your life on television?"

"Terrific. How's life on the boards?" I happened to know that Jane hadn't had a paying part since graduation. Even at school she had had a superiority complex, had called our professors and actors like Al Pacino and Glenda Jackson "colleagues," had thought that any art without struggle was worthless. She would say "television," not "soap opera," because she would not want to admit that she knew what a soap opera was. She had claimed never to watch TV. She had once said she had never heard of Mary Tyler Moore.

"I'm not acting right now," she said. "Ted and I have founded a repertory company at our place in Vermont."

"Really? You have a company?"

"A *wonderful* company. I feel so fortunate. The honor of working with these people . . . I hardly deserve it. We have Robert Hincks . . . do you know his work?"

I nodded. Robert Hincks was a director known for his wild, often violent interpretations of classics like *The Three Sisters*, *The Master Builder*, *The Tempest*. Jane talked on and on, swinging her very long, dark hair in that characteristic, jittery way she had, an affectation meant to suggest that she was a neurotic artist. She spoke in a low, gravelly voice and punctuated her speech with choppy shoulder shrugs and jerks of the head. Her favorite trick was to put herself down, forcing the other person to contradict her.

"Ted and I have a country house, the Battenkill runs across our property . . . you can see the mountains all around you. We have an old barn, a massive old barn, which we have made into a theater . . . we have already started rehearsing *The Cherry Orchard.* The place is so lovely. So . . . serene. You absolutely must come to us. It seems to . . . affect people's artistic spirits."

I knew exactly what someone like Jane must think of the artistic spirit of a soap opera actress. "Thank you for inviting me," I said.

"Ted and I feel so fortunate to have such excellent colleagues," she continued breathily. "We have Trent Lieber, who trained at Yale, Sligo Mallory, who came to us from Trinity in Providence, Hoya Armstrong, who's worked at the O'Neill workshop six summers in a row—we were so fortunate to get him—and Julius Kramer, from the Guthrie. He did that Pinter in New York last season. Did you see it?"

"No, I didn't." I noticed that everyone Jane had mentioned was male. She had always had a retinue of men at Juilliard; she seemed to draw them with her husky voice, her self-effacing manner. I would say she drew them like "moths to a flame," but she was so mothlike herself, flitting through the conversation, trying to convince the world she was more spirit than human.

Susan came to rescue me. "Una, I want you to see Stan's new painting. 'Scuse us, Jane." She led me away from the kitchen, into the part of the loft which belonged to Stan and Daria. "Was she telling you about her artists' colony in Vermont?"

"Yes, you can see the mountains from the stage."

"Louis and I went up last July. She had a big party, where we were all expected to help build the stage. I'm not kidding you! She was really pissed off because we'd forgotten to bring hammers—she didn't have enough to go around. So her boyfriend taught me how to use an electric saw, and I spent the afternoon sawing wood for the seats. The audience sits on benches. 'Rough-hewn benches,' according to the brochure."

"Very basic—the performances are so mesmerizing, you're not supposed to notice your ass is killing you."

"Listen. I had to go into her house, to use the telephone or something, and you'll never believe it. Jane has a Betamax. *And* an Atari."

"I don't believe it."

"I swear it. It's hooked up to this enormous thirty-six-inch color TV in her bedroom. That's where the phone was."

"Sure it was." I smiled at Susan's blush. She hates to admit she likes to snoop.

"But the best part is—the actors all live in her house. Something very kinky is going on up there. Ted acts as if he doesn't care, but the air was *electric*. I mean, Jane was moving in her typical slinky way, and the actors were rubbing against her, trying to get her alone. It was so animalistic. And she was having a very open affair with one of them—Sligo, I think."

"I notice Ted's not with her tonight," I said. Susan and I were standing in Stan's studio, which was painted black and smelled like paint thinner. His canvases were huge, covered with nightmare images of howling skeletons. "Jesus, Susie— how can you have this stuff in the house?" It made me feel creepy, as if the skeletons could come alive.

"They're about Auschwitz," Susan said. "He's been dreaming about it for months now. We wake up and hear him screaming . . ."

I shuddered. "I don't see how you and Louis do it, living with four other people."

"It's what we can afford," Susan said briskly, and instantly I felt terrible.

"I know," I said, trying to smooth my gaffe. "I just mean that it must be difficult. If I have to face anyone before I have three cups of coffee and a look at the *Times*, forget it . . ."

"You're lucky you can live alone," she said.

"Well . . ."

"You are."

"You're lucky to be in *Hester's Sister*. Is the play in shape yet? How's it going?"

"Fine," she said. She warmed to me again, and her hazel

eyes sparked with excitement. "I mean *really* fine. Keep your fingers crossed, Una. I think it could be a hit."

"That's great," I said, but why did my heart sink? Susan was my best friend. I wanted her to succeed. This is all because of Jane, I told myself. Jane always made me feel cheap, like a sellout, acting for money while everyone else is acting for passion. But I knew it wasn't only Jane; for her to make me feel that way, it had to be the truth, didn't it?

Susan and I returned to the bosom of the party. She told me to check out the men; she had invited several she thought I might like. I danced a few times. Every so often Louis would find me with a refill for my glass of Scotch. I found myself thinking of Lily and Margo. They understood me. I was always at my best when I was with them because they knew what to look for. Standing at the edge of the dancers, I found myself thinking of how wonderful it would be if Lily did marry the Dutch heart surgeon and move to New York; we could be one another's built-in support system.

I danced a few times with David Hammarslough, a man I had dated at Juilliard. David is tall and dark. He cuts his own hair and always wears the same thing: jeans and a ratty black turtleneck. Sometimes I think he looks like a prisoner, but he has soft black eyes that are kind and knowing. He has appeared in two successful Broadway plays and one Canadian movie. At Juilliard we took dance class together and spent numerous hours staring at each other's bodies before finally going to bed together, the same night we played opposite each other in Gorky's *Enemies*.

The night of Susan's party was the first time I had seen him in four years. I had drunk too much Scotch by the time I finally spotted him, and I pressed my body close to his while we danced.

"You really look great, Una," he said.

"I think of you a lot. I keep reading reviews of your work, and you keep getting better."

"Have you seen it?"

"Some of it. The movie and one of the plays." I had felt overjoyed when I saw how good he was in each of them; I hadn't felt at all envious until the middle of each following night.

Dancing with him to a synthesizer version of "Moon River," my nose nuzzled below his armpit, and his smell made me think of sex. We lurched out of the loft onto Pearl Street and found a cab heading north. David told the driver to take us to the Village. He lived in a narrow brownstone that had once belonged to Edgar Allan Poe.

"You've got to come in," he said. "I have this cask of cognac, it's supposed to be more than a hundred years old." He was as drunk as I was. Staring straight ahead, at nothing in particular, he fumbled for money to pay the driver. "They say Poe wrote 'The Raven' in the room where I sleep," he said, kissing one of my eyebrows. "You don't believe in ghosts, do you?" he asked.

"No," I said. The image of my father in bermuda shorts scuttled in and out of my mazed brain. It's okay, I told myself. I've known David for years—*I used to love him.* That makes it okay.

I sat on an overstuffed couch in his cluttered living room while David assembled snifters, a candle, and the wood cask. "Now to open it . . ." he said.

"Oh, maybe we should forget the cognac," I said. I felt dizzy and faintly nauseated.

"No, it's great stuff, it's supposed to be more than a hundred years old," David said, then turned suddenly and looked at me. He was kneeling beside the coffee table, trying to figure out how to open the little cask. Smiling, he walked across the floor on his knees, and kissed me wetly. "Great to see you, Una," he said.

"Great to see *you.*"

"No, I really mean it." He kissed me again, and began pulling down my pants' zipper.

I remember crashing into his bathroom and throwing up into his toilet. When I returned to the living room, David wasn't there. I found him passed out on his king-sized bed. For about ten seconds I considered walking home to Chelsea, but I was positive I would be taken advantage of, the state I was in. I took off everything except my shirt and lay beside David on the bed.

We wakened holding each other. We both had dry mouths and terrible hangovers, and I was embarrassed to kiss him before I went to the bathroom and rinsed my mouth out with cold water. David had to catch a plane to Los Angeles, where he was about to begin rehearsing a part in the new Robert Altman movie.

"We deserve to feel this way," he said, with his arm across his eyes. "I'm sorry about last night."

"For what?" I asked, laughing, hoping I hadn't missed anything.

"For losing it."

I told him I had to go home to do my laundry. Outside a fine drizzle was coming down. David and I kissed goodbye, promised to stay in touch. He was tender, but I had the feeling he was just as glad to see me go as I was to leave. I walked eleven blocks through the cold November rain. My hair and the clothes I had worn to Susan's party smelled like cigarette smoke, and I wanted to get rid of it. I bought a Sunday *Times* at a place on Ninth Avenue.

Inside my apartment I threw my dirty clothes into the washing machine. I lit a fire in my small fireplace. While the washer hummed, I spread the paper out on my lovely tattered Chinese rug. Prokofiev played on WQXR. Clean, grey light streamed through my big windows. Drizzly Sundays were the best. Reading the article on Bill Forsythe in the Arts and Leisure section, I thought how wonderful it would be to have someone I loved to talk with about the article, about reviews of books I wanted to read, about Russell Baker's column. I thought of Susan and Louis, and I felt a jolt of jealousy until I remembered the party. They couldn't settle down to read together until they had cleaned up that mess—the empty bottles, the spilled food, those ashtrays. My own life wasn't terrible the way it was. I looked around the room. It was spare, with tall ceilings and windows, furnished with castoffs. Wicker chairs that had once rocked on my parents' porch in Connecticut, low mahogany tables that had belonged to my grandmother, bookcases filled with books I had had since childhood.

I loved living in Chelsea, but that grey November morning I realized that I had been living in that apartment ever since I had started on "Beyond the Bridge." I could afford something much better if I wanted it. The boulder of change, dislodged that day in Newport, had gathered momentum. I could feel it rumbling behind me. A new apartment was needed. I opened the Real Estate section and started to read.

M Y decision to move marked me as a lonely woman. I spent the month of November and the first weeks of December socializing more than I had in years. With real estate agents, co-op boards, and friends who owned their own apartments. My free time was filled from the minute I left the studio until the time I arrived at home, exhausted, often after eleven o'clock. Every morning I ignored the *Times* and drank coffee while gazing at maps of the city, learning the boundaries of neighborhoods I hadn't known existed. I asked myself questions: Do I want to walk to work? Is a view important? Would I like to be on a high floor, or will I be too afraid of fires in the night? Brownstone or high-rise? One bedroom or two? Doorman or not? Four-room layout or open space? I wished that I had my father, that real estate wizard, to advise me.

At first I ruled out the Upper East and West sides, but one Sunday I decided to explore them. Snow had fallen that morning. I dressed in warm grey flannel slacks, a navy V-neck sweater over a yellow turtleneck, and my long black coat. I wore an enormous silk scarf wrapped around my entire face except my eyes, and a blue ski hat. The taxi drove me to East End Avenue, and I walked along the promenade over the East River. Chunks of ice swirled below in the swift current. I stepped carefully over snow-glazed cobbles which led to Carl Schurz Park. Parents pulled small children on sleds, joggers swaddled in bright suits ran past, dogs romped with their owners through copses of birch, maples, and pines. I was spellbound. This wasn't New York City; this was a Christmas card. I felt as though I had discovered a substation of New England.

Sitting alone on a bench, I began to think of things I would buy my family for Christmas. We would spend it at my

mother's house. I wanted it to be one of those wonderful
Victorian-style Christmases you read about in Dickens and
women's magazines but which don't really exist: felt, gilt,
tinsel, walnuts, raisins, sleighbells, roast goose, fir trees, *The
Nutcracker Suite*, snow on the ground, and good will. Looking
east that fine, snowy Sunday, it seemed possible.

My house hunt was interrupted by Christmas shopping. At
the studio we had filmed episodes through the end of January,
and I had a six-day vacation free of any public appearances.
For my mother I bought an extravagant peach silk robe at
Saks, a four-record set of birdcalls, and a set of sable watercolor brushes. For Margo I bought an enormous book on
Rodin, a pair of gold ginkgo-leaf earrings, and an antique
silver fox jacket. For Lily I bought a tiny original madonna
by Tomassi, a second-tier Cinquecento artist.

The madonna was exquisite. I found her in a gallery on
Madison Avenue, and she spoke to me. Round-cheeked, dim-
pled, wrapped in an ivory mantle and smiling at her golden-
haired child, she was beautiful. I wanted that woman as my
mother, my sister, my daughter, and myself. Lily loved
sixteenth-century Italian art; it was her area of expertise.
Aside from being wholly appropriate as a combination
Christmas-graduation present (in December she completed
her final semester of graduate school), it was the most beautiful thing I could give her.

LILY, MARGO, and I were set to arrive at my mother's
house on Christmas Eve. Staring at my brownish reflection in
the train window as we clattered past Guilford, I thought of
how this was our first Christmas without my father. We would
all find ways to circumvent any discussion of the matter. I
knew that for sure. Whenever the word "Dad" came up, the
subject would change. For although we never quite succeeded,
all the Cavan women had the same vision of a Victorian
Christmas, and talking about death would drive it away.

My train stopped at the small blue Old Saybrook station.
Carrying shopping bags and my suitcase, I slogged down the
aisle and out the door. My sisters stood at the far end of the

platform. Margo tore toward me calling, "Baby, baby, you're *home* again!" We hugged mightily. She smiled and tilted her head. Lily was walking toward us with her arm linked with the arm of a very tall man.

"Una," Lily said in a refined voice I could hardly recognize. "This is Henk Voorhees."

I looked up at him. He was blond and stern. His black coat on his tall thin frame made him look like a stovepipe. We shook hands, and as an afterthought, he bent down to peck my cheek.

Lily was giggling, burrowing her round face into that black coat. "Should we tell her now? We can't not tell Una—"

"Tell her," Margo urged, practically jumping on one foot. The station was bathed in eerie yellow light from the lamps along the platform. Our clouds of breath in the cold air dispersed like sulfurous fog.

"Tell me what?" I asked, trying to smile.

"Henk and I are getting married," Lily said.

"DID you know he was going to be here?" I asked my mother while we were cooking dinner. Her kitchen is cozy and warm, with pale wood walls and indirect lighting. She leaned over the oven and checked the codfish.

"Not until this morning. Apparently it was a last-minute decision."

"Seems that way," I said, but she ignored the irony. "Can you believe they're getting married?" I watched my mother's face for some sign of joy or disapproval, but she gave nothing away. My mother hoards her feelings in the name of politics.

"It is rather sudden," she said.

W E drank cocktails in the room that overlooked Long Island Sound.

"What wonderful architecture you have here," Henk said, looking all around the room, as if his head were attached to his neck with a ball joint. "You make superb use of the space."

I glanced at the long beam, which my mother had had reinforced with steel when I lied and told her that I had read about a place very like her house which had collapsed under the weight of the first heavy snowfall.

Lily sat on the floor at Henk's feet. She rested her elbow on his knees and gazed adoringly at his face. Margo caught my eye and stuck her tongue out at Lily.

"Lily tells me you live in New York," I said to Henk, deliberately not looking at Margo, so I wouldn't laugh.

"Yes, I do. I live off East End Avenue, on Gracie Lane."

"East End Avenue! Oh, I just spent a day there two weeks ago. It's lovely."

"It is," Lily said. "You can see the Sound from Henk's apartment."

I turned cold; Lily hadn't called to tell me she was in New York. "When were you there?"

"Oh, just a couple of weeks ago."

"Whenever she has some free time, I spirit her to New York," Henk said, stroking her yellow head as if she were a golden retriever. "*Liebchen*," he whispered. Lily refused to meet my eyes.

"You do?"

"Henk, you must have a terribly exciting practice," my mother said, adroitly steering her family past the trouble spot as always. "What is it like to save lives *every day*?"

Henk waved his hand in the scoffing manner Margo had described. "Oh, it's not every day. If I did surgery every day, I wouldn't last long. No one does that. But saving lives—yes, that I do. It is an awesome power, a responsibility."

"And his patients are so *grateful!*" Lily said. "They come from all over the *world*. Where was that woman from, darling, the one who . . ."

"Denmark."

"Yes, she's Danish, and she came to Henk. He's so well known." Lily beamed.

"You're an American citizen?" I asked.

He stared me down. "I am a citizen of the world."

Seeing that Henk's glass was empty, Lily leapt up and ran to refill it with Genever gin, which he called "Dutch stuff."

"When is it you're getting married?" I asked him.

"Oh, I think we must let Lily tell you that," he said, winking, making me feel uneasily as though I had just been admonished.

Lily returned and settled herself by Henk's feet. He cupped his hand around her ear and whispered something.

"Oh," she said. "We have set a date. I thought I'd announce it tomorrow, but since you ask—we're getting married on New Year's Day." She giggled, and everyone else gasped. Even Margo. "We're taking our honeymoon first, getting married at the end of it."

"Yes, tomorrow night we take off for The Hague," Henk said. His wide mouth spread into a linear smile, no lifting of the corners whatsoever.

"The Hague?" my mother asked, frowning. "Tomorrow night?"

"Yes. We're eloping to The Hague!" Lily said wildly. She looked at me, then Margo, then my mother. She read the shock in all our faces, and then she turned back to Henk. "Darling, do you like the horseradish spread? Have you ever tried it before?"

"It's nice," Henk said. "Very, very spicy."

"I HATE his fucking guts," I said to Margo later. We were drying the dishes while my mother wrote down telephone numbers of where she could reach Lily and Hank in The Hague. Henk was telling her that he would leave messages with his answering service in New York, and she could get information from them.

"He's not that bad, Una," Margo said.

"Why didn't *you* tell me? If Lily wouldn't, or couldn't?"

"Listen, it all happened really fast, and they wanted to fix the details before spreading the word. Lily felt so guilty about not calling you."

"She should have."

"The problem is, Henk's insecure. He was afraid you and Mom would object if they told you before you met him."

"He strikes me as imperious, not insecure."

"Well, I think that's a smokescreen," Margo said slowly.

"Lily tells me he's very insecure, which makes him appear possessive. He's never come across sisters like us before. I can tell I make him nervous. And you know how *accommodating* Lily is with men—she picks up signals they don't even know they're sending. She's got this new upper-crust accent, the perfect voice for a doctor's wife. It's really funny."

"Hysterical."

"But it won't last. She'll be back to normal soon. You know she's dying to get married, and once she is, she'll let him know what's what."

"I hope so, but can you believe the wedding plans? Who do they think they are, blowing off to Holland?'

"His mother's old, and he wants her to see the ceremony. She's not well enough to travel. We're invited, you know."

"Actually, I didn't, but I can't fly to Holland on ten minutes' notice. Next week I have a busy schedule. I have to show up at four malls to give autographs, plus I'm in the midst of buying a new place."

"I'm not going either. I have a paper due next week. It's *overdue*, actually. The last few weeks have been crazy with Lily."

"*Plus*, I can't believe she's been in New York without even calling me."

Lily walked into the kitchen. She hunched her shoulders and stood very close to me and Margo. I glared at her.

"Why didn't you call?" I asked.

She straightened up and looked back coldly. "Oh, I wasn't aware I was expected to answer to you."

"Lily, don't be bitch eyes," Margo said.

"Well, I've been slightly preoccupied, falling in *love*, in case Una hasn't noticed. Frankly, I wanted to spend time alone with Henk. He works incredibly *hard*, and he doesn't care to socialize after operating."

"He just said he doesn't operate every day."

"He's very modest. He has an amazing schedule. Can you imagine how emotional it is to consult with a patient who could die at any moment? Unless you do something?"

"Just like the gods," I said.

Lily shook her head. "If you think about it for a minute

you'll realize how important it was for us to spend time alone.
I'm sorry if we hurt your *feelings*."

"You did."

"Well, I'm *sorry*."

"She didn't go to New York that often," Margo said. "Sometimes Henk came to Providence."

"At least I'll be moving to New York," Lily said, smiling,
cuddling against me.

My arm went around her in spite of myself. "You think
you can bear to see me then?"

"Oh, I think it can be arranged," Lily said, slipping her
other arm around Margo and gathering all three of us into a
tight knot.

MRS. JAMES F. X. CAVAN

IS PLEASED TO ANNOUNCE

THE MARRIAGE OF HER DAUGHTER,

LILY ELIZABETH CAVAN,

TO

HENK O. VOORHEES, M.D.

THE CEREMONY WAS HELD ON JANUARY FIRST

IN THE HAGUE, THE NETHERLANDS,

AT THE HOME OF DR. VOORHEES'S MOTHER,

MRS. JAKOB VOORHEES.

AFTER JANUARY FOURTH,

DR. AND MRS. VOORHEES WILL BE AT HOME AT

ONE GRACIE LANE,

NEW YORK, NEW YORK, 10028.

I RECEIVED the announcement in the mail, just like everyone else. Mine, however, had Henk's unlisted home number
written at the bottom in Lily's perfect, tiny, upright handwriting.

IN FEBRUARY I found a co-op in a small building on Hudson Street in Greenwich Village. On the fifth floor, it had two
bedrooms, polished wood floors, a new kitchen, and large

east-facing windows that admitted plenty of light. Heather Dobek, a smart broker who had shown me some nice places over the past months, brought me to it. "The only problem with this place," she said, "is the co-op board. They're real tough. They do everything but smell your shit before they let you in."

"What won't they like about me?"

"You're an unknown quantity. Not yet thirty, unmarried, in show business, etcetera."

In all my years as an actress I had never thought of myself as being in show business. Those words meant Las Vegas or Atlantic City. They conjured feathers, pasties, and show tunes. They had nothing to do with Soundstage 3 and "Beyond the Bridge."

"So what?" I said. "It's none of their business."

Heather shook her frosted hair. "Una, honey, if only you knew what I know. Nothing in the real estate business is fair."

I thought of my father and his favorite saying: "If you give them a chance, people will usually do the right thing." (All except his daughters' suitors.) My, these real estate people were a confusing lot.

"I want this place," I told Heather. "I'm prepared to make an offer."

Lily, who hadn't found a job and had loads of free time, came to see the apartment one afternoon after my offer had been accepted but before I had met the co-op board.

"It's a fantastic place," she said. She pulled a bottle of champagne from her Hermès bag, an incidental present from Henk. We drank out of the bottle because she had forgotten glasses, and the bubbles kept going up our noses.

"I want it, but they might not let me in. Actors are undesirable, it seems. We attract the wrong crowds—we're a pretty noisy bunch."

"That's crazy," Lily said. She paced off each room and told me what size rugs I should buy.

"How's your job search?" I asked.

She giggled. "At a total standstill. I'm not looking at all anymore. Henk and I are so happy, having dinner together every night. I'm cooking the most wonderful meals—Una, you don't know how great it is to call the butcher and say, 'send me your boned duck breast.' Or lemon sole from the fish market. Blueberries all year round. If I started working, I wouldn't have time to cook."

I stared at her and tried not to scream. Lily's voice was coming out of Lily's body, but the words belonged to someone else, an airhead out of the soaps. I had played Delilah to characters like that before.

"Henk has a housekeeper," Lily went on. "She's been with him since before his divorce, and we're not going to fire her. But Henk was so tired of sauerbraten and roast chicken—apparently that's about all she ever made. He loves the things I do."

"What about you? Do you love it?"

Lily glowed. "I adore it. Una, in case you haven't noticed, Henk is very rich. I am having the time of my life. Instead of working in a museum, I have time to wander through them. A different one every day, if I want. I just stare at the paintings. Yesterday I spent hours in the Frick. When I leave here, I'm going straight to the Metropolitan.

"And I love Henk. We're so much in love." Her eyes filled with tears.

Lily seemed genuinely happy, but why did I mistrust her? She sat on the wood floor and wept, smiling all the while. I held her hand and thought, this is not real. This is not Lily. I hardly recognized her. She was an actress playing Wife.

"You have to see our place soon," she said, drying her big eyes. "I know it's terrible—we've been home for a month, and you haven't even been invited."

"That's okay." I felt the frown on my face and tried to get rid of it.

"It's just that, we didn't have a real honeymoon, and we've needed time together. You understand, don't you?" She looked worried.

"Sure I do."

"Henk really likes you. He's so glad you live close by. We're going to have you over very soon."

"I honestly cannot wait."

T H E co-op board sent me a letter saying that they held their meetings at 7:30 P.M. on the third Tuesday of every month, and that they would see me at their next meeting. Heather suggested that I wear "something conservative." I chose a pair of black pants and a white angora sweater. Pearls at the throat. Gold shrimp earrings, a Christmas present from my parents my last year at Juilliard.

The board convened in the apartment of Monica and Chip Krane, a spacious two-bedroom filled with brand-new early American furniture. Monica greeted me and offered coffee. We sat beside each other in identical rockers.

We smiled at each other. Board members straggled in. A husky man with a tangled mop of red hair seemed to be in charge. He wore a spongy maroon jogging suit over expensive blue running shoes. Carrying his coffee to a wingback chair, he sat down and started scratching his head with the round end of his spoon.

"The electric heat at my office makes my goddamn head itch," he said when he saw me staring at him.

I nodded sympathetically. Monica made introductions. The redhead was Joe Finnegan. He was president of the co-op's board as well as vice president of a company that manufactured and distributed sports equipment.

"Una—what kind of a name is 'Una'?" he pronounced it "Youna."

"Irish, Mr. Finnegan. I'm surprised you didn't know."

I tried a little coy flirtation. Joe Finnegan looked like a man who would warm to an Irish flirt.

"With a name like 'Cavan,' I'd say you're a mick, but off-hand I'd say even Dublin's not overflowing with girls called

You-na. And call me Joe. We don't bite, even if we do hold your future in our hands."

Everyone laughed, and Joe checked me out in a studied maneuver I was not supposed to miss.

"Questions from the floor?" Joe asked.

"Yes, I have one," Monica said. "We have one concern, Una. We all lead pretty quiet lives here. We—"

"Speak for yourself, Monica honey," Joe said.

Everyone laughed. Monica blushed and continued. "We are not your typical Greenwich Village artsy types, if you know what I mean. We are all business people. We've been careful to keep that sort of profile."

"I assure you I lead a very normal life," I said.

"One man's 'normal' . . ." Joe Finnegan said.

"I don't work crazy hours. The show is filmed during the day. I have to be at the studio early, so I go to bed early. I have friends who are actors, but I also have friends who are in business. My sister—" As Lily and her respectable credentials came into mind, I felt I'd been given a solid gold gift. "—lives on East End Avenue. She's married to a heart surgeon."

One of the board members who had not previously spoken leaned forward. He was of the pin-striped suit contingent. "What's his name?" he asked.

"Oh, that's right," Monica said, nodding. "You're Type A, aren't you, Pete? What'd you have, a bypass?"

The man nodded.

"Dr. Voorhees. Dr. Henk Voorhees," I said.

The man nodded and settled back in his chair. "Sure, I've heard of him. He didn't do me, but I believe he consulted. He's got a great reputation." He looked all around the room making eye contact with all the other board members. One by one, I ticked them off by the expressions that crossed their faces.

The official tally remained to be taken, but I knew already: I would be accepted into the co-op by the silent intervention of my brother-in-law. They sent me into the tidy bedroom where healthy plants in macramé holders hung from hooks in the pressed-tin ceiling and bits of Americana (cast-iron trivets, a brass eagle, a crewel sampler, two color photographs of two different lighthouses at sunset) hung on the walls. The apartment had such a grownup, sedate air to it. I hadn't known that people of my generation still decorated like that. My friends' places were comfortably, handsomely furnished, but they were hodgepodge, unfinished. The pairing of an art deco étagère with an empty wire spool from the phone company, of industrial black metal shelving with an antique curly maple dining table, seemed arbitrary and aimless. *This* was a home. *Here* I felt safe. I could imagine raising children here. It made me want to take the first taxi to Sloane's and purchase matching living room, dining room, and bedroom sets.

"*Les jeux sont fait*," Monica called when the vote was over, and I rejoined them.

"You're in, Una," Joe Finnegan said. "Welcome to our madhouse."

"Oh, thank you," I said, beaming. I walked around the room, shaking hands.

"We're anything but a madhouse," Monica said. "That Joe—*he's* crazy."

Joe crossed the room and put his big arm around my shoulders. "We've got our own little TV star now," he said. He had sad, liquid brown eyes, just like the eyes of every uncle and parish priest I had ever known. "I'm divorced, you know," he said.

"How very sad." I smiled at him. I knew that he was trying to pick me up, and I didn't care. I had grown up surrounded by Joe Finnegan types, men who alternated insults with flattery and probably had them confused in their own minds, men who had been told too often by their own mothers, "You have that Irish charm." The trouble was that they believed it.

BEFORE I moved in, Chance and Billy Schutz asked if they could come over to see my new place. I finished filming my scenes for the day. The Schutzes picked me up at the studio in their black stretch limousine. I sat between them in the back seat, an alpaca lap robe across our legs.

"I think this is very exciting," Billy said in her deep, smoky voice. Her voice reminded me of Jane Valera's, but Billy is wonderful. She is a talented, devoted potter who spends most of her days on Duane Street, in a dark studio where every surface is caked with clay. She sells her pieces at galleries and shops in New York and around New England. She has upswept auburn hair streaked with grey, the color I hope mine will be when I'm fifteen years older. She wears no makeup on her freckly skin, and she cares nothing about the latest styles.

Chance is the fashion plate, not Billy. He is a true fop. Whenever he enters a room, heads turn; his expensive citrus scent precedes him, but his appearance is worth the wait. Every article of clothing is custom-made. Billy once told me his underwear is silk, hand-stitched by schoolchildren in Mongolia. He loves gold, good leather, cashmere, and silk. It is a challenge to find the tiny monogram you know exists on each shirt, each jacket, each scarf: like the "Ninas" in a Hirshfeld drawing. His grey wolf eyes look as though they could devour you, but he is capable of true tenderness.

We stopped in front of my new apartment building. People coming home from work glanced at the car with fake indolence. Chance loved the attention, but Billy was indifferent. Riding to the fifth floor in the small self-service elevator, she practically shimmied with anticipation.

"I cannot wait to see it!" she said.

I caught Chance nervously watching the floor numbers click upwards. I could read his mind: PRODUCER AND WIFE PLUNGE TO DEATH IN CREAKY ELEVATOR.

"Okay," I said, pulling the keys from my pocket and unlocking the three locks on my apartment door. We stepped inside.

"Now, this is super, don't you think, Chance?"

"Very nice," Chance said. He walked through the rooms looking skeptical. He and Billy live in a penthouse on Park Avenue; Billy once told me that he rarely ventured south of Fifty-sixth Street, that he cannot bear the squalor of her studio, that he feels unsafe without a doorman, elevator man, and marble lobby.

"I wish I had some furniture, so I could invite you to sit down," I said, babbling. "Let's see, this is the kitchen, of course . . ." I let loose a crazy giggle. "Here's the living room— I thought I'd put my couch here, my stereo here . . ."

"Wonderful. And it will get the morning light," Billy said, grinning.

"What's this, the fifth floor?" Chance asked, pressing his face to the sooty window, doubtlessly looking for the fire escape. He pulled back, and there was a smudge of soot on his forehead. It was so incongruous on his pink skin, I nearly laughed. Billy licked her fingers and wiped it off. My doorbell rang.

"Oh, that must be Rudy," Billy said. Rudy was their chauffeur. "I asked him to bring something up."

I buzzed Rudy in, but before he came up in the elevator there was a knock at the door.

Joe Finnegan stood in the hallway. "Who's the brass?" he asked.

"My producer," I said coolly.

"Nice car."

"Look, why don't you come back later, Joe?" I felt as unwilling to introduce Joe to the Schutzes as I would to introduce an unsuitable boyfriend to my father. Just then Rudy stepped out of the elevator carrying one of Billy's bulky pots.

"Jesus H. Christ," Joe said. "It's a fucking birdbath."

"Shut up, Joe," I said, standing aside to let Rudy in, then closing the door in Joe's face. He stopped it with his foot.

"Okay, okay, I'm going. I just wanted to invite you up later, to welcome you into the house. For a nightcap."

I let him peek around the door. "As you can see, I'm not moved in yet. I'm still living at my other place."

"When're you moving in? Listen, I can get a crew together and get you in here in one morning. I'll even supply the truck."

Closing on the apartment and a heavier-than-usual shooting schedule had kept me too busy to think about movers. "Who are they?" I asked.

"Guys from the warehouse and my brothers. The kids are

in college—slip them a couple of bucks if you feel like it."

At the mention of brothers I warmed to him. I couldn't help it. The idea of a close family appeals to me more than anything.

"Okay, Joe. I'll think about it."

Joe smiled at me and walked away. I noticed he was wearing a heathery tweed jacket, rare apparel for a New York businessman. Even my father, who had lived in Connecticut, had worn only dark suits.

Inside, Chance and Billy flanked Billy's pot like dignitaries at an awards ceremony. Rudy, in his black uniform with gold braid and tasseled epaulets, stood solemnly in the corner.

"To our dear friend, Una," Billy said, her blue eyes sparkling with tears. "May you be as happy in your home and your life as we have been in ours."

"Oh, thank you," I said, starting to cry. The idea of Joe's brothers, so close to him that they would help move in a stranger, and the sight of Chance and Billy, still deeply in love, made me feel sorry for myself. My father was dead, my mother was insulated in a haze of watercolors, one sister lived in another state, the other lived across town and never invited me there. I sat down beside Billy's pot and wept.

Chance handed me down a crisp, snowy linen handkerchief. It was starched and folded, solid as a book, perfect and unusable. I took it, then looked up at him. "I can't use this," I said.

"Of course you can't." Billy, understanding, handed me a wrinkled blue tissue from her pocket. She crouched beside me, stroking my back with her chapped hands, her fingernails black with clay. "What is it, Una? Do you have the moving-in blues?"

"That must be it," I said, snuffling. "I've never bought a house before." That made me think of Monica and Chip's homey place two floors below, and I started crying again. I hate Early American furniture and could never live with it, but it symbolized things that would last.

Billy patted my back until I was calm. She hummed a sad tune—"Once Upon a Time." "Chance, remember when we moved into our first place?"

"In Darien." I could see his sharply creased pant leg out of the corner of my blurry eye.

"Yes, it was a tiny place," Billy went on. "We closed on it in early April. Upstairs there was one little room where I was planning to set up my studio. It faced north, and like *all* artists, I wanted a studio that faced north. The day we moved in was beautiful. It was sunny, and new leaves were on the trees. While the men carried in our furniture, all I cared about was setting up my studio. I ran upstairs, and I almost died. Outside the window was a maple tree—I hadn't even noticed it when we first looked because it had no leaves. Suddenly there was the maple, covered with baby leaves, blocking every bit of light. I cried and cried."

"What did you do?"

"We pruned the tree," Chance said. His manicured hand stroked his wife's hair.

I loved that story. I felt sodden with tears, and I felt as though I could fall asleep with my head on Billy's lap. Through my closed window the traffic steering downtown on Hudson Street sounded distant, and a jet of steam whistled out of my coiled radiator.

"Sounds like a good heating system," Billy said.

"It does," Chance said, nodding vigorously. "This is quite a place. I think we'd better celebrate. How does dinner at Café des Artistes sound to you two?"

"Oh, Lord," Billy said, frowning, looking down at her hands. "I hadn't planned on cleaning my fingernails tonight."

FEBRUARY, because of Valentine's Day and the Washington's Birthday sales, is a big time for soap opera actors to make appearances at department stores, malls, and anywhere else the general female population might be inclined to spend money. I tried to reason with Art Panella: if Delilah is supposedly at large in the wilds of Lake Huron, won't the viewer think it peculiar to find her signing autographs at the Rose Garden Mall in Stamford? Art admonished me, saying I should give him credit for some brains. They *know* that Una

Cavan is not *really* Delilah Grant. I understood that, but I had something more important on my mind: that night I was invited to Lily and Henk's apartment for the first time.

Two long black limousines bearing me, Stuart MacDuff, and my soap opera lover, Jason Mordant (a.k.a. Beck Vandeweghe), along with a camera crew, stopped at the entrance to AmbiMart. A group of mall employees unrolled a red carpet that stretched from the car to the store. Wet snow was falling. We stepped out of the car, and a woman four inches shorter than me held a flowered umbrella over my head; she had to struggle to make sure it covered both of us. It took great willpower for me not to grab the umbrella away from her and hustle both of us inside. The crowd, mainly women of all ages, called "Delilah!" For weeks there had been posters in the stores and thirty-second spots broadcast on radio and local TV stations, promising all patrons of the Rose Garden Mall that Paul, Delilah, and Beck would soon be in their midst.

A man wearing a green sports jacket and holding an over-sized microphone greeted us at the electric doors.

"Well, hello you folks from 'Beyond the Bridge!' " he said, and the words boomed from loudspeakers the length of the cavernous mall. "On behalf of all of us here at the Rose Garden, as well as all our shoppers, let me, Larry Hicks, welcome you to the largest, the wildest, let me say the *best* mall in southwestern Connecticut!" The crowd cheered. Larry Hicks took my arm and led me to a wide stage draped in white plastic and decorated with red cardboard cutouts of hearts, cherries, hatchets, and profiles of Cupid and George Washington. He covered his microphone with one hand.

"Did they tell you what we have in mind, dear?" he asked me.

"We usually sign autographs and do a scene or two from the show."

"Perfect, absolutely perfect. You just fill the time until two o'clock any way you see fit, but make a lot of noise. We want the shoppers at the south end to know you're here."

"That sounds fair," I said, staring at Larry Hicks. He had

the most unnatural skin tone I had ever seen, and his toupee
looked solid instead of a mass of individual hairs. If the wind
blew, none of it would move or the entire thing would crash
off his head.

"I see you've noticed my tan," he said, touching one
wrinkly brown cheek with his left hand. "Mum's the word,
but Tropical Tanning is giving you and the guys some free
gift certificates—a couple hours under the sunlamps. It'll
make the months till summer go by a little faster."

"Great."

"Tell you, I think you soap stars have it great, all the perks
you get. I know it's not kosher to take free gifts, but quite a
few of the stores here have gift certificates with your names
typed in." He winked.

"How super," I said. It was the same everywhere; the mall
managers offered us free merchandise, gift certificates, promises of fifty percent off retail price at stores in the mall. They
always treated it like buried treasure: no one was to know
where we had found it. I had stacks of gift certificates that I
meant to use one day, but I most often wound up throwing
them out.

A line of autograph seekers had formed behind a red velvet
cord. When Stuart, Jason, and I were seated in tall red chairs
that resembled thrones, the line started to move.

How I loved my public! For the first forty minutes or so I
smiled and chatted with them. They said such nice things.

"I love you, Delilah."

"I want nothing but happiness for you and Beck."

"Oh, I hope your life takes a turn for the better . . ."

I signed notepads, business cards, and shopping bags. The
women were high school girls, retired schoolteachers, grand-
mothers, secretaries with TV sets in their lunchrooms, lawyers who watched during their vacations. From years of meeting my viewers, I had begun to know something about them:
they were lonely. Whether married, single, young, old, em-
ployed, unemployed, they watched "Beyond the Bridge" and
the characters became their family and friends. We appeared
before them every day. They knew our greatest fears and

joys, our most intimate secrets and lusts. Our lusts were their lusts. Women would take my hand and say, knowingly, "I *know* what you're going through with Beck." They had been through it themselves.

But after the first forty minutes, the procession of fans started to make me feel unreal. I am *not* Delilah Grant, I wanted to tell them. I am Una Cavan, I am not in love, I live in Manhattan, not Mooreland. They knew the difference, of course, but they loved Delilah Grant, not Una Cavan.

A small woman with tight grey curls stepped forward. She wore a black wool coat with a white fur collar and handed me a greeting card. "Will you sign the back, Miss Cavan?" she asked. No one ever called me "Miss Cavan." I smiled at her. "Who shall I—?"

"Make it out to Mary Finnegan," she said.

I looked into her brown eyes and recognized her son. "Are you Joe's mother?" I asked.

"Oh, yes. I'm so surprised you made the connection, with all the Finnegans around. I'm a fan of yours—have been ever since you came on the show. I don't like that stepmother you have."

"No, she's a pip, isn't she?"

"I could not believe my ears when Joe said you had moved into his building. What a small world we live in!"

"Joe looks like you."

She chuckled, passing a thin hand across her eyes. "No, that's the joke—he looks exactly like his *father*. But everyone says he looks like me, at first glance only."

Although I usually signed my autographs simply "Delilah," I wrote, "To Mary Finnegan with the fond wishes of Una Cavan." Mrs. Finnegan read it, then slipped the card into her black vinyl purse. She glanced back at the line behind her, appeared to debate with herself whether or not there was time to have a longer conversation with me, and decided to move on. "Now I'll have to buy another card," she said. "I was planning on sending this to my sister-in-law in Hartford. She isn't well."

"Oh, I'm sorry," I said. We waved at each other, and she walked away. I gave the next woman a wide smile.

STUART was meeting his wife Margie at the Showboat for dinner, so I rode back to Manhattan alone with the driver and Jason Mordant. Jason was thirty-eight, gay, and in the process of being dumped by his twenty-one-year-old lover. He rested his cheek against the window and watched the Manhattan skyline come into view.

"What's on for tonight?" I asked.

"Evisceration," Jason said. "Mine or his, I haven't decided."

"When's he moving out?"

"Moving out? He moved out last month. His body's still there, but his mind's long gone." Jason had a receding hairline. He was a very handsome man, with a warm smile and expressive blue eyes, but he blamed everything on his receding hairline. I had seen him regarding Larry Hicks's head with undue interest. At various times he had told me he would be playing Warren Beatty-type characters, finding more satisfying and longer-lasting love matches, and not feeling suicidal so often if only he had more hair.

"I'm having dinner with my sister," I said.

"Oh, you'll like that," Jason said, smiling at me. "I know how you love your sisters."

It was true; the prospect of seeing Lily was part of the reason my spirits were so high. Generally autograph sessions could depress me for days. But crossing the Triborough Bridge I felt elated, ready for anything. I thought of Mrs. Finnegan; she was hardly a familiar face, but I knew her son, and the connection seemed comforting. Mrs. Finnegan, Lily: two connections in the same day. Presence is everything.

I WAS admitted to the twelfth-floor apartment of Dr. and Mrs. Henk Voorhees by a statuesque woman of sixty dressed in a black uniform at least one size too small. "*Velkommen*," she said coldly, engaging my eyes, standing aside and allowing me to enter the black-and-white marble foyer. Gilded pedestals bearing chipped antiquities stood around the oval room. An enormous, unmistakable Van Gogh filled one wall; the painting was familiar, a swirly green-and-yellow landscape. Transfixed, I stood there, turning around and around, stunned by the grandeur of my surroundings. Lily rushed in wearing a silvery chiffon caftan.

"Dahhhhling," she said.

"All you need is an ebony cigarette holder." I kissed her and handed her the bouquet of roses I had been presented by Brierley's Florist in the mall.

She gestured at the painting. "Henk loves Van Gogh. He is an ancestor." She smiled at the elderly maid. "Thank you, Ilsa. That will be all."

The maid nodded sharply and took my coat and the roses away. "What is with her?" I asked.

"Let's just say she hasn't *taken* to me yet. Henk says she thinks I'm too young for him. She thinks I'm after his money."

"Henk talks to his maid about his wife?" I asked, regretting my question instantly.

"Ilsa has been with him for a long time," Lily said. "She is very devoted. I have to understand that."

"Oh, I know." I rubbed my palms together, trying to bring the conversation's tone back to what it was when I entered. "So, what's cooking? I'm starved. Am I going to get one of your gourmet meals?"

"Unfortunately not." Lily's tone was cold. "I was busy all day, so I had it catered."

" 'It'? Is this a party?"

"No, it's dinner for three. Relax—you're in the lap of luxury." Lily relaxed as she showed me around the apartment. It faced south and east, with views of the East River, the Sound and the Atlantic, the bridges, the Chrysler Building, Citicorp, and the Empire State Building. The apartment had seven bedrooms, five bathrooms, two kitchens, two living rooms (each with two fireplaces), a library, a formal dining room, an informal dining room, a breakfast nook the size of my bedroom, and Lily's morning room.

I liked the morning room best. It faced east and would get the morning sun. It contained a Queen Anne writing table, two chintz-covered armchairs flanking a small tile fireplace, and a chaise longue. Watercolors of Paris hung around the room, and the walls were covered with pale-gold-and-white-striped fabric. The Tomassi madonna hung above the writing desk. Lily had filled the bookshelves with her art books, and she had erected an easel in the corner.

"This is where I spend my days," she said. She pointed at the chaise longue. "That is where I lie when I have the vapors."

With the toe of one maribou-trimmed mule she stepped on a tiny button. Ilsa appeared immediately, as if she had been lurking in the hallway. "We'll have drinks in the library," Lily said. Turning to me, she added, "It's so much more intimate than the big living rooms."

"The big ones, yes," I said. Then, suddenly noticing Henk's absence, I asked where he was.

"Oh, at the hospital. He works incredibly long hours. He's never home before ten o'clock. I hope you don't mind eating late."

"What will madame have?" Ilsa interrupted rudely.

"Are you talking to me?" I asked.

"Yes, madame."

"I'm not married. You'd better call me 'mademoiselle.' "

"Very good, mademoiselle."

"I'll have a malt Scotch on the rocks," I said.

"Oh, give her the Laphroaig, Ilsa," Lily said. "I'll have my usual."

"Very good, madame," Ilsa said, walking out of the morning room.

"That one has *got* to go," I said.

Lily giggled weakly. "You shouldn't push her, Una. I have this feeling she was a Nazi."

"*Is* a Nazi. She's here all day?"

Lily nodded, smirking. "Watching my every move. She's afraid I'm going to steal the silver."

"Why don't you get Henk to fire her?"

"Like I said, she's the loyal family retainer." Lily led me down the long corridor to the library, where everything was made of mahogany and red leather. A fire crackled in the marble fireplace. Lily and I sat at opposite ends of the red leather sofa. We sipped our drinks and stared at the fire. For the first time in my life, I did not know how to start a conversation with her. Was it the austerity of our surroundings? The unfamiliarity of the terrain? A blazing birch log snapped and crashed between the brass andirons. Like a Noel Coward heroine, Lily walked to the fire and stirred it with an exceptionally long poker.

To her back, I said, "I've missed you. Thank you for inviting me here."

Lily turned and smiled skittishly. "You *know* I've missed you, too. But being married—" she shrugged.

"Being married what?"

"It's time-consuming." Defiant, chin tilted ceilingward. "I have new loyalties."

"But they don't replace old ones, do they? Look at Henk— loyal to you, loyal to Ilsa."

"That's not it at all," Lily said, her voice growing high and strained. "You don't understand. Henk warned me that you and Margo would be *jealous* of him at first. He sees families in *crisis* all the time—when a man is dying, his wife and sisters and children always fight over who has the most *rights*. You know, over who gets to stay in the room, who should talk to the doctors, who gets to determine what extreme *measures* can be taken. There are bound to be conflicts like that between members of a family. The old family and the new one."

That speech left Lily breathless. I sat absolutely still, my lips pressed to the rim of my Scotch glass; I found it extraordinary that Henk should compare families and marriage to families and crisis. Lily sat down on the couch. We drank without speaking; we were sipping our drinks when Henk walked in ten minutes later. He kissed the tops of our heads and settled himself in a red leather wingback chair beside the fireplace.

"*Liebchen,*" he said, patting his knee. Lily flew across the room onto his lap. Ilsa, tight-lipped, walked into the room with a glass of Genever gin on a silver tray.

"This is a lovely apartment, Henk," I said, thinking how

handsome, how blond they looked together; what a stunning couple they made.

"I want to make a good home for your sister," he said. Stroking her pink cheek with the back of one hand, he murmured, "Beauty."

"Well, you're succeeding," Lily said. She kissed his lips, then gently eased off his lap and returned to the sofa.

"Tell me about your day," she said.

Henk took a large swallow of gin, then smoothed back his blond hair with both hands. His fingers were long and slender, and he wielded them with arrogance. The hands of a surgeon, I thought.

"Oh, it was a monster. You don't really want to hear about it."

"Of course I do!"

"Well, Mrs. Lavoise went into crisis late this morning. I spent six hours with her on the table."

"You must be exhausted!"

Henk waved one hand. "No, it's over and done with. She's fine, the procedure was fine, we're all fine. Now I'm home and all I want to do is kiss my pretty wife. Come back here." He patted his knee again and Lily, dimpling, charged to his side. I watched this with pure incredulity. Could it be possible, Lily simpering? Was this what marriage was all about? Maribou mules and a hostile maid? The good little wife on the husband-daddy's knee? Was I privy to a secret scene of marital life, enacted only in private or in front of sisters? I finished the Scotch in my glass and looked away. No wonder Ilsa was sick at heart.

Henk noticed. He laughed uproariously. "Una, dear. Are we embarrassing you?"

"No, not at all," I lied.

Lily rested her head on Henk's chest and regarded me through sleepy eyes. I could see her enjoying my discomfort. She was getting me back for years gone by when I, the oldest daughter, had gotten riding lessons, new party shoes, first pick of the doughnuts on Sunday morning. For years I had appeared daily on national TV. But now Lily had something I did not have: an adoring blond husband. I felt like sticking my tongue out at her and screeching, "Nah, nah, I would *hate* to be fawned over." Instead I smiled politely. I tipped my empty Steuben glass. Henk, the vigilant host, touched a button on the mahogany side table. Ilsa appeared immediately.

"Another drink for Miss Cavan, please."

"Very good, sir."

"Oh, am I the only one having more?" I asked.

Lily gave me an exaggerated roll of the eyes. "One drink before dinner, that's our limit. Right darling?"

"Absolutely. 'One makes the blood behave, more are tickets to the grave.' A little cardiovascular humor," Henk said, grinning. He, too, had something I didn't have—Lily.

"We never eat red meat either," Lily said. "Henk's taught me so much about diet. Did you know that increased fiber lowers the risk of cancer as well as heart disease?"

"Yes, I've read that."

"And forget salt!" Lily eased herself off Henk's lap and came across the room. She displayed her left hand. I held it, feeling the faceted surface of the enormous pear-shaped diamond with my thumb. "Not that," Lily said. "Notice my fingers."

Her nails were long and opalescent. "You had a manicure?"

"Yes, but the fingers them*selves*. See how much thinner they are? That's since I quit using salt. You wouldn't believe how much water it makes you retain."

I stared at her fingers, but I couldn't see any difference. Lily had always been thin. "I'll have to cut down on the stuff," I said.

"Give it up entirely," Henk commanded. "That's the thing to do. It's poison to the system. Give up eggs too."

"Okay, I will."

For dinner we had curried chicken, hearts of romaine in tarragon vinaigrette, and fresh peach chutney. Lily assured me that it did not contain one pinch of salt. It was delicious. I drank one glass of Gewertztraminer, and the Voorheeses drank Ramlosa water. We ate in the baronial dining room, with Voorhees coats of arms on one wall and a moosehead over the blazing hearth. I sat in the center of one side of the long table; Lily and Henk faced each other at the ends. Ilsa stood against one wall, watching us eat. My sister and her husband were totally absorbed in each other; it was almost as if Ilsa and I were not there.

Suddenly Henk smiled broadly at me. "Forgive us, Una. Are we ignoring you?"

"Well—"

"A little, I can see that," he interrupted. "You are too polite to say. Like your sister, so polite, so well bred. You were an example to her? Growing up?"

I glanced at Lily, who smiled encouragingly at this exchange. "I suppose I was. We were very close. By that I mean emotionally, as well as in age."

"Ah, how I envy that. A close family. My brothers and I have no respect for each other. They are mechanics, if you can believe that, with no love for art or culture or any of the things that make me happy. They think I am a doctor only for the money. Thus, sometimes it is difficult for me to understand the bond between siblings. The sibling relationship. I marvel at it. When I see it, say, between a patient and his healthy brother? It is a wonderful phenomenon," Henk said.

"I hope that we can become closer, Henk," I said. "Now that you're married to Lily. My brother-in-law!" I began to relax, to enjoy the conversation.

"I'd love that! It's exactly what I'm hoping for!" Lily said, excited. "I've been planning—"

But Henk interrupted her with a seemingly urgent question about a telephone call he was expecting from a patient in Japan. Lily stared at him, her mouth dumbly open, her cheeks pink.

"There has been no call from Japan," Ilsa said.

"Oh, good. I'm sorry, go on darling," Henk said to Lily. He resumed eating.

As Lily launched into a plan for buying season's tickets to the Metropolitan Opera for her, Henk, and me, I tried to convince myself that Henk's question had been urgent, not a ploy to wreck the flow of Lily's sisterly enthusiasm. He watched her, eyes wet with adoration, occasionally reaching out to touch her hand, her cheek. And Lily basked in it. She loved him back. I could see it in the way she watched for his approval, the way she couched her idea for making me an extravagant present of the tickets in great theatricality for his amusement. I didn't trust this new situation enough to know whether I was jealous of Lily (as she had told me Henk had prophesied) or suspicious of Henk. Maybe Margo was right and he was insecure. Maybe my perceptions were off. But I felt the caution to navigate my brother-in-law the way a mariner navigates shoal water.

JOE FINNEGAN had volunteered to move me to Hudson Street, and I took him up on it. I phoned his office, and his secretary located him in a conference room. "Don't interrupt him," I told her, but she put me through anyway.

"What's up, Tiger?" he asked when he heard my voice.

"Listen, if you're in a meeting, I can call back later."

"Hey, any of you guys watch 'Beyond the Bridge?'" he asked the people in his meeting. "I've got Una Cavan on the line." Then, to me, "What's on your mind?"

"Joe, did you mean that about the moving men?"

"Joe Finnegan never says anything he doesn't mean. I hear you had a nice visit with my mother."

"Yes. She's delightful."

"She's a real fan of yours, I'll tell you. Spends the entire afternoon watching soap operas. So, when's moving day?"

"Well, I thought some Saturday—"

"Okay. How's this—me and my brothers be at your place this Saturday at eight A.M. That too early for you, hotshot?"

I laughed. "Not at all. But you don't have to be so prompt. Don't you have other plans?"

He lowered his voice, but not enough to keep the others from hearing. "Hey, the sooner I get you into the building, the sooner I start making moves on you. Don't say Joe Finnegan doesn't give fair warning."

"Here's the address," I said, feeling incredibly nervous. I felt more as though I were making a date than arranging for movers. There was something exciting about any man who had that much bald confidence. I thought of the resolution I had made in Newport, already semibroken with David Hammarslough. Did it make any difference that Joe Finnegan was Irish Catholic and sort of reminded me of my father? No, in fact that made it worse.

JOE FINNEGAN arrived in Chelsea with two brothers who looked exactly like him, only younger and thinner. "Meet Dan and Tim," he said, walking straight into my living room and gazing at the stacks of boxes. He wore his maroon jogging suit, and I doubted he had combed his wild hair that morning. "What do you figure, five hours to move this place?" he asked.

"Oh, I don't know—" I answered, but he wasn't talking to me.

"I say four, tops," Dan said.

"So, where do you go to college?" I asked.

"Fairfield," Joe answered for them. "All the Finnegan men go to Fairfield."

"Naturally," I replied.

"Why don't you brew some coffee?" Joe asked. "Let us get started."

"Because my coffeepot is in that box," I said, pointing, "and besides, I want to help load the truck."

Dan and Tim, gazing with boundless adoration at their brother, giggled.

"Leave that to us, Tiger," Joe said, touching my forearm. I felt the sort of thrill I remembered from high school when Jack McCarthy would bump me in the hall. Joe winked at me, but I lifted a box and carried it past him to the street where they had parked a truck marked "Celtic Sports, Inc."

After one hour, when I felt my feminist persona had been duly noticed, when my arms ached with the buildup of lactic acid, and when Joe, Tim, and Dan had finished with the cartons and started moving the heavy pieces of furniture, I sat down for a rest. With men like Joe Finnegan, I always feel obliged to lift the heaviest boxes. When I was thirteen, my parents bought a new rug to cover the living room floor. They drove it home from the store and left it in the car while they ate lunch. I remember the smell of hot dogs frying. I snuck out of the house and dragged the rolled-up rug and its horsehair mat out of our station wagon. Heaving the rug over my shoulder, I dragged it up the hill, over the rock ledge, around the garden. Then I went back for the mat. When my parents finished lunch they came outside and found me panting beside the rug. My mother gasped, scolding me for doing possible damage to my "female insides." My father told me I shouldn't have done it, but he did not sound convinced, and his eyes sparkled with pride.

On Hudson Street, after we had unloaded the truck, I passed out beers. "This is monkey piss. You should buy imported," Joe advised.

"Thanks for the information," I said.

"Ahh, don't listen to Joe. He's full of gas," Tim said. It was the first time I had heard him speak. He and Dan started a little punching match.

"This beer's fine. We drink it by the keg up at school," Dan said, landing a punch on the side of Tim's head. Boys horsing around always made me nervous; I'm afraid of things like ruptures, brain damage, lawsuits. I looked at Joe.

"These two clowns don't know what's good. They haven't lived yet, have they, Una?"

I smiled at Joe. "We're not that much older."

"Sure we are. You're an old broad. You'd better face it."

Irish humor, especially among athletes, is often a series of insults. I let it ride. "Are you the oldest?" I asked.

"Damn straight. Me, then two sisters, then these jokers."

"Really? I have two sisters."

"No boys?"

"No."

Joe shook his head. Dan and Tim, alarmed, stopped fooling around. "Oooh, your poor father," Joe said. "I don't know what I'd do if I had all girls."

I remembered that he was divorced. "Do you have kids?"

"No, thank god. She couldn't. At the time it was terrible, but now it's a blessing. I'd never have gotten divorced if there were kids. You just don't walk away from your own flesh and blood."

"I can think of circumstances," I began.

"No way. No circumstances. What the hell are circumstances compared with a kid?" Joe finished his beer. He shot a look at his brothers. "You two better get going. Get ready for your dates tonight. You got dates?"

"Yeah," Tim said. "Remember Marianne?"

"That wop? Get rid of her. She seems like a dope. Ma can't stand the sight of her. Una, you got a phone?"

"Not yet."

"Then you find a pay phone, Timmy, and you break your date with her. She's a royal loser."

I handed Dan and Tim fifty dollars each. They protested a bit, but Joe told them to keep their mouths shut since I was a big TV star and could afford it. When they had left, Joe turned to me with tears in his eyes. "It's up to me to keep those two in line," he said. "The old man died last year."

"Really?" I said, moving closer to him. "My father died a year ago January." The bond was becoming stronger by the minute.

FOR THE first month I lived in my new place, I saw Joe Finnegan only in the lobby. With Delilah the focus of a new plot twist, I was busy filming every day. Joe was busy because the NCAA basketball playoffs were underway and the baseball season would soon start. One morning we met at our mailboxes and he told me that his business boomed whenever anything of national sporting interest occurred. They sold more tennis rackets during the U.S. Open, more basketballs when the Knicks won, more baseball bats during the World Series. I related that to my own life: according to Chance, more people bought our sponsors' products during periods when Delilah was threatened by or rescued from a violent experience.

Delilah had been rescued from the fur trapper by Beck, and now she was safely home in Mooreland where she had mysteriously earned the credentials to become a psychotherapist. Little did she know that one of her patients, a reporter who worked under Beck at the Mooreland *Tribune* and had been referred to Delilah by Beck, was madly in love with him. Yet another cub reporter, out to bash Delilah. For that first month, I was too exhausted to unpack many boxes.

One rare night when I was home before nine, I sat amid brown cartons, eating Chinese food out of the box, watching a movie on television, when someone knocked on my door. Instinct told me it was Joe. I hunched in my seat, trying to decide whether or not to let him in. The TV's sound was turned low; he had no way of knowing I was home unless I answered the door. But then the telephone rang and gave everything away. I cannot listen to a telephone ring and ring without answering it. It is different from someone knocking at the door. A knock at the door brings a visitor, while a ringing phone brings news, good and bad, from home.

"Hello," I said into the receiver, and instantly Joe called, "Hey, Una, what gives?"

"I'll be right there," I called to Joe.

Margo was on the line. "Hi. I miss everyone," she said. "Now I know how you must have felt when Lily and I both lived in Providence."

"But I hardly ever see Lily. She's busy with Henk."

Silence on the line. "You hardly ever see her?" The concept was as strange to Margo as it had been to me when Lily had first moved to New York and never called.

"I've only been to her place once, and she's only been here once." For the first time since the dinner, I wondered what had happened to the Metropolitan Opera tickets.

"Do you talk on the phone a lot?"

"Never. I work all day, and Henk's home at night. She doesn't like talking on the phone when she can be with him."

"Jesus. I can't believe it. I was picturing you two running all over the place together. I pictured Henk practically adopting you, calling you both '*Liebchen.*' "

"No, that's not it at all," I said quickly, trying to ignore Joe's light tapping on the door, his voice calling "Una, Una," over and over. "How's everything with you?"

"Fine, I guess. I'm going out with someone now. He went to Brown, and now he owns an inn at Watch Hill."

"How'd you meet him?"

"You know—the typical. He was in Providence trying to steal a chef away from the Market Café, and he came up to Brown to take a stroll down memory lane. We met in the library."

"Oh, that's romantic," I said, delighted by the shy excitement in Margo's voice and by her idea of a typical meeting.

"It's pretty great. His name is Matt Lincoln. You've got to see the inn—there is a room in the turret, and you can see out to Martha's Vineyard." Joe's tapping had become loud knocking, and Margo heard it. "Is there someone at your door?"

"Actually, there is. I'd better answer it. I miss *you*, you know."

"I know," Margo said. We blew kisses to each other through the phone. I envisioned New York in relation to Providence, and hated to think how much water our kisses had to travel under in order to reach each other.

"Ooooooooo-na!" Joe called again. I pulled the door open to find him standing in the hall, dressed in his jogging suit. His red curls straggled damply across his forehead. "Got a beer for a dying man?" he asked, one hand over his heart.

"Only domestic." I stood aside and let him in.

"You have got to be kidding me," he said, looking at the piles of boxes. "My brothers and I busted our gonads to get you moved in here, and you haven't even *unpacked?*"

"Haven't had time. Mind if I finish my dinner?" I gestured at my Chinese food.

He shook his head. Then he helped himself to a beer out of my refrigerator and sat at the end of my sofa that wasn't piled with books. "Haven't seen you around much, kid," he said.

I marveled, watching him down half the beer with one gulp, the way he had the day he moved my stuff. Beer trickled from one corner of his lips. "Just ran to Wall Street and back," he said.

"My brother-in-law would approve of that, but not of the beer."

"Who, the heart surgeon?"

I nodded.

"What a crock of shit. Those guys are always telling people what they can and can't do, but they don't know everything. What they know is how to collect the fee."

I must have sighed, because Joe suddenly leaned forward and peered into my face. "What's wrong?" he asked.

"I don't know. I'm tired. It's been a long week."

"Oh yeah?" He placed his beer on my bare oak floor. "You just relax and let Uncle Joe do his thing." Joe had a particularly crass way of expressing himself, but I was succumbing to his charms. I had no idea of what "his thing" was, but I was willing to let him do it.

He cracked his thick knuckles and slipped off my grey knee socks. Then he began to slowly massage my feet. Facing me, he propped my heels on his knees. His thumbs circled the balls of my feet, pressing down to the bone, then touching so lightly that it tickled. He ran his fingernails down the calloused skin from my toes to my heels, then brought them back up along the soft, tender skin in my arches. I continued to eat dinner. With squarish chopsticks, I maneuvered a peapod into my mouth A bit of sauce dripped on my shirt, but I hardly cared. Joe popped all ten of my toes.

"You have a high arch here, Una," he said softly.

I stared at my small foot sandwiched between his rough hands. His thumbs rubbed my ankle bones. "Really?" I said stupidly, buying time. Joe's red hair was drying in corkscrew curls. He was gazing at my foot, his mouth half open. I could see the tip of his pink tongue.

"You know what this is leading up to, don't you, Tiger?" he asked.

I slid my foot out of his hands and planted it on the floor. Joe Finnegan, my heritage. My first communion partner had looked very like him; the more I considered that, the more it seemed possible that the boy's name had been Finnegan. Or at least Joe. Joe Hannigan, possibly. I twirled my fingers in this Joe Finnegan's curls, and he stood. He pulled me out of my chair. We kissed. His mouth seemed to cover my lower face. Closing in, he pressed his pelvis against my thigh. We rubbed slowly against each other for a minute, then suddenly he lifted me into his arms and rushed me into the bedroom, like a thief stealing a sack of grain from a bakery in the dead of night.

"What are you doing?" I asked, laughing.

"Carrying you to bed," he said seriously. Perhaps I could have taken that literal answer as a bad sign, but I didn't.

Undressed, we lay on the sheets and admired each other in the light slanting in from the street. Joe kissed my breasts or held them, even while he was slipping one finger in and out of my cunt. "Are you . . . prepared?" he asked.

I laughed again. "Do you mean birth control?"

"Yes. Do you want me to . . . use anything?"

"Tell me you don't have rubbers in your wallet?" I asked, really laughing now. Actually I felt nervous, as though we had flashed back ten years to high school or the years just afterwards, when boys carried rubbers around and did things like feel your breasts (second base) or touch your cunt (third base) instead of truly plunging in.

"Of course I have rubbers," he said, rolling on top of me, laughing also. "But if you're telling me I don't need one . . ."

"Give me a minute," I said, heading to the bathroom to install my diaphragm. When I returned I lay beside him on the bed. He kissed me once, and then his thick cock was inside me before I had any idea that we were ready. He moved in slow, thrusting motions, and at intervals he whispered, "Is that okay, baby?"

"Yes," I grunted back, trying to slide my arm between our bodies. He lay on top of me, not taking any of the weight on his own elbows. I couldn't get a good breath. With one hand I began to lightly tickle his balls, and he began to squirm. He reached down for my clitoris, but the instant he found it he crashed into orgasm.

A three-minute rest, during which he must have felt the tension in my body, and then he went down on me. After a certain point, when I know whether or not I am going to come, I become aware of the time. I think of the man huddled between my legs, his tongue going, his fingers spreading my labia majora, my pubic hairs tickling his nose, and I imagine how his jaw must ache. How his neck muscles must cramp.

Oh, I feel so sorry for him that no orgasm is possible. I lie on my back and reach down to touch his shoulder. That expectant look. I shake my head and smile. "It's all right," I whisper. "I didn't need to."

Relieved, he slips upwards on the bed, presses his still dripping cock against my leg, and kisses my shoulder.

"That was wonderful," Joe said.

"It was," I said. It was, too. I didn't come, but it still felt wonderful. It did, it did, I thought.

"Do you have a hard time coming?" he asked.

A difficult question. Not a hard time, exactly. But I have to get to know a person. Or I have to love him. But I'm afraid of egos. I hate to hurt feelings. I hate so much to hurt feelings that I have faked a couple of orgasms in my day. Who will ever know? That's the way I thought the times I did it. But I knew. I lied. And honesty in bed seems crucial. So much is bared anyway, a lie seems magnified. It seems twice as harmful. But still, I am afraid of egos.

"No, I don't always have a hard time," I said carefully to Joe. "But my body has to get used to yours."

"I did something wrong." Sullen. Bad boy!

"You did not! You were wonderful, honestly. It's very complicated."

"Right. You went to Catholic school, and you can't come until you're married or at least engaged."

No man had ever hit me with that assessment without hearing my entire history. It was a shockingly intimate moment. "That is it," I said. "You look like the boy I made first communion with—but I'm not even Catholic any more. I don't even believe in God."

"You don't?" He pulled back a bit, shocked.

"No. You do?"

"Well, sure." He sounded puzzled, as though nonbelief had never occurred to him. "If you're not a Catholic, I guess you shouldn't mind the 'out of wedlock' bit."

"Listen, Joe. These things linger. My whole life, three things got drummed in: family, scholarship, and chastity."

"Which ones do you have left?"

I lay on my back and thought about it. Leaving Juilliard I

had forsaken scholarship; messing around since the age of eighteen, I had forsaken chastity; and though I would not, would never, forsake my family, I had neither begun a new one nor succeeded in staying close enough to my old one.

"I guess I . . .," I began finally, feeling panicked and alone.

"You've always got family," Joe said, wrapping his arms around me. "Didn't your parents tell you that? No matter what happens, your family will always be there."

Unless they die. Unless they move to New York and never even call you. Telling such things to Joe seemed impossible. Tears choked my throat so I wouldn't have to.

"Shhh," Joe said tenderly, licking the tears from my cheeks. "Husha, husha little baby." His cock stiffened as he soothed me, and presently he was gliding inside me again, kissing my damp cheeks, continuing to say "husha, husha," even though I was no longer crying.

LIVING on different floors of the same building as your lover presents certain problems. Such as: do you spend every night together? Do you eat meals together, and if so, who cooks? What about the awkward feelings which arise when you meet at the mailboxes after a long day and want to go upstairs alone? What about when one person seems to spend all his time in *your* apartment, thus requiring *you* to clean and pick up, while his remains relatively uninhabited? What do all the neighbors think about all this?

"I think I am proving Monica's worst suspicions about actresses," I said to Joe one Sunday afternoon when we returned from brunch. "Did you see the way she looked at us?"

"Who the hell cares? Fuck her and everyone who looks like her. It'll give her another chance to bitch, and Monica's happy as a pig in shit when she's bitching." Joe dropped the paper on my table and dove straight for the sports section. "She's jealous," he said.

"Why? Because I have you and she doesn't?" I asked, teasing.

"Frankly, yes. She's made more than one play for me. After

board meetings, down in the storage area. She's a horny broad, and I doubt Chip has one clue about what to do about it." He sat on my sofa.

I thought of Monica and Chip's apartment, filled with homey Americana, and knew that Joe was exaggerating, if not lying. I smiled at him. "You're such a riot," I said.

"God as my judge," he said, raising his right hand. He draped the sports section like a tent over his knees. "She's after me."

"Right." I started unpacking one of the last boxes. Joe watched me crouch; I felt very sexy. I moved slowly, stretching to place things on my desktop, shifting my ass as I rummaged through the box. Joe and I had spent every Sunday morning for the last month together, and I loved the routine: brunch, an hour or two reading the *Times*, bed. Sex on Sunday mornings felt delicious and leisurely. I always came on Sunday mornings; Joe said it was because I knew I should be at Mass.

That Sunday Joe walked across the room; he reached down for my hand. Instead of rising I pulled him down, and we undressed each other on the floor. Carpet fibers scratched my back. I thought suddenly, I'm *always* on my back. Lovemaking with Joe was nothing if not consistent: he was always on top. I tried to roll us over then, but he resisted. He lowered his head to my breasts and sucked my nipples. I tickled his balls. He came, and for the first time since we had started fucking on Sundays, I did not.

"Why won't you let me go on top?" I asked as soon as he had rolled off.

He looked surprised. "I'll let you. It's not a question of *letting* you."

But I saw the way he avoided my eyes and knew I was right. He propped himself up on one elbow and stirred the things in my box.

"What have we here?" he asked, holding up a framed photograph of me, Lily, and Margo. It was ten or so years old; Margo still had braces, and Lily had her short-lived pixie cut. My father had taken it on the beach in front of our house.

"You're the prettiest," Joe said, kissing the top of my head. "Which is the sister who lives in the city?"

"Her. Lily. The other one is Margaret."

"I know, I know. Lily and Margaret, your two sisters. When am I going to meet them?"

"Good question," I said, feeling sullen. At that moment I felt angry at Lily and Margo for their distance, angry at Joe for asking about them, angrier at Joe because shortly he would leave, as he did every Sunday, for dinner with his entire family at his mother's house. I began to cry. Often after sex with Joe things would make me cry.

"Hey, what are you doing this afternoon?" Joe asked, reading my mind.

"My laundry. Reading next week's scripts. Nothing."

"Ma'll kill me for not warning her, but how about coming to Norwalk for dinner? Everyone will be there, and I've been wanting to show you off."

"I'd love to," I said.

JOE's mother and brothers lived in a ranch house in a neighborhood of similar ranch houses. Mrs. Finnegan and her two daughters greeted us at the door. Joe had called ahead to say I was coming, and he warned me: all three were avid "Beyond the Bridge" fans. They were dressed in Sunday's best. Mrs. Finnegan wore a floral pantsuit over a ruffled blouse, and Joe's sisters, Corinne and Erin, wore velvet dresses that strained across their ample bosoms.

"Oooh, hello Una!" Mrs. Finnegan called gaily, clasping her hands. We were, after all, old friends from the Rose Garden Mall. She had tied a pink bow in her grey hair.

"Hello, Mrs. Finnegan," I said, and she pulled my head down so I could kiss her.

Erin Mankiewicz, the elder sister, shook my hand vigorously. "I can't tell you how thrilled we are to finally meet you. We have watched the show for—what, Cori?"

"Since grammar school at least," Corinne said.

"It's a pleasure to meet *you*," I said. "I've met your mother, and your brothers, of course, and Joe has told me about—"

Joe, standing behind me, his hand on my waist, interrupted. "Jabber, jabber. What's a brother got to do to get a few kisses around here?"

His sisters and mother swarmed on him like bees. "We're having roast beef, Joey," Erin said. "And little Joey brought you some pictures he did at school. Did you happen to remember the catcher's mitt?"

Joe grimaced with anguish, then grinned. "You bet I did," he said slyly.

"He's such a joker," Mrs. Finnegan said, turning to me, her arms draped around his neck.

We walked through the front door, directly into a small living room that was packed with people. Dan and Tim sat on the couch, two men sat in overstuffed chairs, and four kids were tussling on the floor. A golf tournament on the large TV screen cast green light on the viewers' faces. The brown floral draperies were closed.

The men stood when we entered, and Joe made introductions. Stan Mankiewicz was Erin's husband, and Paul Haggerty was Corinne's. Joe rushed to sit between his brothers on the sofa. "Relax, fellas," he commanded with a wink at me. "Ma and the girls want to take Una into the kitchen and pick her brain about the show."

"Oh, he's fresh!" cried Mrs. Finnegan.

We walked toward the kitchen. Around the house were various statues of Jesus and Mary, framed Mass cards for Mr. Finnegan (every time we came upon one of these, Mrs. Finnegan would strike her breast and murmur, "God is good"). There were calligraphed prayers on parchment. Ruffled cotton curtains were pulled across each window. The smell of roasting beef filled every room.

"Not very grand, but it's home," Mrs. Finnegan said. The sentiment was lovely, but already I was feeling claustrophobic. From the living room came hoots and shouts as someone sank a long putt. "His putter has a goddamn graphite shaft!" Joe yelled.

The house is dark, I thought. Electric lights were on everywhere, but very little natural sunlight penetrated the curtains.

In the cramped kitchen all three Finnegan women donned

aprons and began to work, dodging each other, moving in mystical rhythms no doubt established over long years of preparing roast beef dinners while the Finnegan men watched golf tournaments. In what appeared to be an elaborately choreographed ritual, they crisscrossed the kitchen at least three dozen times. They opened canned peas, stirred flour into the roasting pan to make gravy, poured water into the coffeemaker, frosted a chocolate cake, sharpened knives, stirred up brown bits from the bottom of the pan, tasted things, and asked me endless questions about the show:

"How did you get the part?"

"Will Delilah ever marry Beck?"

"What's this new thing, with Delilah being a psychiatrist?"

All three women hated psychotherapy, believing that it taught patients to hate their mothers.

"Are the Grants Catholic?"

"Thank God Delilah had that baby, even if she was out of wedlock, instead of aborting."

"What's Stuart MacDuff like in real life?"

"Do you think you'll ever go into the movies?"

"Why do you do commercials for *those* garbage bags instead of *these* garbage bags?"

I sat at the kitchen table drinking sweet red wine. Erin and Corinne, hungry for information, paused now and then, their eyes sparkling.

"Have you ever been married, Una?" Mrs. Finnegan asked. "In real life, I mean." She showed none of the deference she had that day at the mall; here she was on solid ground, in the midst of her five grown children. She kept her eyes on me.

"No, I haven't."

"The kids getting married today have such an advantage," she said. "The church provides counseling. That's something no psychiatrist understands."

"Like what Paul and I went through," Corinne said.

"Even better! Father gave a sermon at early Mass a week or so back, and he told about how we've entered the computer age. The young man and woman fill out very thorough questionnaires, takes about an hour and a half, giving their inner-most thoughts on all sorts of problem areas—finances, sex, nuclear war. Then the forms are handed in to a computer in New Jersey, and the computer figures out which areas they're weak in. As a couple, I mean. You're Catholic, aren't you Una?"

"Well, no."

Mrs. Finnegan was about to speak, but Erin cut her off. "Ma, *computers* don't figure out problems. People do." Then, to me, "Stan's a programmer."

"Oh," I said.

"But anyway," Mrs. Finnegan went on, "the couple goes through six months of counseling, with the computer and Father, and by the time their wedding day comes, they are *ready*."

The kitchen walls pressed in, until the room was as close as a suitcase, trapping me, the three Finnegan women, and the smell of roast beef. I excused myself to go to the bathroom. Sitting on the fuzzy gold toilet seat cover, I pressed my fore-head against the cool tile. Out of the corner of my eye, I glimpsed the golden toilet paper holder with two ornate rose-buds guarding each end of the roll. The Finnegans used pat-terned toilet paper. This is nothing like my house, I thought. Nothing like my family. In this house the women cook the dinner and the men watch golf. In this house, you have to un-screw two golden rosebuds just to remove the empty toilet paper roll. In my house my mother cooked the dinner and my father, when he was home and not suffering from Black Ass, did the dishes. My sisters and I studied or played together. My mother never owned an apron; she owned an easel and watercolors. Our house was quiet. There weren't crucifixes and religious artifacts all over the place. When we cooked roast beef, the smell stayed in the kitchen.

Joe knocked on the bathroom door. He did not say, "Are you all right?" Instead he said, "Hurry up—I have to take a whiz before Hale Irwin tees off."

I sat on the toilet, my head in my hands, and knew: if I had finished Juilliard, this would not be happening. I would not be sitting in a bathroom while two rooms away three of my fans argued over the doneness of a rump roast. I would not be listening to my lover telling me to "shit or get off the pot" in order that he be able to catch the tee-off. If I had graduated from Juilliard I would be happily married to a man who loved me, a kind intellectual who would speak softly, who would gather my mother and sisters with me to his heart and keep us together. Who would be a father to my children. Like my father Joe was imperious, full of his own greatness, and had the makings of a patriarch. But those were not qualities I cared about.

Then I heard Mrs. Finnegan asking Joe to carve the roast and felt ashamed of myself. Joe padded down the hallway; I recognized the sound of his bare feet. The Finnegans were a lovely family; their love and devotion for each other were enormous, if oppressive. But I was making the same mistake with them that I made with all close families: I was holding them up for comparison with the Cavans. Splashing cold water on my face, I opened the bathroom door and went out to dinner.

I began avoiding my apartment and spending as little time in the building as possible. I told Georgie Attwood, my agent, to book me for nighttime appearances at malls; I did one game show in Los Angeles and talk shows in Chicago, Phoenix, and Seattle. Chance loved it; whenever stars from "Beyond" made guest appearances in distant cities, our ratings in those cities soared. I tried to see Lily and Susan whenever they were free at night: anything to avoid Joe. Lily was busy with "The Spring Rambles," a charity ball intended to raise money for cardiac research, and wasn't available to see me. Performances of *Hester's Sister* were scheduled to start in two weeks, at the end of April, and Susan was busy with rehearsals. She had quit waitressing in order to see more of Louis, but she said she would meet me at the Bridge Café one evening after work.

The night was balmy. Walking south on Broadway I noticed all the open windows in the apartments, lofts, and studios. Spring had arrived in New York City. In my travels I had seen daffodils, new leaves, and crabapple blossoms. A steady breeze blew north off the harbor, but I was comfortable in my thin cotton sweater.

Susan waved to me from a table in the corner. The Bridge Café stood across Water Street from her loft; she apologized for not inviting me there, but she had been too busy to keep it neat or stock provisions. She and Louis ate out nearly every night.

"How've you been?" she asked. I could tell from her tentative tone and wrinkly brow that she knew something was wrong.

"Not so great," I said.

She held my hand on the red checked tablecloth. "What?" Deep breath. Exhalation. Glancing around to see if anyone was watching. "I'm in big trouble. You know how I told you about that guy in my building?"

"You slept with him and now you can't stand him and you're afraid to go home," she said.

I stared at her for a few seconds, mystified and grateful. Like Margo and Lily she had that ability to zoom straight to the heart of my matter. "Exactly. Well—not exactly. I can *stand* him, but that's about it. I'm actually afraid to talk to him. He's left about fifteen messages on my machine. Then I call him back when I'm sure he's out and leave messages on his. I sneak into the building at off hours, terrified I'll meet him in the hall."

"What a horrible way to live."

"I know," I said, miserable. "In bed at night I hear him knocking on my door. It goes on and on, and I keep thinking about all the people who *know*—they all hear him knocking, and they know. Then he finally leaves."

"Who cares who knows?"

"I do."

"How bourgeois," Susan said, frowning.

"I know it is." I said. "I'm disgusting myself. I deserve everything I'm getting."

"You do not," Susan said sternly. Then, "What are you getting?"

I looked up at her. "Did I tell you that I had two visions of my father? Every time I fuck someone, I'm afraid he's going to show up again and start yelling. Joe's Irish Catholic. I thought that would make a difference, make it less sinful."

"You think it's sinful?"

"I don't know. I'm not sure."

"Actually, I'm more interested in your visions. You see your father?" Susan looked at me with deep concern in her hazel eyes, and I suddenly felt positive that I was crazy. Can you imagine telling your best friend you have seen your dead father? I felt my hands trembling and held them on my lap.

"Not recently. Last summer I did. But I keep thinking I'll

see him. Every time I—I don't know. Anything. I'm afraid he can see me even if I can't see him."

"Una, that does sound a little crazy, honey."

"I know it does." Oddly I felt calmer. The relief of unburdening. I had killed two birds with this conversation: I had told Susan that I was afraid to see Joe, afraid to see my father. Sitting opposite her at our corner table, the two birds looked disturbingly alike. Just then a young woman with a punk haircut and wearing a black leather skirt walked shyly over. "You're Delilah Grant, aren't you?" she asked, holding out a paper napkin for me to sign.

Susan and I both laughed. I signed the napkin. "You are so famous it cracks me up," Susan said when the girl walked away.

"How's the play coming?"

"Fantastic. I'm getting nervous." Then she turned pink and started blinking her eyes. "Did I tell you about our angel?"

In stage language, "angel" means benefactor. When a show runs into financial trouble, such as not having enough money to pay the actors or buy costumes or rent the theater, an angel comes along and makes everything dreamy. Angels are usually rich businessmen who love the romance of the theater.

"No, who is it?" I asked.

"You know him," Susan said. "It's Henk Voorhees."

I sat there without speaking, trying to decide how I felt about that. Henk and Lily did not know Susan or know that I knew Susan. Henk "loved the arts," as Lily had told me often enough. Naturally he would contribute to arts' organizations. But he had never asked me about acting. I had assumed that theater was not one of his passions. Of course I had no illusions about "Beyond the Bridge" being theater, but I had gone to Juilliard and had plenty of friends on the legitimate stage. I remembered thinking that "loving the arts" could mean loving museums, opera, ballet, performance art, literature, whatever; it did not necessarily mean theater.

But here was Susan Russell, my best friend, telling me that my brother-in-law was about to finance her starring role. I sat there feeling jealous. Susan knew it. She understood the insecurities that motivate actors too well not to. I watched her lower her head until her halo of frizzy brown hair caught the red neon light cast by the sign in the window. She stared at the wide plank floor.

"The play probably won't do anything," she said, but her tone told me she already knew the play could be a hit.

"I hope it does wonderfully," I said. I did want Susan to do wonderfully, but I wanted myself to do better. "Have you met Henk?"

"Not yet. I've heard he's met the director, but he likes to keep a low profile. Have you seen him or your sister lately?"

"No. They're busy with 'The Spring Rambles.' Henk is quite the fund raiser—money for research, money for theater."

"Your sister snagged a rich one." Her voice was bitter, and I looked up, shocked.

"What does that matter?"

"Una, if you were thirty and still waiting on tables to pay the rent, you wouldn't have to ask. You know what Louis is doing right now? Running movies at a theater on Thirty-fourth Street. He does that three nights a week."

That, in a nutshell, told me why I had left Juilliard. I lacked the dedication to starve for my profession. By my junior year I had heard three or four stories of recent alumni who had done well, had starred in Broadway plays or Hollywood movies. I had, however, heard two hundred stories about alumni who were pioneers in "artists' colonies" on the Lower East Side and across the rivers in Williamsburg and Hoboken because they could afford no better, who waited tables between shows, and who finally gave up acting entirely to become affluent bankers, ad writers, insurance salesmen, car salesmen.

A waiter came to take our order. Neither Susan nor I felt like having anything. The waiter stood by our table for a few seconds, until a group wanting another round of drinks caught his eyes. He glanced over his shoulder at us and walked away.

"I'm jealous, you know," I said.

"I know."

"*Really* jealous."

She looked furious. "Don't you think I've ever been jealous of you?"

"For what?"

"What do you think? For having girls like that—" she nodded her head at the punk rock autograph seeker standing at the bar "—know who you are. For working every blessed day of the week."

The punk rocker had been watching us; she waved when we looked her way, sending Susan and me into a fit of giggles. "I see your point," I said. "That *is* worth something."

We decided not to order any food. On the street outside we hugged tightly. The Brooklyn Bridge soared overhead and a neon replica glowed in the café's window. Susan felt thin as a bird, and I didn't let go for a long time. When we parted, we just said, "See you." There was no need to apologize further.

THAT night Joe Finnegan's knocking would not let me sleep. I lay in bed, curled under the covers, while spring air blew through my open window. I waited for him to leave.

"I know you're home," he called. "I saw your goddamn light go out fifteen minutes ago."

Wearily I walked to the door and opened it. He stepped inside, into my living room where street light cast long shadows shaped like surrealistic furniture on my bare wood floor.

"What is it?" he asked, holding my face between his hands. The magic of human contact. His face looked mournful. Sometimes I felt so lonely, any tenderness was better than none. I pressed my head against his chest, wondering how to explain that I didn't like him. I would rather avoid him for the rest of our lives than explain anything like that.

But we didn't bother with words. He didn't ask me what was wrong, and I volunteered nothing. We walked straight into my bedroom, stripped, and climbed into bed. Our bodies cleaved together and we held tight to each other all night. Several times I wakened in the night feeling empty and nauseous, and I pressed closer to Joe thinking that closeness could drive the feelings away. His arms were wrapped around me; one hand held one of my breasts. I kept glancing at the alarm clock's illuminated dial, dreading the approach of morning and the spoken word.

Dawn light streamed through my window, catching me and Joe wrapped in my white sheet like an overexposed photograph. My right arm was asleep; it had no feeling at all. I lay awake, waiting for the alarm to go off, and felt utterly vacant, as lonely as I had ever felt in my life. Turning to watch Joe sleep, I found him watching me.

"Morning," he said.

"Good morning."

"You feel like explaining things to me, Una?"

Barely awake, I felt glad that Joe was getting to the point before I had a chance to drink some coffee and begin to dread what I had to say.

"I'm going to tell you something I've never told another woman: you're hurting me," Joe said, rising on one elbow to see me directly. "I wish you would just tell me what's going on."

"I don't think it's working between us," I said, unfamiliar with the language for ending a relationship the man wished to continue. "We're not making each other happy . . . enough."

"That's fair," Joe said. "Couldn't you have gotten around to it sooner? Instead of hiding from me?"

"I'm sorry," I said, feeling surprisingly good. Giving it to him straight came easier than I had anticipated. Why hadn't I ever learned that men could take the harsh truth so well? Emboldened, I continued. "I've enjoyed spending time with you. You're wonderful company; we've had fun times together. But do you think we have enough in common? We don't exactly see the world the same way." I smiled. "And that's an understatement. Also, our living arrangements leave a lot—"

Joe placed his hand on my arm. "Una, this is very hard. Could you give me a second to digest it?"

"Of course, Joe. Sure," I said. Turning red. Wishing that I was not always the victim of my own excesses.

HESTER'S SISTER was a tremendous smash. I sat in the audience with Lily and Henk, spellbound by the coastal stage set, the eerie lighting, the not at all eerie relationship between Hester and her sister Anne (played by Susan). They were two sisters who lived on Massachusetts' northern coast, who constructed fishing nets for their living, who had never married. Both were young and beautiful. Hester snubbed a town elder who wished to marry her. The men in town, not understanding why two beautiful women would choose not to marry, found reasons to say that Hester was a witch. The local women, jealous of the sisters' beauty, believed the stories; Anne's friend, Prudence, tried to convince Anne. She had proof: the nets woven by Hester developed holes and let all the fish swim through, then repaired themselves when pulled in. Her father, a fisherman, had sworn it was true. At the play's end, Hester is burned, not knowing whether Anne believes in her innocence, and the audience is left with the sense that Anne will be burned next.

After the final curtain, after Susan's eight curtain calls, Lily and I sat still, holding hands, too disturbed to cry.

"Some play, eh?" Henk said, still applauding madly.

Lily and I stared straight ahead. We were reading each other's mind: I love you. I love you, too. I thought of Anne and Hester, of how much they had loved each other and of how much they had doubted each other in the end. How confusing were facts! Presented with facts, Anne had mistrusted a truth she had known since birth. I squeezed Lily's hand.

"Time to go to the party!" Henk said, boisterously throwing on his black coat. "Come on, let's get going."

People gathered around us, congratulating Lily and Henk for their involvement in such a wonderful play. Henk grinned magnanimously, but Lily was tight-lipped and pale.

"What is wrong, *Liebchen*?" he asked, bending over her.

"The play! It was so . . . it reminds me of *me and my sisters*!" She started to sob.

A look of pure alarm crossed Henk's strong features, and he bundled Lily backstage to some secret place. I stood alone beside our seats, guarding Lily's and my coats, watching the audience file out. No one there recognized me; I felt glad and resentful all at once.

At the party, hosted by Henk and other angels at a restaurant in SoHo, everyone recognized Susan. Louis preceded her into the room. A hush traveled across the tables, which then erupted with wild applause, hooting, and cries of "Brava!" when Susan entered. Susan, wearing a tuxedo, looked incandescent. An enormous smile wreathed her pale face. She walked from table to table, accepting congratulations. At our table she embraced me and kissed Lily and Henk.

To Lily she said, "Any sister of Una's is a sister of mine."

Lily held her hand and said, "That was the best play I've ever seen."

Henk placed one firm hand on her left shoulder and said, "Marvelous. Just marvelous."

"I'll be back later," Susan said, allowing her director to spirit her along.

Then the early editions of the next day's papers arrived.

"We already know what the reviews will say," Henk said, scoffing. "Don't even bother to read them."

But he listened avidly as an unidentified young man read parts of each review to the crowd. " '*Hester's Sister* is a cauldron bubbling with darkest emotions, home truths, and terrible secrets.' 'Everyone who has ever been a sister—no, make that *everyone*—will weep at Susan Russell's stunning performance as *Hester's Sister*.' 'A chilling portrait of two sisters and their bleakest hour. Don't miss Susan Russell.' "

"You know," Henk said contemplatively, "I have helped bring many shows to the stage. All arrive at a moment of truth—just before opening night, you have a sense, a clear sense, of what will happen to the show. Some you know will fail. Simple as that. Others you hope have a chance for greatness—few do, but you hope. But this play. You just knew." He waved his hand. "It was perfect, the way each element coalesced."

"You've been an angel before?" I asked.

Henk tossed his blond head back, amused. "Oh, many times. I did *Favorites*. You've heard of that, of course."

"Of course." *Favorites* had been the hottest show on Broadway two years ago. A waiter delivered champagne to our table. I sipped, feeling myself grow lighthearted. The play's sober effects were wearing off. Across the room people were toasting Susan, and she was grinning with delight. I felt truly ecstatic for her.

"Well, here's to Susan," I said. Lily and Henk clinked glasses with me.

"A *real* actress," Henk said.

That triggered an alarm in my brain. Was he talking about me? I tried to meet his eyes, but he was smiling at Susan.

"She is wonderful, isn't she?" I asked, prodding.

"Marvelous. A *truly* devoted artist." (The "truly" digging in.)

"Oh, I have to use the bathroom. Want to come?" Lily asked me. (A touch panic-stricken, I thought.)

Was I paranoid? I stared at Henk, wanting some clue before I plunged in and extracted things he might not want to say. Yet he seemed to be saying them, however obliquely. I would move slowly. "Henk, did you know that Susan and I were at Juilliard together? Did Lily tell you?"

His controlled blue eyes finally settled on me. "Yes, of course. But you weren't there for long, were you?"

"Well, for three years."

He nodded, his attention moving back to Susan. "Yes, most likely you did not feel the need to graduate. For that TV program."

A definite barb. Quite poisonous. I hated myself, but blood rushed into my face, revealing my hurt feelings to Henk. Lily prodded my foot under the table; I followed her to the bathroom where ferns hung from black pipes and purplish plant light flooded the pink-tiled room.

"He didn't mean it the way it sounded," Lily said. "He's just a terrible snob."

"Yes, I can see that."

"He really hates soap operas—I don't know why. He says he can tell everything about his women patients by whether or not they watch soap operas."

Actually that made some sense to me. Lily, Margo, and I had once discovered you could tell plenty about a person by the shoes he wore. A person who watches soaps is sensitive, probably lonely, and probably female. "My producer says that most of our audience are college graduates. I wonder if Henk knows that."

Lily patted my back. "I doubt it. He just has this thing about soaps. He does love you, though."

"*Oh sure he does!*" I said, shoving Lily against the tiles and starting to babble. "You've been married to him since *January one* and this is only the *third* time I've seen you it makes me sick we're supposed to be *sisters* what the hell's the matter is he keeping you *prisoner* does he *hate* me oh god that play really got me."

Lily and I hugged, weeping together. My head was resting on her shoulder, and I could see my tears spreading in a deep circle on her mauve silk blouse.

"He doesn't hate you," she said. "I swear it. He just wants me alone for awhile. We're newlyweds . . ." Sob, sob, sob.

"I'm trying to understand that," I said, calming myself. "But when you consider how close we have always been, this new business is shocking."

Lily began to regard her face in the mirror. She was trying not to hear me. I recognized the mechanism; denying the problem could make it disappear, the way I had tried to handle Joe.

"Can you please talk to me?" I asked.

"All right. Henk seems to need me to himself right now. Like he told you—he's not used to close families, close sibling relationships."

It was the old line Henk had handed me at dinner that night, yet the phrase "sibling relationships" sounded too clinical, too textbook perfect to describe what went on among me, Lily, and Margo. And here was Lily, repeating it like a prize student.

"One important fact you seem to neglect, my sweet: Margo and I are the siblings. Don't you think we'll do our best to make him comfortable?" I made myself sound surer than I felt. "Don't you think we'll welcome him with all we're worth? And don't say he's insecure."

"I wasn't going to," Lily said, looking surprised.

The bathroom door opened and Susan flew in. "Henk said you guys . . . oh, Jesus. Exit, stage left."

"No, wait—it's okay," Lily said nervously. "I'd better get back to the table." She left in a hurry.

Susan and I stood in the middle of the bathroom. Her face and the starched white front of her shirt appeared lavender in the strange light. I made a great effort to smile. "See what you can do?" I asked, gesturing at the bathroom door through which Lily had just left. "Your play is so powerful, you're stirring things up between me and Lily." It was true.

She looked dubious. "There's more to it . . ."

"So what if there is? You're the catalyst. Now let's go out there. Louis must be dying of pride for you right now."

"He is a bit puffy."

"I've got to go kiss him." We walked into the restaurant where a few people started applauding instantly. We headed for Louis, who was hugging a fat champagne bottle to his portly chest. I bent him over backwards, planting a wet kiss on his full lips, and then I rejoined Lily and Henk, who were cuddling at the table and hardly even noticed when I sat down.

"Listen, Una," Henk said, his eyes concerned. "I didn't mean to hurt your feelings. You ran away so fast, we didn't have a chance to discuss everything."

The harder I tried to relax, the stiffer I became. "Oh? What should we have discussed?"

"Come on, Una," Lily said. "Try to get—"

"*Liebchen*, this is between me and your sister. It is important that she accept me as a member of the family," Henk said. "I see the problem constantly with patients."

"Wait one minute—do you think I haven't accepted you?" I asked, fuming. "I would love to be friendly with you. Haven't I said that a million times?" I looked to Lily who nodded but clearly didn't want to cross Henk by speaking.

He patted my shoulder. "My dear, we somehow started on

the wrong foot. It makes my beloved so sad when you and I quarrel. We can start over," he said sincerely, smiling in a way that cajoled me to join him. "So, we had a misunderstanding tonight. What about it? What's the harm?"

Wanting to be clear, I asked, "What *was* the misunderstanding?"

"Oh, about the medium, your TV program. I attacked the soap opera, not you. Lily tells me you're the best actress performing on TV, and I believe her. If she says you're the best, you're the best."

I said nothing, trying to determine whether I had just received an apology. Whatever it was, Lily's eyes begged me to accept it. I smiled, leaning across the table to shake Henk's hand. But I wondered. Lily needed him too badly. And even as I smiled at him, his eyes held me at bay. Lily could delude herself, but Henk and I knew just where we stood. He pretended to pull, but he was pushing with all his might.

O<small>N</small> "Beyond the Bridge" Delilah's life was once again building toward a homicidal crescendo with her, naturally, as the upcoming victim. Her patient, Nancy Vaughn, appeared to be merely a neurotic cub reporter when in fact she was a psychopathic killer. She had killed before, and she would kill again. She had killed a landlady, an indigent amnesiac, and a previous lover. She had left a trail of bodies from California to Mooreland, along with an equal number of identities. She had been Joralemon Trabert, Mary Smith, Mary Smitten, Gayle Horton, Gail Appleby, and Sandi Greene, but it was Nancy Vaughn who would attack Delilah. Delilah had no idea. Her relationship with Beck was going well, and that made her happy.

Why didn't Delilah marry Beck? The real reason, according to Chance, was that their often thwarted love match made the show's most popular story line. Chance feared that if he ever let the marriage take place, the viewers would let out little sighs of contentment and immediately switch the channel. Thus, the scriptwriters kept throwing spanners into the works of romance, taking Beck and Delilah close to the altar, then giving one of them amnesia, a new love interest, or a death threat as a way out.

During those weeks when spring turned to summer, I continued my crazy pace. I flew around the country making appearances whenever my shooting schedule allowed. Susan and *Hester's Sister* were featured in the arts sections of newspapers from New York to San Francisco. The play had already been booked for Broadway in the fall; there was talk of a national tour and a movie. I would read those articles and fight down my envy. Susan was having exactly what everyone dreamed about when they began drama school: artistic success. Remaining true to one's ideals while making a bundle in the process. Alone in hotel rooms at night I would get half-hearted urges to call Joe or Mrs. Finnegan and listen to them tell me what a wonderful actress I was. But that would be no different from the waitresses, stewardesses, women wearing business suits on the streets of St. Louis, Phoenix, and Denver saying, "We love you, Delilah." It was lovely, but I kept thinking of Edmund Wicklow saying of Susan in *Manhattan News*, "What an exceptional talent!"

When I did return to New York, I slept or worked. Susan had performances every night as well as matinees on Wednesday. Lily had been skittish with me since the opening night party. I spent all my free time alone, but I no longer tried to avoid Joe. When we met in the building or the stores along Hudson Street, we would smile grimly and say hello. There was nothing left to discuss since that morning after our last night together, but at least we had resolved matters between us.

I was lying on my bed one warm night early in July when my phone rang. It was Margo.

"You promised me you'd come stay at Matt's inn," she said.

"That's right. I did. I remember that."

"Well, my school year's over, and I'm in Watch Hill for good. When can you come?"

"I'll talk to Chance and see what I can do," I said, and then I listened to Margo coo about Matt.

"Anything new with Lily?" she asked after a while.

"Not really."

"Well, she called me the other day. We talked about Henk."

"Did she tell you about the things he said to me at the party?"

"Yes. She doesn't know what to do about it. My theory is, he wants to scare us off. He needs her all to himself . . ."

"Margo, if I hear that one more time, I'll punch a wall. Henk has about four phrases in his vocabulary, when it comes to our family, and they keep going around and around. He thinks his Dutch accent makes them sound less insane."

"Well, we have to give Lily a chance. She will convert him. From everything she says, he's quite—"

"Don't say 'insecure.' "

"Okay, I won't." She giggled.

"They've been married for six months. Don't you think a pattern has been set? *My* theory is that he uses mind control. He exerts a charming sort of influence over her. Every time we've been together, Lily has gotten excited over something about our family. And *every time*, Henk nips it in the bud. Cuts her right off. It's true."

"Should we rescue her? I mean, do you think she's being brainwashed or anything? Like Patty Hearst or a Moonie?"

I thought about it. "I do think she's being brainwashed, but willingly. We can't rescue her. She's in love with him. *That* much is obvious."

"I'll never let her go," Margo said fiercely.

I said nothing.

"I'm serious about this," she continued. "You've alerted me—I can't say I notice anything alarming when I talk to her. But you're there. I trust your instincts."

But were they sound? It was the question I asked myself each time I encountered the Voorheeses. Is Henk evil or am I crazy? Or *am* I jealous of Henk for having Lily to himself, of Lily for having a handsome husband who loves her?

"Who knows?" I said to Margo. "We'll talk more when I visit."

"Call soon to let me know when?"

"I will. I promise. I love you."

T H E annual "Beyond the Bridge" staff picnic was held the following weekend at Chance and Billy's summer place at North Haven, the peninsula just beyond Sag Harbor on Long Island's east end. I sat beside Stuart MacDuff on one of the three buses Chance had chartered. "Where's Margie?" I asked.

"Margie MacDuff is sitting in the back of the bus with Pauline the makeup girl. Says she sees enough of me at home, wants to mingle."

I chuckled, thinking of Margie and her no-nonsense way of handling Stuart. "Beautiful day for the picnic."

"Mmmm."

I leaned back in my seat to read the *Times* and let Stuart sleep. He was notorious for taking quick naps on the set whenever he could find time. I gazed out my window and watched suburbia give way to the Long Island landscape of scrub pines, sand hills, and marshes. "We there yet?" Stuart asked when he wakened.

"Not quite."

"So, who's along on this jaunt, anyhoo?" he asked, craning his neck and turning his leonine grey head from side to side, nodding regally at the people he saw. Stuart was loved by the entire cast; he reminded everyone of their fathers or the fathers they wished they had. "Don't see Jason, but maybe he's on one of the other coaches. He say whether he was coming or not?"

"He wasn't sure. He wanted his friend to come, and he said his decision would depend on that."

Stuart shook his head. "Poor kid. He goes through hell for that friend. I say he should give him the bum's rush."

"Jason's worried about his age. He's afraid of getting old."

Stuart smiled at me, his eyes twinkling like Santa's. "Aren't we all? That's the secret Jason should take note of—not one of us is getting any younger."

Chance and Billy were standing on their front steps when the buses drove into their circular drive. Billy wore one of Chance's old shirts over her bathing suit, while Chance looked as if he had stepped directly off the yacht club dock: pressed white duck trousers, a navy sports shirt, spanking-white deck sneakers.

"Welcome, halloooo, you're here!" Billy called.

She and Chance greeted each person and directed them to the bathhouses. Then she came toward me. I liked to think the Schutzes had a special feeling for me; they certainly seemed to. No matter what the gathering, they sought me out and insisted I sit at their table. Billy told me that Chance felt a particular pride for my work since he had "discovered" me. She quickly added, "Of course you were destined for success, but you can imagine how much pleasure it gave him to offer a green kid like you a star spot on the show."

"Una, dearie," she said, kissing my cheek. "Chance tells me you've been quite the jetsetter."

"Oh, my public appearances," I said, striking a campy pose.

"She's done very well for the show," Chance said, grave as always, giving me a formal peck on the lips. "Ratings are higher than ever, and we may win some awards this year."

"Awards?" I asked. That was the first I had heard of it. Usually when "Beyond" was in strong contention for an Emmy nomination or an award given by one of the other broadcasting organizations or publications, the grapevine grabbed onto it early.

"Just a possibility," Chance said, enigmatically. Of course, he said just about everything enigmatically.

"You must get right into your bathing suit," Billy said, patting my bottom and pushing me toward the bathhouse. "The water is heavenly."

Such an idyllic picnic! The Schutzes had set up volleyball and badminton nets, a croquet court, and a lawn-bowling area. Two bars equipped with everything from chilled Russian vodka to fresh lemonade stood at opposite ends of the beach. Wearing my black tank suit, I walked along the sea wall to the steep flight of stone steps, and descended to the beach. Scallop beds lay just offshore, and the sand was covered with silver, apricot, and umber shells. I picked up a few small ones and rattled them in my hand. All around me my colleagues were frolicking—in the water, on the beach, on the lawn. I tried to be objective: if I were in a Broadway play and were having an outing, would it be better than this? No. Certainly not. But perhaps it would have been better deserved.

I spotted Jason lying beside a young Oriental man on a green wool blanket. Both wore low-rise bathing suits and had tremendous tans.

"Darling," Jason called to me. I walked toward him and was shocked by his feverishly happy expression. I hadn't seen him look that way for weeks. "Una Cavan, meet Terry Matsomo." Terry and I shook hands, then Terry went back to playing indolently with a seagull feather. Inviting myself, I sat down beside Jason. We watched Marilee Duncan, the actress who played Nancy on the show, try to pull up the blue-

and-white striped sail on a windsurfer. Down the beach a few sound technicians and cast members were playing volleyball with a huge yellow beachball. Margie MacDuff and Art Panella walked past with tall glasses of strawberry daiquiri.

"My, such a colorful party," Jason said, "and so handsomely cast."

"It is," I agreed, suddenly recalling my old fantasy about the "Beyond the Bridge" cast as a family with Chance and Billy as our parents. It seemed particularly true that day; the jitneys had transported us to this peninsula far from the city, across the causeway, Beyond the Bridge to this Brigadoon time warp. On the bus people had been dozing and talking in low tones, and I sensed that we all felt the same warm comradery. On the show we played characters who were lovers, family, enemies; we saw each other nearly every day, during which we filmed intensely intimate scenes with each other. It was impossible for that not to carry over into our real lives. Certainly Jason annoyed me when he forgot his lines, just as Art annoyed me when he forced me to redo a scene because I hadn't been "vulnerable enough." But I had been on the show for eight years, and the bonds had grown strong. Like members of a family, we eventually forgave each other.

"What's that?" Jason asked, watching me rub sunscreen on my arms. "Is that why you're such a ghost all the time?"

"Unfortunately I don't have your deep Mediterranean complexion. I never tan—I just burn and peel. It's my lot in life."

"Oh, but a little *color*. . . . You should go to a tanning salon. They have experts there who control exactly how many rays you get."

Tanning experts made me think of radiation therapists. During my father's treatment for cancer of the lymph system, his radiologist had misjudged how much radium his body could take, and in his zeal to kill the tumors he had also killed my father's intestines. He shrank them to the diameter of straws. My father's stomach turned leathery black, and for the rest of his abbreviated life he had to eat baby food and wear two colostomy bags. I looked away from Jason smearing olive oil on his deep-brown stomach.

Chance strolled along the sea wall with Hank Ahrens, an associate producer. I reminded myself to ask about time off to visit Margo. A current, deeper blue than the rest of the water, bisected Shelter Harbor Sound and twisted around the headland. Beyond the land lay Gardiners Bay, then the Atlantic, and then Watch Hill. Margo was just thirty or so miles northeast across the water from where I rested. I felt sad then, thinking of truth versus fantasy, my real family versus my television family. Still, it was Jason beside me, not Margo, talking in gentle tones about how I could look and feel one hundred percent better if I'd only get a little color in my face. Presence is everything. I reached for Jason's hand and held it, out of Terry's sight, watching Marilee skitter past on the sailboard like a young girl on rollerskates for the first time.

L O O K I N G for Chance, I found Billy on the wide porch. Four wicker rockers lined the slatted floor, looking east to the water. The ceiling overhead had been painted light blue, to resemble the summer sky. I sat beside Billy in one of the rockers, and we propped our feet on the porch rail.

"How's it going?" Billy asked, and I knew she meant the party. She was a nervous host.

"It's fantastic. As usual, everyone is having a ball. Can't you tell?" We listened for a few seconds to the pitch of voices coming from all over the compound. The bash was in full swing: people were playing games, romances were starting up, the beach resounded with jolly noise. "Do you think Chance will give me some time off? I want to visit Margo."

"Of course he will. You've been such a workhorse this year. Chance says you are singularly responsible for at least four rating points." She grinned at me and must have seen something in my expression. "Aren't you proud of yourself?"

"Sure I am." Doubtfully.

"You don't sound it."

How much should you tell the boss's wife, even if she is a very good friend? Perhaps it was the day, my mood, the fact that we were staring at the sparkling Sound instead of the grimy streets of Manhattan; anyway, I decided to risk it. "I'm not sure it's enough. Remember my friend Susan Russell?"

Billy nodded.

"Well, I don't have to tell you how she's doing. I'm sure you've seen the reviews and advertisements."

"In fact, I've seen the play."

"I'm wondering whether I should be doing more . . . *serious* acting."

Billy frowned and looked truly perplexed. "I'm not sure I know what you mean by 'serious.' "

"Plays. Movies."

"Oh, you mean *chic*. It's not fashionable to do soaps."

I watched a large white sloop tack around Shelter Island's southern end toward Gardiners Bay. It made me think of *Manaloa* sailing away from Newport. I tried to decide whether Billy made any sense or not. "I see what you mean," I said, "but that's not all. Wouldn't it be more artful to create new characters?"

Billy shrugged. "If you want to create new characters, then by all means do so. But you are superb at what you do on the show. You should take great pride in that. Certain assholes I meet now and then at cocktail parties ask me why I don't sculpt instead of build pots. They think sculpting is something to aspire to, that pottery is simply a stage I must pass before I qualify. I tell them I haven't *settled* for anything—I don't build pots because I can't sculpt. They're two different art forms, and building pots is the less fashionable."

I truly admired Billy; she could deliver an answer like that with perfect credibility and conviction. Perhaps Billy was as fine a potter as Marisol was a sculptor, but I remained unconvinced of her analogy. I must have shrugged or something, because she continued. "In fact, you have turned Delilah Grant into a living, breathing woman."

"Albeit suffering."

"That's part of Delilah. People believe in her. If you only knew how much mail Chance gets, praising Delilah and your portrayal of her. Not all women are strong, my dear. They respond to your Delilah. And people *certainly* do not respond with that sort of vitality to cardboard cutouts."

I half rose from my rocking chair to kiss Billy on the top of her head. Fine auburn wisps had blown free of her French twist; they glinted red in the sun. "You're right about that," I said. She was. Whenever I felt inferior for acting in a soap opera, I would think of the intelligent women who watched me every day and think, "They can't all be wrong."

For the rest of the day I felt contented and dreamy. I swam the length of the beach and back seven times, then reapplied sunscreen and fell asleep on Jason's blanket. When I wakened I was alone on the beach and the orange sun had started to set; the land across the Sound gleamed in the declining light. A chilly breeze blew across my legs, and I wrapped myself in the blanket. Ghostly sanderlings raced across the high-tide line. Translucent brine shrimp leapt from drying clumps of kelp. From the house a hundred yards away came the first strains of dance music; the orchestra was warming up. The party went on.

CHANCE promised me three weeks off in September. September: my favorite month. I spent the rest of the summer looking forward to leaving. Chance never mentioned my dissatisfaction with soap opera acting, so I guessed that Billy hadn't told him about our conversation. Delilah was in jail. Nancy had charged her with a hunting knife; they had struggled, and Delilah had turned the weapon on her patient/attacker. Now she was imprisoned for first-degree murder. The sentence would likely be death by electrocution. Beck, horrified by the thought of Delilah behind bars and eventually dead, was plotting a breakout. They would go underground and gather evidence to clear her good name, proving that Nancy had been a serial murderer out to get Delilah. Meanwhile, in prison, Delilah was adapting to the life by volunteering to counsel her fellow inmates. The corrupt guards and warden, who passed out drugs and any other contraband for a price, were unnerved by Delilah's probative counseling technique and by Beck's position as editor of the Mooreland *Tribune*. A group of the most violent inmates had paid the guards a gigantic fee, insuring that they could break out without interference, and the warden wanted them to take Delilah as a hostage. Breakouts galore! Delilah, lonely and frightened, was resisting homosexual advances by her cellmate, a lovely radical imprisoned for her part in a terrorist bombing.

I felt pleased that Chance had allowed the screenwriters to incorporate my suggestions into the story line, but the rest of it offended my sensibilities. How could Beck, a smart editor, encourage Delilah to escape and hide out until they could "clear her good name"? That sort of warped logic pervaded the show. In real life, would the Law forgive a prison escape (a felony in its own right) just because the escapee was able to prove herself innocent of the original crime? Have they not heard of the appellate court? As parents through the ages have been telling their children, two wrongs do not make a right. But in Mooreland, the kindly district attorney would take one look at Beck's indisputable proof and offer Delilah a full pardon. Quite possibly along with a new job as head of the newly created Mooreland Psychological Commission.

The show was loaded with those sorts of inconsistencies. For the sake of drama, Beck would keep secrets from Delilah, Delilah would keep secrets from Beck, and, finally learning the truth, they would call each other liars and break up amid tears, accusations, and hurt feelings. Our intelligent viewers would bristle at this, firing off letters that said, "Why can't they learn from their mistakes? I'm so sick of the same thing happening over and over." So was I.

GREENWICH VILLAGE had been vacated along with the rest of New York for the summer. At night I would come home from work, change my clothes, and go out for a walk. The antique shops along Hudson Street were closed now. All spring the owners had filled the wide sidewalks with oak tables, maple desk chairs, walnut cabinets, mirror-front wardrobes, brass coatracks; now the shopkeepers had taken leave of the city to search the Adirondacks, Bucks County, Vermont, New Hampshire, and the Maine coast for new treasures. Walking south at sunset I would see the twin towers standing in pink haze, their lights twinkling like a mirage through the heat and vapors of lower Manhattan. My route took me east along West Tenth Street, past the police garage and the narrow row houses. Often I would stop in the bookstore, where other roamers would line the display tables, reading a few pages or flipping slowly through picture books, taking advantage of the shop's air conditioning. On winter evenings the shop and sidewalks had been more crowded; now people were vacationing or too hot to leave their apartments.

For me, going home was to be avoided. I would browse, then buy something and take it to the Gran Caffé Degli Artisti, where I would sit on the upper level by the wide window, holding the cool glass of iced espresso in my hands and gazing onto Greenwich Avenue with my book open on the scarred wood table. When the ice melted, I would order another glass, no matter how much coffee I had left. Gold lantern light blazed overhead and from the streetlamps outside. People sitting at other tables talked quietly. About: Their weekends in Quogue, East Hampton, Wellfleet. This awful heat. The murder on Bank Street. Falling in love with someone married. The terrible movies around. Have you noticed: the new vegetable stand; the way it seems to thunder every day at three; how fast the ice in this drink melts. I would eavesdrop without seeming to. They were my compatriots, stranded in this hot city while everyone else breathed fresh salt air.

Having drunk much iced coffee, I would feel too caffeinated to go home to bed. So I would sit in the window and watch people pass below. One night I saw Joe with a woman. She had a shag haircut, the likes of which I hadn't seen for ten years, and she wore a sleeveless pastel jersey which accentuated her bountiful curves. They walked slowly along Greenwich Avenue, their arms around each other in an easy embrace. Joe's corkscrew curls glinted in the yellow street light. The couple paused, as if they might climb the stairs to the café, but instead they walked on. I turned in my seat to watch them disappear down Perry Street.

Hardly anyone recognized me on those walks; since Susan's success in *Hester's Sister*, I had noticed fewer people recognizing me at all. I enjoyed that—I was able to move without scrutiny. Yet I also wondered, wasn't recognition supposed to be one of the rewards for acting on soap operas? Other times, usually after signing an autograph, I would feel as popular as ever and see my delusion of obscurity as the paranoia it truly was.

Toward the end of August the hot air lifted. Certain nights were chilly enough to require a sweater. Canadian air masses shifted south; I took that as a sign to mean that I could soon leave for Watch Hill. As an inducement, I bought my train tickets through a travel agent around the corner from Soundstage 3. My predictions had come true: Beck had aided Delilah in her escape just as the corrupt prison officials and inmates were setting their hostage plan in gear. Delilah's lesbian cellmate had cooperated with Beck in diverting attention; she had faked a choking spell by inhaling a generous amount of talc supplied by Beck. Now she was in the hospital, and Beck and Delilah were on the run, pursued by vengeful prison officials and the real lawmen. Would they survive? First they had to hide out for three weeks, casting doubts in the viewers' minds, providing Jason Mordant and Una Cavan with the perfect covers to take vacations.

THE morning I was to leave New York for Watch Hill, my telephone rang at seven. It was Chance's secretary, asking what time my train left, saying that Mr. Schutz would send his car to drive me to the station. I glowed with pleasure. I felt like a celebrity! At nine-fifteen I waited in the lobby of my building with two canvas duffel bags, a suitcase, a tennis racket, and a satchel of new books to read on the beach. The cool black limo glided to the curb, on schedule, with Chance in the back seat. I had not expected him to come along with the car.

My first thought: I am about to be fired.

My second: one of my sisters is dead, and they have sent Chance to break the news.

"You don't look well," he said when I climbed in.

"Is everything all right?"

He covered my hand with his and smiled. "Yes, everything is fine. Don't worry." He directed the driver to Pennsylvania Station, then pushed a button that raised the smoky glass partition between the front and back seats. "I have been meaning to talk to you, but the summer has been hectic."

"I know." Chatter about beaches, parties, summer's quick passing. Soon we were under the canopy between Penn Station and Madison Square Garden.

"Are you happy on the show, Una?" he asked.

"Oh, yes. Very happy." At that instant, about to leave for three weeks, I was.

"Still, perhaps it is time to move on, to follow your natural cycle. Perhaps you would like a new challenge?"

I shrugged. I couldn't get over the idea that I was getting sacked.

"Would you like to audition for a movie?" he asked.

This was Billy's work, I knew. Chance and Billy Schutz, my fairy godparents, were offering me a movie audition. Chance sat beside me, his wolf eyes devouring my wordless ecstasy. I nodded. Then I hugged him.

"I shall call your agent about this. My friend is casting an important new movie in France, and I mentioned your name. He was very interested."

"This is wonderful, Chance. I've been thinking about a movie or a play, you know. I love the *show* of course, and I would always want to come back to it, but I would like to try something new. Just to try—just to see if I could do it. But then return to the show."

Chance laughed at the way I was chattering. He checked his watch, slim as shirt cardboard. "We don't want you to miss your train. I'll arrange an audition for you, through Miss Attwood."

"Thank you, Chance. Thank you for the ride and the . . .

movie thing." We both laughed at my awkwardness. "Who is your friend, by the way? Just out of curiosity?"

"Emile Balfour."

Emile Balfour. So simple—I had an audition with Emile Balfour, indisputably the wildest director working in movies today. He was French and owed as much to Rimbaud and Jung as he did to Truffaut and Fellini. He used vivid imagery, dream sequences, the sea, brilliant color, and unknown actors who became known very quickly. Of the dozen or so directors Chance could have mentioned, Balfour was by far the most exciting.

Finally I was on a train bound for Westerly, Rhode Island, a town just a few miles from Watch Hill. I rode alone until Stamford, when a woman my age sat in the seat beside me. I fought the urge to tell her what had just happened to me: I have an audition with Emile Balfour!

I had seen all his movies. Many were love stories set on the shores of various oceans. In Tripoli, Corfu, Christmas Cove, Labrador, Portillo. An interview I had once read said that he was born in Montreal to French parents, then moved before he turned one to Arcachon, a small town on France's southwest coast. He loved sailing, and he needed the sea for renewal. It inspired his best pictures. I recalled the wind sequence in *The Listener*, which had been shot in Canada. A woman walked alone along a snowy path bordering cliffs over the Bay of Fundy. Her husband had not returned home from a solitary hunting trip. Was he dead? Had he deserted her? At first her expression was calm, but then she began to howl; the camera recorded the desolation on her face, but the screams were drowned out by the February wind. No sound emerged. It was one of the most chilling scenes I had ever seen.

The train chuffed eastward through Connecticut, passing the factory cities west of New Haven, then the seaside colonies beyond the Connecticut River. I tried to think of Margo, of our vacation, but Emile Balfour stayed in my mind. I flipped to the arts section in my paper to see whether any of his movies were advertised. I leaned forward in my seat, straining for glimpses of Long Island Sound, as if they could renew me, inspire me to do a good audition for Emile Balfour. I was so absorbed, I nearly missed the peninsula where my mother lived alone, painting watercolors to her heart's content. I thought of her rarely; all through my childhood she had seemed to wish she were elsewhere. At an easel, on a moor, in the library. We shared something secret and important that we never spoke about: our trips to fetch my father from his haunts. She would have preferred to smooth all wrinkles out of the past's fabric. If my father had been an imperfect man in life, he had become the perfect husband in death. At holidays and over the phone my mother would grow weepy at the mention of his name. "He was a good man," she might say. Or, "Oh, what a fine husband he was." My sisters and I would snicker, and our mother would leave the room in a huff. It was much easier for her to maintain illusions when she was alone, so we obliged and rarely visited.

On the train I leaned forward and strained to see the landmark flagpole that marked the head of her road; the train's speed blurred the trees, rocks, and bay into a wash of greyish blues and greens, and the flagpole never came into sight. My father's ashes were in that bay. My mother had kept them under her bed, in a large can with a lid to be pried off like the top of a cocoa can, and she had scattered them, alone, one year after his death. I pictured her standing on the rocks, dipping her hand into the can, throwing dust into the sea. She had done it at night. I thought back ten, fifteen years, to the time when she and I would search for him. Perhaps if we were different, those sad, weird memories would bind us. Instead they divided; they proved that I knew the truth about him. She couldn't pretend with me.

Some nights, alone in my apartment, I would think of my mother at my age. She seemed to long for my sort of life: artistic and alone. Yet she had married and borne three girls, all the while wishing for solitude. And watercolors. Now that she was alone, able to paint as much as she wanted, she could imagine a past that lived up to her hopes and expectations. The train rushed into a tunnel cut into a rocky hillside, and the bay was lost to my view.

I stepped off the train at Westerly into a brilliant, blustery September afternoon and Margo's arms—all at once. We stood hugging on the splintery wood platform for a long time. Her hair, after a summer of sun and swimming in salt water, was a white halo. It hung loose to her slim shoulders, rippling in gentle waves. "Back together again," she said into my neck. I am five inches taller than she is. The short hairs along her part fizzed up my nose.

"Where's Matt?" I asked, looking around, scratching my itchy nose with the back of my hand.

She stepped away from me and hoisted my heaviest bag. I fought her for it. We both have streaks of machismo, but mine is more finely developed. I won the bag.

"Back at the inn. He was dying to come, but I wanted to see you alone, with my own two eyes, first."

"That was a good idea." I followed her to a rusty blue Land Rover. It had bright plastic decals on the window: the Audubon Society, a four-wheel-drive permit to go on some beach, a Brown University seal, and a long sticker saying "Let's Go, Bruno!" I leaned back against the cracked leather seat, and we drove along the shore road.

"Don't get your hopes up, but I'm trying to arrange a family reunion. I've asked Mom, Lily, and Henk to come for a long weekend."

"When?"

"Anytime they can make it. They all seem to have previous commitments."

The tone in Margo's voice invited me to complain about my mother's permanent isolation and Lily's since marrying Henk, but I felt too blissful. I wanted to watch the road spin along the salt marshes and inlets and take deep breaths of salt air. In New York I used only the top third of my lungs, taking shallow, sooty breaths. Instead I asked Margo about her upcoming year.

"I'm going to live with Matt and do independent study. It's an easy drive to Providence from here, for days when I have conferences with Professor Allen. Plus, there's a lady with a Rodin collection."

"Where?"

"In Watch Hill. She has a huge house with a glassed-in sculpture court. I've visited her a couple of times. She and her husband always have dinner at the inn now, and she tells everyone I'm doing my 'report' on Rodin. I'm getting my doctorate, and people still think I'm twelve."

I smiled over at Margo, but fortunately she didn't see me. Although she was twenty-five, you'd never know it. Her small stature, her pretty blond hair, her shaky way of doing things all make you think she's quite young. She never used to drive. Lily always had. And now, watching Margo maneuver a four-wheel-drive vehicle along the road, I sensed trepidation disguised by bravado. Or perhaps I was just unwilling to believe in my youngest sister's competence.

The turreted Ninigret Inn crowned the crest of a hill which overlooked the Atlantic Ocean on one side and the town of Watch Hill on the other. Its silver shingles had been bleached by the east wind and salt spray; I imagined gales roaring up the bluff, along the promontory between the inn and the lighthouse. Nor'easters to rock its foundations. The inn could once have been a sea captain's house. In the eighteenth century. The captain's wife would wait here while her husband plied the coasts of Brazil, Jamaica, and Florida. She would wear rustling white garments and climb daily to the turret where she would scan the horizon for sails; although she would see many rising out of the waves, she would recognize her husband's instantly. Then she would run (I see her: the sun on her pink face, her fizzy blond hair blowing in waves behind her, her rustling white dress held daintily above her bloomers by small pale hands) down to the dock. Her husband would step off his packet laden with palm fronds, copper, sperm oil, and pineapples. Then they would rush (now she

is in his arms, her glowing face pressed into his blue coat)
back up the hill to their house. I told this to Margo when she
parked the Rover in the inn's yard.

"I've thought that exact thing myself," Margo said, shield-
ing her eyes as she looked up at the turret's pointed roof.
"Her name is Letitia and his is Nathaniel. She fixes him pancakes for his first meal back because he is so sick of fish."

Inn guests sat in white slatted chairs spread around the
grassy lawn. A hedge of wild roses ran along the property
lines. The only trees were a few scrubby oaks and pines. Margo led me to the steps, then proceeded through a wide screen
door into a shadowy foyer. The inn's main public room contained some couches, a fireplace, and windows separated
from each other by bookshelves. Shabby Persian rugs covered
the tile floor. I loved the place on sight.

Ten seconds after the door slammed shut, Matt hurried
down the steep staircase from the second floor. I knew instantly that it was he. Short and compact, he had a fuzzy
brown-gold beard and friendly blue eyes. He wore a faded
flannel shirt over jeans. His handshake was firm and earnest,
and I judged him to be about twenty-six.

"Took you long enough to get here," he said, continuing
to shake my hand. The more I stared at his smile, the more
intense it seemed.

"You can let go now," Margo said dryly.

"No, these first meetings are the most important—they're
when the bonds crop up. Una and I have to have a good, solid
bond."

"I can tell this is an excellent bond," I said, pulling my
hand away; it hurt a little around the knuckles. Then I kissed
Matt's cheek.

"How was your trip?"

"Great. Relaxing. It's nice to be here."

"Wait till you see your room. You're sleeping in the turret," he said.

Margo looked lovestruck and proud as hell at his generosity. She grinned at me. "The turret room is great."

"It's also haunted," Matt said.

Margo's expression slid from pleasure to panic; I knew she was remembering that time, one year before, when I had told her about our father's ghost in Newport. She shook her head and covered Matt's hand with hers, as if he had just committed a really disastrous faux pas and she was taking hasty steps to correct it. "No, that's just what we tell the tourists. For effect. There's no ghost."

"Margaret, just because we haven't seen it doesn't mean it doesn't exist." He smiled at me. "The previous owner swears the place is haunted."

"Oh, when did you buy it?" I asked, changing the subject to convince Margo that I wasn't hooked on the supernatural. That I wouldn't hold a seance in the turret when my travel alarm struck midnight. The Witching Hour.

"Last year. This is my second summer here."

"Matt spent a year at the Cornell Hotel School."

"And then my grandmother died and left me a little money, and I foolishly squandered it on this tinderbox," he said.

Margo rolled her eyes. "Matt's father is a *broker*."

"Real estate?" I asked eagerly.

"No—stocks and bonds. Solid stuff. The brawn of American profit making," Matt said. Then he took the bag from Margo and started to lead me upstairs. What a letdown! I thought how nice it would have been if his father was in real estate, just as our father had been. It would have been a great thing for Matt and Margo. They could talk about their childhoods together and understand without explaining what their fathers' business lives had been like. Knowing Margo and Lily for so long had taught me the value of being understood without having to explain.

Flanked by Matt and Margo, each laden down with my luggage like Sherpas on a Himalayan trek, we climbed four of the steepest flights I have ever encountered. The steps rose at nearly vertical pitch, like stepladders. I grasped the wood railing to haul myself up; dance class had not prepared me for such dizzying feats. By the time we reached the top, I was panting and trying not to show it.

"Prepare for the vista of your dreams," Margo said.

"You ready for the notorious turret room?" Matt asked.

"She can handle it," Margo said.

Then Matt flung open the door. The turret room was truly splendid. Circular, its ceiling was a cone, like a silo's. Miraculously curved windows faced the glistening Atlantic.

"We put diamonds on the water for you," Margo said, nodding toward the sunlight flashing on the waves.

"How divine," I said, kissing her. The room was sparely furnished, with no pictures on the walls to detract from the view. A bed with a white chenille spread, a scarred wood bureau, two faded chintz armchairs, and a rickety table filled the round space. There was no rug on the painted wood floor, no curtains at the white frame windows. Of course, the room was the highest point on the promontory, and no one could see in.

"I guess we should let you get settled," Matt said, backing toward the door.

"She's settled!" Margo said. "Just put on your suit and let's take a swim."

"Wonderful," I said, but as glorious as the room was, I felt a chill after they left me to change. Matt was right: it was haunted. I felt my father's spirit, but it was a spirit yet to come. I sensed it fleetingly, the way one whiffs honeysuckle on a drive through the country when only hayfields are visible out the window. My father would visit me in this room. I knew it for sure, but just as surely I knew it wouldn't happen tonight. I felt that a visit had been promised, but it wasn't imminent.

TEN minutes later, dressed in my black tank suit and covered with sunscreen and one of John Luddington's discarded white dress shirts, I met Margo on the inn's wide, curved front porch.

"Do you like your room?" she asked, lighting up a cigarette.

"I love it," I said, carefully avoiding my revelation.

Leaning forward, her tone conspiratorial, she said, "Matt wanted you to have it. It is the most expensive room in the place."

"I know. I'd pay a lot for it."

She held up her hands and shook her head. "No—I didn't mean that. Are you crazy?"

"I know I'm not supposed to pay, you knucklehead. I'm just telling you I realize what a snazzy place it is."

"Good. Matt's dying for you to like him. He does not want to be another Henk."

We both laughed. " 'Oh, *Liebchen*,' " I said, deepening my voice. "We both know there could only be *one* Henk."

"Thank god," Margo said.

Suddenly the implication of her words hit me: another Henk? Another brother-in-law? I glanced at her and knew that I was right. She was blushing madly. "Are you serious?" I asked, craning to see her ring finger, which was bare.

She nodded. "Matt, we have to tell her!" she called.

Matt poked his golden beard out the office window. It caught the sun. Margo walked across the porch to stand beside his protruding head. They both grinned. "I want you to know, Una," Matt said, "you're not losing a sister—you're gaining an inn."

I hurried over to kiss them, and Matt climbed out the window to hug us. The three of us stood in a tight bunch, cooing and kissing. Both Matt and Margo were crying. "We're planning a Christmas wedding. Here at the inn, maybe," Margo said.

"Yeah, it's going to be great. We'll probably have a polka band with at least one accordion, and think of the matchbooks! Our names are perfect—Mmmmatthew and Mmmmargaret," Matt said, drawing out the m's. He turned away and blew his nose on a blue bandana. "We'll have a whole bunch of cocktail napkins and matchbooks printed up, and we can even use them here."

"We went to his old roommate's wedding at the Chateau de Ville, and he still can't get over it," Margo said. She smiled like an imp—making excuses for her betrothed. She reminded me exactly of an affianced twelve-year-old.

"I know—I can't. I mean, why would someone want to make their wedding day into a really tacky occasion? With a fake waterfall and ushers with ruffly shirts?"

"Oh, god, and the announcer," Margo said, giggling, grabbing Matt's arm. "Straight from Las Vegas—can you imagine an announcer at a wedding? Better than a game show."

It seemed hard to believe, but at twenty-nine, I had only been to two weddings. I thought about that fact, watching Margo and Matt giggle wildly at their memory. None of us Cavan girls had had much use for ceremonies. Weddings and funerals—they had seemed like crazy rites of passage whose importance eluded us. Take away the religious, and what is left? Bunting, banquets, moments of silence, tears shed by people you wish would leave you alone. Better to celebrate or grieve in private, with the people you really love. But I didn't say anything as I listened to my sister and Matt tell me their plans for a Christmas wedding: the Cavan and Lincoln families and all their friends from Brown, Watch Hill, and the hotel trade in attendance; mistletoe and laurel roping everywhere; a pig roasted on a spit.

WHEN Matt went back to work, Margo and I headed down the path to the beach. It cut through a thorny grove of bayberry, wild roses, and beach plum. We emerged on a flat strand of beach stretching to a rocky headland at one end; we walked in the opposite direction, north, toward the open sand. Finally Margo dropped her towel, and without consulting each other, we stripped off our bathing suits. Swimming nude was a Cavan sister tradition; we did it whenever the beach was relatively deserted.

The September sky was so clear, it left the water nearly colorless. Diving, I could see Margo's slender legs, vertical, treading water. On land they had looked tan, but here they were pale. I passed beneath her, then came up for air. Unable to touch bottom, we faced the open ocean and trod water.

"Now I feel purged," I said, slightly breathless.

"Purged of what?"

"Of everything. Let's see . . . New York—*hot* New York. Work. Lily."

Margo siphoned seawater into her mouth and squirted it

out between her teeth. "I can't believe you have to purge
yourself of Lily."

"You're absolutely right—how can I purge myself of someone I never even see? What did she say when you told her
about getting married?"

Margo's head rested back on the water; she turned to look
at me. "I haven't told anyone yet. Only you. Matt only asked
me last night."

"Really? What a gas!" I said, secretly tickled to be the first
to know.

"I mean, we had *talked* marriage before, but he never actually proposed until last night. He wanted us to be able to
officially tell you."

"That's dear of him. I like him a lot."

"You never talk to Lily?" Margo asked.

"Hardly ever. Once every couple of weeks."

A long pause. "Because she calls me fairly often. Every
few days. I've been afraid to tell you."

I thought about it. Lily and I lived in the same city; we
had the same area code and lived within each other's calling
area, yet we rarely spoke. "Maybe that's because you're at
the inn during the day when she's alone. I work then. She
never calls at night, because Henk's home."

"I think she feels safer talking to me. I haven't seen Henk
for ages—since before their wedding—and she can pretend
with me. She makes their life sound idyllic. Apparently Henk
loves tennis, so they play at Forest Hills. He just bought her a
Renoir watercolor. Sometimes they take picnics to Central
Park and lie on the grass and eat chicken wings. She makes it
sound so wonderful."

"I've told you, Margo—it probably is." I felt uncomfortable, as if I'd been caught spreading vicious, false rumors
about the marriage of the century. A Renoir watercolor?

"No, it's not. Lily's different. She's always happy when I
talk to her now, as if it's a big act. She's afraid to let anything
real show—everything sounds rehearsed. She was never like
that before, no matter how much in love she was. I think
you're right about her being brainwashed." She paddled on-

to her back, and her small breasts bobbed like lobster buoys.

"Why would she let it happen?" I had wanted to feel relief, having my suspicions supported by Margo, but instead
I felt small and horrible. The suspicions were correct: the
prognosis was bad.

"Because of Dad."

"*Dad*? You're crazy."

"No I'm not. Lily has always wanted to be married—much
more than you or I. I knew she'd wind up marrying the most
dependable man around, with the biggest house, the most
family heirlooms. You must admit—Henk is the exact opposite of Dad. Can you see Henk with Black Ass? Drinking his
brains out in some dive?"

"No—plus he *is* older, sort of a more stable father figure,"
I said, eagerly joining in the analysis.

"Not to mention a doctor. What could be safer than life
with a doctor?"

"True!"

"One ray of hope: Lily always asks about the department at
Brown. I think she misses art history."

"She has the Renoir, and she says she goes to museums," I
said doubtfully.

"Una, that would be like you watching soaps instead of
starring in one. We have to hang on to the possibility that
Lily will break out of this some day—she'll get tired of being dependent. She'll resume her career."

"God, I hope so," I said, feeling bleak.

Trawlers, their outriggers fitted with nets and spread like
wings, were heading back from Georges Bank. The pulse of
their engines traveled across the water. Their nets made me
think of Anne, Susan's character in *Hester's Sister*, of how
she made fine nets and her sister made faulty ones.

"If any of those fishermen have binos," Margo said, "they'll
think they're seeing sirens of the sea. Mermaids."

Suddenly the open ocean seemed terrible. I imagined the
trawlers' catches: marlin, tiger sharks, monkfish, conger eels,
manta rays. Dangers lurked in the deep. Long ago I had loved
to look through books on marine life and frighten myself with

images of gigantic sharks; strange, sightless creatures that exploded when brought above a certain depth; electric fish that flashed red and zapped their prey. Without saying anything, I swam toward shore and Margo followed.

On the beach we wrapped ourselves in towels and sat on the pebbly sand. The outgoing tide had sliced a bight parallel to the land in the wet sand. Water tore through it like a river. "That swim made me thirsty," I said.

" 'Bring me glass of water, Sylvie, Bring me glass of water now . . .' " Margo sang.

When we were little we would watch a program called "Sing, Children, Sing" on educational TV. The folk greats like Leadbelly and Woodie Guthrie would sing their songs, and Margo and I would sing them back. A few years later, when Margo was really twelve instead of still looking like it, my parents had been distracted by some trouble or other, and had not been able to attend her spring concert. I was the only person from her family there. Her class had sung "Bring me glass of water, Sylvie," and hearing it reminded me of my parental attitude toward her. Overhead the sky was still brilliant blue. I lay down on my towel and put a small pebble into my mouth to suck. Somewhere I had read that sucking a pebble is one way to stave off thirst.

"Does Matt's family come from Rhode Island?"

"No, from Portsmouth, New Hampshire. Both of his parents are still alive."

"Does he have any sisters or brothers?"

"One sister, two brothers. He's the oldest."

After a while we walked back to the inn. We walked into a lattice-enclosed shower. A soggy wooden pallet served as the floor. Margo turned on a faucet, and tepid water came out of the spout. Through the latticework I could see guests heading back from the beach. "Do they have to use this shower too?" I asked.

"No, they get hot water inside. But Matt doesn't like too much sand going down the drain. So the family has to take their showers here." She soaped her hair. She sounded like a good wife already: responsible, not dependent.

T HE next night Margo and Matt had planned a cook-out on the beach. All the inn's guests were invited. At seven Matt and two of the college boys who worked for the inn dragged brambles and driftwood to a pit they had dug in the sand. Then they left me and Margo to set fire to it. Without planning to, Margo and I had dressed like twins: white jeans and blue sweaters. Only hers was turquoise and mine was navy. I stood on the beach drinking a beer, watching Margo strike matches that the wind would blow out. She shifted her body various ways to shelter the matchbox, but the wind sailed around her every time.

"For a smoker, you're not very good at that," I said.

"Little help?" she asked, both eyebrows lifted.

I cupped my hands into an airtight windblock, and the match was struck. Margo flung it into the mass of dry vegetation; it caught the edge of some brown leaves, and the pile went up in flames. Wind blew blazing twigs down the beach. They burned for a while, then turned to ash in the damp sand. Margo poked the fire with the iron claws of a long-handled clamming rake, creating a hot core of embers.

The sun was settling into a bank of bruise-colored clouds, spreading violet light on the beach. Silhouetted against the sunset, the inn itself looked purple, its windows glowing orange with lamplight. The effect was unnatural, like a Max-field Parrish painting. Wind whipped my hair around my head. Margo and I tended the fire without speaking, and I felt a sense of deep satisfaction. The only sounds were the fire cackling like a witch, the breakers rolling in, the wind soaring along the promontory. I was standing on a beach with a sister, with cozy shelter a short distance away.

Matt and the college boys led the guests down from the

hotel. They carried a tape player playing Keith Jarrett and coolers filled with food and beer. The procession approached, looking strange and righteous: the townspeople coming to get the witches. Then, when they were close enough to be heard over the wind, their voices were friendly. Matt gave out beers while Margo and I inspected the foil-wrapped packages: bluefish covered with a mustard-mayonnaise-dill sauce, sweet corn, Idaho potatoes. Margo placed everything on the fire. Then she and I stood with Matt, watching a red moon rise over Block Island.

"Hey, did I tell you I have an audition with Emile Balfour?" I asked, knowing that I hadn't.

"You're kidding!" Margo said, squealing out the word "kidding."

"That is fantastic," Matt said. "Who the hell is Emile Balfour?"

"Emile Balfour is the movie director every actor in the world wants to work with," Margo said. "He is fantastically innovative, right, Una?"

"Right."

"He did *The Listener*."

"Oh, now I know who you mean," Matt said, nodding slowly. "All his movies open with rain falling on the windshield of a car, driving through the night, the wipers going, a voice saying, 'The rain, the rain. I must find shelter from the rain.' Only the words are in French, and you have to read the subtitles. That guy?"

Margo and I laughed. Matt shrugged and looked up at the stars, which were very bright except when the lighthouse's beam arced over our heads. "I love movies, but I can never remember who directed or acted in them. Is that offensive?" He looked at me. "I mean, if you're the star of a great movie, don't you want people to know your name?"

"I guess that's nice," I said, thinking of course I do.

"Of course she does!" Margo said. "You want to be recognized for your work, don't you? Wouldn't you be pissed off if someone thought your inn was owned by Hilton?"

Matt hugged her. "Hilton doesn't own little inns, poopsy."

"You get the drift, though."

"All I know is that I love certain movies, and I don't stop to notice who starred in them. The whole thing has to work together, I guess. I don't know one director from the other . . . it's best when you don't notice the separate elements. Like certain foods."

"Wait, you *always* say you should be able to distinguish flavors in everything you eat. You said that about bouillabaisse, just last week," Margo said.

"Well, a sauce, then. You want a roux to taste like a roux, not a mixture of butter and flour. You never want to taste the flour."

"Oh, god," Margo said, scoffing like Henk. "You're so confused." Then she and Matt excused themselves to check on the bluefish.

I glanced around. There were three couples plus the college boys. I stood there, trying to decide whether or not to mingle. A tall man headed down the path from the inn and stood, in silhouette, looking around. Then he walked over to me. His hair appeared black in the night, and his eyes were wide, startled-looking.

"I just had a nap, and when I woke up, everyone was down here," he said, sounding abstracted.

"Yes, it's a beach party."

"For the Ninigret Inn, right? I hate to crash a party unless I'm sure I won't get kicked out."

"Actually, if you're staying at the inn, you're invited. I believe that's official."

"Oh, you're from the back office?"

"No. I'm Una Cavan. Pretty soon I'll be related to the inn by marriage."

"Uh." He let my inane comment go by with a lack of concentration peculiar to people who have recently awakened from sleeping late in the day. Then he drifted toward the fire where people were starting to fill their plates. Matt brought me my dinner and showed me the best place to sit: on a smooth log he told me had been imbedded in the sand since washing ashore in a winter gale. Then he went back to Margo, who was dishing out bluefish.

After a few minutes the man returned. He held his dinner plate and two beers, one of which he handed to me. "I'm Sam Chamberlain," he said. "Mind if I join you?"

"No," I said, making room on the log.

"You're staying at the inn?"

"My sister helps run it. She's marrying the owner."

"You're Margo's sister?" he peered at me in the dark. Up close he looked thirty-five. His hazel eyes were curious, more gold than green.

"I'm Margo's oldest sister," I said, amused to know that the inn's guests knew her by name. Library research on Rodin seemed a more appropriate profession for her. I couldn't see her as one of those jolly innkeepers who say they got into the business because they "like working with people" (Margo is shy), who like standing behind the front desk, watching the guests trail back from day trips (Margo has no time for small talk), who make pies and hand out free slices to the guests (Margo hates to cook). I was still smiling when Matt and Margo came along. They sat on the sand, facing us.

"Glad you could join us, my good man," Matt said to Sam.

"Good deal—a nighttime picnic," Sam said.

I tilted my head back and tried to identify the constellations overhead. The Milky Way was prominent, and I found the Big Dipper. Noting my interest, Margo said, "You should have been here August twelfth when the Perseid meteor shower was in full swing. It was wild! Matt and I sat on the beach and watched them fall into the ocean."

I gave her a look. "Meteors burn up when they hit our atmosphere."

"Not these. I swear, we heard them hiss. Right?" She turned to Matt, who nodded solemnly.

"You don't see many meteors in New York," Sam said.

"Oh, I'm from New York!" I said.

"Oh yeah?" he glanced at me casually. Everything about him seemed casual: his messy dark hair, his billowing white shirt, his khaki trousers. He had bare feet; the tops were covered with curly dark hair.

"What do you do in New York?" Margo asked.

"I'm an oceanographer."

"An *oceanographer* in New York *City?*" Margo asked.

"Yeah. I work at Columbia."

That struck everyone, even Sam, as being hilarious. Although Manhattan is an island, edging toward the Atlantic at its southern tip and Long Island Sound at its northern tip, it was unthinkable that an oceanographer would spend time there instead of, say, Woods Hole or La Jolla. Where was the sea life? The rock formations? The silt? The water column? The food chain? In Manhattan there were only dark laboratories and offices and libraries, places where an oceanographer could study the sea secondhand.

"I'm there on a grant," Sam said. "But I'll eventually work my way back to Woods Hole."

"Ah, Woods Hole," Margo said, the way I could imagine her saying of Henk when she had first met him, "ah, New York Hospital," ticking off the impeccable credentials of her sisters' potential suitors. She smiled across the small patch of sand at me.

"What do you do in New York?" Sam asked me.

"I'm an actress."

"I have season's tickets to the Ensemble Studio Theater that I never get to use. Seems every time I'm supposed to see a play, someone I'm trying to get grant money from throws a cocktail party."

"I'm a soap opera actress."

"Oh." Deadpan.

Margo chuckled. I looked at her as though I would like to kill her, because I knew what she was going to say. "Una always says 'soap opera actress' as if she's announcing a contagious disease. She is a *fantastic* actress."

"I think I heard a fan talking about you on the porch this afternoon—she said some celebrity was staying at the inn. Must've been you."

"No doubt."

"Not to mention, she has an audition coming up with Emile Balfour." Margo's eyebrows cocked expressively.

"What's that going to be like?" Sam asked. His tone was straightforward; he was asking me about my acting job the

way he might ask someone about their teaching job or me-
chanic's job. Without awe or envy.

"It will be marvelous," I said airily. "He makes great films."

"Films." Sam snorted. "When people say 'film,' they generally mean a movie that's either foreign or doesn't have a
plot."

"It is foreign," I said.

"What's it about?"

It suddenly occurred to me that I didn't know. I had been
so thrilled by the idea of a movie, any movie, I hadn't bothered
to wonder. "I'm really not supposed to talk about it," I said.

"No, Emile Balfour always veils his projects with secrecy,"
Margo said, letting me know she was on to me.

Sam leaned back, sinking his hands into the sand. His arms
looked extremely long, but, then, he was a tall man. "Wow,
what a night," he said, gazing at the white stars. "I miss this
in New York. Closest I feel to the shore is the foghorns you
hear on the Hudson River."

I nodded; I had noticed the foghorns. They seemed incongruous, penetrating the roar of traffic, subway trains, and
planes en route to Kennedy, LaGuardia, Newark, or Teter-
boro. But I listened for them every foggy night.

Margo and Matt stacked our dirty plates and stood. "Emp-
ties?" Margo asked, fitting four empty beer bottles on the
fingers of one hand. Then they walked around to the other
groups, collecting garbage and asking people if they were having fun.

"What kind of an oceanographer are you?" I asked Sam
after a while.

"Marine biologist."

"Did you grow up on the shore?"

"Yes, in Padanaram. On Buzzards Bay. I generally keep
migrating back to southeastern Massachusetts—I went to college in New Hampshire, and graduate school in New York,
and now I'm back in New York. But usually I've worked in
Woods Hole."

"Both my parents are geologists," Sam said. "They go off
on lecture tours and digs all the time. Recently, in fact, they
were studying a vein of something in Colorado, and they

discovered an Indian village. So now they're going nuts, reading up on archaeology. My mother's decided to go back to school and study it. They're in their sixties, and my mother's starting a brand new career." He spoke ruefully, with some amusement, as if his parents were a pair of difficult kids.

"Do you have sisters or brothers?" My perennial question.

"No, I'm an only child."

An only child! Now that was a novelty, a situation to ponder, something to approach with care. I stared at his face, which was lean and angular. He had a rather long nose, like my own. "What's your research on?" I asked.

"I study *Chondrus crispus*, mainly."

"What is—"

"Seaweed. That crinkly brown stuff you see in tidal pools."

"Oh, *that* stuff," I said.

"There's a lot going on in tidal pools."

"I know." I did. Margo, Lily, and I had loved to gaze into tidal pools along the rocks in Connecticut. When we were young we would stare at the periwinkles in their coiled shells, the thicket of mossy seaweed, the bottle-green rock crabs, brittle stars, shimmery pebbles, and play a game: what new things can *you* see? We tried the same game with a patch of grass, but acorns, leaf mulch, and ants were less wonderful than the contents of a tidal pool.

"Want to take a look?" he asked. Sounding like a small boy enticing me to come along to the fire station. A field trip!

"Sure." Leaping up, I followed him along the high-tide line toward the rocky headland. The sea was at midtide, neither high nor low. "Tidal pools are much better at low tide," I said, not mentioning the fact that it was too dark to see anything anyway. The lighthouse beam swung across our path.

"Sure, they're *better* at low tide, but I have something in mind. Wait till you see."

We scuttled over smooth rocks that had been underwater when the tide was full. Bits of damp seaweed clung to them; I felt it with my bare feet. When the lighthouse's beam blinked toward us, it was possible to choose our steps, but then it would swing away and make the darkness total. Thus, we would advance, stop and wait, then advance again. It was a slow progression. Suddenly Sam stopped short, and I crashed into his back. I grabbed for him, but my left foot slipped on a weedy rock, plunging me to the knee into a pool. I felt the barnacles gouge my calf.

"Shit," Sam said, struggling to pull me out. "Oh, shit," he said again when the lighthouse's beam revealed blood seeping from a hundred scrapes. He tore a handkerchief out of his pocket and soaked it in salt water. Then he pressed it again and again to my bleeding leg. It didn't even sting.

"What was it you wanted to show me?" I asked.

He peered at my leg. "Christ, that looks terrible. We shouldn't be out here in the dark. What a couple of crazy—"

"Well, here we are. So show me." I touched his upper arm, to let him know I didn't hold my injury against him.

"Okay," he said, remembering the point of our mission. "Stare at the light."

I did, for five long seconds. When I looked away I saw squiggles of light in the blackness, and the blackness was complete. "Now shade your eyes and look into the tidal pool."

Cupping our hands around our eyes, Sam and I squatted on rocks and peered into the black pool. Tiny waves rippled the surface; the tide was coming in. We looked below them, to the bottom where purplish spangles flashed like neon. "What is *that*?" I asked.

Sam reached into the water and pulled up a handful of kinky seaweed. It was reddish and made me think of Joe Finnegan's hair. "No, what is that sparkly stuff?"

"It's this—*Chondrus crispus*. Irish moss. It's covered with bioluminescence. Tiny organisms that give off a phosphorescent glow." His voice was awestruck.

It was glorious. I cupped my hands around my eyes and watched the purple weed glimmer and dance in the intertidal current. I pulled a bit of it out, but like Sam's handful, it lost its magic when it left the water.

"Unaaa!" I heard Margo calling my name. Bracing myself on Sam's shoulder, I stood and waved.

"We're out here!" I called. Margo stood still until she could fix my position, and then she waved back and walked away. With my white pants and Sam's white shirt, we must have looked like two bright rocks jutting into the sea.

Sam touched my calf. "That's a nasty scrape you've got. But at least you got it in the salt water. It'll heal fast."

It was already starting to feel sore.

THE next morning I wakened to sunrise in the turret room. My calf throbbed with pain under the weight of the covers. I lay in bed watching the light turn from deep red to pink to sparkling blue.

"You awake?" I heard Margo whisper through the door after a while. She knows I'm an early riser.

"I'm awake," I said, and she entered bearing a tray with two cups and a porcelain coffeepot.

"I wasn't absolutely sure you'd be alone," she said. "I know what a romantic night on the beach can do."

I nodded, sipping coffee. I pulled off the gauze bandage to shock her with the sight of my scraped leg.

"What happened?" she asked, leaning closer, a horrified look in her blue eyes. Her mouth looked like a parody of someone staring into a bloody car crash.

"I slipped on the rocks. Like a goon. Made a big fool of myself."

"That looks awful. It'll probably get infected."

"No, it happened in salt water."

"Well . . . even so. Good thing you found the bandages— Matt and I went straight to bed. We were whooped. Did you see the Karsky sunrise? The colors get more magnificent as the weather gets cooler."

"It was extremely Karsky," I agreed, happy that Margo had remembered the old color school.

"You and Sam Chamberlain seemed to hit it off."

"Mmmmm." I felt uneasy, sensing that Margo wanted to propel me into a romance. Maybe with the idea of saying, "and to think it all started at our inn" years later, after we fell in love and married. I drank my coffee. Outside my aerie, fair-weather clouds tumbled through the blue sky. I thought of my father and wondered when he would make his appearance.

"I have a lot of research to do this week," Margo said. "It's just as well that you've found someone to keep you occupied."

"I don't need to be occupied. I brought books to read, and I plan to swim a lot."

"Also, Matt wants to begin to batten down the hatches for winter. Check the shutters. Throw some shingles on the roof, put insulation in the attic. So you'll be alone a lot. I'm not trying to push you into anything, though. But I thought *if* you're free, and *if* Sam's free . . ." she smiled and pulled her yellow hair into a ponytail behind her head. "But meanwhile, I thought maybe we'd take a jaunt downtown later this morning."

I laughed because she was flustered and because Watch Hill's downtown consists of one street running the length of the harbor, lined with a block of pretty shingled stores with geranium-filled windowboxes.

"I have to buy a bathing suit for next year," Margo said.

"Aren't you a little early?"

"Post-Labor Day sales are on. Plus, I have to buy someone a birthday present." She tickled my knee. Margo loves birthdays, and my thirtieth birthday was the next week.

AT ten o'clock, we left the inn to walk down the hill to town. Warmth radiated up from the tar, but even so, we were chilly in our summer things. I wore white sharkskin pants and a big blue shirt, and Margo wore a fluttery sun dress with a skirt in pieces, like petals. We walked the inland route, which was more direct and took us down a street of smallish summer cottages instead of the one that bordered the sea and went past the carousel. Some of the stores had already closed for the season; the others had just opened for the day's business. Margo thought we should try the Mayan Shop first.

While Margo tried on bathing suits, I sat in a wicker chair behind a rack of tawny fall things and thought about Sam.

Can you will attraction away? If so, why would you want to? The year that had just passed had been lonely and rather desperate for me. I thought of Alastair, of Joe, of the nights spent with them and the lonely nights in between. I had been starting to think that love would elude me forever. Weren't there women who were better off alone? Who were happier by themselves than sharing life with a man? I thought of my mother; she cried whenever she heard my father's name, but she seemed more peaceful, more fulfilled, living alone than she ever had surrounded by a family. Then I thought of my sisters, one married, one engaged, each secure in a niche for which I felt too bony, too angular, too jutting to ever fit into myself. Always a sister-in-law, never a bride.

Besides, I was about to get my big break as an actress. My first movie audition! All of the envy I had felt toward Susan would start to disappear after I became Emile Balfour's new star. I had never met the man, but magazine photos made him look glamorous. He wore wraparound shades, smoked constantly, had a handsome, down-turned mouth and an endearing cowlick. His romances with leading ladies were famous; photos would show him with his arm draped proprietarily across the slim, lovely shoulders of his star actresses. In Cannes, Paris, Hollywood, New York, Tokyo. At premieres, openings, society bashes, nightclubs. I had been nurturing a fantasy in which he fell madly, irreparably, in love with me. He would be ruined as a playboy. We would marry, I would star in the rest of his movies, and I would be his artistic consultant. I had been thinking along those lines when I met Sam Chamberlain, and I had already closed my mind to the possibility of attraction to the odd oceanographer from New York.

How different would that sort of romance be from ones with an Australian sailor, a young actor, a sporting goods executive? It would invite another visit from Father Conscience, while I was hoping my father's next visit would be a friendly one. But an affair with a French movie director would be different. It was exciting and pragmatic. It could take me where I wanted to go. (And was that approach so different from Lily's? Whose romance with Henk had taken her to East End Avenue?)

Margo called my name. I walked into the dressing room where she stood wearing a tiny pink bikini.

"You knockout, you," I said.

"That's exactly what I thought. Do you think I have too many hips to wear it?"

Margo's hips were delicately flared, like hips drawn in fashion magazines. "No, you look great."

"Matt will die. He is a true sucker for things like this. You should see what he bought me to wear in bed."

"What?"

"A little black confection with lace and rosebuds. For a woodsy-looking guy with a beard, Matt has very sex-crazed tastes."

"So, you're taking the bikini."

"Yes," she said, gathering up two other bathing suits, both sleek one-pieces. "Plus these. You can't swim in a bikini. The parts feel like they're about to slide off. So I need a couple tanks."

"Then why bother with the bikini?"

"Tanning purposes. I like a tan back and stomach, but I don't like lying out nude at the inn."

I held my words of warning; for years I had preached shade and sunscreen to my sisters, but they refused to listen. They did not freckle, they said, and it was a well-known fact (they also said) that only frecklefaces got skin cancer from the sun. They called it "sun cancer."

Margo paid for the suits. Outside the sun beat down on the green awnings and made the sidewalk scalding hot. Like the middle of summer. We walked down the block, across the street from the tiny yacht club, to the Olympia Tearoom.

"Want an orangeade?" Margo asked.

"Sure," I said, and we pushed open the wide screen door. Overhead ceiling fans turned, circulating cool air through the dark room. A row of huge windows faced the water, but the sun hadn't come around enough to shine inside. Margo and I crossed the black-and-white marble floor and sat at a dark wood booth. A waitress brought menus.

"God, bluefish salad sandwiches," Margo said, reading with a scowl on her face. "At this time you're so laden down with bluefish and zucchini, you'll try anything."

I laughed at the image of anyone laden down with bluefish and zucchini, but it made sense. At the seashore everyone had gardens and went surfcasting, and they liked to share the largesse with their neighbors, most of whom also had gardens and went surfcasting. The young waitress brought tall glasses of icy orangeade, and Margo and I sipped through straws. I saw the waitress notice that I was Delilah, then whisper to another waitress. I smiled at them.

" 'Oh, Delilah, won't you please sign your napkin,' " Margo mimicked. She lit a cigarette and smoked it like a glamour girl.

"Fewer people will recognize me if I do a movie."

"Oh, everyone will always know you as Delilah. No matter what else you do. People will be so disappointed if you quit the show."

"I'm sure they'll get over it. It's not like we're close personal friends or anything. It's not like losing a *sister*." Modesty, however false, made me play down my confidence. "Besides, I probably won't even get the part. Balfour was probably just doing Chance Schutz a favor, offering me a screen test."

"Chance Schutz!" Margo said, nearly choking on her smoke. "Remember when he cornered you after the Juilliard play? And he really pissed Dad off?"

We giggled at the memory. "Dad never felt very happy about my acting on 'Beyond.' " I stated it as a fact, hoping Margo would contradict me.

"No, he always hoped you'd become Ethel Barrymore or some other stage great. He'd love to see you in movies, though."

"I guess that's one of my big regrets—that he never will."

"But the rest of us will, and we'll be really proud. You can be sure of that. *I* can't believe he'll never meet Matt."

"No, but Mom knows Matt, and she has enough enthusiasm for two people." I waited for a laugh.

Margo hunched over her glass and sipped thoughtfully. "You know, Mom was always the stable parent, but even though Dad had Black Ass, I thought he was nicer. 'It was the best of times, It was the worst of times.' I think he loved us more."

"I don't know," I said, but I did know what she meant.

"Let's bust out of here," Margo said, reading my mind.

T HAT afternoon I waved to Sam Chamberlain. He was sitting in a lawn chair, reading a book. Probably some scientific tome, I thought, but when I got closer I could see it was Agatha Christie's *They Came to Baghdad*. Things are not always as they seem, I told myself sagely.

"How're things?" Sam asked as I passed.

"Great," I said, continuing to walk by. I wore all my beach regalia and carried a big bag filled with a blanket, a towel, books, and several different strengths of sunscreen. "Great weather we're having."

"Fantastic."

"Well, 'bye," I said, heading down the beach path into the gorse.

That day I swam the length of the beach, back and forth, until I was too exhausted to move. Then I went up to the turret room for a nap.

That became my routine for the next two days: waken at sunrise, drink coffee brought to me in bed by Margo, spend the morning with her, spend the afternoon alone swimming, reading, and sleeping, then have dinner with Margo and Matt in the inn's dining room. Once Sam walked in just as we were finishing, but the other time he didn't show up at all. Matt said he usually ate early, as soon as the dining room opened. With everything in New York geared to a late-night crowd, I wondered how Sam got along. But I didn't consider asking him, even though I spotted him around the grounds quite often.

ON Friday I walked to the beach after breakfast and found Sam reading a new mystery in a low chair. He wore a long-

visored cap and zinc oxide smeared on his lips. A bunch of
dark hair stuck out the gap above the hat's adjustable strap.
It glinted in the sun.

"Hey, how are you?" he asked, looking surprised and
pleased to see me. His strange greenish eyes lifted when he
smiled.

"Fine. How's the book?"

"It's good, it's good," he said, kicking a few large round
stones away from the sand beside him. "Here, have a seat."

I spread my towel. From behind, his black hair looked almost golden in the sun. I had a crazy urge to run my fingers
through it. I thought of a pirate, dipping greedy hands into
a treasure chest and letting jewels run through her fingers.
The thought made me self-conscious, and I sat right down
on my towel instead of smoothing its corners and anchoring
it with rocks, the way I usually did. I caught Sam examining
my scraped leg. It was covered by a huge blotch of Mercuro-
chrome, which I hadn't reapplied for several days and which
the salt water had faded to sickly pink. "It's healing pretty
well," I said.

"It looks much better."

Our small talk felt comfortable after my fantasy of treasure hair. I stretched out on my towel and asked him how he
liked New York. Then he asked me if I was the oldest sister.
Then I asked him where he had gone to college. Then he said
"Dartmouth" and asked me why I had dropped out of Juilliard. Then I was telling him the story of Chance Schutz and
my father and how my father had died. I stopped short of
telling him my ghost story, just as I realized that it wasn't
small talk any longer. "So, why marine biology and not geology?" I asked him, thinking about the plethora of geologists
in the Chamberlain family.

"Didn't want to compete with my parents. There are only
so many grants in the field, and I didn't want to be any kind
of a siphon from their money. Plus, I'd rather study living
things. Things that move and change faster than rocks. I mean,
there's lava and glacial debris . . . and sludge. My parents make
an excellent case for the thrill of the ice age, but it just didn't
turn me on."

"Do your parents work together?"

"Mostly. My father's really annoyed about how seriously my mother's taking archaeology. He likes it as a sideline, but he doesn't want to give up geology for it. He's afraid she'll defect from the igneous to the anthropomorphic."

"Tragic."

He nodded, smiling. "They love to build mountains out of molehills. Their marriage is always going through some crisis—they're always terrified of being rent asunder by something. Like her getting a grant to study in Colorado and him not. Of course it never happens." He paused. "She had a mastectomy a few years ago, and he nearly went wild. His hair went white that year."

Again, I tried to see whether this was hyperbole, but this time I could see it wasn't. "Really," he said. "He lost weight, went completely white, and broke his arm rolling over in bed. When she got out of the hospital, he looked worse than she did. The idea of losing each other is unthinkable for them."

"Is she okay now?"

"We think so. The cancer didn't metastasize, and if it doesn't recur within five years, she's supposedly cured. It's been four years. Nearly five."

"That's great," I said, thinking of how my father's doctors had told him the same thing. They hadn't counted on the complications of radiation.

"So, you Cavan girls are a close pair," he said. "What about the one in New York?"

"Lily," I said. "She's wonderful, only she's married to Rasputin."

"Yeah? A beast?"

"Not a regular beast. You can never quite put your finger on what's wrong about him. The main thing is that he keeps her imprisoned—on East End Avenue, no less. Which partly explains what I mean about his beastliness; I mean, how can you say someone is *imprisoned* on East End Avenue? When it's such a spiffy place and most people would kill to live there?"

"She's a prisoner of the heart," Sam said.

"Exactly."

"Made worse by the fact that she doesn't try to escape. He's exerting some kind of power over her."

"She makes absolutely no effort to see me," I said, drizzling a handful of sand onto my good leg. It caught in the tiny blond hairs on my thigh. "Maybe I should move to France or California and do movies. Let Lily and Henk alone in New York."

"Seems to me you don't have to go anywhere to do that. You'd better give her a little time to get sick of it. Then she'll let him know what's what."

"Actually, I thought that would have happened before now."

Sam was staring at the rocky promontory, now covered with water. "Hey, it's going to be dead low tide around six tonight. Want to take a look at the tidal pools with me?"

"Great!" I said with as much sarcasm as I could muster, but I had the definite feeling he had said it to raise my spirits.

"You're going to love it," he said, patting my injured leg. "It'll be broad daylight, and there'll be no slipping whatsoever."

MARGO, MATT, and I had lunch on the inn's porch, and then I retreated to the turret room. Although I felt like finishing *To the Lighthouse* for the seventh time since I had first read it at fourteen, I fell asleep on top of the bedspread. I dreamed a wonderful dream. It was winter; the sky was pearly white, opalescent, like the inside of an oyster shell. I was walking on the beach in front of my parents' house with a woman— Susan, Lily, or Margo. The water was flat calm and licked the shore in gentle rhythms. The air was icy cold, ready to snow. Walking along, I had the sudden urge to swim. I dropped my clothes on the sand and walked into the grey water, casting a glance back at my companion. Look at me! Doesn't it amuse you to see me swimming in the middle of winter? I dove and swam underwater, bubbles coming out of my mouth. A glorious azure fish swam by. I followed it, gaining, and caught it in my arms. Then I walked naked from the sea, holding the blue fish like a baby to present to Susan-Lily-Margo.

WHEN I wakened from that dream the sun had gone around the inn. It was late afternoon. I lay still for a long time, trying to analyze the dream's meaning, feeling content, not wanting to lose the restful feeling. I closed my eyes to preserve the color of the fish in my mind. What a lovely fat blue fish! Its scales were radiant, edged with ice crystals that refracted light like rainbows. I had felt so proud to hand it over to my companion. This blue fish is for you, I had thought, and she had known what I meant. I wasn't sure who my companion was, but I knew she was female. Females, beginning with my sisters, had been my most loyal, my most satisfactory companions.

Rising from the bed, I stretched, looking out at the beach. There was Sam, waiting for me. He wore his baggy khaki pants and a blue shirt with the sleeves pushed up. After my brilliant fish, Sam's blue shirt looked bleached and faded. I dressed and walked slowly down to join him, and when I arrived, I could see that the shirt really *was* bleached and faded. It looked decades old. It was made of blue oxford cloth and had ragged places around the neck and elbows where white threads hung loose. It had a soft shapelessness to it; it hung loosely on Sam's lean frame.

"Hi, Una," he said.

"Hi, Sam."

"You just wake up?" he asked, moving one finger close to my cheek as if to touch a crease, then stopping short.

"Yes," I answered, and we just started walking. He seemed to understand that I needed to wake up slowly. The sand flats gleamed in the declining light. Cirrus clouds had started to gather over Montauk; in a couple of days there would be rain. We walked silently along the deserted beach to the rocky headland. Our passage across the rocks was easier than it had been the other night. We crouched beside the tidal pool where I had scraped my leg and saw periwinkles gripping the rocks, feathery appendages wisping out of crusty barnacle shells, weird crabs scuttling away from our shadows, an abandoned moon shell, a colony of blue-black mussels anchored by silken threads to the pinkish rocks, springy brown seaweed.

"What new things can *you* see?" I asked Sam, playing the old game.

"Huh?"

"In the pool—find something you've never seen before."

"I study this stuff. None of it is new."

"Something is. Find it." The pool was still; the ebb was total, a foot lower than it had been, and no waves stirred the surface. It was as still as the water in my dream.

"Oh, there's some starfish larvae," he said, pointing at a microscopic dot of gelatin. "Too bad I don't have my hand lens."

"It's not in your pocket?"

"No, it's back in my room."

I felt disappointed, gazing at the cloudy mass. I would have loved to see the tiny stars. Magnified, they would be as perfect as snowflakes, and they wouldn't melt. "Are you telling me starfish larvae is new to you?" I asked.

"No, but it's new to *you*."

"True."

We sat on the rocks and felt the evening breeze grow cool. Our arms touched. The breeze made the hairs on the back of my neck tingle. I glanced at Sam's weathered brown face, and thought how marine biologists had to spend lots of time in the sun. He had cat eyes and shaggy black hair. Without sunlight it lost its golden glints. He had a habit of brushing his hair out of his eyes with large, careless hands. He did it over and over, but it kept falling back.

Black plovers flew along the ocean's edge, silhouetted against the grey gleam. As dusk approached, the scene took on a mysterious quality. I felt timeless. If I closed my eyes, I could be on the beach in front of my parents' house. Or I could be eighty, spending my last autumn at the shore. The rocks beneath me were giving up their warmth. I started to shiver.

"Hey, look at the black zone," Sam said.

I opened my eyes. The light was fading. "What's the black zone?"

He pointed behind us, requiring me to swivel. Where the rocks met the hill covered with bayberry and beach plum, there were streaks of black. They inscribed the rock with rough, bold bands: a dark message. In the light of early evening, they looked magical and terrible. "The black zone of shore," he said. "It's where the land meets the sea—literally. That stain is made of microscopic plants. Millions of them. It looks dead, but it's alive."

I stared at the markings for a long time, as if they were hieroglyphics in command of a greater meaning. I waited for them to speak to me, the way my father's ghost had. I did not believe in God, I did not trust my own convictions, my own conscience, my own wishes, my own spirit. I looked to the supernatural, to things like my father's ghost, *Hester's Sister*, Margo's vibes, The Black Zone of Shore, to set me on the right track. *To tell me what to do.* I needed permission to follow my own instincts.

"You hungry?" Sam asked.

Food hadn't occurred to me. I stared at him with what must have been a stupid expression on my face.

"I think you've had too much sun," he said, gently taking hold of my hand and helping me across the rocks. Funny man, the sun hasn't been seen for half an hour.

My feet firmly planted on the sand flats, I walked toward the inn. Sam moved his arm around my shoulders. His body felt warm and smelled like sweat and suntan lotion. When we climbed the porch steps and wiped our sandy feet on the sisal mat, Margo looked up from the chair where she had been reading. Her face betrayed no surprise at seeing us together.

"Oh, Una—I'm glad you're back. A telegram came for you." She hurried inside to find it, and I followed her.

I tore open the envelope and read:

CONGRATULATIONS/ YOU AND JASON MORDANT AWARDED "SOAP COUPLE OF THE YEAR" BY SOAP OPERA UPDATE/ PROMO TRIP TO EUROPE IN OCT????/ LOVE CHANCE AND BILLY

THAT night Margo and I decided to run up the phone bill. We had to tell our mother and Lily about Margo and Matt's betrothal and about my award and movie audition. While Matt boiled water for lobsters and Sam took a shower, Margo and I settled on the couch in her and Matt's private quarters. Margo dialed our mother's number.

"Mom, guess what?" (I heard her say, bubbling with excitement) "Matt and I are getting married! . . . Probably Christmas. . . . Well, as a matter of fact, two nights ago. . . . Oh, thanks, I'll tell him. . . ." (Long pause.) "Una's here. She wants to talk to you."

With a sour look, she handed me the phone.

ME   Hi, Mom. Great news, or what?

MOM   Mmmm. She sounds very happy.

ME   Oh, she is! We're ecstatic—don't you adore Matt?

MOM   Well, I only met him that once. He seems very nice.

ME   (*looking at Margo*). "Yes, he *is* wonderful. (*Long pause.*) I have some good news too. I just won an award.

MOM   For—

ME   The show. Jason and I got "Soap Couple of the Year." I mean, I know it's not a *Tony* or an *Emmy* or anything. . . . (*Margo, at this, shaking her head violently, mouthing, "It's great!"*)

MOM   Congratulations, dear.

ME   (*now subdued*). Plus, I have a movie audition. With Emile Balfour. My career is really *moving ahead.*

MOM   I think that's wonderful.

ME   (*fighting strong urges to say terrible things*). Well, I think I hear Matt calling us for dinner. He's a fabulous cook.

MOM   (*with as much enthusiasm as I have heard during the conversation*). Oh, what's for dinner?

ME   Lobster.

MOM   Oh, lobster! Yummy! Bye-bye.

ME   Bye-bye.

Replacing the receiver, I looked into Margo's eyes.

"Not exactly brimming with excitement, is she?" Margo asked dryly.

"We must have interrupted a really intense painting session."

"Gee, I hope the good news didn't wreck her concentration."

Years of being her daughters had taught us not to dwell on it. Margo lifted the receiver and I dialed Lily's number in New York.

"I really wish we had a speaker phone for this," I said.

Ilsa answered, and Margo asked for Lily.

"Baby, here's the scoop," Margo said the instant she heard Lily's voice. "Wedding bells are ringing for me and Matt!"

From four feet away I heard Lily's howl. "When???" she yelled. Margo held the receiver away from her ear and shouted "At Christmas! Talk loud 'cause Una's here and she has to hear you."

"Hi, Una!" Lily hollered.

"Hi, Lily!" I yelled back, leaning close to the telephone. "Put Matt on!"

"He's cooking lobsters in the kitchen!"

"I don't give a shit if he's catching lobsters in the ocean. *I want to talk to him!*"

I ran into the kitchen and found Matt and Sam drinking beers. "Your other future sister-in-law wants to say hi," I told Matt. "Get ready to scream."

Matt and Sam followed me in to Margo. Matt had a few private words with Lily, and then we all huddled close to the telephone, reinstituting the conference call.

"Una's got great news too!" Margo bellowed.

"What cooks?"

"A movie audition—*plus* I won 'Soap Couple of the Year'!" I yelled.

"*Zoap* couple of the *year*? You got an award ceremony or anything? You gonna need a new *zoot*?" Lily loved to replace *s* with *z* whenever possible.

"I don't know yet—"

"She also has a movie audition," Matt yelled.

"With Emile Balfour!!" Sam yelled.

"Who the hell's voice is that?" Lily asked in a lower tone.

"That's Sam Chamberlain," Margo screeched. "Tell you about him *later!*"

"*I have some news of my own!!*" We heard Lily call. "*I'm going to have a baby!!!*"

Margo and I looked at each other. Suddenly Margo pressed the receiver tightly to her ear. There was no more shouting. The conference call was over. This was serious business; we were on the way to becoming aunts.

MARGO, Matt, Sam, and I ate the lobsters on the inn's front porch. All that was visible of the ocean was a white line of breakers. We took turns dipping lobster meat in the communal bowl of melted butter.

"My, what a shock," Margo said after a while.

"I can't get used to it—Lily with a baby."

"So much for her resumed career."

"But you can't be dependent with a baby, can you?"

"She'd better have a girl."

Matt and Sam waited patiently while Margo and I tried to control our wonder. Lily was four months' pregnant; she had known for three, but she and Henk had wanted to savor the secret. At first they had planned to tell us at Thanksgiving, but Lily had been too bowled over by Margo's and my news to wait.

"And you're half of the year's best soap couple," Sam said after a while.

"What a riot," I said, feeling gleeful.

"What do you think Chance meant about going to Europe?" Margo asked.

"Oh, I'm sure he means army bases. He's convinced that lots of our fans marry army guys or join the army themselves, go overseas, and lose interest in the show. Then, when they come back, we lose them to different shows. He's always wanted to send some of the actors to army bases in Europe, just to keep our loyal viewers loyal."

"October in Europe," Matt said. "Not too shabby."

"Not too," I agreed.

While we ate our dinner, I kept sneaking glances at Sam. I focused on his blue shirt, ragged around the collar, a condition I attributed to the coarseness of his beard. His face, clean-shaven this afternoon, was now handsomely shadowed with dark bristles. I imagined the rough hairs tearing the shirt's fibers. When he finished eating his lobster, he held up the carapace and explained how each part functioned. I watched his long finger trace the red shell and listened to the professorial tone of his voice. The pleasure of the conference call remained with me, and I sank back into my chair, relaxed, waiting for the time to pass. The black zone of shore had told me what I wanted to know.

AFTER dinner Sam admitted the possibility for seduction by saying he would love to see the turret room. We climbed the ladder-stairs. Naked bulbs lit the narrow staircase, the stark, whitewashed walls enclosed us, the original doors were now cracked with age. Young guests would be tempted to slip notes through the cracks. The turret itself had no trappings of luxury. I opened the door, and Sam walked straight to the east windows. I had not yet turned on the lamp; the black vista stretched from shore to shore, broken only by lines of rollers. We heard them crashing onto the rocks below.

I gazed at Sam's narrow back. The folds of his blue shirt fell loosely; only his shoulders stretched the material.

"So," he said, turning toward me and smiling. He had a wide, easy grin. "All three of you Cavan girls have happy news tonight."

"You might even say monumental—a marriage and a baby."

"Don't forget the award."

"Hardly in the same class," I said, smiling back.

Still grinning, he drew me toward him and kissed me. His lips tasted like lobster.

"You taste like lobster," I said.

"I'm an oceanographer," he said.

We kissed again, and I ran my hands along his arm muscles. He began stroking my ass. A September breeze blew through the open windows. The bed loomed just beyond the limit of my peripheral vision. Our tongues touched; Sam was quietly teasing the tip of mine with the tip of his. By now I knew we would go to bed, but I wanted to prolong the tingling sense of *not being sure*.

But even as we kissed, the thought snuck up on me: sure of what? Sure we were soulmates, made-for-each-other, or simply horny? What of the resolution I had passed in Newport last summer? Never to have another casual involvement—did the fact that this was my vacation make a tiny fling acceptable? Exploring Sam's arms with my fingertips I found a tiny threadbare patch above one elbow. It seemed touching. It bore a message, like the black zone of shore. It said to me: I am vulnerable too. Suddenly passion surged and I leaned against Sam's chest. I gave myself totally to the kiss.

I wanted to press against him and not do anything else, but he rolled me onto my back and started to unbutton my shirt. His big hands were no longer careless; he kept one around my back and tenderly undid the buttons with the other. Even in the dark his eyes were bright, with gold flecks, staring into me. We relaxed, smiling at each other. Then he looked down at my breasts. He passed one hand across them, back and forth, and then we started kissing again. A chilly breeze came through the window; it made me want to get under the covers.

"Excuse me for a minute," I whispered after a while, trying to remember whether my diaphragm was in the bathroom or still in my duffel bag.

"Hurry right back," he said.

"I will," I promised.

I rushed into the hall, into the tiny white-tiled bathroom. My diaphragm was not there. I went back to the bedroom, found Sam standing where I had left him. We smiled; I shrugged with embarrassment as I hauled my duffel bag out from under the bed. Struggling with the zipper, I finally unearthed the round plastic case from beneath a pile of sweaters. Palming it and the tube of jelly, I hurried out of the room.

In the bathroom's bright glare I inserted the diaphragm and regarded my naked self in the spotty old mirror. My nightshirt (which, like my beach shirt, was one of John Luddington's castoff dress shirts) hung on the back of the door. I slipped it on. I rolled up the sleeves. Not sexy, I thought, and took it off. Buried somewhere in my makeup bag was a tiny sample bottle of Ivoire, and I considered dabbing it between my breasts. But I never wear perfume, and it would have made me feel more self-conscious than ardent. So I returned unadorned to the turret room.

Sam had removed his blue shirt and was sitting on the edge of the bed. Black hair covered his tan chest. He opened his arms, and we hugged as though I had been gone for an hour. Then I unbuckled his belt, but we didn't take off his pants right away. We leaned back on the white bedspread, kissing for a long time, holding each other close.

Sam stood up and undid his zipper, letting his pants drop to the floor. He stepped out of them, and I saw his tall erection as he walked toward the bed where I was already burrowing under the cool sheet and blanket. We pressed against each other. We hugged and tried to fit our bodies to each other, getting warm. Then he touched me, to see if I was wet, and he kept touching me, pressing his erect cock against me. He looked serious, no longer smiling. I let myself float. Tension tugged my shoulder blades, my belly, my knees, but I concentrated on letting it flow out. Lying on my back, I watched Sam above me, touching me with gentle hands, never taking his eyes away from mine. He ran his fingers all along my ribs and breasts. And I arched my body toward him, reaching for his long cock, and stroking it the way he stroked me. Gently and not gently. Around, around, and then I had to stop touching him because he found a perfect rhythm, and I rolled my face toward his shoulder and kissed it while he moved me into crashing lines of waves. Then I looked up at his face, which was smiling again. He slid on top of me and we were zooming together, he wouldn't let me worry about him; suddenly I was unconcerned about time.

We fell asleep embracing.

When I wakened, the morning air was cold and we were in the midst of another Karsky sunrise. I cuddled closer to Sam and realized that we were covered with an extra blanket. Deep in the night he had wakened, gone away from me, and covered us. I hadn't even noticed. I tried to stay awake, but the bed's warmth lulled me back to sleep.

"Did you sleep well?" Sam asked me, sounding polite and tentative when we wakened for good later that morning. Then he hugged me, proving that the tentativeness had been my own illusion. I traced swirly patterns on his skin. I wrote my name, then drew a pine tree. I waited to feel disconnected, the way I usually did in a romance's early stages, but the feeling never hit. He brought his face close to mine and said, "Let's not get up today."

Of course we did get up, but not until we heard voices on the porch below, heralding the lunch hour. I realized that, for the first time, Margo had not delivered coffee to me in bed. Wise sister! How had she known? Sam and I dressed in bathing suits and walked down to the beach. Neither of us was hungry for lunch. We dove straight into the water.

Una, I told myself, swimming alongside Sam, this is love. Then: no, this is crazy. Maybe Sam is just a prop. Then Sam proved I *was* crazy, that he was no prop, by stopping short in the water, treading water as he kissed me with his salty lips. We sank below the surface. Our legs fluttered, and water went up my nose; I came up choking. Then I laughed, but I couldn't help the salt tears that streamed from my eyes.

On the beach we lay on our backs and talked to each other, facing the sky. The cirrus clouds had moved closer; they washed across the sun, leaving us cold and shaded for short interludes. Then the sun would break through.

"You know, sea turtles are dying out in these waters," he said.

"Why?"

"Because they live on a diet of jellyfish, and they keep eating plastic bags thrown overboard by sailors. They think it's their dinner."

"That's horrible."

"Yeah, it's really bad."

Gulls and terns yelped overhead. Sam said, "If you ever come across tern eggs on the beach, you'd better take off. Tern parents are wildly protective about their brood—they attack anything, even humans."

What a riot, I thought tenderly. My own private professor. "What else?" I asked, egging him on.

Sliding closer to me, he rolled onto his side and kissed my right eyebrow. "You swim like a dolphin. And dolphins are the most beautiful swimmers."

Did he mean dolphins the mammals or dolphins the fish? Then I remembered my dream of the blue fish and realized the fish had been a *dolphin*, a blue-green tropical dolphin, the kind that would never be found in New England waters.

"Delilah?" a female voice asked.

Shading my eyes, I looked up. Two young women wearing terrycloth robes stood over me, their heads bent down for a closer look, to see if I really was Delilah. I nodded my head, and Sam struggled into a sitting position.

"We just watched your show!" one of them said. "Just fifteen minutes ago! They announced about your award. We both think you're wonderful—you really deserve it. Don't we, Callie?"

The other girl nodded. I smiled at them upside down. "Thank you," I said. Sam leaned back on his elbows, taking the sun on his chest, watching me. I knew it, but I didn't catch his eye.

"I'm glad you're finally out of prison," Callie said. "But you should watch it here—you're getting really sunburned."

They walked away, and I shot off my back. My arms and chest were a tender pink. "I can't believe I forgot sunscreen," I said.

Sam wrapped a towel around my shoulders, the essence of concern, but his expression was amused.

"It's not funny," I said. "I haven't had a sunburn in more than three years."

He was staring with earnest concentration at my face.

"What are you doing?" I asked, really annoyed.

"Counting all your new freckles," he said.

THE sunburn didn't amount to much. It stung a little, but Margo gave me some vinegar to rub on it. I lay face down on the bed while Sam massaged clear, biting vinegar into my skin. I began to smell like a marinade. "The clouds saved me," I said dreamily.

"Actually, it's possible to get a much worse sunburn through clouds," he said.

"You know so many facts," I said, with true admiration.

WAKING up beside Sam in the turret room two days later, I listened to rain splash on the windows; it seemed to be coming from all directions. Sam was asleep, his wide mouth slightly open, his dark lashes resting on his cheek. I brushed his messy hair off his forehead, noticing for the first time the fine white scar above his left eye. It was tiny, delicate, and nearly invisible. I thought it must have happened when he was very young. I pressed close to him, making our curves fit together. My skin felt stiff from the sunburn. We had touched all night. Once I had wakened, after a dream, and discovered space between us. But then, as if he were awake also (which he was not), or could dream right into my mind, he rolled against me.

By then Margo had started delivering coffee to both of us in the turret room. We were awake, already dressed, scanning the horizon for whale spouts, when she arrived that morning. She called through the door, "Chance Schutz is on the horn." Then she entered to give Sam his coffee while I flew through the door and down the suicide stairs.

"Una, dear. I apologize for the intrusion on your holiday," came Chance's brisk voice through the telephone wire.

"Please—you're not intruding. How are you? How's Billy?"

"Marvelous. We're marvelous. First of all, congratulations

on your award. It is quite a coup. For you personally and for
the show. We are all proud."

"Thank you." I was beaming. I was accepting my Emmy.
(. . . And I would like to thank everyone who made this possible. . . .)

"Secondly, and I hesitate to ask this: would you be willing
to cut short your time away? We could make it up to you
later, of course, but we're thinking of a European tour. Of the
American army bases. Two weeks or so of different cities;
strike while the iron's hot, we thought." He paused. "Also,
it happens that Emile Balfour is at home in Paris this month
and would be willing to see you next week. Would that be
convenient?"

I loved the way Chance used euphemisms like "convenient,"
knowing full well that I would slit my throat to read for Emile
Balfour in Paris. "Of course," I said, burbling, a brook flowing
through a lush green meadow. "Of course it's convenient."

"Now, you understand, I've recommended you to Emile
with the stipulation that *if* you get a part, you will return to
'Beyond the Bridge,' bringing with you new glory." His tone
was half serious; no one who made a big hit in movies returned full-time to soap operas. But I went along with him.

"Of course. 'Beyond' is my spiritual home."

"Now, this little hiatus won't interrupt anything important,
will it? You can resume your vacation later?"

"Oh, yes," I said, but the thought of Sam took my breath
away. Leave Sam? Right now, just as things are getting perfect? My acceptance speech died in midair.

"My secretary will make arrangements for the trip. When
will you return to New York?"

"When?" I repeated dully. The fact of my imminent de-
parture from Watch Hill brought me up short against the
truth. Only I didn't know what the truth was. Had I fallen in
love with Sam Chamberlain? That was a simple question;
why didn't it lead to a simple answer?

"When will you return to New York?" Chance asked again.
"To be truthful, we would like to see you as soon as possible.
Would tomorrow be too soon?"

"No, that would be fine," I said, thinking shit, tomorrow.

"Marvelous. The sooner you get to New York, the sooner you can go abroad."

"Wonderful," I replied without any conviction.

BEFORE ascending to the turret I sat alone on the porch for a while. A few guests sat in the lobby reading the Providence *Journal* and drinking coffee. I rocked myself back and forth on the metal glider and watched the grey rollers, full of churned-up sand and seaweed—*Chondrus crispus*, probably—smashing on the beach. Storms brought all kinds of debris up from the bottom; walking along my parents' beach after storms I've found quarters, shark's teeth, children's sand toys, rubber soles off sneakers, bleached fishbones, battered lobster pots, rusty teakettles. Everything you can imagine. Margo once found a brand-new playpen, with shiny pale wood slats and bright plastic rattles strung across one side on a metal bar. She ran up to the house to tell us all about it, and the same thought clouded all our faces: what had happened to the baby inside? Lily called the Coast Guard to find out if any babies had fallen overboard, or if any yachts with young families had gone down in the Sound, and they said no. But all that spring we stepped carefully along the high-tide line, watching fearfully for small remains.

Rain splashed into the porch, but it felt good. I heard someone sneaking up from behind. "Boo," Matt said, kissing the top of my head. "Big doings in New York?"

"Yes. I have to leave tomorrow."

"Oh, boy. Margo will kill you. She had big plans for a birthday party."

"Oh, well."

"She's loved having you here. So have I. Ever since we met she's been telling me stories about you Cavan girls. How great you and Lily are. How she and Lily used to watch after you."

"They did," I said. "Isn't that weird? I'm the oldest sister, and they took care of me."

"I think you looked after each other."

"Hmmm," I said, thinking how nice it was that I was having a good talk with Matt on the porch while Margo was having a good talk with Sam upstairs. She was probably drinking coffee out of my cup. From the porch I could see squalls blowing in from Block Island. Rain poured from the low, brownish clouds to the sea's surface, and the clouds traveled fast. Lightning slashed out of some of them.

"Tonight we'll have an unbelievable farewell dinner," Matt was saying. "Anything you like. What's your favorite food?"

"My favorite?" I thought about it. My favorite food varied from place to place. In restaurants in New York it was veal, lightly sautéed, with lemon and butter. At my apartment when I was too tired to cook it was take-out Chinese from a small place that did a fantastically hot Capital Chicken with Watercress. At my mother's house it was Connecticut River shad, the first of the spring, with asparagus and new potatoes. Anywhere else at the shore it was *very* fresh sole, caught that same day. "Filet of sole," I told Matt.

"Filet of sole it shall be," he said. "And now you'd better head upstairs and prepare to break two hearts."

"Two?" I asked, wanting him to spell out what he was getting at.

"Your sister's and Sam's. Yes, Sam's," he said, noting my skeptical expression. I am not an actress for nothing; I know how to use facial expression to coax explanations that might otherwise not be forthcoming. "Sam's crazy about you."

"How do you know?"

"The same way I know you're crazy about him. You can't take your eyes off each other. You're together twenty-four hours a day."

"So, what does that mean? We're attracted to each other. This is our vacation—we'll probably never see each other when we get back to New York."

I must have been carrying the naive act a bit far, because Matt threw me a fishy look. "Tell me that in a month and I might believe you. I predict big things for you and Mr. Chamberlain."

I smiled at him, noticing the way he said "Mister," as if he were not quite used to having any sort of authority, as if he wanted to ally himself to someone older. "We'll see," I said to him, then walked upstairs.

Sam and Margo stood by the window, where I had left them, training binoculars on something. "Margo thinks she saw a spout," Sam said.

"It was rain hitting the water," I said, staring at Sam's back. He wore the same rumpled blue shirt he had worn our first night in the turret room.

"No, it could be a whale," he said. "It's possibly a migrating humpback."

"Like a robin heading south for the winter," Margo said.

"Guess what? I'm going to Europe next week, and I leave for New York tomorrow!"

Both of them whirled around. Margo let the glasses dangle on a cord around her neck. She looked stricken, but Sam grinned his loose, wide, smile and opened his arms. "That's great! Your public overseas will—" Spotting my expression, he came toward me. We hugged. "What's wrong?"

If you don't know, I'm not going to tell you, I thought angrily.

"You have to *leave*?" Margo asked.

"Yeah, but Europe. That's great," Sam said.

"This is really lousy," Margo said and walked out of the room.

I pressed my cheek against his chest. I wasn't crying; I felt more like sleeping. Cradled in his arms, breathing his familiar odor, listening to the rain, I thought I might take a snooze on my feet, right in his arms. But that sleepy feeling dueled with one of being very pissed off. He should not be so happy for me, I thought. This confirms my suspicions—all we're having is a fling. He straightarmed me away from him. "What gives?" he asked.

"Nothing." Sullen. A child. If you knew me at all, you wouldn't have to ask.

"Okay, fine. I thought you were excited about going to Europe." Walking away from me, taking up the binoculars. Scanning the drenched horizon.

I sat on the unmade bed and looked through yesterday's *New York Times*. Matt picked up one for me every day at the store. I turned straight to the arts section. There it was, the big ad for *Hester's Sister*. . . . "Starring Susan Russell, Broadway's newest light. A witchy moonbeam glimmering with light, sensitivity, and truth. Takes her audience straight to the play's dark heart." I turned to the classified ads and started looking for a new apartment. I love doing that. All those little ads seemed to promise wonderful new things. Bigger windows, better kitchens, tons more closets, exposed brick walls, huge terraces, working brick fireplaces, more space, more space, more space. Lower maintenance payments. A superintendent on the premises. More tax credits. I threw the paper across the bed and waited for Sam to turn around.

He took his sweet time. During the time he didn't turn around I could have read the editorial page. "Well, *I* didn't see any whales," he said. "Margo must have been mistaken. If there's a whale in the area, you usually see more than one sign."

"I'd better pack my stuff," I said. "I have to leave on a very early train tomorrow."

Sam stretched across the bed and kissed me. "Do you think I'm not going to miss you? Is that what's wrong?"

"I guess." It must be, because I'm starting to cry, you goon squad.

"I thought you could tell how I feel," he said. "This is different for me. I'm falling in love with you."

I racked my mazed brain. Wasn't it supposed to be better if the man said, "I love you" instead of, "I'm falling in love with you"? A boy I had gone out with on the Vineyard had closed a letter to me with "I love you," then edited it to "I love being with you." Growing up with two sisters meant that our house was always full of *Seventeen, Mademoiselle, Glamour, Cosmopolitan,* and *Vogue.* How often had we read each other articles on the dynamics of love? On the Best Words to Tell Him What You Mean, How to Read Between the Lines, and What Is He *Really* Trying to Say? "What are you really trying to say?" I asked Sam.

"That I will miss you like crazy. That I wish we had more

time together, but I'm happy for you. That I love you."

"Really?"

"Yes."

"Because I love you too. And I'll miss you like crazy. Too."

"See, I knew that. It's pretty obvious."

All through my life I've been hot to communicate without words. With a look, with a gesture. I could do it with Margo, Lily, and Susan. But how long had I known them? It took time to develop a secret language, one that didn't need words. I had to learn these things.

"You'll go to Europe," Sam said slowly, "but you'll be back soon. By then I'll be in New York, and we'll see a lot of each other. I'm planning on it. This doesn't change things—we've both known that you'd have to leave for Europe. All this does is move up the clock a little. Right? You'll go to Europe and you'll come back. That's all."

"Yes, that makes sense," I said slowly.

"You know, I never thought I'd get to thirty without being married," Sam said, lying on his back and moving me next to him, with one arm around my neck. We stared at the conical ceiling. "I grew up with great parents. We were really happy. They were always going off on research trips, but we had a great life. I thought marriage was really terrific. Really the tops. I figured I'd go to college, meet someone, marry her, and bango."

My parents hadn't had quite so idyllic a love life, but I had had vaguely the same idea. Bango.

"But then I never met anyone," Sam continued. "I had a few long relationships, but they weren't right. Didn't feel right. And then I went to graduate school and started thinking about spending nine months out of every year on board a research vessel. I stopped thinking about . . . marriage."

He paused before saying "marriage" because he didn't want to give me the idea that he was proposing. I knew that much. I mean, we were just lying on a bed having a discussion. Telling each other a few intimate facts. It was my turn.

"Well, I've had my share of romances too. But I've never been engaged. Acting is very important to me, and it takes

up a lot of time. It doesn't give me much chance to meet anyone. Not that I've been wanting to get . . . married. That's
been far from my mind at all times. I'm not sure I'll ever be
ready for that."

Sam cocked his head. His eyes looked amused. "What is
'ready'?"

I thought about it, feeling embarrassed. Actually, I was
just blowing off hot air. I felt so relieved to be having this
talk, I wanted it to continue. I thought fast. "Ready for marriage? I guess I mean deeply in love and ready to sacrifice acting. Not all of acting, but some of it." Then I thought of
Susan, blissfully married to Louis. What of acting was she
sacrificing? Nothing.

"Yeah? Like what?"

"Well . . . say I fell in love with a man in New York and
got a movie part with Emile Balfour. I mean, what if I had
to work in France?" Tiptoeing around reality.

"Well, movies don't go on forever. You'd come back eventually."

"Even if I kept working on 'Beyond the Bridge.' There are
mall appearances all over the place and even overseas. I mean,
like next week."

"For a couple of weeks. Not forever."

"This is true." Outside the turret the storm was really heating up. Sheets of rain smashed against our windows. A lightning bolt zigzagged to earth mere yards away. It scared me
into a clutching hold on Sam. He wrapped his arms around
me and held me tight. We kissed; it felt like hot rain drench-
ing both of us. Another lightning bolt flashed by, the kind
Zeus would hurl from Olympus, the kind artists draw in comic
strips.

Sam stopped kissing me and we watched the storm. Thunder
cracked all around us. "That last lightning was a close call," I
said.

"This place is grounded," Sam said with confidence. "Didn't
you notice the lightning rods?"

"No, but if you say so . . ." My eyes blinked with every
flash. My breath came from the back of my throat.

"Haven't you always wanted to make love in the middle of a thunderstorm?" Sam asked, beginning to fiddle with my pants' zipper. "Here we are in the turret, with a tempest raging outside."

"Raging," I said, my eyes full of the latest flash. We could be killed, I thought. Sizzled in our very bed for merely thinking about sex. I had a friend who was asleep beside her boyfriend in a house on the Vineyard and was thrown from her bed, clear across the room, when lightning struck. Of course, the bed was metal. My hand reached back, behind my head, to check. It gripped a wooden post. But what about the box spring? Those metal coils. "Listen," I said, hiking up on my elbows. "I don't feel too safe here. I think we'd better go downstairs."

"We're okay, I promise," Sam said. He had unzipped my pants now and was pulling down my underpants at the same time. His fingers were working into my pubic hair, combing it with gentle strokes. "I'm a scientist. I know about these things. Aren't you going to trust me?"

"Yes," I said after a minute, and kissed him. I touched his zipper and started pulling it down. It's metal, I thought, grasping the brass pull, but that thought slid from my mind. The thunder outside was growing distant, the storm was passing. A new storm was gathering.

THAT night Margo and Matt threw me an early birthday dinner. Sitting on the front porch we started with champagne and oysters (Margo and I said, "Dear little oyster from the bottom of the sea" in tribute to Lily, distant Lily). The rain had stopped, but the air was chilly and damp. We wore sweaters and wool jackets; the wind blew our candles' flames, making thick waxy drizzles on the tabletop. I sat huddled against Sam's warm chest on the metal glider, watching Margo get more and more excited as the time for me to open presents approached. I watched her fondly; she had always loved presents. Her own or anyone else's. At birthday parties she always maneuvered to get right next to the birthday girl. She loved the sound of the paper tearing, the recipient's shortness of breath, the squeals of delight. Watching her on the porch of the Ninigret Inn that night, I reminded myself to try to squeal with delight.

"And now for the main course," Matt said, raising one eyebrow at me. His expression was apologetic. Couldn't they get fresh sole? I wondered, and then the waiter wheeled out a cart with four prime rib dinners.

"Oh. Prime rib—how super," I said, staring at my center cut. I do enjoy a slab of beef now and then, but it was a far cry from filet of sole. Matt avoided my eyes as he dished out the crisp green beans.

"What a meal," Sam said. He held his knife in one hand, ready to get started as soon as politely possible. "In graduate school I spent a year aboard the *Knorr* in the Indian Ocean, and I didn't taste beef that whole time."

"Beef is sacred over there," Margo said, passing clean goblets around the table and filling them with red wine from a bottle whose label she ostentatiously allowed us to see: Chateau Margaux, premier cru, 1964.

Sam laughed loudly and brushed his dark hair back. "You don't say *beef* is sacred. You say *cow*."

Margo waved her hand and gave me a significant look. "They're both bovine," she said.

"Great prime rib," Sam said, chewing heartily. I sipped my Bordeaux and smiled at him. Between bites, when he put down his steak knife, he would rest his hand on my knee. I covered it with my own. For Matt and Margo's sake, I made a mighty effort that night. But I couldn't understand why they had chosen beef for my farewell meal.

Finally it was time for the presents. A waiter cleared the table and another waiter, surrounded by the inn's entire staff, came out with my birthday cake. It blazed with thirty candles. Its white icing was decorated with gaudy pink and blue roses: my favorite kind of birthday cake. Everyone sang "Happy Birthday," and I smiled modestly at my hands on the table, adoring the hoopla. No one enjoys their thirtieth birthday, but I did. Everyone was very concerned about my feeling sad, and

I was the absolute center of attention. Sam kissed me before I had a chance to blow out my candles. Margo piled three bright packages on my lap. I blew hard, extinguishing every candle, and my entourage cheered.

"Happy, happy birthday, baby," Margo said, grabbing one package off the pile. "You have to open this one last."

"Okay, open mine first," Sam said. In four seconds flat I had torn off the wrapping: three paperbacks by Rachel Carson. *The Edge of the Sea, Silent Spring,* and *The Sea Around Us.*

"Oh, thank you. I love them," I said, feeling disappointed. I *did* love them, but I had hoped for more. Holding the perfect little package, I had hoped it would contain something fabulous. A tiara? A diamond necklace? I never wear jewelry, but I had secretly hoped for Sam to give me some. Something that would sparkle and tell me secrets.

"Next package," Matt said, tapping a long thin one with his index finger. I opened it, more slowly than I had Sam's. It contained a silk scarf: exactly the shade of the fish in my dream.

"It's exquisite," I said, allowing Sam to drape it around my neck. "Did you pick it out, Matt?"

"I cannot tell a lie," he said, smiling at Margo.

"Well, thank you. Both of you."

"Now, this one's from Lily," Margo said, handing me the small package. "She and Henk sent it, and she made me promise you'd open it last." She placed it on the table, and all of us leaned over it, admiring the shiny silver paper and blue bow.

"Looks expensive," Sam said.

"Here goes," I said, placidly tugging on the ribbon. It came off easily. Then I undid each piece of tape, trying not to tear the paper. I finally gave up and ripped out a navy blue leather box stamped "Tiffany" in gold.

"Holy crow," Margo said.

Lying on the puffy satin was a pair of dangling diamond earrings. They positively dripped with stones. Platinum settings glinted in the candlelight. I lifted them, allowing them to drape over my finger. They weighed heavily on my hand. "Put them on," Sam said.

I stared at them. Nothing about what I felt made sense. Two minutes ago I had been disappointed to get books instead of jewels from Sam, and now I felt like screaming at the sight of diamonds from my sister. Oh, contrary one! Thirty years old, and no accrued wisdom.

"I can't," I said. "These are for pierced ears." I did not have pierced ears. I had never had pierced ears. During our schooldays, when all our friends were going crazy buying "fun studs" at the malls, I had proclaimed the practice of ear-piercing barbaric. Had Lily thought my lobes would spontaneously puncture?

"This is glamorous stuff," Sam said. "Just right for a movie star."

"I can't believe it," Margo kept saying. "I cannot believe that Lily bought you diamonds." She pronounced it "dye-ah-monds."

I closed the box on them. "They're really something."

For the first time all day the gravity of turning thirty struck me. What had I managed to accomplish in thirty years anyway? All that came to mind was the fact that I had once hitchhiked from Old Saybrook, Connecticut, to Princeton, New Jersey, and that I was a pretty good swimmer. Who cared about acting on a soap opera? Who cared that my mentor had bamboozled me into a movie audition? Balfour probably owed Chance money or something. At that instant I felt desolate, and tears filled my eyes.

Sam did not notice, even though I kept my profile canted in his direction. "Come on, Matt," he said. "We'll clear the table and give the birthday girl a chance to enjoy her largesse."

"That's why we have *waiters*," Matt began, but he must have gotten a signal from Margo because he was soon following Sam into the kitchen with an armload of bloody plates.

Margo stared at me. She was slouched in her chair, playing with a wax drip on one candle. I could feel her gaze, even though I was watching the wax.

"What's the matter? Huh, Una?" she asked.

"Nothing. It was a great party." Then, more convincingly: "I'm thinking about my trip to Europe."

"Oh."

"I'm not sure I'm ready for it."

"Huh. Did you like your presents?"

(Laughing, wry shaking of the head.) "Of course. Can you believe *diamonds* from Lily?"

"I think she's showing off. How *rich* Henk is." (Watching my reaction very carefully, trying to determine the source of my misery.)

"It was very generous."

"And what about Sam's books? Aren't they nice? I mean, *paperbacks*, but still . . . I think they're meant to remind you of the times you spent at that tidal pool. I wonder if they're inscribed." She began flipping open the covers. "Oh, this one is." She passed *The Sea Around Us* across the table to me. I read "To Una, Watch Hill belongs to us. Love, Sam." I felt terrible, even worse than I had opening the presents, at that moment. Sam had written a lovely inscription, and I hadn't even bothered to look for it. How disappointed he must have felt, sitting at the table and waiting for me to read his words!

"That's so wonderful," Margo said, reading his inscription.

"It is."

"Hey, did you like dinner?"

"Yes," I said, finally meeting her eyes. "But why did you serve beef? I did love it, but I thought Matt said something about fish."

She leaned closer to the candle. Conspiratorial. Her eyes sparkled. "I was thinking about Sam, actually. I know you're leaving tomorrow, and I wanted to help things along. A little snare—men *love* rare roast beef."

I grinned. Good old Margo. I kissed her and went to find Sam.

OUR last night together before I left. Sam and I lay on the bed in the turret room and touched each other naked. The sky had begun to clear; autumn constellations blazed in the night.

I nuzzled his hairy chest. "That was a dear thing you wrote in my book," I said, my voice muffled.

"Yeah?"

"I know I didn't look for it right away . . ."

He squeezed my shoulders and pulled the covers higher. Cold air swept down from the north to frost the brass monkeys that night. "It was private. I didn't want everyone to read it anyway."

"Even though they did, eventually. Margo saw it, and she showed Matt . . ."

"They feel responsible for us. They feel as though they brought us together."

An understanding thought, coming from an only child. Things about the future filled my mind: what will happen while I'm in Europe? When I get back to New York? When we're not in Watch Hill? I ached with the thought of leaving him. My train pulled out of the Westerly station the next morning at 8:24. What would happen after that? What would happen after? What would happen?

"Did you like dinner tonight?" I asked.

"Sure. Did you?"

"Margo planned it for your benefit. She figured beef would be right up your alley."

"I know," he said, laughing, squeezing my shoulders again. He slid under the covers, until we were smiling straight into each other's eyes. "Matt told me."

A whirlwind tour of Europe, and I could think only of Sam. The Concorde (the flight being Billy and Chance's thirtieth-birthday present to me), Daimler limousines, fine hotels, and a hefty expense account. Also, a weeping Jason Mordant.

Jason had lost his lover, this time for good. On the plane, between nibbles of Beluga caviar and *tarte aux truffes*, he told me the story. Terry had been cheating on Jason with a cast member of *The Fantasticks*.

"A couple of times, that I could stand," Jason said, "but this was love. I mean, they bought a town house together. Off Seventh Avenue South, I don't even feel like saying the name of the street. You can see it from the Buffalo Roadhouse, which used to be our hangout. It really makes me feel sick, Una."

"I'm really sorry, Jason," I said, but I kept my voice closed off. I wanted privacy to savor the memory of Sam. Why hadn't I taken any pictures of him? I always wish I had photos to remind me of how people I love look, but I didn't even own a camera. In my luggage was a pillowcase from the turret room, full of Sam's scent, but that was stowed in the Concorde's hull, and, besides, the scent would soon fade.

The stewardess plumped small white pillows beneath our necks. The lights were dim and yellow, and there was a lulling buzz of the craft flying through the night. The window burned at the touch, from the friction of flying at a supersonic speed. Sam felt more distant with each passing time zone. I kept touching the hot window with my fingertips, to shock myself. Jason was turned away from me, his stifled sobs shaking his thin body. I covered his hand with mine. When one is in love, it is easy to give comfort to someone who is hurt. Their pain

seems alien. It has nothing to do with *your* love. With your
life. On "Beyond the Bridge" Jason's character and mine
shared everything. Our viewers and *Soap Opera Update* had
just voted us "Soap Couple of the Year." Watching Jason
dissolved in agony, I tried to soothe myself with thoughts of
Sam. Finally I had stumbled onto a love that would redeem
me. Sam didn't bring out the macho in me, nor did he require
me to be a little girl. He let my nature take its course. I watched
Jason and thought: I am nothing like you.

Winging east, my father appeared to me. I have never been
hypnotized, but that night I am sure I had the sensation of
hypnosis. My eyes were closed, and I breathed in steady,
sleepy breaths, but I was aware of the flight, the silently moving stewardesses, the sleepless passenger behind me, Jason
dozing. My father wore a white robe. He flew alongside us,
outside the aircraft. He motioned for me to roll down the
hot window, and I did, as if it were a window in the Volvo.

"The Concorde, that's my girl," he said, patting the sleek
hull with one hand. "The Cavans go first class or we don't go
at all."

I smiled at him and reached for his hand. He zoomed
through the sky, parting the air into turbulent black eddies.
There was no body movement, however. He simply zoomed.
Occasionally the plane would gather speed, and my father
would lag slightly behind. I would have to lean my head out
the window and look back at him, watching him try to catch
up, his mouth open like that picture of a man in a wind tunnel, moving in words that were drowned out by the plane's
wind.

"Why haven't you come back?" I asked, when the plane
slowed to a steady speed. "Since that time in Newport? I
thought I'd see you in the turret room."

"I've been busy. Things to do that you can't begin to understand, Una."

"Oh," I said, feeling abysmally sad.

"But I've been watching you, sweetheart. You're doing
great. You've really turned over a new leaf."

Had he been watching me? Could he say that if he knew

about Joe, about Sam? I blushed and shrugged my shoulders.
I had to avoid his eyes, which were sunken into his sockets.
He looked much worse than he had the last time. The sight of
him made me want to weep.

"I know what you're thinking, honey," he said, bringing
his hand to my cheek. "You think I haven't been doing my
job. But I've seen it all. I know you've made some mistakes—
we all do. That's for sure. But you're on the right track.
You're heading in the right direction. That's all I ask."

Behind me the sleepless passenger asked the stewardess for
a glass of pineapple juice. I wondered whether the air from
my open window was bothering him.

"Your movie audition, for example," my father said. "I'll be
right there when you have it. It makes me so damn proud. My
daughter, a movie star! A regular Katharine Hepburn!"

"Well, it hasn't happened yet."

"No, but you're making headway. Not to mention that Sam.
He's a hell of a guy, a real gentleman. I know you two made
a couple moral slip-ups, but I just turned a blind eye. It's the
intention that matters."

"What is his intention?" I asked, burning to know.

"Why, he wants to marry you," my father said, his white
robe rustling behind him like God's or an angel's. "It might
take him some time to ask you, but he will. That's something
I know for sure."

"What do you think about Lily and Margaret?"

My father smiled, and most of his teeth were black. Two
were gold. "Dad, you should see a dentist," I said, alarmed.

He brought one hand to his mouth, exploring his teeth with
one finger, his eyes troubled. "Yes, they're all rotten, aren't
they?"

"Yes."

Suddenly, with a wave, my father veered off into the night.
A swirling black-and-purple wake, glittering with tiny stars
or bioluminescence, followed him until he disappeared, leaving me to wonder whether he had meant his teeth were all
rotten, or that Lily and Henk and Margo and Matt were rotten. Behind me the sleepless passenger plunked down his

empty glass on the tray. I took that as a signal of irritation, and I rolled up the window. But I didn't stop scanning the blackness until much later, when the jet hit an air shear, jostling me out of sleep.

I wakened wondering whether my experience had been no more than a strange dream.

CHANCE had arranged for Jason and me to spend two days in Paris before beginning our tour. Our itinerary would take us to visit United States Army installations at the Supreme Headquarters Allied Powers in Europe, better known as SHAPE, in Belgium; the First Armored Division in Nuremberg and the Seventh Corps Headquarters in Stuttgart, Germany; the 509th Airbourne Infantry in Vicenza, Italy. But first we were directed to recover from jet lag and enjoy Paris. I was to contact Emile Balfour. We had accommodations at the Hôtel de Crillon, the Schutzes' favorite, between the Tuileries and Jardin des Champs Elysées.

Paris in late September. For the first morning I did no more than sleep deeply beneath white percale sheets and feather-light blankets. My room contained pale green-and-cream silk curtains and Louis XVI furniture. The windows overlooked the hotel's interior courtyard. I would waken, glance around the unfamiliar and luxurious room, and fall back to sleep. Finally I wakened for good. Lifting the receiver, I said. "*Café filtre et un brioche, s'il vous plaît.*" Margo had prepared a list of useful phrases for me. We had approached it like a computer dating service, with Margo matching the phrases with my habits. She spent an hour asking me questions like "Do you prefer butter or preserves? What *kind* of preserves?"

I had finished breakfast and had already written a long letter to Sam on the Hôtel de Crillon's cream vellum stationery when I finally called to leave a message with Emile Balfour's secretary. I had not even had time to work mysef into a nervous frenzy when he called me back.

"Miss Cavan," he said in perfect, gracious English. "Welcome to France."

"Thank you." I straightened up, pulling the covers over my breasts, as if he could see me. I had left the window open to let in the cool night air, and now I heard voices in the courtyard. Low, female voices speaking in French. The clink of a china coffee cup being placed on a saucer.

"I know your business will take you to several locations before you return to France. Perhaps you will read for me on your return?"

"I would be delighted to. Enchanted," I said, trying to decide whether or not to say *"enchanté."* I have always disliked using foreign words such as *ambiance, cache-pot,* and *manicotti* because I do not feel I have the authority to pronounce them properly. Who am I to say "manigotte"? "What will you have me read?" I asked.

"Ahhh—" I could almost hear his shrug. "We do not have that type of formality. I will decide on a scene when you arrive. Will that be acceptable?"

"Of course." Emile Balfour, asking me whether it would be acceptable. He came from the same school as Chance Schutz.

"So, listen: are you free tonight? You would like to go to Palace, see something else of Paris?"

"I'd love to!" What the hell was Palace? I pictured some gothic chateau on the banks of the Loire, with crenellations and a moat, towers and balustrades. But the Loire was far away; were there castles on the Seine?

"Great. I will come to you at ten tonight. We will have supper." Then he hung up.

I added a long postscript to Sam's letter, dressed, and knocked on Jason's door. When he answered I could see that I had wakened him. The room smelled of heavy sleep; the curtains and shades were drawn, and the only light was that which slanted in from the hall.

"Want to be my fellow tourist?" I asked. I hung back, not wanting to get too close. I was afraid of what might spring at me from the dark.

"What time is it?"

"Nearly noon. We should get hopping."

"No, I haven't even thought about coffee yet. You'd better go without me."

I stood in the hall, regarding Jason in his handsome dark-silk robe. His tan skin looked sallow in the room's blackness, and there were shadows beneath his eyes. I wanted to yank him into the light, shake his shoulders, tell him to pull himself together. "Well, okay," I said doubtfully. "Would you like to meet this afternoon?"

"Oh, knock on my door if you're in the neighborhood. Don't make any special trips, though."

"Maybe we should plan on lunch. I'll come back around one-thirty—"

"Listen, you're not being paid to keep an eye on me," he snapped, then immediately grabbed my forearm. "Forgive me, Una. I'm a crank when I first wake up."

"That's all right," I said cheerfully, heading down the hall, feeling as though someone had just poured gravy on my head. I hate having people yell at me, especially when I don't deserve it. It reminds me too much of being young, of trying to please everyone in sight.

This was my first visit to Paris. I walked alone on the Faubourg St.-Honoré. It reminded me of a celestial version of Madison Avenue. All the great design houses: St. Laurent, Givenchy, Valentino, Chanel. Shops of expensive hand-painted—embroidered—women—stitched—articles. Jewels. Cafés. I walked into a tiny children's store and bought a fuzzy white lamb. With some difficulty I directed the shopwoman, who spoke shaky English, to send it to Lily in New York. Even on these streets the French women carried shopping bags, the way peasant women did in picture books of French life, only here the bags were of fine leather instead of cotton net, and they contained snakeskin wallets and Turkish cigarettes instead of leeks and turnips. I wandered along the Champs Elysées toward the Arc de Triomphe. It stood before me, carved with intricate reliefs, seeming to block the street. I wished I had had the presence of mind to buy a guidebook in New York. I thought of the Louvre, the Rodin Museum (where I wished to buy something for Margo), Notre Dame. But instead of exploring, I found a small café with wrought-iron chairs and tables on the busy sidewalk beside a flower market and wrote another letter to Sam.

The scent of out-of-season irises, tulips, and peonies mingled with car fumes and the smell of strong coffee. I drank mine black.

DEAR SAM, *I wrote,*

Well, here I am, the American in Paris, watching *tout le monde* (Margo will translate) from this sidewalk café. Gertrude Stein, Gertrude Stein, Gertrude Stein. Are you reading this on the beach? Are you within sight of the black zone? Shouldn't the neap tides be along any day now? I have been reading Rachel Carson avidly.

As I mentioned in my letter earlier, I'm going to meet Emile Balfour tonight. He's taking me to something called "Palace." Do you have any idea? I feel this need to act very cool, very suave with him. After all, if he's going to make me a movie star, I have to act the part. Of course, he's probably a perfectly humble nice guy and Palace is probably his local bowling alley, and I'm all hepped up over nothing.

Two transvestites just walked by.

I can't believe I'm in Paris. I'm actually sitting in the shadow of the Arc de Triomphe. Everything is magnificent, but so far jet lag prevents me from feeling totally fine. I'm walking the streets in a real daze. First of all I can't speak the language. Second of all I don't know anyone except Jason, who's in a blue funk. It's very sad—his loved one left him. I can't imagine being in Paris with a broken heart—

How are Matt and Margo? Margo will be mighty pissed off when you get two letters from me and she gets none, but tell her I'll write from Brussels or somewhere.

I wish you were here with me. I loved being with you at Watch Hill. This trip, by all accounts, will last for two weeks, and then we can meet in New York. After today I'll start sending letters to your New York address. I miss you, Sam.

Avec beaucoup d'amour,
UNA

Margo, along with her pragmatic French phrases, had given me some romantic French phrases to use in letters to Sam. How I love letters! They allow you to say things that might be difficult face-to-face. You can think about the words, erase them if they aren't perfect, hold back if you are unsure. But that day, sitting at my café table in the Paris sun, I did not feel unsure. I pictured Sam, walking along the sand flats. In Watch Hill it would be early morning. He would be walking slowly, his hands deep in the pockets of his khaki shorts, his messy black hair falling into his eyes. He would be looking east, across the Atlantic, facing the shores of France, squinting into the rising sun. We were separated by the mere element of water.

Jason had risen and was smoking a black cigarette in the lobby when I returned. He wore a pale yellow silk shirt with a maroon foulard scarf knotted around his neck, and he wore sunglasses with very dark lenses. *"Eh, ça va?"* he said, standing to greet me.

"Say what?" I asked, kissing both his cheeks.

"How goes it, Una my love?"

"You said all that in three tiny syllables?"

A wave of the hand. "Inflection is *all*. Absolutely all. You can speak volumes in one sentence, if you only have the right tone."

"Like on 'Beyond,' when Beck looks at Delilah and says, 'But *why?*' "

"Exactly." Jason checked his black diver's watch. "My mother's French. I speak *la langue* fluently. Rustily, but fluently."

"Oh, I didn't know that." I marveled at the strangeness of not knowing the first thing about Jason's family. We spent every day working together and were America's favorite daytime couple, and I hadn't known his mother was French. Was she still alive? Did she live in Paris? I wanted to ask, but Jason grabbed his buttery leather jacket and kissed my cheek.

"Listen, I'm off. You don't mind if I desert you?"

"No, not at all." Flustered, I had thought we could spend the afternoon together. I suddenly felt marooned and without options. "Oh, wait," I called just before he went through the door. "Have you ever heard of 'Palace'? I'm supposed to be going there with Balfour tonight."

Jason took a step back and grinned, his foot planted dramatically on the marble floor. "How *chichi*. It's a terrific nightclub called 'Palace des Complines.' Known to cool cats as 'Palace.'" Impossible to get into unless you are with one of the greats. I'm going to Crazy Horse, myself."

"Well, have fun," I said. I wanted to wait by the door, to see whom Jason would meet, but politeness prevented me. Crazy Horse? Palace? Whatever had happened to La Moulin Rouge, Les Deux Magots, Les Folies Bérgères? All the great Paris haunts of legend and song? Of Hemingway, Lautrec, Colette, Scott and Zelda, Matisse, and Picasso? What did one wear to Palace? I ran upstairs to peruse my wardrobe.

w h e n Emile Balfour rang my room at ten that night, I looked fabulous. I had gone to a fancy beauty salon and had my hair washed and twisted into a magnificent chignon. It was very severe and accented my sharp profile. I wore a gold satin tunic with a belt of twisted silk and brass baubles over skinny, straight-legged black pants. On my feet I wore pointed gold shoes, the toes slightly upturned, like Aladdin's. My black stockings were sheer, flecked with gold. The entire ensemble brought out gold highlights in my auburn hair. I thought I looked very modish.

Taking the elevator to the lobby I felt short of breath. I tried to rehearse what I would say to him. Should I call him Emile or Mr. Balfour? Would it be better to appear confident, as a colleague, and say "Hi, Emile," or would it be better to show my awe, to act a bit subservient, and say, "How do you do, Mr. Balfour"? Or "Monsieur Balfour"? Movie directors adored adulation, but he had said on the telephone that he did not believe in formality. When the grand elevator doors slid open, and I was finally standing in the lobby, I was too muddled to do anything but beam when Emile Balfour, tall and wonderfully handsome in his tuxedo, came toward me, kissed both my cheeks, and said quietly into my ear, "Welcome to Paris."

In America, where everyone recognizes movie and television stars, only the cognoscenti know the faces of directors. But everyone at the Crillon knew Emile Balfour. His bodyguard parted a path through the crowd for us. I had the impression of men in black tie and women in evening garb. Orchestra music. There was a ball at the hotel that night. We stepped quickly, blinking at the flashbulbs. When we were safely in the black limousine, Emile leaned close to me, smiling his famous down-turned smile, and said, "Tomorrow all the newspapers will be asking, 'Who is she?' " He looked pleased.

I laughed gaily. This was going to be fun. I felt as though I had already passed my audition and was living the life of a Balfour leading lady. Through the car's tinted windows the lighted fountains of the Place de la Concorde looked dim and green. We spun down the grand boulevards into the heart of Paris. "You know," Emile said, pointing at another fountain, "if you want to impress someone, you pay the city some money, and they will turn on the fountain at a certain time. You synchronize your watches. Then you take your lady to the fountain, which is dry, and you say, 'Our love is so deep, it makes rivers flow, fountains bubble . . .,' and the water suddenly goes on, all lit up like magic. Then she will do anything for you."

I laughed. What a charmer. A traffic jam caught us on a dark one-way street. Bums lurched toward the car from darkened doorways, but Emile was unperturbed. He looked impatiently at his watch, then tapped the glass partition and gestured for the driver to turn down an alleyway. We weaved through the slum, rousing bums who slept on grates and in front of building vents. But the driver never blew his horn; Emile told me it was against the laws of Paris to blow a car horn. The entire time, he spoke without facing me. Finally he glanced in my direction and said, "So, you won an award."

I read his expression, watching for disdain. I had hoped he wouldn't mention the show. It embarrassed me to discuss my

soap opera with France's great director. "Yes, I did," I said.
"We give our viewers what they seem to want."

"Really? What is that?"

"We make them laugh, make them cry, and make them
wait."

"It amazes me that a man like Chance Schutz would con-
descend to an audience like that. It really is an insult."

I felt heat spreading up my neck, into my face. I looked
out the car window.

"I mean, I'm always telling Chance, 'Get out of that stuff.'
He's too talented to waste himself on crap. Your show has an
appeal, certainly, of a campish sort. But apart from that . . ."

The driver stopped in front of a building. A line wound
from the front door around the block. People pressed close to
our car, to see who would emerge.

"Now, get ready," Emile said, ducking his head and hur-
tling out of the car the instant our driver opened the door. I
followed, and when I looked up we were in a darkened palace,
with a rock beat pounding in our ears and a thousand men in
black tie greeting us, leading us to the preferred table, bearing a complimentary (or perhaps Emile's customary) bottle
of champagne, while those who were not prominent enough
lounged glumly in the ground-floor waiting room and craned
their necks to see who passed. I knew that crowd: in New
York I had gone to Area, to Kamikaze, to Limelight, and
watched the famous be whisked by like prize cattle. Occasionally I was among them. On nights when I was not, I de-
plored the system as free advertising, but whenever I was, the
system did not seem so bad.

Emile waved the waiter away and opened the bottle of
champagne himself. Very indolent, his cigarette dangling off
his lower lip, the smoke curling into his eyelashes and making
him squint, he twisted the bottle around the cork and allowed
a thin stream to cascade onto the table. He poured the wine.
A waiter arrived instantly with a white linen cloth and
swabbed the puddle. Emile watched, then leaned back and
surveyed the room. "To art," he said, raising the delicate flute.

"To art," I said, surprising myself by thinking of "Beyond
the Bridge."

Emile had the sharp bone structure and boyish expression of a French sailor. He wore a heavy chronometer on his wrist, an accessory which looked fantastically incongruous beside the trim cuffs of his dinner jacket. His touseled brown hair looked windblown, but I had smelled the lacquer sitting close to him in the car. When he reached the end of his filterless cigarette, he jabbed it with a gold toothpick and brought it to his sensual lips. "Okay," he said. "What were we saying about Chance Schutz? Oh yes—that he had better find a new baby."

"Baby?"

"Baby. Project. Get the hell out of soap operas. He sent me several tapes of your show, by the way. You are a good actress. You've got spark and talent. That's why I want to try you out. I think you will work."

A couple danced close to our table, and a bodyguard materialized out of nowhere to prod them away. I watched with indifference, as if it happened to me every day. "Can you tell me about the movie?"

"It is about a woman alone. Has no one. She lives on the wild shore. Yet she is lovely. What has happened to her? Who has she loved? What did that love do to her? The movie unfolds into her story. It is a compelling script. Flashbacks leading to a new love in the present. Confrontations. But still abstract, like *The Listener*. Totally different than anything I have done before—I'll give you a script before you leave Paris."

"Are you shooting it here?"

"No. I'm shooting my current picture here. Parts of it. I don't like setting a film in the city. I need the ambiguities of nature, the message. The symbolism."

"Yes, I know." I thought of the black zone of shore. I knew precisely what he meant; it was one of the reasons I felt drawn to his work. My eyes sharp with the recognition of a kindred spirit, I smiled at him, but his eyes were scanning the crowd. My father had taught me to never look around a room, trying to see who was there. Let them look for me. I had thought that a man like Emile Balfour would have learned the same lesson. "Where will you shoot the new picture?"

"Corsica. Very wild, desolate." A quick glance. "You could

live for four months without the distractions of a city?"

"Of course."

"I wonder about Chance Schutz's great interest in you. Are you lovers?"

I blushed, even though everyone knows how direct the French are about adultery. "No, we're not. I'm a close friend of his and Billy's. How do you know him?"

"He produced one of my early films. Many years ago, before I was known."

I hadn't known that. I thought of Chance and wondered how many young artists he had taken under his wing. He had transformed me from a drama student into one of America's favorite soap stars. Because of Chance I was drinking champagne with Emile Balfour at Palace. I felt terribly guilty for being ashamed of the show, and I straightened my spine, determined to act proud.

Emile looked vaguely bored; he gazed through the room at the writhing dancers, the dark tables around the perimeter, the waiters stationed like extra police at a parade. At his glance the waiters started toward our table, but Emile shook his head impatiently, and they stopped in their tracks. Statues.

A tuxedoed man approached us, and no one stopped him. By Emile's expression I could see that this was the person he had been looking for. A slur of French, and then Emile motioned for him to sit down. Emile's manner toward me changed drastically. Suddenly he was pressed beside me, one finger tracing the back of my hand on the table, his warm breath on the back of my ear.

"Arnaud, meet Una Cavan. The American actress." He said "the American actress" as if I were in a class with Meryl Streep.

"*Enchanté*," Arnaud said, grinning broadly. He had a shiny bald head and wore round wire glasses. "So delighted to make your acquaintance. Perhaps you will give me *le scoop*?" He whipped out a small cassette recorder, placed it on the table, and switched it on. For several seconds there was silence. Emile leaned over and gave me a long kiss, his tongue entering my mouth, his hand passing across my breasts.

"You ready?" he asked into my mouth.

By the time I had recovered from the kiss and divined that Arnaud was a reporter, Emile had started talking.

"I am trying to persuade Una to accept a role in my next film. As you know, it will be shot on Corsica, and that is all I can say. Una is used to the bright lights of New York. Can such a woman last on Corsica? She needs a lot of action, this one." He kissed the top of my ear. A photographer darted around our table. Arnaud smiled unctuously.

I sat there, growing stiff. I had not traveled to Paris to be used by Emile Balfour, I told myself, but I continued to smile for the camera. I could not move; I was the Petrified Forest of rage. I thought of Sam, having dinner alone at the Ninigret Inn. At that precise moment he was probably hunched over a plate of steamed cod, reading an Agatha Christie paperback. Emile's hot tongue swabbed the rim of my ear.

"What is your best work, Una?" Arnaud asked.

Before I could reply, Emile said, "No doubt about that. She is a cult figure on 'Beyond the Bridge.' It is a daytime serial. Of a very different sort."

A cult figure? Somehow I had never thought of my fans as a cult. I could not believe Emile's approach—first call soap operas "crap" and tear down the people who work in them, then hype them up for the media and make them seem fashionable, cultish. My stomach growled. I was torn between the desire to run away from Emile Balfour and never return, and a strong need for food. Hadn't he said something about dinner? I smiled weakly at Arnaud and the photographer, afraid of showing my true feelings. If I showed them how angry I felt I would displease Emile, and I was not practiced in displeasing men. Emile began to speak in French. For fifteen minutes I stared at his gargantuan watch, willing the interview to end. Suddenly, without a word to me, Emile touched my hand and stood. He rushed toward the door, leaving me to run after him. On the way past our waiter, he signed his name to the bill.

In the back seat of the car, he faced me. His expression was blank. "I am sorry. I can see that you are upset. Aren't you used to interviews?"

"Not . . . that kind," I said in the strongest way I could. I could have said, "No, *I'm not,* you fucker," or, "How dare you use me that way?" or, "Who the *holy hell* do you think you are?" Instead, I shrugged and looked apologetic, because I did not want to offend the man. He had too much power over my future for me to slug him. Emile reached around, patting my cheek tenderly. He turned my face toward his.

"Una, I am very sorry. But you understand publicity, don't you? How reporters must be manipulated, how situations must be made to appear a certain way? You are watched by millions of American women, a market that I would very much like to reach with my films. You are my entrée to that market."

Wasn't that sort of the same as being a doormat? I thought. Emile's voice was cool and soothing. If I had heard it about an hour earlier, I would not be in this state now. I stared at him, squinting with anger. Emile immediately turned away, fishing a cigarette from a leather pocket on the car door, and lit it.

"I'm sorry," I said, as soon as I was able to speak.

"That is all right," Emile replied, benevolent and forgiving. Why the hell was *I* apologizing when he was the rude one? My mind was full of righteous indignation, but my voice was full of contrition. At that instant I hated Emile Balfour. Tomorrow some Paris paper would report that we were having a romance, and I hated him.

The driver drove down a narrow street, barely wide enough for the car. He stopped in front of a tiny bistro with a carved gold snail above the door. Without waiting for the driver, Emile opened the door and we stepped out. An old man, his dress shirt and black tie covered by a starched white apron, greeted us without appearing to recognize Emile. He led us through a narrow room to a dark wood booth. There were no cushions. Emile and I sat opposite each other, illuminated by the green shaded lamp hanging overhead. Kitchen noises clattered a few feet away, and the odor of garlic was omnipresent. My stomach growled loudly.

"They have the best lamb in Paris," Emile said. "Allow me to order for us?"

I nodded, feeling sodden. How could I have expected to dazzle Emile Balfour and become a movie star? What a charade! When the waiter had uncorked a bottle of red wine and taken our order to the chef, Emile settled back against the booth and told me a story about his latest movie. How he was shooting right on schedule, how the leading man drank too much every night but so far had been sober on the set, how Emile would see that the actor never found another job if he screwed up the film. I listened, letting amusement alternate with sympathy on my face. Emile looked pleased, like someone who knew that he was fabulously handsome and famous and had somehow managed to make an hysterical woman calm down before she raised the roof.

The waiter brought our dinner: grilled lamb with rosemary, flageolets, baby carrots, and fried shoestring potatoes. Emile chewed some food, then went on with his stories. Occasionally his eyes would flick charmingly, meeting mine, but mainly they roamed the room. I continued to nod at him, but I was thinking: with men it always came down to the same thing. I wanted things from them, and I would compromise myself to get them. With my father I had wished for devotion. I had agreed to overlook his nights at The Blue Danube as a means of exerting emotional blackmail. I *will* forgive you if you love me. I *will* be a Good Girl if you love me. With Emile I wanted a starring role, and I was, by sitting in that restaurant, allowing him to use me as a publicity stunt. I would pretend to be his new lover if he would give me a job. Suddenly a terrible thought struck me: what if he really expected me to *be* his new lover? My father had always warned me about guys like him. What would I do, how would I react, when he made the pass? Would I go willingly, trying to not think of Sam? Perhaps I had just discovered why Lily and Margo had found true love and I had not; with men, they were not constantly patting their pockets for currency with which to barter.

After dinner we drove to the Crillon. Emile and I sat quietly in the limousine's vast back seat while revelers passed by, peering into the black windows, trying to see through their own reflections. Some of them brought their faces so close to the glass, their noses touched and left imprints. I sat upright, watching the faces, waiting for Emile to touch me. The faces

appeared quizzical, like faces observed through a one-way mirror in a department store dressing room or a police lineup.
As Delilah, I had seen a lineup. About two years ago Delilah
had been raped by a champion golfer, during Mooreland's
annual benefit tournament. Beck and her father had flanked
her while she sat in a small room at the Mooreland police station, watching the men parade onto the stage, standing before
the height lines, their heads resembling musical notes on a
staff. The men had faced the window, which must have looked
to them like a mirror, because some of them had crouched,
peering into the glass, smoothing their hair and moustaches.
The perpetrator had a bushy blond moustache. Delilah had
identified him, but he ended up beating the charge because he
always played in the same foursome as the judge.

"So, now you have seen something of Paris," Emile said,
smiling warmly.

"Yes. Thank you so much." I was stiff, waiting for him to
say, "Now let's go upstairs," but he only smiled. He sat at his
end of the long leather seat, wedged into the corner.

"I imagine your tour will be arduous, but perhaps it will be
pleasant, knowing that you will soon return to Paris. You can
come to my studio and read for me. Of course I say 'read,' but
for an actress of your abilities, that might be insulting."

"I've never acted in a movie."

"No, that is true, and although I trust Chance's judgment
when he tells me you are capable, I have investors who must
see for themselves. Don't worry; they are money men, not
artists. They will see a little show, give us the money, and that
will be that."

"That will be that?" Was he telling me that the audition
was just a formality, that the part was mine for the asking?
I felt a slight surge of adrenaline, and held onto the seat.

But Emile shook his head and smiled wryly. In the dim
light, his face looked very young. "Well, I am afraid we must
do a little test. As you say, movies are different from television.
I like to improvise in my work, to give the picture more
creative range, so perhaps we will see how you improvise."

I love to improvise. "Fine," I said. Now that business was

concluded, he would touch me. Perhaps he would slip his hand around the back of my neck, pulling my face into his lap. Right here, with all the voyeurs outside. But instead he tapped the glass partition behind the driver's head, and the driver sprang out of the car. He opened my door and leaned inside waiting for instructions.

"Walk Mademoiselle Cavan to the elevator," Emile commanded. Almost as an afterthought, he reached for my hand and kissed it.

"*A bientôt,*" he said.

"Goodnight," I said, backing away from the car, waving at him until the driver slammed the door and left me staring at my own reflection in the black glass.

Shouldn't a grand tour of Europe be electrifying? Especially when one has just fallen in love? I had expected it to be. I had expected to fly through the cities with my eyes wide open, taking in the richness so I could write to Sam about it. I had planned to stand before the little pond in the Tuileries and watch the children sail their model sailboats and describe the bright hulls, the fluttering of the cotton sails, the music of the children's language, in long letters. The barges puffing along the Seine. Breakfast alfresco beneath grey-and-white umbrellas at the Crillon. But in Paris I had developed narcolepsy. How could I write long letters to Sam when I kept falling asleep? From the moment Emile Balfour had dropped me at the hotel, I could not keep my eyes open. I had slept until noon the next day, had barely stayed awake through breakfast with Jason, had fallen asleep, upright, in the limousine on the way to the airport. Emile had sent the script to me by messenger, but I had no will to read it.

On the plane to Zaventem, I slept. In the cab, driving southwest to Brussels (a city I had never visited), I slept. We finally reached the Ste. Claire, a tiny hotel adjacent to the Grand' Place. I rested my elbow on the grimy mahogany front desk while Jason checked in, and I fought to stay awake. Only a few minutes, and then I'll be alone in my room, I told myself, listening to Jason's voice rise in anger and not caring why.

"The rooms are on air shafts," Jason told me.

"I don't care," I said. I adored natural light, had never stayed in a room facing an airshaft in my life. The one time a desk clerk had put me in a room facing an air shaft, I had found another hotel.

There was one bellman assigned to carry both my and Jason's bags. He opened the door to my room first. The space

was a cubbyhole with dim, brassy light fixtures and greenish
reproductions of Franz Hals portraits. Not even Rembrandt.
The air shaft was hidden by a heavy brown-and-orange floral
curtain. I sat in the room's single chair (straight-backed), forgot to tip the bellman, and was treated to a guttural Flemish
insult. He slammed the door and I could hear him burping at
Jason in the hall. From a room across the air shaft I could hear
a telephone ringing. I knew Chance Schutz, and I knew that
he would never knowingly book us into such a terrible place.
If I had felt one bit less miserable, I would have raised a stink
and gotten us out of there. Instead I stumbled to the bed, lay
on top of the mustard-colored spread, and fell asleep.

I have never believed that one needs to be *worthy* of love.
But during those first days in Europe, I felt that way about
Sam. Sam Chamberlain, a straightforward oceanographer,
son of upstanding geologists, involved with a scheming harpie
like me. Sam wasn't offering any resistance. I was unused to
simplicity, to love without guile. With Sam I knew the simple
joys. The sea, the shore, the sand, the waves, sandpipers, tidal
pools, clean salt air, lovemaking in the turret room. With Sam
I had not even considered bargaining power.

But what did I know of him, after all? Could you judge a
man by the way he acted on vacation? When he was over a
hundred miles from his permanent residence? Perhaps he
lived in squalor, over a seedy nightclub which he would visit
whenever he was free for the evening. Perhaps he was a com-
pulsive liar; perhaps he was not an oceanographer at all but
a pornographer. The words even had the same ring. Perhaps
he enticed women like me to fall in love with him, then threw
them over for their sisters. In my narcoleptic state I enter-
tained these ideas and worse ones. I lay awake on the mustard-
colored spread as long as I could, until the voices rising up
the air shaft became as spellbinding as a chanting coven of
witches. Their message was "Sleep, sleep." I resisted, playing
out scenarios in which Sam would hurt me, I would hurt Sam,
Sam would hurt me, I would hurt Sam. Then Emile Balfour
would drift into my mind, his lean face and handsome tuxedo,
and I would think of the things I would do to become his new
star. Pretend to be his new lover. Become his new lover. Do

whatever he told me to do. But for now I would sleep.

My telephone jangled sometime later. I struggled up from the quicksand depths of sleep to answer it. First I heard the voice of the hotel operator, and then I heard the voice of Margo. Even though she must have realized it was the middle of my night, she gave me no chance to waken.

"I can't believe you did it, Una. It reminds me of a whore."

"What does?"

"You with Emile *Balfour*."

It had hit the American papers? I suppose I should have anticipated that and called Sam. "That's completely false. The whole thing was a publicity setup. How did you get this number, anyway?"

"I called Chance Schutz. Una, you should try to imagine how Sam feels. He's sitting downstairs now, talking to Matt about it. We read it in the 'Celebrity File.' "

The "Celebrity File"—a highly reliable column in the Westerly *Gazette*. "Don't believe it. Sam doesn't, does he?" I asked, beginning to feel alert and alarmed.

"There was a picture of you sitting at a cozy little table with his arm around you."

"Oh, Christ, we were talking business," I said, glad they hadn't used the one where he was kissing me. "Let me talk to Sam."

"Good. But I'm going to tell him you called here, okay? I think it would help."

I thought about it. It would help get me off the hook, but it would remind me of my father and one of his buddies getting together to cook up an alibi. "No, don't lie about it. I wouldn't be calling now, anyway. It's the middle of the night."

"I'm sorry if I woke you up," Margo said, her voice softer. "But it was quite a shock. Do you swear it isn't true?"

"I swear. Now please get Sam."

Silence on the line. I sat straighter on the bed, touched my cheek which was imprinted with the bedspread's honeycomb design. Voices still sang down the air shaft, and the elevator rumbled through the hotel like approaching thunder. I remembered the lightning storm with Sam and felt a sharpness in my chest.

"Hi there," he said.

"Hi. I hear you saw the paper."

"Yeah. Your sister's pretty upset. She says you're not the type to fall in love on a different continent every other day."

"She's right. The whole thing was a publicity stunt. I didn't even know about it until it was halfway over. I should have called you."

"You probably should have. Are you having fun over there?"

I glanced around my ugly room and my eyes filled with tears. Hearing Sam's voice at the end of a transatlantic cable made me fill sick and lonely. "Oh, sure."

"Did you have your audition?"

"Not yet. We're going back to Paris when we finish the tour." Until that moment I hadn't known that I would want to go through with the audition. I did not like Emile Balfour, but I wanted the part. I still wanted the part.

"Well, good luck, then. Now that I know he's not my chief rival." Sam's voice sounded stiff and a little tentative. He was having doubts about me. I could hear it through the wire.

"He's not. I promise. I miss you—you can't believe how much."

"I miss you, too. I sent a letter to your hotel in Nuremberg."

"I sent one to Watch Hill. Two, actually. I'll send the next one to New York."

"It must be really late for you. You'd better go to sleep. Sweet dreams."

"Sweet dreams." I hung up the phone and found myself cured of narcolepsy. I began to unpack my bag, thinking about the sound of Sam's voice, trying to determine what I had heard in it. Distrust? Disappointment? Jealousy? Regret? Or nothing? How could I know what Sam felt about me when I didn't know what I felt about myself? The call had cured me of narcolepsy, but now I had insomnia.

BELGIUM is full of American personnel, both civilian and military, all potential "Beyond the Bridge" fans. Army, NATO, private industry. Chance had arranged for Jason and me to host a luncheon at the SHAPEHOW Club. (Supreme Head-quarters Allied Powers Europe Homesick Officers' Wives Club.) We would host others at SHAPE and others at NATO. We were driven southwest from Brussels on the Chaussée de Mons. Jason scribbled in his journal while I stared out the window at the warrens of houses and a ruined castle in the distance. Jason and I had reached a silent accord: we would not intrude on each other's misery. I heard his pen scratching paper. It symbolized one of the great differences between us: Jason would immortalize his blackest thoughts while I wanted no record of mine. I kept trying to recall the nuances of my conversation with Sam while at the same time trying to dis-pel them. *Had* I heard distrust in his voice, or was it simply a reflection of my *own*? *Am* I worthy of such a man, and do I want to be with a man whom I need to feel worthy of? By the time we had driven onto the massive base and stopped in front of the SHAPEHOW Club, a pretty brick building, I felt so confused I was tempted to tell the driver to take another spin around the block.

"Remember, we're doing this for our country," Jason said, touching the back of my hand.

"I'll try."

"Una, you look smashing in that black, but take a look at your eyes." He handed me a mirror from his satchel. Peering into it, I saw the violet crescents beneath my eyes. I rubbed them out with a dab of the white stuff Jason carried at all times. Like whiting out a mistake on a college term paper. Poof! I suddenly looked happy and rested, just like Delilah Grant.

The hall contained long tables covered with pink table-cloths and centerpieces of hothouse tulips. Someone had strung a huge banner over the stage: WELCOME BECK AND DE-LILAH! ! ! Everyone cheered when we entered. A tall woman with short dark hair shook our hands as we ascended to the stage.

"Well, hiya! I'm Shirley Morris," she said to us in a deep Texas drawl. Her short hair had been razor-cut—punk style. Lines of gold studs rimmed both her earlobes. I glanced around the room for the buxom, floral-garbed, tightly permed officers' wives I had expected to see, but the crowd was young and attractive.

"Charmed," Jason said. "Now, Una and I thought we'd make a little speech, act out a couple scenes, and show a videotape."

We ran through two scenes together: the fight between Beck and Delilah just after Delilah learned that Beck had kissed her patient, and the love scene immediately after Beck helped Delilah escape from prison. The women loved them. They cheered us. They called for an encore, but Jason plugged in the videotape instead.

THAT night I read the script, entitled *Together Forever*. I took a bath, wrapped my wet hair in a threadbare towel, and, wearing John Luddington's old dress shirt, settled back against the rock-hard foam pillows. The secrets of a hundred hotel guests whined down the air shaft. Arguments, lovemaking, dance music, bathroom sounds. They distracted me for about four minutes, but suddenly the script took over.

It was about Anya, a widow from New York. She travels to Ponci, a wild island in the Tyrrhenian Sea where people live as though it were the last century. Ponci is the ancestral home of Paul, her late husband; upon arriving, Anya instantly feels that his spirit is somehow present. Fierce wild goats and a horse named Gangster terrorize the inhabitants, most of whom are fishermen and pirates. Anya falls in love with Domingo. He is the pirate chief. At first she waits for him on the hillside, shredding olive leaves and reading Proust, watching for his ship. She adores the black pearls and jeroboams of champagne he brings to her. After a while she sets sail with him, at first observing and then joining in the plundering of yachts. Then, one night, on their way up the hill, Domingo is trampled by Gangster; you get the feeling the horse contains the spirit of Anya's dead husband. With Domingo dead, Anya takes over his pirate vessel. After Paul, there can be no other man for her.

When I finished reading the script, I felt like laughing.

Together Forever had a bizarre sense of humor: black humor. I was left with the sense that Anya's dead husband was haunting her, would never let her be free. And yet, in killing Domingo, he had unleashed a bold primitivism in Anya. It was a fabulous, strange, eccentric story. I sat on the mustard-colored spread and imagined becoming Anya. I wanted that part! The events in Paris, at Palace, rushed through my mind, but now they had a different color. Instead of seeming evil and contrived, they began to serve my purpose. Emile wanted to capture the American female, and I was the person to help him do it.

N E X T stop: Stuttgart, Germany. Where we would meet the wives of men stationed at the Seventh Corps headquarters. On the plane from Belgium I reread Chance's briefing notes and felt high on *Together Forever*. Just to be considered for Anya was a triumph. She was funny, mysterious, and romantic. Delilah's fans would love her. But how could I expect to win such a part? I felt sure that Emile had promised me the audition only because he owed Chance a favor. The papers had already published that picture of us together; perhaps that was all the publicity he wanted from me. My fans would see it, rush to see the next Balfour film, with me in it or not, and that would be that. I ached to bounce my ideas off Jason, but soap opera etiquette prevented me from flaunting movie possibilities to someone stuck in the cast.

I tried to write Sam a letter, but nothing came out right. Why couldn't we go to Nuremberg first, where *his* letter would be waiting? I wanted to see how he felt before I betrayed myself.

I turned the pages over and stared out the window.

"Well, so far it hasn't been too painful, has it?" Jason asked when he saw that I was unoccupied. "I mean, the lunches haven't been bad at all, and Shirley Morris was darling. I love it—a punk army wife."

"It's been okay," I said.

"This will be the high point of my trip," he said, leaning

across me to look out the plane's window. "I plan to forget Terry here. Did you know that Stuttgart means 'stud farm'? Stud garden, literally."

"No, I didn't know that." I glanced at him, amused.

"Well, be forewarned. I intend to raise hell. Fortunately I've visited here before, so I know where to start."

"Jason, what would our ladies' luncheons think if they knew about you?"

"It would disappoint them beyond all measure." He kissed the tip of my nose. Sometimes Jason surprised me; just when he seemed to hit the depths, he would pop up in a great mood. Sitting beside me on the plane, he was humming. "I have to be careful with the army guys, though. They are hostile. I used to live in Washington, D.C., and about five hundred marines stormed into our bar and tore us to shreds."

"Well, marines. They're different."

Jason shook his head vehemently. "No, it's the uniform. It gives people a sense of power. They start thinking they can control everyone's life. I had fifteen stitches." He patted his hip. "Stab wound. I am lucky to be alive. Army, marines . . . they're all the same. It's better to lay low. Of course half of them have prurient interests themselves, which explains why they go so overboard. I mean, you've heard of protesting *too much*? Well, they doth."

I laughed. "Be careful, then. At least we don't meet this group on the base."

"No, in the hotel banquet room. Most likely we shall be spending the rest of this little jaunt in banquet rooms. So I advise you to get loose in your spare time."

Jason cheered me up. By the time we arrived, in yet another limo, at our hotel in Bad Cannstatt, a spa just northwest of Stuttgart, I felt less crazy. I watched the scenery with interest: tall black smokestacks ringing the city; billboards advertising Bosch, Daimler-Benz, and Kodak; finally the woods, gardens, vineyards, and orchards to the north. If Stuttgart was an ugly city, Bad Cannstatt, with its mineral springs and neoclassical Kursaal in the Kurpark, was a lovely suburb. We arrived during the midst of the Cannstatt Folk Festival.

A gala, carnival atmosphere pervaded. Our rooms at the Alfie Haus were neither charming nor disgusting: two double beds, a color TV, and a private bath in a half-timber building designed to look like an American's idea of a Bavarian ducal hunting schloss. We entered, and Jason immediately started talking to our handsome blond bellhop. They were engaged in a rapt conversation (Jason speaking no German, the bellhop speaking very little English, making do with a smattering of French and much body language). One of the carnival's brass bands marched below the hotel's windows. I sat on the edge of one double bed, listening to the raucous music and the receding voices of Jason and the bellhop.

Leafing through the hotel's brochure, I learned that masseuses were available at the hotel's mineral baths. A massage! My neck felt tense and sore from travel and worry. I gathered my bag and a thin white towel and went off to explore the Alfie Haus.

The Alfie Haus: one standard-issue link in a chain of hotels. Probably American-owned. On my travels promoting "Beyond the Bridge" I had stayed in Holland Houses (hotels built to look like windmills); Western Hospitality Inns (motels with an Old West theme: cactus and roadrunner wallpaper, a huge plastic cactus outside the office, tacoburgers in the coffee shop); Galleons (housekeeping cottages whose facades looked like the stern of a brigantine. If you saw these buildings side by side, you would think you were sneaking up on the Spanish Armada). So I did not need directions to find my way through the Alfie Haus. I knew how the pattern red-and-blue carpet would blur to purple in certain badly lighted areas; I knew that the pine-veneer-paneled banquet rooms would flank the hotel dining room (in this case called the Goldene Traube); I knew that the desk clerk would nod at me, then go on watching the festival through the window; I knew that just past the front desk I would find a long corridor which would lead me to the indoor pool, the mineral baths, and the masseuse.

NAKED and choking on steam, I sit with two other frauleins in a vat of seltzer water. Nudity has never bothered me; I stare at their breasts with interest. Each has furrowed pink nipples like mine. Years back Lily started something called "Giving the Tit." Driving down Route 15, she would flash one breast at the oncoming traffic. We never knew whether anyone actually saw it or not, but it exemplified our fascination with breasts. Whenever Margo burped, she would say the word "Brrrrrreast." Lily never burped.

The two German women know each other. Each is holding her brown hair up with one hand, and interrupting the other in a frantic conversation about someone named "Sigi." They ignore me totally. I close my eyes, letting the hot water effervesce against my clitoris, and think of Sam. Alone with Sam in a bubbling mineral bath, visiting Bad Cannstatt for the cure . . . my mouth opens as I await his lips, and here they come, kissing mine; together we sink down into the warm water, pressing together, bubbles everywhere. He is Domingo and I am Anya. The thought is so erotic, I nearly come. If the two women were not here, I would touch myself, give myself an orgasm. White foam hides what goes on beneath the surface; perhaps they would not notice? My hand dips underwater, fingers parting the lips of my cunt, but I don't have the nerve. Sigi, Sigi, Sigi . . . why don't they dry off and finish their conversation in the dressing room? Instead I climb out and pat my pink body dry with my thin hotel towel.

The masseuse, a large strawberry blonde named Wanda, greets me. She spreads some plush towels on a silver table which reminds me of the collapsible metal one my family used to use for picnics, and I climb on. Face down, I close my eyes, and let those muscular arms knead me as if I were dough.

I am pale enough. I would rise into a loaf of white bread, but my crust would never brown. It would look as if someone had scraped my top layer off. The hands push my muscles. Ouch! I say. That *hurts*! But it has to hurt a *little*, Wanda says in good English. You have knots.

I have knots. Knots bind, don't they? Bowlines, half hitches, granny knots, clove hitches, sheet bends, overhand knots, figure eights . . . I knew them all. At eleven I had learned to sail a Bluejay, and I would practice knots by the hour. I could make that boat fast to any dock you could find; I would practice tying knots for hours and hours with a length of clothesline. Even during the winter!

So, you have been here before? Wanda asks in an accent that suddenly, alarmingly, reminds me of Lily and Henk's maid, Ilsa. I don't feel so safe anymore. Perhaps my shoulders got tenser, because Wanda chops then with the edge of her hand.

Where, to Germany? I ask.

Yes. Or to this hotel.

This is my first time in the country. It is very lovely. (I say, although I have seen next to nothing of it, and I have a strange feeling of danger. But I was taught to always be polite to my host.)

I have lived here always.

But your English is so good!

Yes, good, but I learned it in school, not in America or England. The farthest I have been is to Spain. Once I went to the Costa del Sol.

Spain—I've never been there. We're going to Italy later in the trip.

Quit talking now, Wanda says, chopping me again. You have too many knots.

So I close my eyes and pretend that the rough hands are Sam's. They massage my muscles and work their way down my spine. That warm tingle I felt in the bath returns, and I think *go lower*. Go lower! But the hands stay on my back, eventually moving to my legs, but avoiding my ass completely.

THAT afternoon I sent a postcard to Lily and Henk. "Be sure to tell Ilsa that Germany has a lovely countryside," I wrote, certain that Ilsa would read the message herself and save the Voorheeses the trouble.

I strolled through the festival, which stretched through the Cannstatter Meadows along the brownish Neckar River. There were booths attended by women wearing folk costumes, long floral-printed dresses with bodices that pushed their white bosoms up to their chins, spilling like beer froth over the fabric's edge; stands which sold wurst (knockwurst, bockwurst, bratwurst) and lager; brass bands with schoolboys pumping great lungfuls of air into enormous tubas; games of chance and skill; flower vendors. Leaves on the trees had started to change from green to shades of brown and yellow. I found the scene oddly colorless.

A patch of grass beside the river was unoccupied, and I took it. Staring at my notebook for a few minutes, I tried to write to Sam. I told him about the plane ride, the festival, the mineral baths. How I had wished for him to be with me, warm and close in the bubbling water, stroking each other everywhere. Kissing underwater. But the words looked horny instead of erotic. There is a major difference. I imagined Sam, a man I did not (after all) know well, receiving my letter telling him about bathing with two naked female strangers, growing excited and in need of an orgasm, thinking of him while I started to play with myself. "Thinking of you/Wish you were here." No, it would not do.

Absence does not make my heart grow fonder. It makes my brain grow more mazed, my heart grow more distant. I lose the strength of my confidence. Sitting by the Neckar I listened to an oompah band play a polka and felt utterly melancholy. Jason hurried past with the bellhop, now apparently off duty: he had changed out of his uniform into a black turtleneck and tight black trousers. They looked avid, as if they were late for something. Jason would forget Terry in the stud garden. I would moon over Sam while staring at blank paper, but I was far from forgetting anything.

JASON claimed he did not sleep either of the two nights we stayed in Stuttgart. Between meetings with junior army wives, the St. Peter's Mother's Group, and the many factions of officer's wives' clubs, I steered clear of the mineral springs and read guidebooks in my room. I daydreamed about *Together Forever* and reread the script. Lying on one of my beds, all four pillows behind my head, I would keep my ears cocked for Jason. I wished he would drop by and talk to me. *Now* I was ready for a phone call from Margo and Sam, even one reading me the riot act. Why couldn't the 'Celebrity File' have been a few days late in reporting the latest romance? Why couldn't Margo have exploded with righteous indignation now instead of then? Now I was prepared to calmly explain what had happened, to tell Sam that I loved him and that the press was just feeling its oats. Tell him calmly and with some amusement. That telephone call had ruined everything. All I could do now was hope that Emile Balfour would be kind and make me Anya.

OF ALL the places Jason and I visited on our whirlwind tour, Nuremberg was the oddest. I had strange nightmares and a sense of déjà vu the entire time we stayed there. Sliced in half by the Pegnitz River, Nuremberg has an evil, medieval air about it. Moated city, fairytale turrets, damsels in distress, Brothers Grimm, witch's castle, gargoyles, Nazis. The city of Albrecht Dürer, it is also the city of Albert Speer. I felt instantly that I had been there before. I had dreamed of it or had seen it in picture books.

These streets: they echo with the sharp heels of storm troopers. The voices shouting, instructing, recruiting, demanding the citizens to unleash the final solution. Singing allegiance to Hitler. Der Führer. Outside the city is a mammoth stadium where they used to shout the word. Dragging, screaming, scraping, shouting, building, unleashing. Human evil. But there is something else.

DRIVING in from Stuttgart, I asked the chauffeur to stop in front of the Holy Ghost Hospital. It has a Crucifixion Court. It gave me the shivers. I sat in the back seat, leaning forward, staring at the ornate building whose foundations reached into the riverbed, for several minutes before Jason told the driver to drive on.

"What is with you?" he asked.

"I don't know," I answered, but I did. My father had bombed Nuremberg during the war. Before he became a real estate man, before he married my mother, before he sired three daughters, he had been the navigator-bombardier of the Eighth Air Force's lead plane. Perhaps this building, built in the fourteenth century, contained the ghosts who had inspired my father's nights out. The real Blue Danube coursed just a few miles south. Wasn't that significant?

My father trained for the Air Force with a bunch of college-age boys, fighting for their country, afraid of dying, afraid of killing Germans, wanting to kill Nazis. They were sent to England. Misty, green, proud England. Their base was on the Wash, north of London. They lived in a metal Nissen hut which was never free of dampness. They played cards and took leaves in London, where they stayed at the Mayfair, went riding in Hyde Park, got drunk in Piccadilly, saw shows at Covent Garden, kissed girls on Blackfriars' Bridge. They flew missions over Germany and dropped bombs through the clouds on cities they could not see, cities that were only co-ordinates on their charts.

When the bombers flew into German air space like a formation of Canada geese, my father's plane would be at the point of the V. On one mission, he bombed Nuremberg. Sent the wounded, many of them not Nazis, to the Holy Ghost Hospital. My father was twenty-three. No wonder he would always find his way back to The Blue Danube. If you think in terms of *Pilgrimage*, it begins to make some sense.

I thought about my father a lot in Nuremberg. I visualized him not as my father, not as a ghost, but as he had looked then: in his Air Force cap and brown leather bomber's jacket (with the Eighth Air Force insignia and first lieutenant's bars), his big grin and soft brown eyes smiling out of his skinny face, his protruding ears, his long Cavan nose.

Whenever I thought of Sam, whose letter hadn't arrived, I would shake myself up and say how can you think of *that* when your father bombed *this city*. It became the perfect avoidance tactic.

I wished mightily for my father's ghost to visit me. It didn't. Instead I stood on the stage with Jason and talked about my soap opera father, Paul Grant.

DELILAH   Oh, Beck . . . my father will never forgive this jail break. He believes so strongly in the justice system. He promised me I would be free on appeal. In some ways he is so . . . innocent.

BECK   Delilah, darling. Darling. There wasn't *time* to wait out an appeal. We knew about the prison uprising. Did you want to get caught in the crossfire? Don't you imagine that Delilah Grant would make a first-rate hostage? Did you actually think that I would *stand by* and let that happen?

DELILAH   (*docile*). No, I can't imagine that . . . my strong love. You are so good to me. You're risking everything . . . you know that?

BECK   I know that. And your father will understand. Paul Grant is a good man. Soon we will clear your name and come out of hiding. Soon, my love.

Our audience cheered, and some wept. Every woman there had a father and had known, at one time or other, how it felt to disappoint him. Standing on that stage in Nuremberg, entertaining the troops' wives with scenes from my soap opera, I was disappointing my father, James Cavan. He had once told me, Lily, and Margo that we should never visit Germany. Flying alongside the Concorde, he had avoided mentioning my stops in Germany. Of course he would never appear to me here.

BY THE time we reached Vicenza, Italy, our last stop before returning to Paris, I had stopped writing to Sam. Every time I thought about my movie audition, I broke out in shivers. Would I be good enough? Would I be able to improvise? I had learned improvisation, but would I remember how? I felt sure that I would remember *if only* I had graduated. Graduates can improvise, dropouts cannot. Graduates can pull situations out of hats and make them real. If you told Susan Russell to improvise, to act like a drunk mother whose children are home from boarding school for Christmas, she would give you gin and mistletoe. Emile Balfour would tell me to act like a nervous actress auditioning for her first movie role, and I would flop.

I wanted the part so badly, I walked the streets of Vicenza pretending to be an Italian banker, the wife of a colonel in the 509th Airborne Infantry, a lesbian schoolmarm in San Francisco for the gold rush. I wanted to prepare myself for the moment when Emile would say, "Roll 'em!" What harm had been done by that crazy night at Palace? None. I wanted to become his next star. I lay awake in the hotel hoping for it. Voices carried up from the Piazza dei Signori, and I imagined them talking about me. I stared at the white plaster walls, wishing to be adored. I would see my name in reviews and on movie marquees. Wherever I went.

But then my mind would drift to Sam, to our nights on the promontory at Watch Hill when meteors streaked through the black sky and bioluminescent seaweed flashed in the tidal pools, with Sam holding my hand and our toes gripping the salty rocks. We had kissed a lot. We had talked endlessly, and our conversations played themselves for me in my mind. About our families, about New York, about acting and oceanography. I thought of his slim back, his messy black hair, the way his fingers felt on my shoulder. The smell of his skin. The pillowcase I had brought to Europe to remind me of his scent was now as bland as old laundry.

Sam Chamberlain. I thought with wry, detached regret how sad it was that our time together had been so brief. We hadn't had time to forge a strong relationship. We had not really fallen in love; it had been mere romance. It had been the romance of the sea, of September, of the rocks, of the foghorns. Margo the matchmaker: her rare roast beef had been for naught. I lay awake in Vicenza, thinking of how things drift away. My father, literally, was ash, drifting in the sea. My mother, as usual, was drifting in her own watercolored world. Lily had married Henk, and she was drifting toward motherhood. Margo would drift away after she married Matt. And Sam had drifted away as abruptly as he had arrived. The ebb tide was swifter than the flood. One by one, the people I loved would all leave. But if I became a big star, at least I would be adored. *You saw* how they followed Emile Balfour; you saw how they stared at him as if they knew him. They love you as Delilah, I told myself, but that was different. That was limited. Lonely women, American women, who tuned in daily. I wanted to be adored worldwide. Lying in bed I thought of my faceless public adoring me, replacing Sam. He had probably already given me up. I thought that, but I lay awake, watching the headlights of passing cars arc across my ceiling and hoped hoped hoped. Hoped that everything I feared would not be true.

L<small>IGHTS</small>, *camera, action*. Three men slouch in easy chairs, smoking cigarettes, watching the stage, which is only a floor cleared of furniture, with lights trained on it from above. Portable metal spotlights clipped onto heating pipes. One camera records everything. My auburn hair brushes my white throat and the shoulders of my black leotard as I swing my head. I smile at the men, then I smile into the camera.

"Her lines are exquisite," one man, the American, is saying.

I am a ship, a yacht, a white sloop slicing the waves off Napatree Point.

"Okay. We are rolling. Una, how do you feel?" Emile Balfour asks, blowing a cloud of smoke into the air. I see it disperse in the bright light.

"Great. Just fine."

"Turn your face to the left, there," he says. "Now to the right. You ready to talk?"

"Yes."

"Go ahead."

I take a deep breath.

"Just say whatever comes into your mind."

Whatever? Another deep breath. Okay, whatever. "Zoon, zoon, cuddle and croon," I say, remembering one of Lily's favorite nursery rhymes, and then I think of Hecate and the three weird sisters. " 'When shall we three meet again? In wind, in fire, in rain? When the hurly-burly's done, when the battle's lost and won.' " The battle. Battle scars. I think of Nuremberg. I am a young mother, a secret Jew. No one knows. I'm coming home from the market; my bag is heavy with fresh milk, eggs, and crackers. Some bittersweet chocolate given to me at the Resistance meeting. Those Resistance members always seem to have contraband. I cannot wait to give it to my children, little Eric and Susie. But my house is gone. There is a gap where it stood this morning. Plumes of smoke rise from the rubble, and flames lick the timbers. A siren wails. Neighbors hurry toward me, take my bag, push me down on the curb. They press my head to my knees; I am going to faint. All the while I am saying, "Eric . . . Susie." I am in a trance and tears run down my face.

"Good. Whatever that is, it is good," the American calls.

I had forgotten them, my panel of judges. Not forgotten, but transcended. Here I am, improvising like a graduate. The American said it was good. But now my concentration is shot. I can't think of Nuremberg anymore. I'd better come up with something else.

"Tell me, what does your husband do, Mrs. Spock?" Emile Balfour asks. The other men giggle.

"Mah husband?" I ask in a southern drawl, letting my hand dangle in front of my breast. I pat my hair, adjust my collar, let my hands flutter. "Whah, he's a scab. Crosses picket lines all day long. No matter where you got a strike, you just call Ralston, and he'll take the job."

"A *scab*?" Emile asks one of the men.

"Let her go on," the American says, laughing. "So he's a scab. What about you? You work?"

"Yes, I promote birth control." Where did that come from? I feel myself get hot.

"But you have kids, right?"

"Kids? Do I have kids? Honey, you must be joking. I am one of the leaders of the movement. I practice what I preach. No kids. No kids whatsoever."

"No, but you like to get laid, right?"

"Well, of course. Of course. I am a natural woman. Nat—"

"Okay, take it to Italy, babe," the American says. "Do it for Emile. He's a little fuzzy on the Alabama stuff. You're on the boot. In Rome or somewhere."

Italian. I could do an Italian voice. In New York I had an Italian friend who worked for the Metropolitan Opera. She wished to sing, but she worked in the wardrobe, preparing

costumes for the divas. She always had a threaded needle
stuck through her lapel. During her free time she sculpted in
pink clay. She had had several exhibits in SoHo, and she was
terribly imperious.

I screw up my face and slash the air with my hand. "Why
do you copy Picasso, Gauguin? You must learn to be *o-reeginal.*"

"But I want to be an artiste," Emile says, falsetto. He
slouches low in his vinyl seat.

"This is not art. Now . . . to sculpt in pink clay. *That* is art.
That is o-reeginal. Do you understand?"

"Yes, I do."

(Impatient wave.) "He doesn't understand."

"Tell me, Angela . . ." Emile pauses while the other men
giggle. "Are you in love?"

I bow my head, covering my face with one hand. I come up
smiling shyly. "Oh, yes. He is a sailor. He is away for many
months, and then I meet him at the wharf. We *cry* together."
I roll my *r*'s when I say "cry." "I bring him to my house
where I cook him pancakes because he is so sick of fish."

"Okay, Una. Break now."

The camera stops whirring. I blink my eyes as I step out
of the bright light. The men remain low in their chairs. A
full ashtray sits before them on the low table. They look at
me, waiting for me to speak. Finally Emile rises and shakes
my hand.

"Thank you. Now we must wait to see you on film."

"That's it?"

Everyone laughs. The man who has not spoken stands and
kisses both my cheeks. "What, did you think we would say,
'Hey, you've got the job'?"

I scowl, but I turn it into a smile. Of course I did, you
pompous French creep. "No," I say. "I just wondered what
you thought."

"But that is highly subjective," Emile says, his forehead
creasing with amusement. He brings the tiniest nub of a burning cigarette to his lips with a gold toothpick. "We have not
had a chance to get together and discuss it. Perhaps I loved

you, but Jean hated you. You must give me the chance to say, 'But *why* did you hate her? You must love her because she has the spark, the life . . .' You know?"

I nod my head so loosely it flaps. My expression says, "Oh, I am so naive!" It makes all three men laugh. Emile steps a bit closer. He stares directly into my eyes. "Later?" I say.

"At the Crillon."

A L T H O U G H it was just one and a half weeks since we had left Paris, the city seemed colder, more autumnal, full of the rasping sound of leaves blowing down the avenues. At the flower market, where I had sat to write a letter to Sam, I saw bunches of colored leaves and dry grasses instead of the brilliant summer flowers. Autumn is my favorite season; it renews me. But that week I felt tired, as if I might be coming down with the flu.

To reward us for such a successful publicity tour, Chance Schutz had insisted that Jason and I spend three days in Paris, compliments of him and Billy. It was another example of Chance's boundless generosity. He believed in rewarding people for work well done. Our work was finished; I had expected to pay myself for the time I spent auditioning, and Jason had no reason at all to stay in Paris. But we accepted. My new room at Hôtel de Crillon faced the Place de la Concorde; traffic flowed past on the avenue, but no sound penetrated the sealed windows. I tried to open them, the way I had my windows overlooking the interior courtyard, but apparently guests were not to be subjected to street noises. I sat in my Louis XVI chair and rummaged through the desk for stationery. When I found it, I closed the drawer without taking any out.

I paced the sleek room. The heavy architectural details were set off by shades of brown, cream, and black. I should have been wearing a Chanel suit with alligator sling-back shoes. I was in desparate need of an ebony cigarette holder. The room's sophistication daunted me. I grabbed my blue jeans and pulled them on. I didn't even brush my hair. Grabbing my black bag, I hurried down the hall and knocked on Jason's door.

"Yes?" he said, leaning against the doorframe in his silk robe. In my house the fine fibers would have caught on a splinter or a rough spot, but the Crillon's heavy enamel paint made the wood as smooth as metal.

"Let's bust out of here," I said.

"And go where?"

"I don't know. You know Paris, don't you? Will you show me a few sights?"

"Darling, dressed like that you are barely fit for the Latin Quarter. I mean, the Ugly *American*. Is the Latin Quarter what you had in mind?"

"Sure. Anything."

"She who just auditioned for Balfour the Great One," he said, and I didn't reply. "Okay," he said dubiously. "Give me a bit to get ready. We'll take separate elevators down, if you don't mind. You are really too, too déclassé."

"Why don't I just meet you on the wall by the fountain? And spare you the embarrassment."

"Fine. Thirty minutes."

It took fifty minutes, but I didn't mind. I leaned on the concrete wall by the Place de la Concorde and shivered in the chilly air. I felt excited, the way I used to feel when my family would travel to Washington, D.C., for spring vacation and we would prepare to tour the Lincoln Memorial by night, the Smithsonian by day. Cherry blossoms, the Spirit of St. Louis, the Capitol Rotunda, the Botanical Gardens. One time we had seen the Washington Senators play a twilight doubleheader.

Jason's mother was French; he would know all the good places to go. Leaning on that wall, my head tossed back to view the obelisk against the blue sky, I felt independent. The trouble had been (I told myself) that I depended too much on my sisters. On boyfriends. I had not developed a circle of good friends. There was Susan, of course, but soon she would go on tour with *Hester's Sister*. Besides, Susan alone could not be considered a circle of friends. I thought of Sam, and the pain I felt was fresh. I had stopped wondering what had happened to his letter: it was probably lost in the mail, held up at the airport (but which airport? It had to pass through so many), the address smeared and unreadable. It didn't matter. *I* was pulling back. I was the one who didn't trust my old feelings ("Oh, those old things?"). Or the strength of his. Better to simply rise on the crest of a movie audition.

Jason, looking like a smash in his supple leather jacket and matching pants, walked along the promenade. He wore a maroon scarf around his neck and smoked a black cigarette. The wind blew his brown hair straight back, accentuating his receding hairline, but he still looked strikingly handsome.

"My, you're so continental," I said.

He bowed. "And you look like a rube."

"I'm sick of riding in limousines and feeling *très élégante.* Take me somewhere meaty."

"Somewhere meaty? Let's see. The Rive Gauche . . . over by the Sorbonne."

"Is that very blue collar and grimy?"

He shook his head. "No, it's very Greenwich Village. Where the bourgeois mingle with the intellectuals and pretend they're bohemian."

"I'd rather go somewhere different." I wanted him to take me to visit his mother. I could just imagine how thrilled she would be to see us. I pictured her: a stooped old lady, frail, white hair, lace doilies everywhere, a portrait of De Gaulle hanging above the mantel. "Didn't you say you have relatives here?"

He gave me a sharp look. "No, we are *not* going to visit them. My old aunts. They would die if they ever saw me coming."

"Your old aunts?"

"Yes, my mother's sisters. And that's all you'll get me to say about them. Didn't you say you wanted to see the Rodin Museum?"

"Wait, your mother had two sisters? Three girls?"

"Yes, three girls, just like you insufferable Cavans. Now drop the subject, and let's walk. I'll take you to see *The Kiss.*"

"Jason, is your mother still alive?"

"No, dear. Not since I was twenty-six." Taking my arm, he led us toward the Seine. A breeze followed its banks, blowing my hair into my mouth. We crossed a low stone bridge; a sightseeing boat chuffed toward us, the guide's voice wafting out of a loudspeaker.

"Well, I seem to have gotten you onto the Left Bank," Jason said, the instant we stepped onto land. "We'll go to Les Invalides."

Les Invalides. The name reminded me of Nuremberg, of the Holy Ghost Hospital. Jason and I walked through the square, the huge hospital buildings towering overhead. The heels of his boots clicked on the cobbles.

"There," he said, "is the Hotel Biron. Inside is the Rodin Museum. Rodin had his studio there at one time. Isn't it perfect?" Jason regarded the building with one eye closed, as though it were his own architectural masterpiece.

"It's gorgeous," I said, trying to remember every detail so that I could tell Margo. Just as in Vicenza I had visited the Church of San Lorenzo, so that I could tell Lily about the frescoes by Montagna and Buonconsiglio. My private art historians.

Jason and I toured the museum, and I bought postcards and a book for Margo. "You mind if I run to the men's room?" Jason asked when we were standing in the sculpture garden.

"Not at all." I sat on a bench. I pulled a pen out of my bag. I looked through the postcards I had just bought; there were two of *The Kiss*, that most passionate sculpture of two lovers entwined. On the back of one I wrote:

DEAR SAM, I am back in Paris, thinking of you. Soon I shall return to New York. I saw this sculpture, and I remembered Watch Hill. The thunderstorm in the turret room . . . I can't wait to see you. Your letter never arrived in Nuremberg.

Love, U N A

Then I found a French stamp in my wallet; I had bought twelve from the concierge on my last visit. I fixed it to the card. Jason returned a moment later, touching his fly to make sure he had closed it. The motion was surreptitious; he had not intended for anyone to see. But I saw. We walked toward the Latin Quarter. I dropped the card into the first postbox we passed.

THAT night Emile Balfour came to the Hôtel de Crillon to buy me dinner in Les Ambassadeurs, the hotel dining room. I wore a sapphire jumper over a black body stocking. My eyes were rimmed with matching blue shadow, and my eyelids looked like bluebird wings. I had never seen my eyes themselves look bluer. Nothing was too outrageous in Paris; I wanted to make heads turn. Just before Emile rang my room, I tried to reach Sam in New York. His phone rang fourteen times before I decided he must still be uptown, at his Columbia office.

Les Ambassadeurs, just off the hotel lobby, is spectacular. It is paneled in ten different varieties of marble and has the most extravagant flower arrangements I have ever seen. Emile's hand rested lightly on my waist as we passed through the room, beneath the crystal chandeliers and a ceiling medallion painted with clouds. A frieze of cherubs ran around the room; I glanced up at the fat little angels instead of at the tables full of people who were watching us and pretending not to. Little angels watching over me and Emile Balfour, protecting us from evil forever and ever amen. I thought of them as agents of my father. Would he approve of this meeting? Yes, as long as I didn't invite Emile upstairs for a nightcap.

Emile and the maître d' stood erect, like armed guards or subordinates, while I sat down. Then Emile took his seat, and we smiled, listening to strains of piano music.

"Well," he said, still smiling. "I have something to tell you."

I already knew. I could tell by his pleased expression, by the way he tapped his knife with perfectly manicured fingernails. I smiled back with what I hoped was a curious expression on my face. A waiter came to ask what we would like to drink, but Emile and I were engaged in smiling at each other, and the waiter soon left.

"I am prepared to offer you Anya," Emile said. "You will

be perfect for her. You have an elusive quality about you . . . but, you have been told that before, *non?*"

"No, not exactly," I said, my heart racing, wanting to hear more.

"You are well known in the United States, but by a very precious group. Your viewers are dominantly female."

"That's true," I said, seeing an image of dominant female viewers: dressed in tattered loincloths, muscled and brown, sun-bleached hair askew, dragging their men around by their neckties. "Mainly women watch the show, but there are some men—"

Emile waved his hand, dismissing the need to say more. "We want you because you are a newcomer to movies, but a proven talent. With a very loyal following. New but not new. We have it both ways. Also, it is very camp to cast a big soap opera actress."

"Thank you." It took a supreme physical effort to remain seated. I willed myself to not fly to the telephone and call Sam, Margo, Lily, Chance . . . I sat on my hands instead.

"Those men at the studio," I said. "Were they producers?"

"Yes."

"And they liked me?"

"They like who I tell them to like. They give me total artistic control, or they don't get me to direct. You are prepared to spend four months on Corsica next summer?"

Next summer. Now it was October, and I would have all winter to prepare myself for the part and to leave home. Home: Hudson Street, New York, the eastern seaboard, the United States. I had never lived outside the United States before; I had taken vacations in St. Barthélemy, Canada, and Scotland before, and I had just returned from a three-week tour of Europe. But I had never lived in a foreign country. Could Corsicans speak English? I thought of a thousand questions, but I didn't ask them. I just sat there, smiling with ecstasy at Emile while he ordered champagne, and thought of the things I would miss most. *Not* New York in the summer. But other things. By then Lily's baby would be six months old. I would miss half of its first year. And Matt and Margo would be married, and I could take another vacation at the

Ninigret Inn. By then it would be family turf. Sam. I would miss Sam.

"What did you mean when you said it was camp to cast a soap opera actress?" I asked.

"I am already imagining promotion for the film. It will be unlike anything I have done before. No lonely landscapes, no stormy seas. It will be very Forties, with a red heart framing you and your lover, and splashy graphics. It will be fantastic."

I thought this over, feeling slightly disappointed that *Together Forever* would not be a *typical* Balfour film. "Who will play Domingo?" I asked.

"Another unknown. We have not cast him yet. He will be French."

Horrible thought! "I don't speak French—will I have to learn it?"

Emile laughed loudly. "Una, you can't learn French in eight months. I mean, you can learn what the words mean, but forget speaking it like a Frenchman. No, we're filming in English. Everything about *Together Forever* will be new for me. New faces, new style. It will be larger than life. What did you think of the script?"

"I adored it," I said, grinning at the memory. I shivered with pleasure at the idea of being Anya. The part *was* a little camp; it was funny in ways that Balfour heroines never were.

"So, you accept the part?"

I tilted my head. "I'd say yes, but I have to talk—"

"Of course, of course. You need an advisor. But it will mean fabulous things for your career. The next time we dine here, everyone will be looking at you instead of me."

The champagne arrived; this time Emile allowed the waiter to open the bottle. He raised his glass to toast.

"I drink to your mystery," he said.

"My mystery!" I put on my best Mata Hari face.

But Emile was serious. He rested his arm across the back of my seat, waiting for my giggles to pass. "You laugh?" he asked, raising one eyebrow.

"A little," I said, feeling stupid for saying so, so soon after I had had such obvious difficulty stopping.

"But why? When you are so veiled? Isn't that mystery? Do you think I read you wrong?"

"Oh, no." Vehement headshaking. "Not at all. I'm flattered, and I guess flattery makes me nervous. So I giggle." Giggle, giggle.

"You see. That is just what I mean. An actress like you, with millions and millions of fans, and you are uncomfortable with flattery. I find that a fresh quality." He touched the back of my neck with one finger.

Now I knew what was happening. Emile ordered our dinner, speaking to the waiter but watching me the entire time. Bring her to Paris, send out the word that you are lovers, offer her a part, and make your word come true. I would end up in bed with Emile Balfour before the night was through.

Our beautiful food looked like paint on a palette. The delicately sliced vegetables, so bright against the saffron sauce . . . the tiny sprigs of mint . . . the tiny pink sea urchins . . . the thin slices of rare beef. Midway through our entree, a waiter whispered something to Emile. He raised his eyes toward the medallion of clouds, then leaned toward me. "A telephone call which I must take. You will excuse me for a minute?"

"Oh, of course."

I prodded julienned bits around my plate, creating wells of sauce. Moments passed, and tension flooded my brain. I felt that I had a very short time to decide *what to do*. All through this trip I had lamented tradeoffs. Give me love, I give you sex. Give me love, I give you loyalty. Give me a part in your next movie, I give you anything you ask. It wasn't as if they had to torture me to do it. I went willingly up the golden stairs. All the men I had slept with had been nice, attractive, loving. I could truthfully say that I loved them all—then and now. Even John Luddington. We had given each other pleasure, and they had given me the feeling of love.

When Lily and I were in high school and Margo was still in eighth grade, we had believed the lyrics of love songs: Richard Rodgers, Carly Simon, Jackson Browne, Cole Porter. I thought of one now and hummed it while gazing at the frieze of cherubs. My sisters and I would drive along, six breasts abreast in the Volvo's front seat, singing songs while Margo smoked and Lily gave the tit to oncoming cars. Would it be so bad for me to sleep with Emile Balfour? I wondered about that for a while, then I hated myself for wondering it. Three weeks ago I had fallen in love with Sam Chamberlain. Did it matter that I hadn't heard from him? I knew it shouldn't. I knew that I should coast on blind faith, counting the days until I could return home again. *His* was the sort of love I had been seeking all these years. Emile was only a director, albeit handsome as hell, offering me a lovely part and loads of lovely money. It was time I learned the difference.

When Emile returned I had eaten all the julienned strips off my plate. I grinned widely. "Anything important?"

"Nothing that can't wait." He summoned the waiter and ordered espresso and glace caramel.

As if given the nod, a tuxedoed man sidled to our table, tape recorder in palm, and spoke to Emile in French. Emile graciously gestured at the empty space across the table, and a waiter whisked over a chair. I figured it out. I was an old hand at this. Emile had tipped this reporter that we would be dining at Les Ambassadeurs, and that he would be welcome to interview us after dessert had been ordered.

The man made a ceremony of clearing a space for the tape recorder, turning it on, and blowing into the speaker. Then, leaning his folded arms on the white tablecloth, he looked solemnly from Emile to me. "There is a rumor," he said without inflection, as if he were about to ask us about graft or corruption instead of a movie.

"Excuse me," I said, "but I don't know your name."

The man looked wildly at Emile, then relaxed. "*Pardonnez-moi*. I am Claude Troublais, Mademoiselle Cavan. I am a journalist."

"But you already knew *that*, didn't you, Una?" Emile asked, twinkling at me. I nodded.

"There is a rumor," Claude began again, "that you have just signed Mademoiselle Cavan to do your next picture. That filming will take place on Corsica. Is that true?"

"Claude, everyone knows I will shoot my picture on Corsica. I have already been quoted in the press. It is truth, not rumor."

Claude cracked his first smile. "Okay, but what about Una Cavan? We have heard that contracts are being negotiated, and here you are at Les Ambassadeurs. Who is your agent, Mademoiselle?"

"Georgianna Attwood," I said, thinking how tickled Georgie would be to read her name in the gossip columns.

"And is it true? That she is negotiating with Emile Balfour's lawyers for your contract?"

"Una would rather not discuss that, Claude," Emile said, cupping my hand with his. He patted it, keeping it under cover. "Let us just say that if we are lucky we shall have her."

"Then she said yes?" Excitement danced across his face, as if he were asking his brother or best friend about popping the question.

Emile nodded at me, letting me know I should speak for myself. "Probably," I said.

"*Magnifique!*" Claude said, clapping his hands together. Then he turned to Emile and started questioning him in French, the way Arnaud had that time at Palace. I was excluded, but this time I did not mind. I sat there feeling liberated of indecision. I was Una, not Delilah or Anya. I loved Sam Chamberlain, not Emile Balfour. I would thank Emile profoundly, but I wouldn't sleep with him out of hope or gratefulness. I would act in his movie. People of the world would read "Celebrity File" and think that Emile and I were lovers, but I would know that we were not. Sam would know that we were not, because as soon as this interview was over I would call to tell him. Meanwhile, waiting for Claude to go away, I looked around the dining room, at each diner, at each cherub, and I hummed "Loads of Love." For that moment, I was full of it.

ALONE in my room I stripped out of my body stocking and put on my white nightshirt. Then I sat in my armchair and dialed Sam's number in New York.

"Hello?" came his warm, lovely, Sammish voice, answering his phone with a question.

"*Bonjour*! This is your movie star calling." I bounced on my seat with excitement. I felt so *connected*!

"Una?"

I went a little flat. *He* didn't sound very excited at all. "Yes, it's Una. Do we have a bad connection?"

"No, no. It's fine."

Then why do you sound so strange? I thought angrily. "Guess what? I got the part! I just finished dinner with Emile, so don't worry when you read about it in the paper, it was just a regular business dinner with a reporter for dessert, but he offered me *the part*!"

"That is great. Congratulations. When do you start?"

"Next summer. I have to be in Corsica from June through September. It's an island in the Mediterranean—French, even though it's closer to Italy, supposedly very wild and rugged, and . . ." I was babbling. I took a deep breath and tried to stop thinking what's wrong what's wrong what's wrong . . .

"I've been to Corsica. It's great for snorkeling, except for the currents. They're wicked. I know a biologist, got sucked into a cave by a current."

Here we were, having a transatlantic conversation about our professions. Wonderful. The line went silent for a few seconds. I hated myself, but I had to ask: "Is something wrong?"

Pause. Breath. Longer pause. "No, not really."

"Come on. Tell me."

"I said nothing was wrong."

"Then why do you sound so pissed off?" My voice rose with hysteria on "off." I fought to keep it down.

"Well, I suppose it's the photos I keep seeing of you and Emile Balfour all over the papers."

"*Photos*? I've only been with him twice. Three times, if you count my audition, but then we were in a *crowd*."

"Granted, it's the same photo, but it's all over town. You're the new hot couple."

"I thought *we* were."

"Yeah, so did I."

How touching! Sam was jealous. Instead of feeling warm and loved, however, I felt uncomfortable. I had no idea of how to assure him. I had been away from him for longer than we had been together in Watch Hill. I turned brusque. "Listen, I'm coming back to New York tomorrow. I just wanted to tell you." In case you *care*—what a joke!

"Good. I'm glad. Call me when you get home."

"Of course." Pause. "Goodnight."

"Goodnight."

I had expected him to be thrilled for me, slavering with passion, promising to meet me at Kennedy Airport. When Emile had thought about framing *Together Forever* with red hearts, it had made me think of reuniting with Sam. I lay on my back, looking up at the beautifully molded ceiling. I was sleepless in the Hôtel de Crillon, but it might as well have been that fleabag in Brussels. Sleepless is sleepless.

ON the flight back to New York, Jason asked me all about my audition and plans to leave the show. We talked nervously, as though our words were converging but our thoughts going in separate directions. I imagined bubbles over our heads. Jason's bubble contained an image of himself and Terry, back to back, angry expressions on their faces, and the word "Why?" My bubble contained an image of me and Sam, back to back, angry expressions on our faces, and the word "Who?"

"So, after the four months on Corsica, do you think you'll come back to 'Beyond'?" Jason asked, fidgeting with his ascot.

"I don't know. I guess it depends."

"Yes, you might get another movie role."

"Or maybe Chance will replace me."

"Oh, I doubt that. He's so fond of you."

I tried to think of some polite rejoinder. Chatter was the only way to fill the time, to keep from hoping that Sam had decided to surprise me at the airport.

"He'll have to find a new love interest for Beck," I said.

"What did he say when you told him about the audition?"

"I haven't spoken to him yet. I sent a telegram."

"I can't believe you have a movie to do. In some ways, I could kill you."

"Thank you," I said, smiling at Jason. It was so nice to have the envy of my colleagues. He knew what I meant; he smiled back at me. It was the only time during our flight that we actually connected. But immediately we went back to our waltz of distraction, asking polite questions, giving polite answers, wondering what would happen back in New York.

Terry met Jason at the airport. Coming through customs, we could see him craning his neck and waving madly.

"I knew it," Jason said, exhaling a long breath. His face and neck glistened with a thin sheen of sweat. "I bought him a present in Stuttgart, just in case."

For the first time in three weeks, I had to hail a cab.

MY APARTMENT smelled like dust and old sunlight. I opened a window to let in some October air. Oktoberair. It made me think of Germany and beer. Then I began looking through my mail. Going through the motions as though I were improvising for Emile Balfour: woman returns home alone from Europe. I didn't even have a dog waiting for me at some kennel. For a second I considered calling Margo or Lily, to fill in the details I had been too cheap to include in my telegrams, but I didn't. I sat at my kitchen table feeling very far from home.

I had told Sam I would call when I returned. Dutifully I dialed his apartment number, but he did not answer. He would still be at Columbia, and I didn't have his office number there. I considered calling the switchboard. Then I remembered how hurt I had felt in Paris, and I went into my bedroom to sleep off the jet lag.

Some enchanted promontory . . . sleeping, I dreamed of Watch Hill, Sam, and the black zone of shore. Suddenly I was in a romantic New England Brigadoon . . . Beyond the Bridge . . . over the rainbow . . . where things could happen that would never happen in New York or real life. I slept, wakened, slept, wakened. The word "fitfully" flew to mind in one of those dream-scoured moments of awareness. That same instant I grabbed the phone and dialed Sam's number.

"Hello?" He answered his telephone, as he had when I had called from Paris, with a question.

"Hi, Sam. I'm back."

"You're in New York?"

"In fact, I'm in my apartment." In my bed.

"Have you had dinner yet?"

Dinner? What time was it, anyway? "No, I haven't."

"Okay, what's your address again? I'll be right over with something. Unless you want to come here."

He was coming over. I ran to the bathroom and examined my eyes in the mirror. Cloudy and shadowed. I splashed cool water on them, wishing I had time to lie down and cover them with damp tea bags for ten minutes or so. I pulled on a pair of faded jeans under my white nightshirt and paced the apartment until he arrived. He rang the doorbell downstairs and I buzzed him in. Then I paced in a two-foot-square patch of foyer while I listened to the elevator rise on its ancient, creaky cables. First floor, second floor, up, up, up. Then the elevator doors opened and Sam Chamberlain was standing in my hallway. He was right on the other side of my door. I had been all through Europe and returned to New York, and at last Sam and I were separated by nothing vaster than a door. No ocean, no transatlantic cable, no "Celebrity File." I waited half a second after his knock, then pulled open the last barrier.

We stood there staring at each other. His hair looked longer, not quite as messy as it had in windy Watch Hill. His tan had faded, and there were tiny white lines around his hazel eyes. The eyes of a faun; they gleamed and smiled at the sight of me. I took it all in: the blue oxford-cloth shirt, the brown tweed jacket, his khaki trousers. The only unfamiliar apparel were his shoes, black wingtips instead of holey sneakers or bare feet. He held an aromatic bag of Chinese food in his left hand.

"Hello," he said, stepping into my apartment, swinging his arms around me and pressing the hot bag of food into my back while he kissed me, long and lovingly, our tongues twisting together until I was unsure whether I was melting from the back or from the front.

"It is so good to be back," I said into his mouth.

"It is so, so good to have you back," he said into mine.

I took the bag from him and placed it on my spotless kitchen counter. Holding hands, we walked into my bedroom, to my bed still warm from my recent, fitful sleep. Warm orange light from my reading lamp cast cozy shadows around the room. The lampshade was amber glass painted with two frolicking figures; I had bought it from an antique dealer who had told me it dated back to the 1800s. Sam looked at it, then at my bookshelf, my tall mahogany bureau, my wicker rocking chair, getting acquainted with it all. Then he looked back

at me and we started kissing again, as though we had an un-
spoken agreement to not break physical contact for more than
seconds at a time. Pressing close, I could feel his erection
through our clothes. It dug into my belly. Our mouths partly
open, our kisses were softer now, because we knew we had all
the time we wanted. They made me feel as if I might faint.

We drew apart. Sam's expression looked startled for an instant, as if he hadn't quite expected to see me standing there.

"What?" I asked, amused, but he only smiled and shook his
head.

"I can't believe you're back."

"I can't either. This feels different from Watch Hill."

"It's not." He stared directly into my eyes, beginning to unbutton my shirt buttons. I wore no bra; Sam lowered his head
to my breasts and began to kiss my nipples and then to suck
them, circling them with his tongue. He undid his belt. I heard
the scratchy sound of his zipper going down. He eased me onto
the bed; I lay back, watching him undress in the orange light.
His erect penis stood at a sharp angle to his flat belly, bobbing
as he bent to pull off his pants, then as he came to me and
pulled off my jeans. He gazed at my body which I knew was
very pale. I made a self-conscious move to cover my breasts
with my hands, but he took my hands in his and held them out
on the bed. Lowering himself onto me, his body felt hot. It
made me forget the cool October air swirling around us. He
kissed my throat and the hollow of my neck and then my
mouth until I felt as though I might faint again. He kissed me
all the way down my body. I closed my eyes and felt him let
go of my hands. Then he was gently probing my cunt with
his tongue, pushing open my lips, revealing my clitoris, then
licking it in small circles so that suddenly everything was
circles, my cunt, my clitoris, his cock, his ass, my breasts, our
mouths. His fingers found my nipples and caressed them until
I shuddered into a violent orgasm.

But he wouldn't let me rest. He knelt above me, so that I
was looking straight up at his body, at the underside of his
cock and balls, the semicircles of his ass, and I reached for his
narrow hips, pulling them down so I could kiss his penis. I
felt its purple pulse throb against the tip of my tongue. I was

shivering from the chilly air because I no longer had the heat of his body against me. He must have known; he came down beside me and rolled me onto my side. His cock pressed into the furrow of my ass. Reaching down, he guided it into my cunt and began to move in a slow rhythm like waves of good jazz. He thrust in and out; we had never done it that way before, his front pressed against my back, and I shivered with boldness. I touched myself with my own fingers, which excited him further and made him move urgently, reaching around to touch my breasts, rolling the nipple of first one, then the other, between his fingers, making me groan with pleasure. I felt myself starting to come, and as I began to, I felt it growing in him, felt him grip one breast, and heard his sound, a fierce exhalation that made me think of a warrior, and we both climaxed, I about twenty seconds later than he.

They were the longest twenty seconds of my life.

During them, I nearly lost the edge. I was on the verge; I had the most delirious sensation of being in synch with the man I loved, the man with whom I had just reunited after three difficult, lonely weeks in Europe, but then his cock pulsed and spat and I was alone, masturbating while he lay limp within me, his head peeking over my shoulder, willing me to come, cheering me on. My middle finger hesitated. I had never done this in front of a man before. It was a night of firsts: reunion after troubled separation, fucking on our sides, and masturbating in full view of my lover. Well, not really masturbating; I mean, weren't we making love? My finger waited for the signal from my brain. It was greased with fluid from my cunt and Sam's semen, and it nearly slid out of control, like a delivery boy crashing on a patch of glare ice, without the message from above. But then came the moment of hesitation. Sam's dark, satisfied eyes watched to see what it would do. My own eyes watched as well, but they could see only my pale thigh and my soggy pubic hair. Do it! my brain said like a drill sergeant, and the finger took its command like an underling.

"Well," I said, really embarrassed, rolling onto my back and slipping my arms around Sam.

"That was really exciting," he said, grinning, pressing his still or already erect cock against my thigh.

False alarm. We gathered a bit of steam, then decided it could wait. We had all night. All week. And longer, in fact.

"Now are you convinced that the 'Celebrity File' was a bunch of crap?" I asked, snuggling under the covers into Sam's armpit.

"Yes. I'm very relieved. I know it sounds mental, but you should have been here, walking into a drugstore and seeing your face smiling up from every tabloid in town. With Pretty Boy Emily."

"Emile," I corrected. "He's not bad at all. He just wants some free publicity."

"Oh, sure. But I bet he made a pass at you."

I still was unsure of how to interpret that last night at the Crillon, when Emile had touched the back of my neck. My father would have said it was a pass. In any event, I wanted to test my powers. "Well, a little one. But it was firmly rejected."

"But you were probably tempted. After all, you and I haven't been together for long, and you couldn't have felt as though you had much of a commitment to me."

"Well, yes and no," I said, suddenly feeling profound. "I mean, we haven't pledged undying love to each other, but on the other hand, we *did* say that we loved each other. Which isn't exactly a commitment, but isn't Jell-o either."

"Jell-o?"

"Well, chopped liver. In other words, I did feel a strong bond with you. Even though I didn't get one letter the entire time."

"You're kidding. I sent a bunch to Nuremberg. The day you left, in fact, I wrote a long one in the turret room. Matt and Margo insisted I stay there."

"They did?" I had a great image of Sam, alone and lonely in the turret room, writing me a letter on the same bed where we had made torrential love during the lightning storm. "I never got any letters at all. Did you get mine?"

"Three of them," he said. "They kept me from completely believing that news story about you and Emily."

"I am really sorry about that," I said, not feeling sorry at all. It was wonderful to know that Sam had suffered the same doubts I had. Insecurity had not been mine alone, a fact which caused me pause and relief.

"You are forgiven. Now tell me about the movie."

I spared no details. I synopsized the story, then told about the audition, the offer, the arrangement for next summer.

"Four months, huh?"

"Yes, four months, which seems like a long time but probably won't feel like it." I spoke breezily, trying to disguise my fear that the idea of an upcoming four-month separation would prove to be more than our precarious reunion could take. But I had a fantasy: that he would get grant money to study seaweed on Corsica or nearby Sardinia, and that we could live together like Anya and Domingo in a white bungalow with bougainvillea dripping over the windows. We would get married by the black-clad parish priest (his sturdy hat topped by a black pompom), and spend summer afternoons shredding olive leaves and giving each other open-mouthed kisses on the hillside. The steep hillside. Keeping Sam/ Domingo away from dangerous underwater currents and Gangster. Marriage to Sam. The thought made me wiggle closer to him.

THE next day Sam left for work while I slept late. I called Lily just before noon.

"Darling, welcome back!" she said in a tone so sure and confident it made me suspicious. No one her age should have the authority to say "darling."

"Did you get my lamb?" I asked.

"Yes, we did. It was sweet. Henk loved it too. You were so darl—dear to do it."

"I'm glad you liked it." Alarms were ringing. Lily sounded less like Lily than she had the last time I had spoken to her. There was a veneer, a coating that was not quite dry, and I would see if I could crack or at least bend it. "Will you and

Henk come for dinner? I'd love to see you, and I want you to meet Sam. Remember Sam?"

"The voice from Watch Hill?"

"Right. How's tomorrow?"

"Tomorrow. Hmmm. I'd better see. Can you hold on?"

"Sure." I waited patiently while Lily covered the mouthpiece and shuffled through some papers.

"Actually, it turns out, tomorrow isn't very good." Lily paused, and I could hear her sharp breath, as if she were crying.

"Lily, what's wrong?" I asked.

Pause. "Nothing at all. What makes you ask *that*?" She made it sound as if *that* was the worst question in the world.

"I don't know. You sound . . . upset."

"I'm not upset." More wobbly breaths. "We got your telegram. Congratulations on the movie." Her tone was flat and nasal.

"Thank you. As a matter of fact, I'd love to celebrate with you. How's about I take you out for lunch? I'll buy you a milkshake. Are you supposed to drink lots of milk?"

"I thought you wanted to have dinner with me *and* Henk," she snapped, ignoring my question. "What's the matter— don't you like Henk?"

"I do like him. But I'd like to see you alone once in a while. Aren't we allowed to tell a few secrets?"

Snort. Bitter laughter, the sort Delilah would laugh when she wanted to drop hints to Beck: you don't understand *at all*. "Una, I know you're not married, so I can't expect you to understand. But no. I don't have secrets from Henk. If you want to see me, you'll have to see both of us."

This was bizarre. I felt as though I were having a carousel dream, the sort where you keep going round and round, never getting anywhere, unable to get off. If I asked Lily and Henk to dinner, she declined. If I asked her out to lunch alone, she accused me of hating Henk. *Did* I hate Henk? I was beginning to think so.

"Okay," I said. "I would like to have dinner with you and Henk. When will it be most convenient?"

" 'When will it be most convenient?' " Lily said, mocking

me. "You're so formal. I swear, Una. I feel as though I don't know you."

"I'm beginning to feel the same way about *you*," I said, listening to my voice rise to a screech. It was out of my control. Lily and I sat at opposite ends of the phone wire, at opposite sides of the city, weeping.

"Please tell me what's wrong," I said.

"Nothing. Honestly. I'm sorry, I'm just tired. Being pregnant makes me so tired."

"I really want to see you."

"I really want to see you too. And I want to meet Sam. Margo says he's great."

"He is."

"Okay. I'll call you tonight—after I talk to Henk. All right?"

"Okay," I said, hanging up the phone and falling into the sleep of the jet-lagged. But Lily never called.

DURING the weeks that followed, I introduced Sam and he introduced me to some of our closest friends.

At the Schutzes' brunch one Saturday morning, in honor of the show's awards and of my role in a Balfour film, Sam and I stood in the stark grey living room of the Park Avenue penthouse, staring out the terrace window into the November fog, while Billy held both Sam's hands in hers.

"Chance, Billy, I'd like you to meet my friend, Sam Chamberlain."

"Delighted, Sam," Billy said, twinkling. She had changed from her grimy turtleneck into a muslin caftan for the occasion, and I could see goosebumps on her arms and throat. Dampness clung to everything in spite of the heat whistling up the pipes. It had rained for seven days straight.

"Oh, is that one of your pots?" Sam asked, leaning toward a tilting vessel full of bayberry and stalks of marsh grass. Without letting go of his hands, Billy led him closer. I watched the two of them, feeling as though I had brought Sam home to mother. He spoke to Billy, flattering her pottery, regarding her earnestly, with his long arms folded across his chest, as though she were telling the best, most entertaining story in the world. Taking his hand again, Billy led him into another part of the room where more pots, all empty, were displayed on a tall shelf. By the way they were standing, I could tell that she was letting him pick out one to take home. Then I thought of my real mother. I had no doubt that when I finally introduced Sam to her, he would be as charming and kind to her as he was to Billy. But she would be different. She would be friendly enough, in a perfunctory way, but she would turn skittish if Sam were *too* nice or got *too* close. Then she would bolt like a mustang.

s a m's office at Columbia, midway down a dark second-floor corridor in a huge Gothic building, surprised me. Approaching it for the first time, I made the same mistake I had that day in Watch Hill when I had seen Sam reading a book and expected it to be an oceanographic treatise instead of *They Came to Baghdad*. I had expected Sam's office to be institutional, dusty, the sanctuary of a scientist, with piles of Latin-titled books covering the linoleum floor and piles of papers covering the wide desk. I hadn't imagined pictures on the wall or curtains at the window.

I was right about the clutter. Every surface was covered with manuscripts, paper, books, and journals. But there was a hominess about it, a personality that one would never expect to find in such a grim building. Sam had hung a giant Matisse print, one of the bright jazz cutouts, titled *Les Bêtes de la Mer*—The Beasts of the Sea. There was a black-and-white photo of boats in Padanaram harbor, a faded collection of flaking wildflowers, preserved in a glass frame. White rice-paper shades, somewhat yellowed, hung crookedly in the large windows. I had come to meet Sam for dinner, and I couldn't stop looking around. It was the first time I had visited him; usually he came to my place and, of course, we had met at the family inn.

He introduced me to his research assistant, a pretty, over-weight Columbia student named Christie Clendennin. Christie wore a man's blue chamois shirt, the nap worn down to a comfortable sheen, over green denim pants. Her blond hair straggled into her wide brown eyes, and she didn't bother to brush it away. She moved languidly, as though there were all the time in the world. In New York, where every movement, every gesture, was efficient, Christie was an anomaly. She would make a fine oceanographer, taking sun lines from the deck of a gently rolling ship.

"Hi, Una," she said, giving me a wide smile when Sam introduced us. Then she neatly placed the banana she had been eating onto the discarded peel, still atop a bunch of crumpled papers in the wastebasket, and wiped her hand on her pants. Her handshake was firm and sticky.

"Hi, Christie," I said. "I've talked to you on the phone so often, it's nice to match your voice to a face."

Lily still had not matched Sam's voice to his face. I thought of that; of how, to the important people in each other's lives, Sam and I were still voices. But that was changing. Here I was, smiling at Christie.

"Sam, we're going to have to do something about that seminar at Yale," she said, running her finger down a calendar page on Sam's desk. "You going to give that talk or what?"

"You find me a topic big enough to fill five days yet?" Sam asked.

"Five days? When?" I asked.

"Early in December," Christie said. "If he ever gives me some ideas about what he wants to do."

"Listen, they don't give a shit what I talk about. When visitors come here, what do they talk about? Obscure research, that's what. And my research is just as obscure as anyone else's."

"This is true," Christie said, nodding her head at me. "Sam's probably told you how crazy this stuff is. Sam doesn't necessarily care about Professor Schmo's research any more than Schmo cares about Sam's, but they have to act nicey-nicey to each other just so they can get grants from each other's institutions."

"Hey, that's not completely true, Christie," Sam said. "I care about other research."

"Sure, *Willander*'s?"

What senses of humor, I thought. How could two people engaged in such weighty matters as *oceanography* have such flip attitudes, when I, a soap opera actress, could not see the funny side to "Beyond the Bridge?" There is something to be learned here, I told myself.

"Want dinner?" Sam asked.

"Take her to the Symposium," Christie said. "You like Greek?"

"Well, sure . . ."

"They have the best stuffed grape leaves," Christie said,

beginning to salivate. Her eyes misted gently. "And *souvlaki*. Or better yet, *moussaka*."

"The owner painted every surface in the place," Sam said. "Even the lightbulbs."

"Jesus, if that isn't just like you, Chamberlain," Christie said, letting out an impatient sigh. "Dinner means food, not painted lightbulbs. No wonder you're so skinny."

"Fatten me up," Sam said to me.

I smiled, and we left Christie to retrieve her banana and continue eating it while working on the latest grant proposal.

In the hallway we met Victor Parkson. He was staring at a green bulletin board covered with papers which luffed like sails in the breeze from an overhead heat duct. Fluorescent ceiling light buffed his bald pate, which he stroked abstractly. Markings decorated the back of his head. From a distance I had thought he was old and tattooed, but up close I could see that he was younger than me.

"Vic, this is Una Cavan," Sam said, stopping by the bulletin board. Sam's dark hair stirred in the heat-breeze.

Vic's smile bunched his face into folds of loose skin. I could see the shape of his skull perfectly; I could imagine how he would look as a skeleton. I knew immediately that he was a receptor of chemotherapy for some cancer or other. "Sam told me you're an actress on that soap opera. My girlfriend watches it."

"It's so unusual to be recognized in the halls of academia," I said, knowing that that was a lie. Visiting Margo and Lily at Brown two years earlier had been the pantheon of my fame. All the students had known me. But I wanted to talk, to keep Victor from knowing that I knew about his condition. There were red and blue arrows on his neck and skull, indicating where the radiologist should aim the rays. Simultaneous radiology and chemotherapy; I began to feel sick.

"How's your treatment, Vic?" Sam asked.

Don't ask. Why did you have to ask? I thought, peering at a notice over Vic's shoulder.

Vic shrugged. "Sickening. But better than the surgery, I think. Who knows? Have you met with Desmond today?"

Sam rolled his eyes. "Desmond, what a horse's ass. Making us all sweat."

"Who's Desmond?" I asked, happy the subject was changing.

"Department head," Vic said. "He keeps our Sammy on his toes."

"Someone has to do it," I said, steering us further from more talk about Vic's condition. But Sam turned us around. He squeezed Vic's forearm.

"You take care of yourself. We're all pulling for you, you know."

"I know," Vic said.

When Sam and I were in the ugly, dark stairwell, I walked very fast, about two steps ahead of him. I could hear him falling behind with every step.

"What's the matter?" he asked, not catching up to me until we were outside in the twilit courtyard on Morningside Heights.

"Oh, nothing," I said.

"Did Vic bother you?"

"He looks like he's about to die."

"He's very sick. He has a tumor in his tongue, but he's not about to die."

"Are you sure he wants to talk about it with everyone who comes along?"

"Well, I'm his advisor, Una. We talk about it all the time."

"I'm not his advisor, though. We just met. It must be humiliating to talk about it with a stranger." I thought of my father, of how carefully he had guarded the secret of his colostomies, even when the shit was gurgling into the bags. Whenever possible he would blame it on the nearest source of water.

"Vic needs support. I don't think he cares where it comes from."

"I wonder about that," I said, no longer feeling like having stuffed grape leaves or viewing hand-painted lightbulbs. I felt like going home alone, pulling the quilt to my chin, and watching an homogenous night of television. First the bland, anonymous disasters on the local news, then a game show or two, and finally situation comedies, one after the other, that would finally blend into one hilarious whole. But instead I let Sam drag me to the Symposium where he ordered Demestica for us. Demestica made me think of Domestica, and I started wondering, do I really want to stay in love with Sam, hoping for domestica and marital bliss when one day within the next forty-five or so years one or both of us will die? Even the bright swirls of poster paint on every surface in the noisy restaurant made me think of the blue and red arrows on Victor Parkson's head.

"s o, you're an oceanographer," Henk said, somewhat smugly, staring at Sam from his usual seat of honor in the library. Sam sat in another wing chair flanking the blazing hearth while Lily, of fine and rotund proportions, and I sat on the couch. Every time she felt the baby kick, she grabbed my hand and placed it on her belly.

"That's right," Sam said.

"Eh, a doctor of the sea. Hey, we have another doctor in the room," Henk said to Lily in a wry tone which meant to suggest only *one* of us is a real doctor.

"I think oceanography is fascinating," Lily said, grabbing my hand and planting it on her right hip. "That's the head," she said to me. Then, to Sam, "I was always most interested in plate techtonics. Continental drift and all that."

"Yes, the geophysical branch of oceanography," Henk said. "When all the world's landmasses were one grand place called Gondwanaland."

"You're interested in geophysics?" Sam asked.

Henk raised his hand in a scoffing manner. "Well, not interested, precisely. I just picked it up from somewhere. Probably from a patient or something."

How brilliant one must be to "pick up" geophysics, I thought.

"Henk has such fascinating patients," Lily said. "Dear, tell them about the *diamond merchant*."

And Henk whirled off into a long tale about a patient who, he admonished Lily, was not a diamond merchant at all, but

a diamond *broker*, the richest in all of Amsterdam, in fact. He
had paid Henk's fee in cash along with a handsome collection
of unset diamonds, which was now in the vault along with
the rest of Henk's bounty. Patients were so *grateful* when you
saved their lives.

"And I hear you're an art historian, just like your other
sister," Sam said to Lily. I watched Henk's expression, hoping it would reveal chagrin at being cut off in mid-self-
glorification, but he remained stone-faced as ever.

"Not practicing, however," Lily said.

"No, but you must be one of the best-informed museum
visitors in New York," Sam said.

"She might become a docent somewhere in a few years,
after the children are raised," Henk said, pursing his lips in
a smile.

"Or maybe even a museum curator—and get paid for it," I
said.

"We think highly of public service in this family," Henk
said, glaring at me, daring me. But to do what? Whenever I
faced Henk, I felt as though I were being invited to do battle
over some secret issue. (The issue, of course, was Lily, but I
was slow to recognize this. Or afraid to.)

"What sort of public service?" Sam asked.

"Fund raising, volunteer work. People in our positions, as
professionals, have that responsibility, don't you think?"

"I don't have much time for volunteer work," Sam said.
"But I know fund raising. Christ, do I know fund raising. Any
scientist does—grants pay the way."

"Yes, but grants pay *your* way. You must start using your
talents to raise money for the needy, for the arts."

Sam smiled across the wide, rosy expanse of Persian carpet
at me. "Well, I contribute to the arts in my own way."

Henk looked blank for a second. "What, you mean Una?"

"Yeah. She's about to drive the critics crazy in *Together
Forever*."

"I see," Henk said, staring at the ceiling.

But Lily was proud; that was all I cared about. Movie roles
were what she, Margo, and I had always hoped I would eventually corner. And with Emile Balfour! She squeezed my

hand, then pulled it onto her navel. "Feel it?" she asked.

A wee appendage poked out, then retreated. I nodded, feeling tears gather in my eyes. A little half-Cavan was alive in Lily's massive belly. It was half-Voorhees as well, but with Lily as its mother it would be wonderful. I didn't even care if it was a girl. It seemed astonishing that I had not seen the pregnant Lily before now; suddenly she was magnificently huge, and the last time I had seen her she was as skinny as a bride.

"I still cannot believe you're going to have a baby," I said quietly.

"Naturally I am—I'm fertile as the plains of Kansas," she whispered back. Her eyes glowed, and although her yellow hair had lost some of its sheen through a temporary transferal of vitamins to the new baby, her skin looked as though it never came into contact with New York air. I kept my hand on her stomach, waiting for the next bit of action. I was smiling at Lily, who was smiling around the room at Sam and Henk, when suddenly she went as stone-faced as her husband and pushed my hand away. I looked up just in time to see the tail end of Henk's disgusted scowl.

Everyone stared at the fire, trying to ignore Lily who was starting to silently sob. An iron basket on the marble hearth held thin driftwood branches; I wondered which beach Lily and Henk had gathered them from. Or whether they had bought them at a florist. New York florists sell every sort of vegetation from Ficus trees to tumbleweeds. Suddenly Henk let out a mighty puff of air. "For Christ's sake! Will you do your crying in private?"

Lily stood with immense dignity, considering her girth and the fact that she was heaving with the effort of not making noise, and walked quickly out of the room, passing Ilsa as she went. I stood to follow.

"You stay here," Henk commanded me.

"Shut the fuck up," I shot back and ran after Lily. I could hear her footsteps clicking on the marble tiles of one hall or another, but I could not see her. I was in the maze at some Frighthouse. I darted in and out of rooms I had never seen before: a sewing room strewn with flimsy paper patterns and snippets of gingham and velvet; a flower room filled with stainless-steel sinks and the disgarded stems of a veritable acre of gladioli and irises; a TV room whose walls bore spiked metal helmets, pearl-handled rifles, a lance, and several portraits of the same man in full military regalia—some warrior ancestor of Henk's, no doubt; one pristine guest room after the other, all done in shades of green and yellow. Sweating and panicked, I finally found Lily at the end of one long corridor, far enough from the library that she knew her sobs could not be heard. They were primitive, wild, and terrifying. I will never forget how they pierced me.

She lay on her back on a massive bed, her pregnant belly rising like an island, like Corsica, out of the sea, her toes pointed daintily at the ceiling. She wailed as though her child were dead.

"Lily?" I said, sitting next to her, taking her hand. She gripped mine so tightly it started to hurt. Then, when her cries subsided, her hand went limp. I had time to gaze around the room, at her dressing table covered with jewel cases and tiny crystal flagons of makeup and perfume, at Henk's valet stand bearing his dark suit and black shoes (apparel for the funerals of his less grateful patients?), at the tiny gold-framed oil paintings hanging on each wall. "Lily?" I said again.

"What." Her voice was flat, as though she were totally defeated.

What? I tried to think of diplomatic ways to phrase the question that was pounding in my brain: what are you doing with a fascist like Henk?

"What's wrong?" I asked as mildly as I could.

"Nothing. Pregnancy has made me very emotional."

"Didn't Henk *like* me feeling the baby kick?"

At that she started to struggle into an upright position, but I patted her shoulder and she sank back onto the pillow. Her eyes glared at me. "Well, can you blame him? I mean, pregnancy is an unbelievably intense time for a couple. They really don't want any intrusions."

"They," as if the word had nothing to do with Lily—as if "they" were Henk and some automaton wife.

"Maybe, but don't you think we want to be involved? Me, Margo, and Mom, I mean."

"I'm sure you do, but do you honestly think it's your right?" She assumed that haughty tone I had heard so often on the phone, made more extreme by the sudden nasality of crying.

"Actually, yes. I'm not taking anything away from Henk by wanting to see you once in a while. I understand that he's your husband . . ." (stating the obvious, to reassure her) "and that he wants to protect you. And that you're . . ." (choke) "happy together."

"We are. Very."

"So why won't he let me feel the baby kick? My little niece is in that belly." I smiled, but Lily exploded.

"And that's another thing! Hasn't it ever occurred to you that we might want a *son*?"

"I'm sure Henk does." It slipped out, and I knew I couldn't call it back. Lily regarded me with satisfied eyes.

"You see? You *don't* like Henk. He's known it all along. Just because the Cavans have a dynasty of women, that doesn't mean that I want to carry on the tradition. Henk and I are together in this, Una. Right from the beginning he knew you couldn't stand him. I don't know whether it's jealousy or—" she sailed right on, past my grunted protests "—the fact that he thinks soap operas are inferior to the stage. I mean, that he doesn't respect you professionally. You don't seem to be able to separate it in your own mind—the fact that Henk likes you as a person but doesn't think much of your work."

"Henk thinks nothing of me as a person. He's wanted to keep you to himself ever since you met him. That's why you call Margo in Watch Hill but never call me in New York—because I'm too close for comfort."

"Excuse me, Una, but that is ridiculous. It's just another example of how warped your logic is when it comes to Henk. He loves me, and he loves the Cavan family." The Cavan family—Lily had seceded from us; I could hear it in her voice. Lily, defending a man who had just forced her to make

her delighted sister (me) stop patting the kicking baby, and
had then driven her from the room in tears. The strength of
it made me drop my own head and begin to cry. Only then,
when I was weak and she was on top of the world, could Lily
give me comfort. She twisted a strand of my hair around her
finger.

"It's okay, Una," she said in a low voice. "My getting married has been a big change. I know everyone needs time to
adjust."

I nodded, swallowing tears.

"And I do like Sam. Margo was right about him."

I nodded again, kissing her forehead, and slunk back to the
library. Henk and Sam were standing in the doorway. Sam
was wearing his coat and holding mine. He held it toward me.
Henk nodded in the Prussian manner. "I shall thank you
never to say 'fuck' in my home again," he said.

"I shall thank you for thanking me," I said, accepting my
coat from Sam and letting him propel me toward the foyer.

"Imbecile," Henk muttered under his preponderate breath.

"Fucker," I muttered back.

On the cobblestone walk overlooking the East River, Sam
hugged me while I yelled into his ski jacket. A wisp of down
protruded from a seam, tickling my cheek. My fury blurred
the lights of the Queensborough Bridge. From the East River
Drive, below our feet, came a blast from someone's horn. Or
perhaps it came from a dark tug on the river. Sam stroked my
hair.

"What a bastard," he said.

"I know. I told you he keeps Lily a prisoner."

"You weren't kidding."

"And she is so great! Or *used* to be . . . I can't tell anymore.
She might be ruined for life."

"People do change."

I pulled back and stared into his pale green eyes. "It's not
like that—Lily is wonderful. This has to be temporary. Did
you like her?"

"Yes, but she didn't say much. I had the feeling she had
been programmed; or that she had programmed herself."

I shook my head, violently unwilling to believe that. "No,

it's Henk. Jesus, I wish she'd divorce him. Before it's too late."

"Too late for what? It's November, and she's going to have a baby in January."

"That's not what I mean."

"Then what do you mean?" Sam asked.

I scowled and shook my head. "Never mind," I said, but only because I had no idea.

O N E night on our way upstairs to my apartment, Sam and I met Joe Finnegan and a pregnant woman at the mailboxes. I had not seen Joe for months, since before I had left New York for Watch Hill. For several seconds I felt tension in my spine, behind my eyes, while I tried to anticipate the things Joe might say to Sam. I expected him to leer at me behind Sam's back, but instead his eyes flooded with tears and slid to his pregnant companion. Her hair had grown out of its shag cut, and she had gained at least twenty pounds, but I recognized her as the woman he had been strolling along Greenwich Avenue with that hot night last summer.

"Una, let me introduce you to Patsy Connor," he said.

"Happy to meet you," I said. Then I took hold of Sam's hand. "This is Sam Chamberlain. Joe Finnegan—Patsy Connor."

"How do you do," Sam said.

"Well, I'm going to be a daddy," Joe said, the tears welling over his lower lids.

A daddy? He *had* said Patsy *Connor*? What would a macho guy like Joe be doing with a woman who would keep her own name after marriage? Was it possible—? I considered the notion of parenthood out of wedlock, but the staid image of Mrs. Finnegan and her Computer of Catholicism came to mind and drove the hideous idea away.

"Well, congratulations, Joe," I said.

"That's great!" Sam said, pumping Joe's hand the way only another man can pump the hand of an expectant father.

Patsy smiled demurely at Joe. "And we're getting married over Christmas."

Joe flicked some tears away with his index finger. "Yeah, the kid wants to do things back-asswards. Her whole damn family has to be there for the wedding, and one of her brothers's not getting back to the States till December."

"He's in the navy," Patsy explained.

"So, I knocked her up in August, and she's taking her sweet time, pickin' out bridesmaids' bouquets. You know me, Una— I always did go for the unconventional types."

I laughed politely.

"Yes, big talker there," Patsy said. "He's having a major anxiety attack over whether we should serve filet mignon or prime rib at the reception. *He's* more excited about the wedding than I am. Admit it, Joseph."

"Ahh, you're full of shit." He pinched her cheek. "Seriously, though, it'll be a pretty good party at the Wamataug Country Club out in Nyack. Hope you two can make it. Ma'll kill me if I don't invite you, Una."

"Thank you, but we already have a Christmas wedding. Margo is getting married."

Joe shook his head so that the red pipecurls unscrewed, then sprang tightly back. "Jesus H. Christ, you Cavans. Still close as ever?"

"You bet," I said, thinking of Lily.

"Peas in a pod," Sam said.

"You can't beat a good, close family," Joe said. "My brothers are having fistfights over who gets to be best man. I told 'em—you two decide it between ya. The honor goes to the fittest of ya."

Patsy socked his upper arm. "You're such a conceited monster," she said. "The kids probably haven't given it ten seconds' worth of thought. They'll end up flipping a coin the night of your bachelor party."

Perfect, I thought—a woman who gives it straight back to Joe Finnegan. I prophesied a happy, if contentious, life together for them. We said goodnight, and Sam and I walked into the elevator together, leaving Joe and Patsy to argue over who had the mailbox key.

"That one of your old boyfriends?" Sam asked.

"Yes."

"Yes?" He sounded startled. Joe and I were so obviously ill-suited. What would I be doing with such a jokester?

"For a short time. He's a nice guy."

"I'm sure he is. He's thrilled about being a father. Do people always cry when they're about to become parents?"

"I don't know. Joe did, Lily did. Haven't you known any prospective parents?"

"Not many. I think it's because scientists are social retards; we spend so much time in labs and on ships, we never have a chance to meet the Ones of Our Dreams. Until now." He backed me against the elevator wall and kissed me. We stepped into the hallway, and I started patting my pockets for the keys.

"So, I'm the One of Your Dreams?" I asked. I found the key and wiggled it into the lock.

"Yes."

"But what are your dreams?" I asked.

For Thanksgiving, Sam's parents were attending a seminar at San Miguel de Allende, in Mexico, and they sent Sam a blue piñata shaped like a donkey. The Sunday afternoon before the holiday we lay in my bed surrounded by the paper and discussed how we would spend the holiday. My mother had invited us, along with Matt and Margo and Lily and Henk, to her house. We considered that option carefully. Everything in the paper featured family holiday traditions. The food page showed a fat turkey with the author's grandmother's chestnut dressing and the author's husband's grandmother's cranberry orange relish. The wine column listed the best American reds to enjoy with the dinner along with a nostalgic look at the vintages our foremothers might have served with *their* dinners. The architecture page showed a mountain retreat designed by one man to accommodate his extended family at holidays; it contained thirty-four bunk beds, each with a view of Mount Ellen, and a dining table shaped like a giant horseshoe.

But I did not feel ready to see Lily and Henk right away, so soon after our bad scene. Margo's wedding was fleetly approaching, and the family would come together then. I would think of that, and then I would think how how strange it would feel to have Thanksgiving away from my family.

"I can't decide," I told Sam.

"Does your mother make a good turkey?"

"That's not the point. But no; not very. She's never been much of a cook. I'm just not sure I want to see Lily. I *hate* the way she acts with Henk."

"It might be good for you to see her. You can start planning things for Margo—don't you want to throw her a shower or something?"

I shook my head. I have always loathed the idea of showers. Women go to showers and become girls. They collect bows and take their time opening each present, making sure the tape doesn't tear the pretty paper printed with parasols and orange blossoms. They squeak. "No, I don't think Margo's big on showers," I said.

"Then maybe you and Margo can cheer up Lily. It's her first pregnancy; she's probably afraid of giving birth."

"I doubt it. Henk's convinced her she's the Earth Mother."

By the impatient way Sam had started turning the pages, I could tell he was annoyed. I knew why: one minute I was crying because Lily was unhappy, defending her, saying that her change of spirit was only temporary. The next minute I was condemning her, condemning Sam for defending her. I rolled onto my side, giving Sam my back. I was staring at the Arts and Leisure section, but I was thinking: what the hell am I doing with a man who can't sit out a little indecision? Am I supposed to be perfectly consistent? *All the time?*

After a while I began to actually read the article. It was about Kathleen Turner, the comedic actress who had started on the soaps. I started to laugh. Sam didn't ask what I was laughing about, but he slid his hairy leg against mine, letting me know it was fun to be reading the paper in bed with me. It felt lovely and decadent to be lounging around, naked, at two on a Sunday afternoon. We had already risen, eaten breakfast, and gone back to bed.

"Hey, it's snowing!" Sam said.

I rolled onto my elbow, against his body, to see out my bedroom window. Fine flakes slanted through the shadowy sky, a contrast so unremarked, it might not have been snowing at all.

"First snow of the year," I said.

Sam leaned closer to kiss me. "You're such a sucker for the romantic details."

He was right. Things like the first snow, the black zone of shore—mystical forces of nature—represented the mystical forces of my own nature. I read them the way a gypsy reads tarot cards. The first snow was telling me to cook a turkey,

Sam's and my first, and save the family gathering for Margo's wedding. It was also telling me to touch Sam's penis and make it stiff. My own nipples tingled with excitement; I could hardly wait for the winter solstice.

W I T H only three shopping days before Thanksgiving, I had to use Soundstage 3 as my base, running through the city on errands whenever we took a break from shooting. The big rumor was that Beck and Delilah would elope on Christmas Eve. Beginning the first week of December, commercials would be aired hinting to that effect. With a two-week shooting lag, we had the Thanksgiving episode in the can and were moving, with much suspense and elation, toward Mooreland's Christmas season. Our loyal viewers would know what was coming even without the blatant signals. Delilah wore much red velvet and spent long moments staring contemplatively at golden Christmas tree balls while a tremulous version of "O, Holy Night" played in the background. Through the marvels of film editing, Art managed to turn the Christmas tree ball into a tiny movie screen, a bulb of Delilah's memory as it were, across which passed six years' worth of romantic images with Beck. Frolicking on the beach, in the snow, in the fields of Mooreland; their first kiss; Delilah's tears after their first reunion after their first split; Beck's face as Delilah opened the case containing her first engagement ring from him; their recent reunion after her jailbreak. . . . Yes, something was in the air. All of us on "Beyond the Bridge" and all of our viewers could feel it. It was time for Delilah and Beck to marry.

But then what? Ratings soared for weddings and dropped off during the ensuing marriage. It was often Chance's solution to kill off one of the spouses. And with me leaving the show to do *Together Forever*, Delilah was primed to die in late spring. A boating accident, a kidnap and ransom and murder, or simple suicide. Anything, as long as the body was never found and she could be resurrected some time in the future, if I ever tired of movies and wanted to return to the show.

During shooting breaks I bought tall, cream-colored candles; cellophane bags full of nuts in their shells; fresh cranberries from a Korean fruit stand on Broadway; a horrendously expensive white linen tablecloth; waxy turnips; ten pounds of potatoes; loaves of stale white bread; fresh sage; packets of instant gravy—just in case. Each night, laden down with shopping bags, I would take a cab home instead of the subway. I bought a woman's magazine which spelled out the steps to a perfect Thanksgiving dinner.

DAY FOUR: Order turkey, buy unperishables, order pies.
DAY THREE: Make cranberry sauce, polish silver, check china for chips, pick up turkey (if frozen), commence thawing.
DAY TWO: Buy fresh vegetables, pick up pies, chop vegetables and plunge into ice water, set holiday table.
DAY ONE: Prepare dinner and look gorgeous.

Since I had only three days, I had to combine and actually skip several steps. I bought a fresh turkey and frozen peas from the Jefferson Market. On Wednesday night I was sitting at my kitchen table, waiting for Sam to come over, reading the instructions for Day One (Thanksgiving), so that I would be ready to make the gravy, set things to boil at their proper times, and put the bird into the oven early enough to eat at four, when the telephone rang.

"*Allo!*" came the voice. It was foreign, but it sounded close enough to be next door.

"Hello?" I said.

"*Allo!* It is Emile—I am in New York!"

Within two minutes I had invited another guest for Thanksgiving dinner. Emile Balfour was alone in my city; what could I do but the hospitable thing?

"WE DO NOT celebrate 'Thanksgiving' in France," Emile said, putting the word into quotation marks that suggested perhaps it did not really exist. He had arrived three minutes earlier and was sitting beside Sam on my sofa. Emile wore a beautiful yellow Viyella shirt with a black-and-gold paisley ascot. He smoked a cigarette with his elegant gold toothpick. His hair was exquisitely mussed and lacquered. Sam wore his rumpled blue oxford shirt, but with the colder weather he had traded his khakis for buff corduroys. Emile seemed oblivious to Sam's unfriendliness. I, who was tearing around the kitchen, draining boiling potatoes into my sink, shaking nutmeg into all the pots, and trying not to spill anything on my electric-blue velvet slacks and matching satin cummerbund, was not. So I heard everything, especially what Sam did *not* say. He was quiet to the point of rudeness.

"So, here I am, meeting with the money men, when all of a sudden they tell me it's a big holiday. They thought I knew all about it," Emile said. "How did America come to celebrate 'Thanksgiving,' anyway?"

I stood before the sink, a steaming pan of turnips poised over the stainless-steel colander, listening for Sam's response. There was none. I put down the pan and dashed into the living room where Sam had his mouth full of smoked oysters, his cheeks puffed out, his finger held in the air to indicate that he would reply as soon as he could swallow.

"The Pilgrims started it," I said.

"John Alden and Miles Standish," Emile said, laughing, pronouncing "Miles" like "Emile"—Emile Standish. "*Now* I remember the story of your Pilgrims. It was told to me when I was a boy in school."

"You know, Sam comes from Padanaram, in southeastern Massachusetts. That's very near Plymouth Rock. Sam, why don't you tell Emile about Plymouth Rock?"

I wondered whether Emile noticed Sam's monotone as he told about the tourists who go to Plymouth, about the iron fence around the rock, about nothing but the barest details. I mashed the turnips with frustrated vigor.

"I've been out on *Calypso*," Emile said after another long stretch of silence. "One time, before I started directing, I did a documentary on Jacques Cousteau. Wow, what a man he is. He was off Madagascar at the time. What an oceanographer.

He loved the way our film turned out, still says it was the best anyone has ever done of him. We had some trouble, too, I'll tell you that. Lowering the cameraman into the sea. There were many sharks, all kinds. *Now* they have good shark cages, the best, but back then—whooo." I could just picture Emile shaking his elegant head. I sprinkled more nutmeg into the turnips, hurrying so that I could return to the living room and keep the conversation moving.

Sam had not been thrilled to hear that I had invited Emile Balfour for Thanksgiving dinner. In fact, he was furious. I had regretted the invitation almost as soon as I had extended it, but what else could I do? The man who had offered me my first movie role was alone in New York for a major American holiday. I had acted impulsively. Impulses got me into trouble so often, I should have learned. But I never did. I just went on blurting. When Sam arrived at my apartment on Wednesday night, he kissed me and handed me a bouquet of shaggy amber chrysanthemums. Then I told him about inviting Emile: his face drained, then filled with hurt confusion. In the arguments and silences that followed, neither of us had put the flowers in water. Now, wilted as spinach, they lay atop a garbage can in the street. Some bag lady would probably take them home to Penn Station. I hoped they would bring her cheer.

Sam could not understand how I could invite Emile Balfour to *our* Thanksgiving dinner without *at least* consulting him. I should have been touched that he called it "our" dinner, as though we were beginning to merge into each other's family, but I was not. I felt furious with him for questioning my judgment, for being rude to our guest. He felt furious with me for inviting a man the papers said was my lover. I felt furious with him, but I could not show it. I stalked around the apartment, my lips tight, my nostrils flaring, like a drama school exercise: this woman is *hurt*. Sam shot me dirty looks and made angry exhalations when we were alone. He felt furious, I felt furious. Big standoff.

I removed the turkey from my oven and set it on the counter, to allow the juices to gather for thirty minutes before asking Sam to carve it. I was just about to call him into the kitchen where I would act out another scene of hurt and disappointment, when I heard his voice. It sounded amused. It was telling Emile a story about descending into the waters off Montauk in a shark cage. I relaxed and did a last-minute check of the now greasy checklist for Day One.

Sam walked into the kitchen to carve the turkey. I smiled at him, whisking fine flour into the gravy. He smiled at me. Without speaking he rummaged through the kitchen drawer for the leather case which contained my carving set, a fine stainless-steel long-pronged fork and bone-handled Sheffield blade that had been a present from my father the year I got my own apartment. The utensils fit Sam's hands perfectly. He drew the knife through the first joint, and clear yellow juices streamed forth. In the living room, Emile had just turned up the Terje Rypdal music. I knew he couldn't hear us. Standing behind Sam, I circled his waist with my arms. I rested my cheek on his back. He carved one perfect slice after another.

"Not a bad turkey, huh?" I asked.

"Mmmmm," he said pleasantly. I thought he'd snitch a piece of meat, but he did not.

"Things going better with Emile? I heard you talking about sharks."

"Fine."

The single, clipped word set off an alarm in my brain. "What's wrong?"

"You shouldn't have invited him," Sam said, continuing to carve.

I leaned around him, to see his face, and I looked into his frozen eyes.

DINNER was, in its own way, a success. The food was delicious. The gravy was slightly greasy and the peas were mushy, but no one said so. Only I noticed. Sam and Emile exchanged stories about seaside locations. It turned out that Emile had shot movies in spots where Sam had studied the marine life. Emile told Sam about *Together Forever* and said that he was welcome to visit our location on Corsica. Sam smiled and thanked him.

I made sure both men took second helpings while at the same time making sure Sam noticed I had barely touched my first. Sitting between them I stared at my new linen table-cloth and counted the stains. Red wine had sloshed out of Emile's glass; a blob of cranberry sauce looked lurid, un-naturally pink; a small puddle of grease had gathered around the base of the gravy boat. That tablecloth would never look clean again.

"Did Una tell you about the photographers in Paris?" Emile asked. "They swarmed on her."

"I saw the picture myself—everyone in America did," Sam said. "You two at the nightclub."

"Well, don't let it worry you." Emile chuckled and patted Sam's shoulder. "Una wanted no part of it; she wanted me to chase them away. Right, Una?"

"Right." I felt desolate; the tension at my table felt oppressive and familiar. I tried to identify it. I glanced at Sam who was smiling at Emile, as if they were the founding brothers of a new fraternity. Men stick together. Why had I worried that Sam would be rude to Emile? That initial silence had been no more than getting to know the lay of the land. Sam's fury had nothing to do with Emile. Emile was probably feeling sympathy for Sam, for getting stuck with a bitch like me. And I *was* acting like a bitch—even though it did feel justified. Sam gave the turkey carcass warmer glances than he gave me. I was being punished.

I poured more Grizzly Creek Cabernet Sauvignon into my glass. It caught the candlelight and turned ruby-orange. I sipped, and then I knew why the strife felt familiar. It re-minded me of being a child at my father's dinner table. When fits of Black Ass would strike him, he would head straight for The Blue Danube. Then for days afterward he would give everyone at home the cold shoulder. At the dinner table he would politely ask how was school, how was painting, would you please pass the pepper? He gave all of us the feeling he

was terribly disappointed. Not angry, precisely, but let down.
That he had expected more of us; of life; of the dinner. And
that was how Sam was making me feel: as though I had let
him down.

Emile departed immediately after pumpkin pie, and Sam
came into the kitchen to help me with the dishes.

"You don't have to do that," I said. Cool, noble.

"It's okay." He scraped turnips into the garbage pail. "Dinner was delicious."

"Good," I said, noting the adjective "delicious"; it referred
only to the food, not to the company or atmosphere.

We scraped plates for a while. The only sounds were forks
against china, food thudding into the trash, water running,
my stomach rumbling. I was starving; I had a mad urge to
grab a drumstick and start gnawing, but Sam had to observe
my self-denial. Then he would know how bad he was making
me feel.

"That turkey was really moist," he said.

"Good." All through dinner he had made sure I knew I
was the bad girl, and now he was tossing me a compliment.
"Why were you so awful during dinner?" I asked, trembling
from hunger and anger.

"I told you; I was upset."

"You could have been nicer to me. Emile knew something
was wrong."

"I was nice to you."

"Barely!"

"Una, I was really pissed that you invited him. I was looking forward to having the dinner alone with you. You want
me to pretend nothing happened?"

"You were *fine* to *him*."

"I thought you wanted me to be friendly to him."

"Oh, god." I glared at the turkey pan. I knew I should have
bought a throwaway roaster.

" 'Oh, god' what?"

"You made me feel rotten, being nice to him and cool to me.
Like you were punishing me, teaching me a good lesson."

"I was mad at you. That's all."

Neither of us spoke for a while. Sam started washing the dishes in soapy water and I started drying them. I felt flat, as though everything were gone. My great romance, like all its lesser predecessors, was ending. I could tell by the quick way Sam dipped the plates into the water and swiped them with the sponge, that he could hardly wait to leave. My harsh overhead light illuminated us like a spotlight on actors playing tragedy.

When he finished with the dishes, he reached for the turkey pan.

"Don't bother with that," I said.

"Who's going to do it?"

"I'm throwing it out," I said, lifting it off the sideboard and dumping it into a brown grocery bag.

"Shit, Una, it was full of grease," Sam yelled, crouching down to wipe my kitchen floor with the sponge. Clear yellowish fat oozed from the bag's pores, dribbling onto Sam's pants leg.

"Get away from it," I said, prodding his shoulder. "Just leave it alone."

He stood straight, gazing at me as though I had slapped him. "Fine."

"Leave if you want to."

"I didn't say—"

I threw yesterday's newspaper onto the floor to absorb the mess. The instructions for Day One had said nothing about this contingency. I moved slowly; the moment seemed superclear, as though it were already making its mark as a turning point. I could have been seeing it in a dream: the way my Formica counter reflected the overhead light, the shadows made by the stove and refrigerator on the tile floor, the sopping newspaper. Sam's breathing. The clock ticking (but I had no clock in the kitchen). My heartbeat.

"Well. Do you want me to leave?" Sam asked.

"Do you want to?"

"Do *you* want me to?"

"I don't care." Shrug.

"You don't *care?*" Sam started washing his hands. He grabbed the damp dish towel. "Jesus, Una, say what you mean. You want me to leave? I'll leave." He walked out of the kitchen. I heard his footsteps: sharp on the tile, muffled on the Chinese rug in my living room, sharp on the wood floor in my foyer. A door opened; he was taking his coat out of the closet. *Leave*, I thought. *Go ahead, leave.* Never come back. NeverNeverNeverNeverNeverNeverNeverNever. I was still thinking Never when he walked out the door. I grabbed a hunk of stuffing and started chewing.

T H I N K I N G Never when the one of your dreams walks out the door is bad luck.

But in the days that followed, I felt oddly vindicated. As if I had suspected the worst about human nature and been proved right. Without the frenzy of Thanksgiving preparations to make, my days felt vacant. I trudged to the subway, rattled underground to the studio, stood before the cameras, and gazed soulfully into Christmas tree balls.

"Did you have a good turkey day?" Jason asked one afternoon between scenes. We were sitting on a sofa on the set, drinking cups of the syllabub Margie MacDuff had sent in with Stuart.

"No."

"Neither did I. Holidays bum me out royal. But I *am* psyched for Christmas. Terry and I are going to Aruba."

"I would hate Christmas without snow."

"That's rude of you. You're supposed to say, 'Lucky Jason!' Or something."

"Oh. Lucky Jason!"

"Something is wrong in your world, Una honey, and I hope it rights itself soon," Jason said, peering at me with concern.

B U T what would it take to right it? I spoke to Sam every night. His feelings were hurt because I hadn't stopped him from leaving; mine were hurt because he had left.

"You in a better mood?" he asked me one night over the phone.

"Yes, I'm fine," I said, feeling detached.

"I didn't want to leave, you know, but I was so mad—"

"I know you were."

"Do you understand how I felt about Emile? I mean, he's a nice guy, a little self-absorbed, but he's the last person I wanted to spend Thanksgiving with."

"I told you, Sam—I'm sorry about that. But I couldn't help it. I had to invite him." I spoke coolly, with great control. They say that cancer patients in terrible pain are sometimes given hallucinogenic drugs. The drugs do not make the pain stop, but they make it seem removed, as though it were sitting two doors down from the patient instead of inside his skull. That was how I felt, talking to Sam. Bad, but able to speak with some objectivity.

"Listen, Una," Sam said, his voice rising. "Will you *talk* to me? Tell me what you're thinking?"

"I'm sorry about everything."

"Quit saying you're *sorry*! I don't want you to be sorry— it's over and done with."

"Okay," I said, thinking why did you walk out? To ask would be to provoke more anger. My quandary felt the same as it had during the old days when my father would stay out and I would be afraid to yell at him. But Sam did not suffer from Black Ass. He had not run to The Blue Danube. He had not acted out of pique or desperation. He had *reacted*. To the fact that I had invited Emile Balfour to our Thanksgiving dinner. The more I thought about it, with Sam silent at the other end of the wire, the more I realized that *I* was suffering from a variety of Black Ass. Where drinking at the bar had been my father's emotional crutch, maintaining harmony with every man in sight was mine. Even if it meant inviting Emile, whom I hadn't really wanted to come, just because it was easier than not inviting him. Less likely to cause hurt feelings and bad vibes. Of course I knew that I would eventually have to reckon with Sam's wrath, but I took each incident in the order of appearance. I traded truth and intimacy for temporary peace.

"I can't have dinner with you tonight," Sam said.

"Why not?" I asked, jolted back to reality, the pain no longer two houses away.

"Christie and I have to go over the seminar I'm giving at Yale. I leave for New Haven on Thursday."

"*This* Thursday?"

"You knew that."

"I did?" I knew he was going away for five days, but so soon?

"'I'd like to see you later tonight, though," he said.

"We could have a late dinner. If you don't mind waiting."

"I hoped you'd say that."

O N M Y way home I took the subway to Fourteenth Street and walked west, toward the Hudson. All the discount stores and souvenir stands throbbed with Christmas lights and carols played to a salsa beat. A cardboard Santa grinned through a delicatessen's steamy window. I hugged my bag to my side; in New York, in cities everywhere, Christmas is the season for muggers.

At Bestfood I pushed my cart through the aisles. First I thought I would make spaghetti for dinner, but when I reached the pasta aisle, nothing looked good. I thought of sautéed chicken breasts, of steak sandwiches, of stir-fried vegetables. But each time I reached the shelves where the ingredients were located, I would stare until the boxes blurred and then walk away. I envied the shoppers whose carts were full, who grabbed things off the shelves, who had planned tonight's meal last night—or earlier.

In the front of the store, beside a display of salt-free wheat biscuits, a woman wearing a German folk costume reminiscent of Bad Cannstatt was handing out samples of the biscuits squirted with Bavarian Cheese Spread—beer-flavored cheese food out of an aerosol can. Hanging onto the handle of my cart, I watched her. She smiled at everyone who passed. "Super for cocktail parties!" she said to a woman in a black business suit. The woman took a cracker off the tray and walked on without thanking the fraulein. How embarrassing, to be thirty-five and forced by your employer to wear a folk costume. Whenever people were not passing, the woman stopped smiling. She shifted her weight, as though her feet hurt. I

wondered whether, behind the cardboard booth, she was wearing little Bavarian slippers. I walked over, put a box of biscuits
and a spray can of cheese into my cart, and smiled at her. She
smiled back.

Outside the store brakes screeched. All I had in my basket
were the biscuits and cheese spray. I stood in the express line
and decided we would order pizza or Chinese food for dinner.
A woman asked me to sign her copy of *Soap Opera Update*,
and two other women then grabbed copies from the rack beside the register and thrust them at me. I wanted to go home,
stretch out on my sofa, and sleep until Sam arrived. The
cashier rang up my order. When she pressed $4.32 for the can
of cheese, I nearly told her to forget the whole thing.

At home, waiting for Sam, I changed into jeans and one of
Sam's old T-shirts. My radiator had been on all day; I turned
it off and opened some windows. The winter had been humid
so far; I wanted a dagger of icy air, but instead it felt vaguely
warm. It smelled of exhaust and pretzels; it felt damp, and I
knew any precipitation would be rain, not snow.

I turned on my radio, but that song where geese honk out
"Jingle Bells" was on, and I turned it off. I decided to call the
train station, to find out the timetable for trains to Watch Hill.
Margo was getting married in two weeks. The Ninigret Inn
would be full of Cavans, Lincolns, and friends from hither and
yon for the marital/Yule fest. Margo had said that Matt had
ordered one hundred and twenty-five yards of laurel roping,
a twenty-five-foot blue spruce, and a three-hundred-pound
pig for roasting.

When I called the station, I got a recording telling me all
lines were temporarily busy but that my call would be answered by the next available ticket agent. I hung up. I walked
into the kitchen, stood in front of the refrigerator, and wished
I had bought something for dinner. Or at least for a snack—I
didn't count the cheese spray. I wondered what time Sam
would arrive. Holding the box of biscuits, I walked into the
living room and began to watch TV. I watched the network
which carried "Beyond the Bridge," although I had no real
interest in the program that was on. It was a dramatization of

some plane crash in the Andes. I watched out of loyalty, or ennui, or the hope that the network would show one of the "Beyond" ads, hinting about Delilah's elopement. There were three such ads, and I appeared in all of them.

When Sam arrived I was asleep. He turned the key I had given him in the lock and stepped into the apartment. It woke me. Lying on the couch I listened to him take off his coat, drop his briefcase on the floor. Sleep pulled me down, but I raised myself on one elbow. He was standing in the doorway, watching me. His brown hair straggled across his eyes, and he had a wide grin.

"What time is it?" I asked.

"Eleven-thirty. Work took longer than I thought it would."

I started to get off the couch. "We should call for Chinese— I think they stop delivering at midnight."

"Are you really hungry?"

"No. Just sleepy."

"Me too," he said. Holding my hand, he walked ahead of me into the bedroom.

We stood beside the bed in the dark room, kissing. "Don't turn on the light—" I said, grabbing his forearm. "I look like a wreck and a mess."

"Too late. I already saw you in the living room."

I climbed under the covers while Sam cleaned out his pockets. He kept his wallet in one pants' pocket, his checkbook in another, his datebook and pens in his breast pocket. He was extremely organized. There was a decent chance that, when he was in high school, he had been the sort of boy to use a plastic pocket protector. I considered asking him, but I didn't. I snuggled under the covers, making a nest. It had been many nights since Sam was last here. While he went to the bathroom, I thought of all the Cavan women who were making nests that night, all except my mother. Margo was snuggled beside Matt in Watch Hill, Lily was snuggled beside Henk uptown, and I was making a warm spot for Sam.

He came into the bedroom and turned out the light.

"I'm sorry about everything," he said when he was beside me.

"So am I. It seemed like you weren't coming back."

"I've had to work on my seminar."

"That's the only reason I haven't seen you?"

"Yes."

I didn't argue, but I knew it wasn't. It scared me to know that Sam had the capacity to stay away. No matter how upset I felt, I would always choose the other person's presence, even if it was filled with silences, shouting, whatever. Presence is everything. I could never go away: to think, to be alone, to think things through, to cool off, to calm down. I could never go away for any reason. Lying beside Sam, I could hear him breathing steadily, falling asleep. I slid my arm beneath his head, hooked it under his chin. He wasn't going anywhere.

D ELILAH married Beck the week before Christmas. Billy, making a cameo appearance as Judge Deborah Buell, officiated. Although the happy couple had planned to elope to a ski lodge in Utah, Paul Grant had gotten wind of their plans and made some plans of his own. No way was Delilah, his favorite daughter, going to get married without him giving her away! So, the night before Beck and Delilah were scheduled to leave for their "vacation," Paul and his wife (Selena, who was beginning to poison Paul by adding smidgens of arsenic to his nightly Scotch) threw a dinner party—with all the Grants, a few Moorelands regulars, and Judge Buell as guests. He asked Delilah, as a special favor to him, to wear her pretty white sundress.

"My sundress?" Delilah exclaimed. "Daddy, it's *Christmastime.*"

"Indulge me, darling," Paul said, a twinkle in his eye.

When Delilah showed up at the Grant mansion, twenty minutes late, she was amazed to find Beck and her father in tuxedos.

"What is this, a black-tie affair?" she asked.

Paul kissed her cheek. Then he offered her his arm. "Shall we?" he asked. He tilted his head toward the living room, where all the party guests were seated, looking expectantly over their shoulders toward the foyer where Delilah, Beck, and Paul stood. Beck kissed Delilah's other cheek and went into the living room to stand before Judge Buell at the Christmas tree. An organ began to play "O, Holy Night." Delilah's eyes filled with generous tears as her father handed her the bouquet of holly and white roses.

"Oh, Daddy," she whispered. Jennifer, her little illegitimate daughter, dressed in red velvet, tugged on the lacy white hem of her dress. "Mommy, are we getting married?" she asked.

Delilah laughed through her tears. "Yes, sweetheart, we are." And then the music swelled, she squeezed her father's arm, and the three generations of Grants walked down the aisle.

MY TEARS were real. I cried all through the ceremony. I truly felt as though Stuart MacDuff, as Paul Grant, were giving me away to Jason Mordant, as Beck Vandeweghe. They got mixed up in my mind with James Cavan and Samuel Chamberlain. I do, I do, I said. No wonder a girl loves her wedding day: she is given the ultimate illusion of protection. She gets to walk down the aisle once with her father and then with her husband. Her father passes her, like valuable chattel, into the hands of another man. He actually hands her off: here, take her, but take good care of her. Or else. Standing at my own TV wedding, I felt as though I were the center figure in some primitive ritual. A virgin bride, all in white, the love object of father and husband. My head spun with Freudian implications.

Billy, dressed in a black robe, looked solemn and urgent. She held a black Bible open in her hands, but she spoke the words of a civil ceremony. Some of her pots had been placed around the room to hold holly, fir boughs, and poinsettias. In the list of credits at the show's end, it would say, "Pottery by Willimore Schutz." She looked into my eyes as I gasped my vows. Then she looked into Jason's. She had appeared on the show before, once as an undercover agent, another time as a madam. She nodded and told us we could kiss. Jason took my face in his hands. He looked at me for several seconds, and then he kissed me with more passion than he ever had before. His lips were wet; his tongue entered my mouth. When I pulled away, I tried not to let the camera catch my surprise. Jason was crying.

After we wrapped up the episode, Chance led us into an unused part of the studio, where long tables holding food and liquor had been set up. Our voices and Christmas music echoed through the cavernous space. Billy, still wearing her black robe, rushed over to me. I was unused to seeing her with any makeup, never mind stage makeup.

"You make a beautiful bride," she said. "When do we see it for real?"

"One wedding at a time—Margo gets married next week."

"Yes, but what about you and Sam? I like him."

"So do I. But there are no plans—"

Billy touched my cheek. "There will be," she said.

I found Jason drinking bourbon at the bar. "What happened?" I asked.

"You mean the kiss?"

"That and you crying. What's going on?"

"Oh, the usual holiday blues, I guess. Plus, I got turned on by your white dress."

I tried to see whether he was kidding, and he rolled his eyes. "It's no big deal—I've kissed women before."

"Well, you've never kissed me like that before," I said, embarrassed, wishing I hadn't called attention to it. He was looking into his bourbon with severe intensity, as if he had just seen a gnat land in it.

"When do you leave for Aruba?" I asked.

"Oh, that's off. Our charter got canceled, and Terry's going to San Francisco instead. He's considering going from there to Okinawa, to visit his grandmother who's dying."

"But he's coming back?" I asked, wondering why Jason was sounding so desolate.

He nodded. "He promises to be back for New Year's Eve. We're throwing a party—want to come?"

"Oh, thanks. But I'm not sure what our plans are."

"You're still tight with Sam?"

"Yes," I said, knowing it was true. And getting tighter all the time. "But he's away for five days. At Yale."

Jason pretended to cringe. "Don't say that four-letter word." Jason had gone to Harvard. I smiled, happy to hear him joking. In Europe he had shown me how jokes could pull him up.

"Hello, my children," Stuart MacDuff said, putting his

arms around our shoulders. His steely hair, purple as gun-
metal, glinted in the bright stage light. He always used a blue
rinse, to keep it from getting yellow. "Now listen, Beck. You
going to take care of my girl here?"

"I promise to love and cherish." Jason signaled the bartender for another hit of bourbon. The bartender tried to catch
Jason's eye, but Jason looked away.

"Tell me all your Christmas plans," Stuart said, watching
the door. I supposed that he had told Margie about the party
and was waiting for her to arrive.

"My sister's getting married in Watch Hill."

"And I'm not going to Aruba."

"Would you like to have Christmas with the MacDuffs,
Jason? The whole brood should be there. You like ham?"

"I adore ham, but I wouldn't want to intrude on your holiday. I wouldn't want to expose myself to the stable family
influence."

"Nonsense. You like fig pudding, boy?"

"Love it."

"Well, needless to say, Margie MacDuff makes a superla-
tive figgy pudding. And you know how much she would love
to have you at our table."

"Thanks, Stuart," Jason said, placing his hand on Stuart's
shoulder. Both men looked handsome and archaic in their trim
black tuxedos. "I promise to think about it."

"Good boy. You have a happy wedding, Una." He looked
puzzled. "Didn't your sister just get married, though?"

"That's my *other* sister."

"Ah. You girls travel in a pack, I guess. You'll be next.
Well, have a merry time." He kissed my cheek and went to
greet Margie, who had just joined Billy.

"What a father figure," Jason said, smiling as he shook his
head. I noticed that his brown hair was showing grey strands
along the part.

"You should go there for Christmas. He really meant it."

"They live in Westchester," Jason said dismally, as though
that fact alone would prevent him from going.

"That's okay. Westchester will be like the country. You can
pack a little overnight bag, pretend you're snowed in."

"In Westchester I probably *will* be snowed in. Snowed in with Margie MacDuff—help me."

We laughed, and Jason got me a glass of spiked eggnog.

"Are you and Sam truly in love?"

"Yes."

"Do you think you'll stay together?"

"I don't know, Jason. I hope so—but who can know?" I spoke cautiously. For a second I had a fantasy of Jason going straight, provided he had a chance with me. All I had to do was tread lightly.

"I'm always looking for love," he said. "Something long-term."

"But you've been with Terry a long time. Longer than I've been with Sam."

He stared at me a few seconds, trying to gauge how much truth there was to what I had said. Then he shook his head. "No, it's different. I can tell by the way you talk about him. You expect it to last. Even when you were suffering, right after Thanksgiving, I could tell you knew it was just a matter of time before you worked things out. I was so jealous of you, even though things were good with Terry then. Our charter didn't get canceled, you know. Terry backed out."

"I'm sorry."

"He does this all the time. He leaves me, and then he comes back. And I always take him back. Always."

"But you don't have to. If he treats you this way, maybe you should break up with him."

"The problem is, I love him. Even though he treats me like shit." Jason made a clown face. "So, what do you think of that?"

I kissed his lips. "I think you deserve better," I said. And then Jason walked away.

THE morning we were to leave for Watch Hill, it was snowing, and Sam surprised me with a rental car. He said he was going out to buy bagels for breakfast, and he came back with a subcompact. We ate breakfast while driving north on the New York Thruway. Our trunk and back seat were full of suitcases, wedding and Christmas presents, bird books, binoculars, and snow boots. Dry flakes hit the windshield and the wipers whisked them away. Six inches had already accumulated on the shoulder. Traffic crept along; Sam drove, hunched forward, both hands on the wheel. The defroster did not work well, and I kept wiping the inside of the windshield with a paper napkin.

"Now I wish I'd surprised you with train tickets," he said.

"Want me to drive for a while?"

"Not yet. Tell me a story or something. Or turn on the radio."

I told him the story of Vigil and Ante, of how Lily and Margo had been my emotional bodyguards.

"I can't imagine Lily slitting someone's tires," he said, laughing and fondling my knee.

"But she did. She acts so *genteel* now, but that's just a cover."

"You girls must have been something."

"We still are. I can't believe Margo's getting married. I can't believe it."

"Your youngest sister, getting married before you." He slid a smiling glance at me.

"Who cares? I'm glad she's marrying Matt." Something in his glance made me shiver, as though he were thinking about our wedding instead of Margo's. I was thinking of it too.

"Well, I'm married on the show."

"Mrs. Delilah Vandeweghe."

"No, I'm keeping Grant. Now that I'm a successful psycho-therapist. I'm pretty worried about Jason." I told Sam about our conversation. "They say Christmas is the biggest time for suicide. People remember how happy they were when they were children, and they expect the same things."

"Maybe you should call him from Watch Hill. Stay in touch until you get back to New York."

"That's not a bad idea," I said, and then Sam told me about some article he had read in the *Times* that morning. I swiped the windshield with my napkin. I wanted to slide closer to Sam, but in such a snowstorm it could be dangerous. He took his right hand off the wheel and held mine for a few seconds. I started singing "Hark, the Herald Angels Sing," and Sam joined in. Then he placed his hand back on the wheel. Safety first.

s n o w covered the roof, porches, and lawn of the Ninigrit Inn. It covered the rocks out to the lighthouse and the beach down to the water's edge; it was high tide. Waves pounded the shore. White snow fell on the sea's grey-green surface. I felt a thrill and wanted to run down to the beach with Sam, but our arms were full of packages.

"Welcome, you two," Matt said, coming past a huge un-decorated Christmas tree in the foyer. I thought he looked dif-ferent, and when he kissed me I realized his friendly gold beard was gone. "Everyone else is already here. Your mother stayed last night, and Lily and Henk came in this morning."

"Where are they?"

"Everyone is in the living room. My family's not coming till tomorrow, so you Cavans have the run of the place."

"The family reunion Margo planned for last September—" I said.

"Better late than never," Matt and Sam said at once.

We walked into the living room where Margo, my mother, and Henk were standing before a roaring fire. Laurel roping tied with red ribbons decked the mantel, banisters, and window frames. Lily was stretched out on a wicker chaise. Margo came to kiss me; everyone else looked vaguely disturbed, as if they were trying to remember my name.

"Mother, this is Sam Chamberlain," I said, standing between them with my arms outstretched, like a windmill.

"Hello, Mrs. Cavan," Sam said, shaking her hand.

"Please call me Grace," she said, then, "Hello dear," kissing me, keeping her pelvis well away from mine.

"Isn't this a perfect place for a wedding?" I looked all around the room.

"Pardon me, don't I know you from somewhere?" Lily asked.

I leaned down to kiss her. She looked the same size she had a month earlier. "How are you? Still due next month?"

"Still takes nine months, no matter how hard you try."

I smiled at Lily, then stood and nodded at Henk. We did not speak to each other. He looked annoyed, and I tried to imagine why. Then, as soon as the greetings had died down, he resumed his discussion with my mother. She gazed at him, entranced.

"So, as I was saying, I have quite a famous collection of French watercolors—mainly Degas and Renoir."

"Oh, Renoir," Lily said. "I love his women. They are so maternal."

Margo gave me a loaded eyebrow. Sam squeezed my hand.

"Yes, you don't think of Renoir as a watercolorist, do you?" my mother asked mistily.

"I assure you, these are superior watercolors," Henk said, laughing.

"Oh, I'm sure they are. I didn't mean—" my mother said, flustered, smoothing over any feelings she might inadvertently have ruffled.

"You two want to freshen up after your drive?" Matt asked. "Or whatever?"

"Where is our room?" I asked.

"Oh, the regular," Margo said. "In the turret, of course. It doesn't have any heat, but we're supplying extra down quilts. Sam has to supply the body heat."

"With pleasure," Sam said into my ear.

Everyone, including my mother, laughed. In two days, Sam and I would be the only unmarried couple in the family. If Margo was the type to throw a bouquet, she would whip it in my direction.

"Let's take our things upstairs. We can come right back down," I said.

"Fine," Sam said, following me.

We climbed the narrow, steep stairs, feeling colder with every flight. I could see our breaths. Sam paused, smiling at me, when he reached the door to the turret room. Then he flung it open. First I saw the view, the icy green sea spreading to the white horizon. Then I noticed the bed, covered with a mound of puffy white comforters. The room had a familiar, musty smell. It smelled like old wood, salt air, and summer. Then I saw the ice bucket which held a bottle of champagne, its neck tied with a red ribbon.

"It must be frozen!" I said. My own fingers were icicles.

"I think it's a fairly recent gift," Sam said. He lifted the bottle out of the slushy ice and pulled a small white card from the ribbon. It said "Una." He handed it to me. I turned it over and read, "This is in place of the bouquet I won't throw. I love you. Margo."

"I don't think we need the ice bucket, do you?" Sam asked, placing the bottle on the bureau. He hugged me close to him, my head turned so that I could see the water. Snow was still falling on its surface; I thought of the shooting stars last summer, of how Margo had said they fizzled the instant they hit the surface.

"Do I sense a little tension downstairs?" Sam asked.

"Maybe a little."

"Then let me tell you what to do. As soon as I can, I'll get Henk busy in a conversation. Then you, Margo, and Lily go off together."

"Go off where?"

"Anywhere. Just be together."

"Okay. I'll try."

"But first . . ." Sam said, fixing me with his greenish eyes, pulling me down onto the bed's chilly white hills.

THE SUN was starting to go down. The inn's living room, on the northeast side, was cold in spite of the red fire. The embers were dark as garnets. My mother sat erect in a wicker rocker, staring at the fire. Lily had her head in Henk's lap, and Henk was stroking her yellow hair. Margo sat across a big armchair, her back against one arm, her legs over the other. She was reading a murder mystery with a splashy cover.

"Maybe I ought to crank up the boiler," Matt said. "Warm this burgh up."

"Where's the boiler?" Sam asked.

"In the basement. Who wants a tour of the boiler room?" Matt asked, and instantly I knew Sam had enlisted him in our mission.

"Oh, I'll go," my mother said. She understood that whenever someone offered a tour of the house, the polite guest accepted. Everyone loved showing off property.

"Count me out," Margo said. "I spend too many of my waking hours in that basement, doing hotel laundry."

"Why not?" Henk said, easing out from under Lily's head.

He, Sam, and my mother trooped after Matt. We could hear their footsteps on the wooden stairs.

"The tour has begun," Margo said, climbing out of the chair. "Let's take a sea cruise."

"Oh, I'm so comfy," Lily said, folding her hands over her belly.

"I insist you come," Margo said. She walked to Lily and looked down. "I really insist."

"We must insist," I said, standing beside Margo. After the last scene in New York, I wanted Margo to do the pushing. I wanted to stay cool. Lily looked as though she thought we might be crazy. The snow had stopped falling, but perhaps some of the roads had not been plowed. She was about to give birth, Margo was about to be a bride. There was so much to lose.

"If we go, we have to leave a note," she said, hopping off the couch with admirable speed. "We should say we have to get something important at the store. Something very convincing."

"How about a garter for Margo?" I asked.

"No, say we have to get tampons," Lily said. "No man can quibble with tampons."

"Lily, no one is going to believe you need tampons," Margo said, laughing.

"No, but *you* might. Don't worry. It'll do." She began adjusting the line of buttons down the front of her coral velour dress. Margo and I did not look at each other. It was too sad that Lily had to write Henk a convincing note. We headed for the closets and put on our coats.

"It's going to feel weird, getting married without Dad here," Margo said, slipping on her snow boots. They were rubber with battered leather uppers.

"Maybe Una has an inside track—think he'll make an appearance?" Lily asked, touching my shoulder.

"It's possible."

"Okay, I'll get the car," Margo said, running across the yard to the rusty Land Rover.

I wrote a hasty message: "Be right back—need tampons." We left it on the foyer table. I held Lily's elbow as we made our way across the wide porch. Snow had drifted under the glider and railings; a film of dry snow covered the slatted grey floor. The waves roared down the beach. Margo wheeled the Rover close to the steps, and I climbed inside, straddling the gearshift. Lily climbed in beside me. Margo had already lit up, and smoke filled the vehicle. We were six breasts abreast, but a tighter fit than usual.

"Something is wrong here," Lily said. "I should be driving."

"No!" Margo and I said at once. Margo started to shift into reverse, but Lily reached across me to grab her wrist.

"Don't tell me you can drive a standard," Lily said.

"I can."

"Give me the honor," Lily said, opening her door and coming around to the driver's side. Margo shrugged and got out. She climbed in beside me. "Don't worry—" Lily said, ramming the stick through the gears. "Pregnancy doesn't keep you from driving. How do you engage the four-wheel drive?"

"It's engaged," Margo said.

Lily revved the engine. Through the inn's door I could see

that Matt, Sam, Henk, and my mother had returned to the living room. They were standing in a semicircle around the fireplace. Henk had his back to the door; he had noticed our absence, but he must have thought we had gone upstairs, to look at Margo's dress or something. His head swiveled from side to side. I saw Sam looking at us, wishing us godspeed. I remembered kissing him for the first time.

"Tonight we fly!" Lily said. She threw out the clutch.

The Rover shot down the drive, kicking back snow, an overloaded broomstick trying to take off. The Cavan coven. We tore around the bend. There we were, free on the shore road, dumbstruck. Our half-open mouths wore expressions of people who have just wakened or defied danger. We stared out the windshield, our heads snapping in perfect unison whenever the dark Atlantic appeared in the spaces between the big summer houses. Suddenly we were on a sea cruise, and how had we gotten there? We were playing it over in our minds, the way Margo and I had set up the dare, the way Lily had accepted it without giving herself too much time to think. Even now Lily's green eyes flicked to the side of the road, perhaps looking for a way to turn around.

She did not turn around. A mile from the inn she switched on the radio and found a raucous rock station.

"I'm so sick of the Christmas spirit," she said, scoffing in the manner of her husband. "A station like this won't have Bingo singing 'White Christmas' every ten minutes."

"Have you heard Dino singing 'Rudy the Red-Nosed Reindeer' yet this year?" Margo asked.

"Spare me," Lily said. She drove us past the deserted summer cottages on the road toward Point Judith. Snow covered every surface except for rocks rising out of the land. Wind had cleared those. In spite of the loud synthesizer band on the radio, all three of us were humming "White Christmas." When the streetlights went on and we all knew we had gone far enough, Lily pulled into a driveway. Backing out, she pointed the vehicle toward the family inn.

On the way back we were silent, thinking about what could happen when we returned. I imagined Henk with their lug-

gage and a taxi waiting, ready to push Lily into the back seat
and take her straight to New York to await suitable punish-
ment. I thought of Sam, pleased with his part in our escape.
Wedged between Lily and Margo, my left arm rested against
the baby in Lily's belly. I gave it a nudge. Lily smiled.

"Tell me about marriage," Margo said.

"It has its ups and downs," Lily said. "But one thing for
sure is, you always have someone to carry your bags."

Margo and I both looked at her when she said that, I because it proved that she and I had obviously been thinking
the exact same thing about Henk—waiting with the luggage.

"Is that a joke or what?" Margo asked. "I'm getting married in a matter of *days*, and I wouldn't say nay to a little
reassurance."

"Okay, it's great, but it does take some getting used to. Like
anything major."

"It's very major," I agreed.

"No kidding—if you could just see our bill for the *greenery*
for this fête," Margo said.

When we started up the hill to the inn, we again became
silent. The Rover slowed down. Matt had turned on the floodlights. They illuminated the drive and the inn's snowy lawn.

"Do or die," Margo said, and Lily shot her a sharp look.

We stood together on the sidewalk. Margo, Lily, and I
linked arms, with Lily in the middle, forming a cortege according to age and height. It has always seemed appropriate
that I, the oldest, am also the tallest. We marched through the
snow. Henk stood at the door. The light shined on his back;
his face was shadowed. I painted it with anger. The door
opened and Henk, coatless, stepped out.

"*Liebchen*," he said sternly, "we have been waiting to deco-
rate the tree." I felt shocked to see his eyes look so sad.

Margo and I both started to take the blame, to explain all
about tampons, when suddenly Sam in his ski jacket rushed
around Henk. He grabbed me by the arm. We ran into the
yard, past the floodlights, gathering speed, down the narrow
path between the leafless gorse bushes. Briars snagged our
trousers. The inn behind us glowed, but the path was black.

We knew we had hit the beach when we felt soft sand yield beneath our snow boots. Taking a sharp right, we ran until we reached the tidal pools, dizzy with lungs full of winter air. Shapes flew through the sky. They were patches of cloud, spots before our reeling eyes, ghosts of our loved ones, the Aurora Borealis. Sam's eyes were smiling, golden. He wrapped his arms around me, put his lips on mine. We were breathless from running. He held me so close. The shapes kept moving.

THE next day was brilliantly sunny and frigid. Static tingled through my hair and along the fibers of my wool sweater, making me itch and shake my head. Sam and Matt went outside, to shovel all paths on the inn's property. I reclined on a couch in the living room, changing position constantly and wishing I had something good to read. Lily and Margo played checkers on a low wicker table; Lily, unable to bend, directed Margo which of her checkers she wished moved when it couldn't be easily reached. Henk pretended to read a medical journal while watching Lily. My mother dozed in the armchair beside me, a blanket across her legs, a mystery open on her lap.

As if the static were invading my body, I felt anxious, though I couldn't think why. All of my loved ones were near. I could hear Sam's shovel scraping the pavement outside. Since Lily's decision to follow her instincts and take the sea cruise with us last night, I could even, by a generous stretch of the imagination, feel benevolent toward Henk. Right now he was regarding Lily with an expression of pained adoration.

My mother wakened suddenly, startled but smiling. "What a dream!" she said to me.

I smiled, encouraging her to tell it.

"It was about the tower in this inn—where you and Sam sleep. Only in the dream it was a library, and your father was there, dressed in his Glen plaid suit—you know, the one from the Collins Shop—waiting for you to return your overdue books."

"How odd!" I said, but it was only four minutes before I found the opportunity to excuse myself and fly up the ladder-stairs.

The turret room was empty, ice-cold in spite of the sun streaming through the windows. My heart crashed. I had been positive my father would be here; ever since last summer I had thought he would appear to me in the turret. Shivering, I stood in a patch of sun. Down below I could see Matt, foreshortened by his thick clothes and my angle of vision, rolling a ball of snow, building it into a snowman. Sam was nowhere in sight. Pressing my face to the cold pane, I strained for a glimpse of him.

Suddenly a cloud covered the sun. I peered at it, a cumulous cloud, impossibly high and fluffy, alone in the sky. It was a summer cloud; it had no place in the December weather pattern. I stared at it, silhouetted against the sun. A bird perched on its edge. A seagull, perhaps, flapping its wings. Or a wisp of vapor, breaking free. Or a figure gesturing wildly. I squinted, then tore downstairs for the binoculars.

Fortunately they stood on a bookshelf at the foot of the stairs. I avoided everyone. Tearing back to the turret room, I had the glasses pressed against my eyes even before I reached the window. There, on the cloud's rim, stood my father in his Glen plaid suit, waving. Throwing open a window, I waved like a maniac. My breath came in gasps. For so long, since my transatlantic flight, I had saved up things to tell him, questions to ask. Trying to shout, I croaked instead. The glasses wavered, then found him again. He was pointing deliberately at his mouth, as if he wanted me to read his lips. Panic boiled inside me. What could this mean? Did he actually expect me to lip-read? This visit, like the last, was celestial. Had he become permanently skybound?

I stared through the binoculars. He held a navy blue wool coat with a raccoon collar, a far cry from his usual Chesterfield, over one arm. He gestured at his watch, then pointed again to his mouth.

"Get *down* here, goddamn it!" I yelled.

"I can't," my father said quite clearly.

How bizarre! I thought, watching his lips and hearing his voice. "Can you hear me?" I mouthed.

"Speak up, sweetheart—I can't hear what you're saying."

I spoke in a loud voice, leaning out the window. "Dad, are

you coming to Margo's wedding? Is that what you want to tell me?"

"No, I'm not. I'm not able. This is my cloud. What I want to say—"

"Your *cloud*?" I choked. "Dad, you're not stuck on that cloud alone—forever, are you?"

He grinned and shook his head. I heard him chuckle and felt glad to see he had had his teeth fixed. "Now listen, because we don't have long. It's getting harder to reach you, my angel. I must leave; I know you're happy."

"Oh, I am. I love Sam, Dad."

"I know that. And Margo loves Matt, although I never thought she'd fall for a guy with a beard. I'm glad he shaved it."

"What about Lily? Is she happy?"

"Well, she's getting happier. Finding her way, just as we all do." He chuckled again, reaching up to touch the rim of his left ear, the way he always did. I chuckled along with him. "Henk is okay, Una. A real horse's ass, but he means well. He's insecure."

Then I did scream. "If I hear that once more . . ." I shouted.

"But you will hear it. Because he is, and he needs your patience. Your *love*, in fact, Una," he said sternly. "Make him part of the family. All right? Will you?"

"All right," I said sullenly, thinking my father had a hell of a nerve ordering me to like a man he had never even met.

"It will be easier than you think," he said, reading my mind.

Watching him grin on his cloud, though, made me smile back. "Dad, you seem happier," I said finally.

"Well, I am."

"Did you come into Mom's dream? Is that how you reached me this time?"

He hesitated. "Yes, and it wasn't fair." He shook his head, as if trying to dispel a painful thought. "It wasn't right. She still . . . loves me too much. The way I love her. Troubled, unfinished business, Una. I can't get her hopes up. I'm not coming back."

"Never?"

"Not for a long time. But I'll always know. What you're doing, whether you're happy."

"I love you, Dad!" I called out the open window.

"I love you, sweetheart!" he called. "Now look away, before I drift out of sight. Make yourself busy, so you don't see me go."

I studied his face through the binoculars. Oddly, it was getting younger. The skinny cheeks, the curly hair (now browner than it had been before he died), the lively eyes. It bore a striking resemblance to the Air Force photos of young James Cavan. His grin was wide, steady. "Remember!" he called.

"What?" I asked.

"Everything! Now go get busy."

I waved without seeing, closed the window, and walked to the door. Sam was rushing up the stairs. We hugged tightly, and although he had just come in from outdoors, I was colder than he.

"Put on a jacket," he said. "We'll take a walk."

When we stepped outside the sky was sparkling, and I felt sad to see that it was cloudless.

Walking east toward the promontory we watched glistening black cormorants drying their wings on the rocks. The sun had melted all snow from the beach, though it clung to the hillside and lawns along the bluff. Sam wore a heavy winter sweater and leather ski mittens. His windburned face gleamed. I brushed his red cheek with the back of my hand. Removing one mitten, he clasped my hand and put both our hands into the pocket of my ski jacket.

"Matt is excited. He considers this his high point as an innkeeper—entertaining at his own wedding," Sam said, squinting into the sun. "This sky—it reminds me of summer."

"Yes, it does. Me too."

"We're on the same wavelength." He squeezed my hand. Glare ice frosted the promontory's rocks and seaweed. The tide was low.

"I'd fall for sure today," I said, gesturing toward the tidal pool where I had slipped last September.

Sam stopped abruptly, then walked away from the water,

toward the brush bordering the sand, pulling me along. From a bayberry bush, wind-whipped and denuded of leaves, he pulled two rolled blankets.

"I took a break from shoveling and hid these here," he said. "Somehow I thought we'd need a break from the others. Though the visit is going very smoothly."

We shook out one blanket, laid it quickly on the sand, then stretched out together and pulled the second blanket around us.

"You're fabulous to think of this," I said, my teeth chattering as my body, warm from the brisk walk, became as one with the frozen beach. But presently, pressing against me, Sam's body heat permeated our myriad layers of cotton, wool, and feathers. He gave me a long, warm kiss.

"Now you can tell me," he said.

"Tell you what?" My jaw was growing rigid again with the effort of not chattering.

"Why you were yelling out the window of our room. I could hear you all the way down the beach—I ran back to the inn, and that's when I met you on the stairs."

How could I tell him that I had been having a conversation, my last for a long time, with my father, long dead? For that matter, why didn't I feel sadder about that fact? Subdued, perhaps, but content; he had promised to watch over me forever, and perhaps no daughter could ask for more than that. I studied the bright flecks in Sam's eyes and thought of gold dust swirling in a green torrent. His eyes were smiling, waiting.

"I was talking to my father," I said.

"But your father is—"

"Dead." Oh, how I hated the word! His body was dead, but now he was an angel. I wanted to explain it to Sam. "Can you understand that I talked to him? That I looked out the window and saw him in the sky?"

Sam hesitated, then laughed. "Maybe I can. If my parents died I might look for them in the sky. Did you really see him?"

"I swear it, Sam. And it wasn't the first time, either."

Sam laughed loudly. He pulled me so close my lips were against his neck. His dark hair contrasted startlingly with his creamy white sweater. Our legs entwined, and Sam still laughed.

"I believe you, Una," he said, and we laughed together for a while, lying under the blanket. Looking past his shoulder I watched the tide rising, waves licking the rocks. I saw the black zone of shore glistening under ice, like onyx, like moonlight shining on a bottomless black lake.

"You love your father too much to let him go," he said finally.

"That's one way of explaining it. Would you still believe me if I told you that it's more complicated than that?"

"You've come to the right man—I've made a career out of studying seaweed. Do most people consider seaweed complicated? We scientists keep very open minds."

"Thank you," I said.

"My love," he said before kissing me. His lips tasted warm and salty and made me think of last September. We lay on a winter beach beneath a summer sky. Nestled together, we were perfectly warm now. We went on and on, and the seasons whirled.

"This is it," Sam said. When I opened my eyes, his were open, watching me. The sky was dazzling, cloudless.

This is it: I knew what he meant. This moment, lying together on the sand, was a moment of truth. Years later we would remember it absolutely. Clear and fair, like the first line in an architect's design, this moment would serve as a cornerstone. I recognized it for what it was because I had known others before. They have perfect clarity. Nothing occurs to mark the passage of time; I looked around and saw no ships trailing smoke across the horizon, no clouds skidding through the sky, nothing growing closer or more distant to show the seconds ticking by. The day held still. I knew what I had to do.

"Did you ever think we'd be spending Christmas together in the turret room?" I asked.

Sam hesitated. "I can't honestly say I considered it impossible."

"Really?" I asked, thrown off guard. "Tell me why."

"I trust my instincts. I remember spending time with you

last September, wanting to know everything about you right from the start. You talked about your sisters in a way that seemed fierce, and it made me jealous. To be loved that way—"

"But I *do* love you that way," I said, frowning at the way his eyes looked hard and worried. "In fact, I love you more than anything."

Sam relaxed his eyes and hugged me hard. I thought about what I had just said, about loving him more than anything. That meant more than Margo and Lily; until Sam, that concept had been impossible. I thought of my sisters and their changes, major changes like marrying and having a baby, and I loved them more than ever. Then I thought of my mother and of the tender way my father had spoken about her, and I felt overwhelmed. Thinking about love in quantities too great to measure or apportion seemed talismanic, a sign that I was right in thinking of the interlude as a moment of truth. I glanced around, to make sure time was holding steady. A tanker, or perhaps a freighter, was coming into view near Block Island. But it appeared stationary, far enough away to preserve the illusion.

"Sam," I said, looking straight at him. "Will you marry me?"

He stared back without flinching, and I slowly turned ice-cold. I believe I felt drops of sweat spring from my forehead and instantly freeze. Then I saw him start to smile, a smile which changed to a grin: the best grin I have ever seen. He said nothing. Instead he kissed me.

He wanted the kiss to go on; I could tell by the way his body pressed close to mine, the way his hand worked through my hair to squeeze my neck. I felt colder than ever, and I began to tremble. Was this kiss a way for him to gather his thoughts, to buy some time before declining? I pulled back.

"Sam," I said, trying to quell the panic. "*Will* you marry me?"

"Yes, Una," he said, grinning again. "I will marry you. This is great—you're really proposing to me?" He looked delighted and amused.

"I really am," I said solemnly, quietly.

"I've had this feeling that we were taking it for granted, the future and everything. I guess that stems from the fact that I can't imagine being without you. Can't imagine it." Still beaming, he shook his head. Sun struck his wavy hair, turning parts of it golden.

"Taking it for granted? You mean you didn't consider a proposal necessary?" I asked.

I must have been frowning because Sam's finger traced my lips until I started to laugh. "Here I am," I said, "feeling embarrassed about proposing to a man who has just accepted."

"You have a way of homing in on the worst parts," he said fondly. "When I said I take our future for granted, you should have listened to the next part: I can't imagine being without you."

I kissed Sam's neck, to let him know I understood, but I was watching the ship steam closer. It was a freighter; I could see its rusty hull, its yellow derricks. Smoke twisted from its stacks and dissolved in the pure cold air. Its approach had started the clock, but our interlude, Sam's and mine, held steady.